The Home Stone

The Home Stone

Stephen Mossop

PRESS

VULPINE
PRESS

Published by Vulpine Press in the United Kingdom in 2025

ISBN: 978-1-83919-606-5

Cover by Vulpine Press

www.vulpine-press.com

For Brenda
Always and Forever

Part One

The Road to Bridie's Bridge

1

Bridie's mum always knew when her daughter was thinking. Bridie would always stare at her feet, and that's just what she was doing now. She watched her daughter for a while.

The book Bridie had been reading was laying on the grass next to her, and a half-empty cup balanced on the uneven ground, just under the wrought-iron garden chair she was sitting in.

Hilda Ambrose smiled, as she watched her, and thought to herself how similar she had looked to Bridie at the same sort of age. She had the same brown eyes, the same round face, and the same shade of light brown hair. Her own hair had been a similar sort of length as Bridie's when she had been thirteen too. Only their clothes differed dramatically.

Hilda's mum had always insisted that she wore dresses rather than trousers, and ribbons or bows in her hair.

'You never know when you might meet somebody important,' her mum had always told her. She never did, of course, and was never likely to, hidden away in this little back corner of the countryside, but that had made no difference to her mum.

Bridie, on the other hand, was far too independently minded to obey any sort of dress code her mother might have liked to impose on her. Jeans, and either a T-shirt in the summer or a jumper in the winter were Bridie's style.

Actually, other than her much hated school uniform, it was pretty much her only style.

Hilda reflected and sighed, thinking about the new party dress she had asked her sister-in-law to make for Bridie to wear at Christmas. She'd popped into Brenda's dress-making shop in town a month before and had picked out some nice-looking fabric that she hoped Bridie would like. All she had to do now, was to wait until December, then she could take Bridie's measurements and let Brenda know, for her to make it ahead of the holidays.

She groaned, forever hopeful, that Bridie would like it. And even more so, actually wear it! If she didn't, she knew that it would gather dust on the back of Bridie's bedroom door.

Thinking about school, she wondered if the book on the grass was part of her weekend homework. She would have to ask her.

Bridie really hated school. Wearing a uniform skirt showed her knees off, and Bridie hated showing her legs. She kept saying that they were too thin, and Hilda kept trying to reassure her, that her legs would grow as she got older, just like the rest of her body.

So far, that reassurance had fallen on deaf ears. Just like, she was sure, the argument that would ensue shortly after when she asked what her homework was about. Bridie really resented the fact that she had to do homework, especially at weekends. She would do almost anything to avoid getting it done.

Ah well, she thought. *Here goes. No doubt another peaceful Saturday afternoon spoiled.*

'So, Bridie,' Hilda began, 'what are you thinking about?'

Her daughter stirred in her seat, and raised her head. 'Not much,' she said, blandly.

'Well, it looked like you were miles away just now, so it must have been important,' suggested her mother.

Bridie sighed. 'It's this homework,' she said, 'we're doing Romans this term, and it's so…boring'

'Why?' Hilda retorted.

'Well,' her daughter continued, 'I hate their names. They've all got long names. And I hate that they came here and just sort of took over.'

'Well, I don't suppose they could help their names,' her mum said. 'Their parents probably just thought that long names would make them sound important. What do you think?'

Bridie's eyes widened. 'Well, they weren't important at all!' Bridie stated. 'They were just bullies, this book says all about it. They just came and had fights with the people here and then started throwing their weight about.'

'I'm sure they must have thought they were doing the right thing,' Hilda replied. 'You know, building roads, and all?'

'No,' Bridie said emphatically. 'They were just bullies. They came to steal land and stuff. You know you told me our family have been here for years and years. I hope they didn't try to take our land!'

Hilda laughed. 'Well, I certainly haven't heard that they did, but I don't really know.'

'You know you told me that one of our ancestor ladies had brought her Home Stone here and buried it under the bridge? Was that before the Romans or after them?'

'Oh, it was a long time before they arrived,' Hilda reassured her.

'Good!' said Bridie. 'Else they would have tried to steal that too!'

Hilda laughed. 'Yes, they probably would have!'

Bridie looked over at her mum, a frown was etched across her face. 'What's up?' her mother asked.

'It's just, well, you told me about how the bridge started.'

'Mmm?'

'Well, how did it get here, the Home Stone? Where did it come from?'

Here we go, Hilda thought, *another ploy to get out of doing her homework.*

'Mum?'

'Alright then,' she sighed, resignedly. 'I suppose I'll have to tell you sometime. And I guess you're about the same age as the girl in the *beginning* of the story.

Bridie smiled. 'So?'

'Alright. Well, it all started with a girl with no name...'

'What?' Bridie asked, a puzzled look on her face. 'Everybody's got a name. Why didn't she have one?'

'Look,' Hilda huffed a little. 'It's a long story. I'll get to that in a bit, OK?'

Bridie nodded.

'So, are you going to pay attention?'

Bridie nodded again, making herself comfortable in her chair.

'So, no interruptions then. If you've got questions save them up until I've finished the story, otherwise I'll forget where I'm up to, OK?'

Bridie smiled and nodded more vigorously this time, content that her mother was about to share the story.

'Good,' came her mother's reply. 'Then I'll begin. They were moving fast. The girl with no name had to trot quickly to keep up, time was short. They had to move quickly, if they wanted to stay alive. There was no time to wait for stragglers. If any couldn't keep up, they would just have to take their chances. If they managed by some miracle to avoid the beasts, then the hunters would find them. If they couldn't keep up, they were as good as dead!

'Normally, the families moved at a comfortable walking pace.

'They would wake in the morning, eat breakfast, gather their things and start to walk. They followed the great herds, as they migrated across the homeland. The hunters would run ahead. They would pick off what beasts they could, with their flint spears, then they would light fires and wait until the family caught up.

'Then they would build a stockade and eat, and sleep. Normally, they would repeat these things day after day. Not now, though.

'They all knew that if they delayed, if they lingered, then they soon would be the *hunted*. And the Great Father's hunters would be merciless.

'There were lots of them. More families than she could count on her fingers and toes. She'd tried to count them, the night they were told, but she'd run out of toes and couldn't count any further. She counted, like everybody else, using her fingers.

She'd counted their fires as they burned brightly all around her. Each family was allowed just one fire at the Great Gathering. All of the wood for miles around had been gathered, until there was no more to be found, within a day's walk.

'Usually, families would make two fires. One for the men, and another for the women and children. First on one hand, then on the other, she counted. When she ran out of fingers, she touched her first toe. Then she started counting on her fingers again. When she reached her last toe, she could count no further. There was no way anybody could count further. And she hadn't counted nearly half of them. That meant that there were countless numbers of families, all around her, all moving fast.

'The girl with no name coughed. The dust raised by all those feet in front of her was making her choke.

'She could see only the backs and legs of those in front of her. She dared not stop to catch her breath, let alone sip from the water skin she carried on her back. Her legs ached, but she wouldn't dare stop.

'Ahead of her, through a momentary gap between the crowd of people's backs, she saw a small child stumble and fall. Its mother shrieked as she reached down to grab them, but it was too late.

'Those behind could neither stop, nor avoid them, and they were quickly lost beneath the sea of people's feet.

'The girl with no name only just managed to leap over the broken and bloody bodies, and then they were gone! Left behind like the left-over bones and gristle from a campfire.

'Every now and then she heard others shriek, and she knew that another child would never grow, or another man would go uncomforted that night. But there was no time to mourn over their loss. They were moving too fast. Time was too short.

'She ran with her family, keeping close to them. If she lost them now, she may never find them again.

'She would be prey to any of the men who wandered between the sleeping bodies throughout the short night, looking for comfort. Then she would have no value to the Family Father.

'Men would not want to buy her, and she would never have a family of her own, when the time came, she may have no future. Her family would cast her out. She would never have a name. Life was hard and short enough already, without having to scavenge from other families for leftovers. Especially, with no fire of her own to warm her, and with no man's sleeping skins to cover her at night.

'Other men would find her and steal comfort from her. Soon, without the shelter of a family stockade, the animals would find her. She had seen it happen to others.

'There was only one more night to go, before the Great Father's hunters would track them. So, they moved fast. And she moved fast with them.'

Bridie continued to listen to her mother, feeling entranced and captivated by her mother's words.

'It was getting dark by the time they were allowed to stop. She knew they had covered a great distance that day. They had started early in the morning, rising with the sun, and had paused for only a few minutes in the middle of the day.

'The rest of the time they had spent either walking as swiftly as they were able, or, like her, trotting to keep up.

'They had left the plains behind, late into the afternoon, and they had started to climb their way into the hills that marked the edge of the Homeland.

'Gently at first, the hills had grown steeper, as they moved forward, until everyone had to slow their pace. They weren't used to walking on hills, and the girl with no name had suffered, along with everyone else, from leg cramps and an aching back. But still they had moved forward. They'd had no choice.

'The coming night marked the end of the time the Great Father had given them. His hunters would already be on their way towards them, and they all knew there was little time left.

'Still, the Family Fathers all knew, that if they were to climb higher into the hills and make it safely down the other side, their families would have to rest. They had been ordered not to make fires, in case they drew those hunting them even closer and more accurately to where they rested.

'In the fading light, the girl looked back down the slopes and across the valley. Even to her untrained eye, the beaten track left behind by so many feet would be clear enough to follow, probably even by night. Nothing could be done about that though, and she knew that she would have to rest and be refreshed by the time they had to set off again in the morning.

'They were already further from any place she had ever been before. Tomorrow they would descend the other side of these hills and walk away into the *Nothing*. As far as she knew, nobody had ever been there before, and the thought of it made her flesh crawl with fear.

'She arose and followed the women to a small stream. She would be able to drink her fill, to clear the dust from her aching throat and lungs. Like the others, she would also fill her water-skin, in case there was no water in the Nothing.

'The stream was crowded as she approached, so she followed it a little way upstream. Hopefully there, the water would be a little cleaner, and less muddied by the splashing of so many people eager to drink.

'She stepped carefully into the water, thankful for its coolness on her feet. She would never have done so in the larger rivers she was familiar with, and certainly never in the Great Water in the middle of the Homeland, for fear of the gnashing teeth that lived in deeper water.

'She had seen grown men being dragged to their deaths by those teeth, and the people were always very careful to keep watch, whenever they were near deep water.

'She had no fear of small streams like this one, though. Streams like this one were too shallow for any beasts to hide themselves in, so she revelled in the relief the cool water gave to her feet and legs.

'After she had drunk, and filled her skin, she sat down in the stream to wash some of the dust from her body. After the heat of the day, the water seemed freezing on her back and arms, and she shivered slightly, but she was reluctant to leave for the sleeping-skins. Not just yet. This would be her last night in the Homeland, and she wanted to remember every minute of it, for as long as she could stay awake.

'The thought of leaving here, of leaving the Homeland, was just so horrible that it made her feel ill to think about it. She was exhausted, and every part of her body ached with the exertion of the last few days, but that was nothing compared to the ache in her heart. And to the feeling of hollowness and fear that gurgled in the pit of her stomach.

'Maybe she could hide in a gully somewhere? Or maybe her family could? They could stay there quietly for a while, until they were sure that the storm the Great Father had unleashed on them had passed.

'Then they could wander, quietly, around the edge of the Homeland. They would have no friends, no community, no contact with the rest of the people, but surely that would be better than what they were facing by running down into the Nothing.

'It was called *the Nothing* for a reason, after all – there was nothing there.

'The Homeland was the whole world. Everything they needed, everything they had ever known or wanted, was there. Outside there was nothing, nothing at all. They would all descend down the other side of the mountains and fall off the edge of the world. They would all perish. The Great Father had sentenced them all to death.

'She had overheard the Family Father and his men talking about this, when they camped the previous night.

'She had listened intently, hoping against hope that one of them would know the answer.

'They had talked over every suggestion, but in the end, the Family Father had explained patiently, that the Great Father's hunters had been told to follow them, to kill any stragglers, to hunt through every gully and fissure, every cave and glade, and to make sure that none remained. Any they had found were to be put to death instantly, their bodies left for the animals to gnaw at.

'There was no escape other than into the Nothing.

'If they wanted to have the chance of life, they had no choice but to go, to leave the Homeland forever.

'The girl with no name sat in the stream and sobbed.

'Her tears ran in rivulets down her face, to drip unheeded onto her chest, from where they would cascade down her body, until they blended with the stream-water and were lost forever.

'She found that thought strangely comforting. Even if it was only her tears, then something of her would remain forever in the Homeland.

'Her hands rummaged idly against the bed of the stream.

'To and fro, to and fro, rubbing against the pebbles under the water. She lifted one of the pebbles and gazed at it, her eyes were still blurry with tears. It was about the size of her palm. She moved it around in her hand. It was shaped like a bird's egg, its edges were smoothed and rounded by the weathering of the currents.

'She was fascinated by it, she contemplated how long it had laid there, hidden at the bottom of the stream. She marvelled at the thought of whether it had been waiting all this time for her, waiting for her to find it.

'*Forever*, she thought, *a thing from the beginning*.

'She blinked away her tears to inspect it more closely, and even in the last disappearing rays of daylight, she could see that it was a beautiful thing.

'She dipped it briefly under the water, she could make out a myriad of colours – greens, reds, blues, purples, some colours she had no names for, but they were lovely!

'When she removed it from the water, she noticed the colours quickly fading as it dried. The colours were still there though, fainter of course, but nevertheless still there...

'She could hear the women calling to her to hurry up. They had to get back to their camp before it was dark, and she knew she had to go. She knew she had to leave the Homeland, but she felt within her heart, she couldn't leave the unusual stone behind. She made up her mind to take it with her. It would go where she went. It would always stay with her. It would always be a little piece of home that would stay with her, forever.

'She decided it would bring her comfort, and she felt that it would eventually bring her home again.

'As she picked up her things from the edge of the stream, she slipped the stone into her bag of nuts. Nobody would know it was there.

'It would be her secret.'

2

She woke to the commotion of noise and activity. All around her, people were scrabbling in the gloom to find their belongings; men were kicking exhausted bodies awake; mothers were hustling crying babies into pouches on their backs.

Frightened children were scurrying around, desperate to find their mothers. Desperate to find anyone they recognised.

'What's going on?' she asked nobody in particular, her eyes still bleary from sleep.

She spotted Berry, and shouted to her. 'What's going on?'

Berry's eyes were wide and darting, and even in the gloom she could see that fear was etched into her friend's face.

'Far-Sighted Boy saw them!' Berry blurted.

'Who?' she asked, starting to panic as she realised that she already knew the answer.

'The hunters!' Berry shouted. 'The hunters are coming!'

In the confusion and bustle, she managed to decipher that Far-Sighted Boy had woken early and had seen with the first small hint of daylight, a host of hunters moving towards them across the plain below. They were at a great distance, but seemed to be moving fast.

So, they had come. On the final day of their march, they had come.

The Great Father had sent them, and they were here. They had come to draw the final line under their story. She knew then that what her Family Father had said was true. Any that weren't swift enough to run over the top of the ridge and down the other side were doomed. The hunters would slaughter them, even as they ran away.

The light grew brighter, as the sun rose steadily behind them as they fled.

Many fell to the wayside, exhausted, to await their fate. Nobody could stop to help them. By now, even men were carrying children, in their panic to save as many as they could. Every now and then someone would risk a frantic look behind, and wailing could be heard, spurring them on, as the realisation dawned that the hunters were so quickly closing the gap.

Abruptly, they had reached the top.

The girl with no name slowed, along with the rest, as those in the lead looked down the other side of the ridge into the Nothing.

She edged her way through the crowd in front of her, to catch a glimpse of the mysterious unknown.

Except it wasn't 'nothing.' It was, 'something.'

In the distance, she could make out a wide plain. There was grass, trees dotted here and there. And, if the clouds of dust were anything to go by, there might even be the fuzzy outline of herds.

There was *something!* She was relieved. They weren't going to fall off the edge of the world. But first they had to get down.

A long, very steep slope of loose scree stood in their way. If it had been grass, or even trees, she felt that they could simply have run down to safety. But the edge of the Nothing was going to be the biggest barrier they would have to cross. And, judging from the growing wail of cries behind her, they were going to have to do it quickly.

She edged back through the deepening crowd towards her family. Her Family Father would know what to do.

They waited, anxiously, while the most intrepid of the men on the ridge started to pick their way down. She could no longer see over the top, so had to rely on any news passed back down through the crowd.

The first men were part-way down. Some had slipped on the loose stones, bloodying their backs and buttocks on the sharp stones, but they had recovered and were able to creep down further. One man had stumbled, and had disappeared from view, in a rush of loose stones.

His wail had come to an abrupt end, making everyone shiver with fear.

More had started to edge down, and were moving more quickly now that they'd seen how their comrades had managed.

Some women had moved forward onto the scree. Some of those were soon lost, overbalanced by their heavy burdens and clinging children. More managed to scramble downwards until they were lost from view.

As far along the ridge as she could see, families were gathered, readying themselves to make the descent. Many more gathered behind them, pushing and shoving, shouting encouragements and warnings, eager to get away from the approaching hunters.

Amongst the fray, she could hear screaming, she could make out a distant warning that the hunters were starting up the foothills towards them. So many people, none of them wanting to leave the Homeland, but none of them wanting to die either at the hands of the hunters.

She looked back down the hills they had climbed so rapidly, so painfully, just a few short hours before.

She was sure she could make out bodies moving fast, with urgency.

Sometimes she was convinced she could hear their excited yelps, just like those she had so often heard while watching her own family's men hunt.

She remembered the shouts, the yelps of the hunters, the anticipation, the excitement of it all. The hunt, the chase, the kill. It was all exciting to watch, but now that they were the hunted, now that *she was the hunted*, it was not exciting at all. It was fearful, horrible.

Panic regurgitated in her throat, until it threatened to stop her breathing. She needed to breathe. She was breathing hard, panting, panicking.

The crowd surged forward above her. She could sense, almost hear, the hysterical mothers and children starting their descent.

There were no more shouts of encouragement and endearment, no more calls of good luck. Now the shouts were threats. People were no longer being helped; they were being forced. She could hear their screams. She could feel their fear. She felt it in her very bones.

The hunters were almost upon them, and she wanted with all her heart, to be away from here. *Anywhere but here*, she thought.

She could almost feel the sharp flint spears penetrating her back. In her imagination, she could feel the heavy wooden clubs beating down on her head.

Along with everyone else, she pushed and barged her way through. They were in her way, and they needed to be moved. Almost before she even realised it, she was standing again on the top of the ridge, gazing down into the abyss.

Below her, more people than she could possibly count were scrambling, falling, sliding down the slope of sharp loose stones. Dust was everywhere and the suffocating clouds of dust hung in the air above them all.

She heard her Family Father shouting. He was telling them to go, to run, to jump, to get away. She glanced over her shoulder.

The hunters were running at them now, spears, clubs, knives and shouting, yelling, yelping. The scent of kill flared their nostrils. They were mad and wild for the kill. No one could stop them now, only the drop into the Nothing would prevent them following the families, stabbing, clubbing, ripping hair with tooth and nail.

With the rest of her family, she started down the scree slope. Far-Sighted Boy caught hold of her hand, and shouted that he would look after her. She had no idea how he might do that, but she didn't care. If he said he would, he would. She had to believe him.

She slipped and slid and scrambled down across the sharp, stinging, ever-moving stones.

She struggled to keep to her feet, and more than once felt the stab of stones into her buttocks, as she fought to regain her balance. She sensed, rather than saw, the hunters gathering on the ridge above them. They were yelling at them, screaming at them, frustrated to have lost the chance to kill.

She noticed larger stones tumbling past her.

They were throwing boulders down after them. Wasn't it enough that they had already left the Homeland? Wasn't it enough that they had already lost so many in the panic to get down the slope into the Nothing?

Why did they have to do this, to throw stones, to try to kill even those who were already dead to their Great Father?

Still holding Far-Sighted Boy's hand, she stumbled over a protrusion half-way down the slope.

Her arm jerked painfully.

Far-Sighted Boy had pulled her towards him. He had managed to slide to a stop just below the protrusion, and was pulling her to a halt beside him.

Far-Sighted Boy was fighting the slope, to try and stop both of them. Her feet slipped and slid as she tried desperately to gain some grip.

Her arm was hurting dreadfully, almost wrenched from its socket as he tried to stop her.

She scrambled to her feet, until she reached him, carving a wide arc below them as they slid to a halt. As she felt his arms encircle her, pulling her body into his and down into a crouch against the sharp stones, she saw huge boulders leap past them, over their heads, down to the side of them.

She watched, fascinated and appalled, as the boulders slammed into the backs of men and women in her family. She heard the impact of stones on heads, the sharp crack of bones breaking, the screams.

She heard the dreadful, fearful sound of the scree, as it started to landslide down the steep incline. It carried her family with it.

Far-Sighted Boy scrambled to climb higher up the slope, determined to reach the shelter just below the protrusion. He pulled her with him. It was hard work.

Their hands and feet slipped over and over, as the shifting stones constantly threatened to run them down the steep slope.

They moved carefully.

Eventually they reached the point of safety.

Only then, did they stop. They cowered beneath the protrusion, trying to keep as still as they could – every movement caused stones to slide, threatening to dislodge them, and give away their position.

All around, boulders rained down. Some bounced off the protrusion, flying close over their heads to land just where they had been a few minutes before.

Scree scattered over them, as the boulders struck the protrusion, stinging their bodies and their faces.

She buried her face into his shoulder, as dust and rock debris burned her eyes. He wrapped his arms protectively around her, though it had little effect.

Eventually the number of boulders thrown from above slowed, and then stopped altogether. She heard him give out a long, shaky breath of relief. She went to move, but he held her even more firmly.

'No!' he whispered. 'Not yet. They'll still be watching. Keep still, until I tell you.'

She did as she was told. She was too afraid to do anything else.

'I can feel the stones move,' he whispered, almost inaudibly, 'almost every time I breathe.'

As he said it, she realised that she could feel the stones move beneath her too.

She exhaled a careful, shallow breath.

Sharp stones were digging into her, wherever her body touched them. It was painful, but she dared not move. She made her mind up that moving wouldn't make any difference anyway.

If she managed to move one stone beneath her, another would just take its place. So, she kept as still as she possibly could. She clung to him, afraid that if he loosened his grip, she would slip and be dragged by the stones to her death.

3

After a while, she found it hard to ignore the discomfort she was in. It was excruciating. She felt that she couldn't bear another minute. But still she dared not move.

'How much longer?' she whispered.

'Until I say,' he whispered back, hoarsely.

'Why are we still waiting?'

'Because they're waiting for us to move. If we move, the stones will move. Then the boulders will fly again, and we will fly with them.'

She groaned, but she knew he was right. He was usually always right. She'd known him all her life. He never said much, certainly not to her, but when he did speak, he was nearly always right. She had to trust him.

The afternoon sun baked down on them.

She started to hallucinate. As her mind wandered, she dreamt of her family.

She remembered running through deep grass on the plain with her mother, laughing, eager to be amongst the first to the kill.

Her mind drifted to the skinning knives in their hands, the smell of blood in their noses, anticipating the taste of meat in their mouths. The Family Father standing proud beside his kill, smiling. She felt the warmth of the fire as it roasted the meat. Her mouth dribbled, waiting for her share. He had already disembowelled the beast, and they fell upon it, like eager vultures.

Her mother had shown her the parts that were dangerous to eat, and they left them alone. Those parts would be left for the wild dogs.

Everything else, other than the bones they could not crack, would be used. They would unravel the intestines, cut them up and dry them on stones in the sun. They would keep those in case they grew hungry on their marches. They would offer the raw liver to the hunter who had made the kill.

That was the best part, the very best part. There was so much goodness in the liver, and the killing-hunter would need that goodness, if he was to hunt well again tomorrow.

The rest of the meat was cut up, and cooked over fires.

The whole family would live off the remains for the next day or so. The men would take their pick first. The women would choose the parts they liked. The boys would be next, then the girls. Children would make do with whatever their mothers gave them, or whatever they could chew, from what was left over.

Everybody would eat. Everybody would live for another day. He was still holding her.

'Can you reach your waterskin?' he asked.

She could feel the bulk of it behind her, its thong cutting into her neck.

'Shall I try?'

'Gently,' he whispered, 'very, very gently.'

She drew the skin from behind her. Gradually, she drew it from her back, underneath her arm, until it rested on their stomachs.

They were bunched so close together, she almost felt as one. She had disturbed no stones. He was relieved. He smiled at her, their faces close together. His lips bled where they cracked from the moving of them.

Her waterskin, like everybody else's, was made from hide, carefully and painstakingly chewed, until it was soft enough to work. Sewn together with sinew from the same animal, it was so tightly sewn, it hardly leaked at all through the join.

Her mother had made it. She was very, very good at making water-skins. At one end, a small piece of hollowed-out horn had been sewn in, the hide stretched around it and moistened, so that as it dried, it gripped the horn tightly. That was the only place water could get in, or out of the skin. When it was empty, she would fill it from a stream. She would dip it into the water and pull the sides apart. Water would be pulled into the skin. She would do this again and again, until it was as full as she could make it.

When she needed to drink, she would put the horn into her mouth and squeeze the skin gently.

Sometimes, if she was very thirsty, she would suck on the horn, pulling the liquid into her mouth, but air would bubble into the skin when she removed her lips, and that made a noise.

They couldn't make a noise. So, she squeezed the skin gently.

Water, warm from the sun, trickled into her mouth. She nearly spluttered as the liquid coated her dry throat. She struggled not to cough. More than anything, she struggled not to let the water dribble from her mouth.

She couldn't waste it, but she couldn't breathe. She forced her stomach and her throat to drink, and not to convulse. She held her breath, and allowed the warm water to dribble down her throat and into her stomach. Then the retching stopped, and she went to take another draw from the skin.

He stopped her, wrenching the horn from her mouth.

'No!' he whispered sharply. 'Just one sip at a time. Otherwise, you'll throw it all up again.'

She was desperate to drink. She dreamt last night of the stream. Why hadn't she drunk her fill then? But of course, she had done so.

This was another day. Things were different now. Things had changed; he was right.

He was nearly always right. But she hated him in this very moment. She listened as he took his one sip from the horn. He choked, as she had done so, as the water met his parched throat.

She hated him for taking her water, but she knew he was right. The promise of evening brought the relief of shadows.

The heat lessened with every growing shadow. She could feel him relaxing as the shade grew.

She relaxed with him, knowing that their ordeal was almost over.

'Can I move now?'

'Not yet. They'll still be waiting. Listen!'

She listened. There was a breeze that circled towards them from the plain below.

It was a warm breeze but still cooling. The same wind carried any noises they might have heard from above, away into the Homeland. She could hear nothing.

'I can't hear anything,' she offered.

'That doesn't mean they're not there,' he whispered into her ear. 'I've been thinking that if I was them, I would wait until I was absolutely sure. So, they'll be waiting, like I would.'

'Waiting for what?' she asked, feeling bewildered.

'For us to make the stones move. For somebody to try to climb back up and into the Homeland.'

'Well, we haven't made the stones move! Nobody's tried to climb back up! Why would they still wait?'

'The Great Father would have told them to make sure. To wait until they were absolutely sure that nobody was left. That nobody was going to get back. Only then, would they dare to go home.'

She knew he was right. It didn't stop the pain in her side though.

The stones beneath her seemed to be digging in even further. She was sure she could feel herself bleeding from their stabbing. She wanted it to stop. She wanted very much for it all to stop. But she would wait, because she knew he was right.

In the darkness she stayed nestled to him. He was her lifesaver. He had promised he would look after her. She knew he would keep his promise.

'I think you are ready to be a man now,' she whispered into his ear.

'Do you think so?' he answered, distractedly. 'Why is that?'

'Because you are brave,' she uttered. 'Because you hunt well.'

She had watched him hunt. Boys weren't allowed to hunt with the men. Not until they had been proven during their ceremony. But sometimes a group of boys would go out practising their skills. She had watched them.

She wasn't supposed to, but she had always watched them. So had several other girls. They had all gone to see who would be worth flirting with, in the hope of persuading them to make them a necklace. She had observed the boys, fascinated, as they had encircled a small group of antelope. They had worked together, moving silently through the long grass. They had surrounded the group and on a signal from Far-Sighted Boy, had moved in for the kill.

As one body, the antelope herd had become jittery and nervous, smelling, or at least sensing, some unseen menace stalking them. They had danced away at a gallop; jumping, skittering, squealing away to safety.

The boys had pounced just at the right moment. One or two had managed to spear their prey.

Far-Sighted Boy was one of them. He had held onto his spear, and had run alongside the antelope.

The beasts had moved very fast, but Far-Sighted Boy had managed somehow to keep pace with them. He had gradually managed to pull down his prey, and had stood over it triumphant, panting and sweating, but triumphant. His kill. Nobody else's.

She had decided at that moment that she would have him.

She would make sure, somehow, that he bought her. She had chosen him. How else could it be?

'You hunt well,' she continued, 'and you are kind, and you are wise.'

'What?' he asked, surprised.

'You are wise,' she whispered. 'Men listen when you speak. I have seen them.'

He made no reply.

'So,' she continued, 'do you want to be called Far-Sighted boy, or Far-Sighted Man?'

'I don't know,' he whispered in reply. 'I haven't thought about it. What do you think?'

'I think probably Far-Sighted Man,' she replied seriously.

'Nah,' he said, 'I don't think so. It sounds clumsy.'

She thought for a while.

'How about just Far-Sight then?'

'Yes,' he said, nodding his agreement. 'That sounds much better. I like to keep things simple.'

'So can we move now?' she asked hopefully.

The shadows had quickly dissolved into night. Now it was starting to feel cold. She shivered, despite the heat from his body.

'Wait a minute,' he told her.

He gently eased his back, stiff from chill and the enforced stillness, and moved cautiously, until he could push himself up from the ground with his hands.

Some small stones skittered away into the darkness. He stayed very still for a moment, but could hear nothing from above.

He eased himself upwards, until he could raise his head above the protrusion.

His sharp eyes searched along the ridge high above them. He could see no heads silhouetted against the starlit sky, but he could make out the soft glow of fires on the other side of the ridge.

'It looks like they're camping,' he said quietly. 'We'll have to wait until they go. It would be too dangerous to try to get down now anyway. It's too dark to see, and in this quiet, any noise we make will alert them.'

'Can I at least sit up a bit?'

'Yes,' he mumbled, 'but very quietly. Don't disturb the stones, otherwise they'll hear.'

She gently eased herself into a sitting position. Only a few stones moved. It was uncomfortable, sitting on the sharp stones, but it was a relief not to feel them cutting into her side.

She eased her back and her arms, stretching the muscles to relieve the cramps in her limbs, but otherwise, she sat very still and made no noise. She gazed out from the cliff.

'I can see no fires down there,' she said flatly. 'No camps. Maybe we're the only ones left?'

The thought filled her with horror.

The events of the day had overwhelmed her; being chased over the edge of the cliff by people she had probably played with or talked to, or had seen at the Great Gathering. Friends, she had thought. All part of the same Great Family. It all seemed so alien to her that it was difficult to make sense of.

Then the awful sights she had seen and sounds she had heard, as they tumbled and fell on the steep slope of sharp stones. Worse still, was recalling the boulders that had thrown so many to their deaths in front of her eyes. She tried to sob.

Her eyes stung but no tears came. Her body was too dry for tears.

She felt his arm drape across her shoulders, pulling her towards him. It was comforting, him being there with her, but the thought of all the rest of them, the countless numbers of them, all lying dead at the bottom of the cliff, made her feel sick.

She knew her family would be amongst them. Her mother was bound to be one of them. She couldn't bear the thought of it. Her heart ached. She wanted to be home. She wanted things to be normal, ordinary, like she'd always known. But it would never be again. Nothing ever would be normal again! There was certain death if they tried to go back. She feared what they would face if they tried to move forward. But she knew they had no choice.

'I think there will be lots of people down there, out on the plains we saw,' he told her reassuringly, 'but I doubt they would have wanted to build fires.'

He looked thoughtful for a moment. 'I wouldn't have wanted to either. The hunters would have seen the fires. They might have been told to follow us into the Nothing, to hunt us all down, to kill us all, to make sure we couldn't come back ever.'

As her eyes searched the darkness below them, looking for any clues, any movement, she hoped he was right. She was sure he was right. He was nearly always right.

'Do you want some nuts?' she asked, realising how hungry she was. She'd almost forgotten her other bag, her nut bag.

She unslung the bag from around her neck, pulled the top open and offered it to him.

'What's this?' he asked, as his fingers found the stone.

'Leave it,' she said. 'It's my memory stone.'

'What?'

'My memory stone. I found it in the stream. It's a part of the Homeland. I brought it with me, to remember.'

'You do the strangest things sometimes, girl. Why on earth would you want to carry a lump of stone around with you?'

Her eyebrows knit in confusion. 'I told you, to remember. And anyway, it's not just *a lump of stone*. It's beautiful, it is special. It's from the Homeland. I will carry it with me wherever we go. That way I will always have a piece of Home with me.'

'Whatever.' He shrugged nonchalantly, not sure that he'd ever really understand her.

'Just don't expect me to carry it for you, when your arms get tired!'

'Oh, I won't,' she said firmly. 'Don't you worry about that! When you make your first kill in this new place, I will take some of the hide and make a special bag for it.

'Then I'll hang it around my neck and I will be able to keep it with me always. Always and forever.'

'So, we're travelling together then, are we?' he asked, realising what she had said.

'Don't you want to?'

'Hadn't thought about it,' he replied. 'I suppose we could?'

She smiled in the darkness.

She laid down beside him, wincing as the stones dug into her, and tucked her arm over his chest.

'I think we should,' she whispered. 'We're all that's left of our people now. We should stick together.'

'That sounds sensible.'

'So will you make me a necklace?' she giggled.

'Don't push your luck,' he muttered.

'Anyway, with that stupid stone hanging round your neck you'd probably break it,' he added.

'Please?'

'Please what?'

'Please make me a necklace?'

'Oh, for goodness' sake. I suppose so. Anything for a quiet life.'

She smiled; her beaming face shone as pale as the moonlight that gleamed over the cliff face.

A comfortable silence hung between them, but their reverie was interrupted from the sound of an ardent scream.

She cowered against him, shaking, as a body flew past where they lay.

They couldn't tell whether it was male or female, young or old.

Sharp stones slid and skittered all around them, as the horrified squeal echoed into the shadows.

They heard faint laughter from the ridge above.

They had not gone. He was right. He was nearly always right.

So, they would wait on the cliffside, moving as little as possible, so as not to disturb the stones. They would wait until he was sure. Then they would make the journey down to the plain.

'Blue stones,' she whispered, shivering in the freezing night.

'What?' he answered, his voice dragging back from his dream of gazelles and buffalo.

'Blue stones,' she repeated. 'I'd like blue stones in my necklace.'

'Where on earth do you think I'm going to find blue stones?' he asked, in an exasperated tone.

Why couldn't she be like the other girls, satisfied with kill-teeth and whatever stones he could find?

'I don't know,' she said, dozing again, 'but I know you will, somehow.'

'Why should I bother, anyway? You should just be grateful for whatever I give you.'

'I will be,' she stated simply. 'But I'd still like blue stones. And you'll find them for me because you like me.'

A small smile tugged on his lips.

She could be very difficult to understand sometimes, but she was right. He did like her, so, somehow, he would find some blue stones.

Bridie jumped as her mother suddenly slapped her hands on the arms of her chair.

'Right!' Hilda said decisively, pushing herself up and out of her chair. 'I need a cup of tea. Come on, you can help.'

Bridie groaned, and followed her mother indoors.

'But you haven't finished the story yet, Mum. What did they do next? Did they find her family? It would be horrible if they didn't. I wouldn't like it if my family was lost and I couldn't find them. Even my stupid brothers!'

Hilda smiled.

'We can finish the story in a bit, but I'm not saying another word until I've got a cup of tea in my hand. It's thirsty work, this story-telling!'

'I bet you're not as thirsty as the girl in the story, though!' Bridie told her, as she eagerly raided the biscuit tin.

'And why did she want blue stones anyway?' she asked.

Hilda looked at her, as an exasperated expression crept over her face.

'How should I know?' she said. 'Maybe she just liked blue? Anyway, come on. You bring the biscuits, if there's any left. I'll bring the drinks. I'd best get on, or I won't have time to finish the story before I have to start dinner.'

4

She was thankful for the sun. It thawed the chill in her bones. It had been a cold night. She couldn't remember ever being this cold.

They had no sleeping skins, so all they could do to keep warm was to lay cuddled together, their arms around each other, sharing one another's heat. Still the cold had penetrated deep within them.

The early sunshine had brought relief, but it also brought problems. They had a few nuts left, but the water-skin she had brought with her was empty. They'd had barely enough to drink all the time they had been there, laying painfully on the sharp stones.

Now it was all gone.

When the sun rose high enough, they would be in trouble. So, they would have to find some water somewhere, very soon, or perish.

As soon as it was light enough, Far-Sighted Boy had peeped over the edge of the protrusion, trying to see as far along the ridge as he could, looking for heads, or for any sign that the hunters might still be there. As the sun had risen higher, he had looked again, and again. So far, he had seen nothing.

'We will wait for a little while longer,' he informed her. 'Then we'll go down as quietly as we can.'

When the sun was almost directly above them, he announced that it was time to go.

As they stood, gingerly, and started to brush the smaller stones from their skin, she had never felt as relieved about anything in her whole life. Just to stand up was a joy. The prospect of finally getting off this cliffside made her quite euphoric.

Until she remembered what they could expect to find below them. The broken, still, battered bodies of their family. They were going to find the aftermath, whenever they descended.

It was still a joy to stand and be moving, even though she feared to hear rocks and boulders land behind them at any moment.

The boulders didn't move. There were no rocks. There were no spears thrown. There were no hunters. She was sure of that. He had waited until the right moment, and she was grateful for that. This time he was completely right and *not nearly*.

As she looked down the steep scree slope, she could see that they were still only about halfway down. There was a long way to go, and the rest of the descent looked even steeper than she'd remembered from before. But it had to be done. They had to get off the cliffside.

They were already thirsty, and their thirst would only increase and get worse the longer the sun beat down on them. Whatever happened, whatever was thrown at them, whatever they might find when they reached the bottom, they had to leave. They had to go now.

It was a very long and difficult journey. Every step they took seemed to send a small landslide of stones tumbling down before them. The sharp stones of the scree tore into their feet and legs, cutting even through the tough skin of their soles.

They tried creeping straight down, but the steepness of the slope and the instability of the stones made her feel at any moment that she would fall head first off the cliffside.

They tried sliding down on their buttocks, but after only a few brief moments of trying, they decided that was not going to work.

The jagged rocks and stones would rupture their skin, leaving a smear of blood behind them.

The only way they could find, that seemed to work, was to traverse the cliffside, creeping gently across and downwards, then turning gently to do the same thing the other way.

It was still painful, and it was still slippery, and it was a dreadfully slow process but when they paused briefly to rest, she could see by looking back up the cliff towards their protrusion, that they were making progress.

He held her hand as they crept downward, steadying, reassuring, comforting.

Even so, the pain of the stones cutting into her feet and the cramp in her legs were almost unbearable. As they made what she so hoped to be their last traverse, before reaching flatter ground, he spoke.

'So, I've been thinking,' he said quietly, 'if, when we find some of the others, we'd best be wary. We'll need to have a good story.'

'Why?' she whispered, her throat dry and her voice hoarse from dust.

'Because,' he continued, 'if they find out we're without a family, they might well attack us, or worse, chase us off.'

'Why would they do that?' she asked. Most of her experiences of meeting other families had always been on friendly terms. They'd share meat, exchange news and stories, and often the families would camp near to each other for a couple of days, before going their separate ways again.

'Well, have you seen any game yet?' he asked in return.

'No,' she said. She hadn't really thought about it until now, but though she'd seen grass at the bottom of the cliff, and some trees on the far-off horizon, she couldn't remember seeing any game at all, even though their painful, uncomfortable perch high up on the cliffside had offered an excellent vantage point.

'Exactly,' he said. 'I haven't either. If there's no game, there's no food. If there's no food, they'll likely be hungry, maybe even starving.

Why would they want to share anything they might have with a couple of strangers?'

'Oh, right,' she uttered. *This put a different light on things.*

'And if we were just a couple of unattached kids, then what would they do?'

'Dunno,' she sighed, shrugging her shoulders. 'Shout at us?'

'Probably,' he said, 'but after that?'

'How should I know?' she said, getting increasingly irritated by his questions.

'They would do what they'd do if they found a boy wandering across the plain,' he retorted. 'They'd either chase me off, or peg me out to attract beasts they could kill and eat.'

She didn't say anything, so he continued.

'It's you I'm more worried about,' he said flatly.

'Me? Why?'

'What do they do with girls they find wandering about by themselves?' he asked. 'Especially if it's a pack of lone men we come across?'

'Oh,' she said, knowing straight away what he meant. 'They'd use her for comfort, and then ignore her. There would be no food, there would be no future.'

'So, what do we do, then? Make sure we're not seen? Go off somewhere far away and hope nobody finds us?'

She couldn't imagine not having the company of others, not having other girls to talk to, to giggle with. Not having women to learn from, or to take their advice. She couldn't imagine a life without a certain type of maternal comfort. But if there was no other way...

'What we need to do,' he said, 'is pretend. I pretend that I'm already a man. You pretend you're already a woman. My woman.'

'Oh!' she exclaimed, surprised by his words.

33

'Oh! I hadn't thought of that…but I'm not sure it would work. You can easily pass for a man, but how could I possibly pass for a woman?'

'Easy,' he said, simply.

'Not so easy!' she snapped. 'I don't even look like a proper woman yet! And anyway, I don't even have a kilt! 'No, it's just not possible. It would never work.'

'Well, you look like a woman to me,' he said. 'And we can soon find you a kilt. Didn't you say your mother had made you one?'

'Yes, but…she's down there. She's dead, Far-Sighted Boy. She's never going to give me my kilt now.'

Her eyes stung. If she hadn't been so dry, tears would have been running down her face.

He stopped and turned to her, taking her in his arms.

'I know,' he said sympathetically. 'But even so. If we can find her, we can find your kilt. Once you're wearing that, nobody would even question that you're a woman.'

'It just doesn't seem right,' she said, 'passing myself off as something I'm not. Passing myself off as a woman. Your woman. It just doesn't seem right.'

'Can you think of a better plan?' he scowled slightly.

She didn't respond. She stared first at him, then at the ground.

'Look,' he said, more urgently. 'It's just pretend, alright? I'm not expecting you to really be my woman. Not properly my woman. It's just *pretend*, honest.'

Her bottom lip was quivering now.

'So, you don't really want me at all?' she asked, looking him in the face. 'You never did? All those things you said up there?'

'What?'

'Up there!' she said, glancing back toward the cliffside, and the protrusion.

'You told me you wanted to make me a necklace. That was *pretend* too, then? You didn't mean it at all?'

'No,' he said, startled. 'No, I mean yes. I mean of course I meant it! I…Oh! Why do you always have to twist things around? That's not what I meant at all – I just meant I don't want to make you do anything you don't want to.'

'So, I'm alright as a *pretend woman*,' she scoffed, looking away, 'but you don't really want me as a proper woman.'

'That's not what I meant at all, and you know it,' he said desperately. 'I just want to keep you safe. I just thought that if people think you are my woman, then you'd be safe.'

She just snorted.

'Oh, come on,' he said impatiently. 'Let's get off this cliff. We can talk about it later.'

'Hmph,' she looked irritated. From the look on her face, he realised that she obviously wasn't talking to him now. He went to take her hand again, to help her down the last few metres. She shook his hand away.

The sun was lowering in the sky by the time they eventually reached the bottom of the cliff. At last, they found more level ground. And at last, the stones beneath their feet only crunched, but weren't threatening to cause a landslide that would carry them to their deaths.

She could see grass now. There was still a wide expanse of stones to cross, but at last there was grass.

First, they had to drink.

Her mouth and throat were parched and clogged with dust. She tried to swallow, but had no saliva. Her head was beginning to ache from the lack of water, and she knew that he must be feeling the same pain.

Without any great hope or expectation, her eyes searched the stones, for any sign of water. Perhaps a spring, or a small stream. But of course, that would have been too much to expect. There was no water here. They would have to move on.

And then she saw them. Her family. Her eyes had caught some movement in the lengthening shadows, birds.

As she concentrated, she could make them out. Carrion birds, vultures. She had found them. She had to see. She didn't want to see, but she had to. They were her family, she was drawn to them.

They clapped their hands as they approached. They couldn't shout, their throats were too sore, but she hoped that clapping their hands might scare the birds away. But they were feasting, and had no intention of being driven off easily. It was horrible to watch as they pulled pieces of skin from the bodies, and buried their heads deep inside for more tender morsels. They clapped even louder.

Still, the birds would not go. Far-Sighted Boy motioned her to stay where she was, while he approached the decaying bodies.

He waved his arms from side to side, and threw stones at them. Eventually, the birds flew off to a respectable distance, but all the time watching and cawing, waiting for their chance to return.

He approached the bodies with his hand covering his mouth and nose against the plague of flies that surrounded them. He looked around briefly, and picked up some items from the ground that surrounded them.

Watching him, she knew she would have to do the same. She knew that he would only pick up what boys would think were useful: water, tools, weapons, but she wanted the things that he wouldn't have thought about. Things that were important to women, but not to men.

As she got closer, she had to steel her stomach against the smell, and tried as best she could not to see the damage that the boulders and the fall from the cliff had done to them, let alone what the birds and other beasts had inflicted on them since.

36

She could clearly make out her mother's arm, protruding awkwardly from a bed of stones. She knew it was her mother from the bracelets that decorated the arm. If she had any moisture left in her, she would have cried. If she had had any voice, she would have wailed long and loud. But she had neither. All she could do was mourn from the depths of her soul.

Then she spotted what she had hoped she might find. It lay not far from her mother's hand. It was her mother's bag. The bag held everything she wanted to find, everything she would need, and other things she would use just to remember her mother with.

She picked it up gently and hugged it tight to her, nodding silent thanks to her mother for her last gift. She stepped back and looked around again.

Their Family Father was there, broken and bloody on the ground, his body covered in grazes from where he had slid down the sharp stones. His head had caved in from the impact of the boulder that had killed him, high up on the cliff.

Others that she knew were there also, women, children, boys, girls. They were all gone. She counted as many as she could see. The number was still less than the number she knew her family had been, but then she realised something. There were no babies here, and not many children.

She could only imagine that they were either buried deep under the stones, or had been carried off whole by scavengers. She decided that she was probably right. She and Far-Sighted Boy were the only ones left.

He came to stand by her side as she backed away respectfully. He passed her a water-skin he had found in the debris, mercifully undamaged. They each drank from it gratefully, clearing the dust from their mouths, easing the pain in their throats.

'Are you alright?' he asked gently.

She shook her head.

'I'm not sure I'll ever be "alright" again,' she said simply.

'Did you find what you were looking for?' he asked.

'Yes, it's all here in my mother's bag,' she replied. 'Most of all, I wanted to find the kilt she made me. I'll need that to show that I'm a woman.'

One last look along the stones revealed more and more flocks of birds.

There was a large number of bodies lying broken and battered. She shivered at the sight.

'Have you got your axe-head?' she asked.

He nodded. It was in the bag hanging from his belt, together with his eating-knife. He had made both of them, painstakingly forming them from plain stones. He had completed the knife, but had yet to bind the axe-head with thin strips of thong to a piece of antler. He would do that while the leather was wet, so that it would tighten naturally as it dried.

'Then give it to the Father.'

'How? He's dead!'

'It doesn't matter,' she said. 'If you're going to buy me, you have to pay the Father.'

'But you're worth far more than a single axe-head,' he protested.

'I know,' she said, smiling faintly. 'Have you got anything else to offer him?'

'No, not really.'

'Then give him your axe-head. You made it, and you made it well. I'm sure he would appreciate that.'

'You've made up your mind, then?' he asked. 'You really want me to buy you?'

She nodded. He did as she'd suggested.

'It's getting dark, we should go.'

She made one more glance at her mother's body, one last nod of her head, and they left.

It was very nearly dark by the time they reached the grass.

They walked a short way, when she told him she had to sit down for a while. They had been on their feet for hours. Her legs were cramping, her stomach ached, and her feet were sore and blistered.

'We can't make a fire,' he told her. 'We're too close to the cliff. I think the hunters have all gone now, but I don't want to take any risks.'

She just nodded, too tired to speak.

'I'll watch while you sleep,' he told her.

She knew he must be as tired as she was, but she was too tired to argue. She was thankful for the sleeping-skin he'd recovered from the stones. It was one of the few things she properly approved of, though she knew that he would need the spear and the collection of knives and other tools if he was to impress anybody they might meet.

It was still dark when she woke. The first glimmers of sunrise were just about visible in the gloom.

He was still sat were she'd left him, he had remained awake, though his head was visibly starting to nod.

'Feel better?' he asked.

She nodded. She'd dreamt while she was asleep. She'd dreamt that she was sat by the Women's fire, talking to her mother.

She'd smiled, even in her sleep, listening to her mother's chatter. But then her mother had turned her face more fully towards her, and in the firelight, she could see the dreadful wounds that the birds had made. She'd woken in a cold sweat, relieved to know that she was awake, still alive, with him still sat by her side.

'You had better get some sleep,' she instructed him. 'We only have a couple of nuts left, so you'll have to go hunting.'

He nodded as he laid back onto the soft grass.

'Hmm…' he said softly, closing his eyes. 'Though I suppose we could always try eating that stone of yours.'

By the time she'd returned his smile, he was asleep.

As she sat on the grass, she unpacked her kilt from her mother's bag. In the growing daylight, she turned it over and over in her hands, admiring the detail of the leather-work, the beads sewn onto it, the fine stitch-work. She had seen it before. She had watched her mother as she'd made it.

She'd listened, awestruck with anticipation, to all the stories that she'd been told while her mother had stitched; the traditions, the legends, and what it had meant to be a woman.

Now, with joyful reverence, she wrapped it around her waist and pulled the fastenings tight. It felt strange. After all her imaginings of what it would feel like to wear it, now she actually knew.

Now she was actually, properly a woman, she thought. Only now, she could hold her head proudly in the company of other women, and claim her place by the Women's fire. More importantly, she would be responsible for preparing her man's meat, and for bearing his children.

She pulled a face at that thought, she had practised cooking meat, but the thought of bearing children was more than a bit scary.

That was something that all of the women she had ever known were scared of. They had no choice in any of it, either the getting of babies or the delivering of them, but she knew, along with the women before her, how difficult and dangerous it was. Women were lucky if they lived long enough to see their sons become men, and their daughters become women.

She shivered at the thought. Still, if her mother hadn't died on the cliff, she would have been there to celebrate her new woman-hood. If her mother could do it, then so could she. She would make sure that she did.

She sighed deeply again, as she thought of her mother. The mother who had given her life, who had nurtured her through her childhood, who had guided and advised and taught, and who she had watched, horrified, being thrown off the cliffside by those huge boulders.

Tears ran down her face as she was reminded of her loss. She looked over at where Far-Sighted Boy slept. He was sleeping soundly. It was different for him. He was a boy. It was different for boys. Boys thought differently to girls. They had different things to learn. She remembered when he had come to them. He had been fostered to her Family Father when he was very young.

That was how it worked. Young boys were taken from their mothers and given to other families. It helped to harden them, to teach them how to be men, hard men, men who would unfailingly provide for their families.

He was about the same age as she was, she thought. Although she didn't know quite how old she was herself. Nobody bothered to count the number of summers a child had. It was only important as they grew, and even then, the number of summers didn't matter much. What mattered most, was when a boy was big and strong enough, to go through the ordeal that would prove him as a man. What mattered was when a girl was big enough, and when the signs told the world that she was a woman.

They'd talked about this ordeal.

He had been worried that he hadn't proved himself. She'd suggested that what they'd been through on the cliffside must surely have been worse than anything the older men might have invented for him. He'd been satisfied with that. She reminded herself that he was no longer Far-Sighted Boy. He had proved that he was ready. Now he would be called Far-Sight. And that, she felt was right.

Now they were bound together.

He had promised her a necklace. She shrugged at that, it didn't matter. If anybody asked, she would just say that she'd lost it on the cliffside. He'd make her one eventually, maybe one with blue stones, but it didn't really matter. Not now. He'd bought her now, so that was that. She didn't mind. If he hadn't, somebody else would have eventually. And she was secretly, very pleased that he had.

He was clever, and strong. She'd watched him hunt, in the days before the Gathering. He was good at it, so she had no doubt that he would provide for her. Anyway, he was different to the other men, in a nice way. He thought about things. Most of them didn't.

Most of them thought about hunting and eating and taking their comfort wherever they could get it, with any girl they could catch. She had listened to them laughing and shouting to each other around the fire, boasting about their prowess.

He'd joined in, but nothing like as loud as the others. He was usually quiet, thoughtful. He preferred to listen. He even listened to her, sometimes, and that was unusual too. Girls were not supposed to be able to think. But he always listened to her when she spoke, though he was careful not to let any of the others know.

She liked him, she thought he liked her too. She thought he cared about her and that made her happy. There was a lot that she would have changed about the last few days, if she could, but not this. Being bound to him made her feel content. She hoped he felt the same way. *I'm sure he does*, she thought, as she gazed at his sleeping form.

They walked as quickly as they could, but even so, it had taken an uncomfortable amount of time to cross the plain. It was a strange place.

There was grass, but it was short and thin and sparse. It was green, but not any colour of green that she had seen before. This grass was pale and unhealthy-looking. She had seen the grass from the cliffside, but it had been difficult to tell how far it stretched.

His sharp eyes had seen trees and low hills, though far off in the distance. She couldn't see that far, but she trusted his eyes, so she would follow him, knowing that he was sure that he was leading them to a better place.

Not many could see as far and as clearly as Far-Sight could. Most of them would have only seen the grass plain, shimmering in the heat, devoid of herds.

Perhaps that was why they called it 'The Nothing,' because that was all they could see. *Nothing*. But he had seen something, so that was where they were going. They couldn't get there quickly enough for her.

The small amount of water they had recovered from the stones around the Family would not last very long. It was hot, and they were thirsty again. Their stomachs growled with hunger too. For days, all they had eaten were the nuts from her small bag. Now, all it contained was the stone she had found in the stream, her Home Stone.

They couldn't eat that. So far, they had seen no animals at all, and they couldn't stop long enough for her to search out any insects or burrowing creatures that might have helped to take away the pangs of hunger.

There were plenty of flies, though. Small, irritating flies that stung if they weren't brushed off quickly. They hadn't slept much, either, which didn't help their mood. They had to sleep one at a time, with one keeping watch, while the other slept fitfully under the sleeping-skin. It was cold at night. If they'd been able to build a stockade, they might have both been able to sleep at the same time. But there was nothing here to build a stockade with.

Even if they'd had the time and energy to do so, there was nothing to make a fire with either, even if he would have allowed one.

During the day, the haze from the heat helped to conceal them from anyone who was not already close, but at night, even a small pin-prick of flame would have been seen for miles.

He didn't want to risk even the smallest chance that someone might be watching from the ridge to see if any had survived the cliff-side.

He feared that if they showed themselves, a troop of hunters might be sent down into the Nothing to finish them, and even though there was nothing here to help them survive, they were still very much alive, and he wanted them to stay that way for as long as they could.

So, their days passed.

They spent them tired, hungry, thirsty and hot, and as the days darkened into evenings, so their nights passed, only now, they were tired, hungry, thirsty and cold.

Until one evening, almost without her realising, they found them-selves within walking distance of the trees he had seen, from so many miles away. They were real!

As they passed beneath the branches, grateful for the brief shade, and made their slow progress between the hills, they could clearly see a wide valley stretching out below them down a gentle grassy slope.

This time the grass was more like the grass she was familiar with, lush and green and soft beneath her aching feet.

Birds flew among the branches, the first they had seen and heard since their charge down the cliffside. Proper birds, not the horrible, carrion-eating vultures who had greeted them so disdainfully when they had tried to approach the bodies of the Family strewn out across the sharp stones.

She smiled, despite her cracked lips. This was not 'nothing', this was 'something'. Here, she was sure they would be able to hunt and survive, whatever else might happen.

She glanced at Far-Sighted Boy, and quickly corrected herself. He was Far-Sight now, and he had proved himself worthy of the new name.

He was scanning the valley, looking for streams or springs where they might find some drinkable water. He was looking carefully for signs.

His eyes scanned for places where the vegetation was thicker and where the green was deeper. Then he pointed, and took her hand to lead her to it.

Later, after they'd slaked their thirst and washed some of the dust and grime from their skin, they sat on the bank of the small stream he had found. As they soaked their weary, badly grazed feet in the soothing water, he turned and smiled at her.

'It looks like we're not alone in the world after all.'

'Really?' she exclaimed, instantly alert.

'Over there,' he said, pointing in the general direction of a small group of trees, 'I saw the remains of a stockade.'

'I didn't see that!' she gasped. 'Show me!'

It wasn't very big, but it had clearly been a stockade.

In the middle were two patches of burnt soil, the remains of overnight fires. Small bones were scattered here and there, some burned to ash amongst the debris of the fires.

'Two fires!' she said happily. 'Two fires! That means it was a Family. Men and women!'

He leant down and smelled the ashes, and crumbled some pieces of charred wood between his fingers.

'Last night,' he said, 'or the night before. They won't be too far away. I'll look for signs of tracks, and we'll follow them.'

She was almost beside herself with joy and relief. 'Don't get your hopes up,' he said, 'it might take us a while to catch up. And even when we do, we'll have to be careful. We'll have to be clever.

'I know, I know,' she said, 'but still – there are others! We're not by ourselves after all!'

5

He followed the tracks carefully, she followed his footsteps, wishing he would hurry up. Daylight was fading. Soon they would have to stop, unable to follow any further until the morning.

When he stopped suddenly, she very nearly fell over him.

'Why did you stop?' she asked, startled from her day-dream.

'Aren't you hungry?' he asked simply.

'Of course I'm hungry!' she replied, irritated. 'What a stupid question!'

'Then shut up and keep still!' he ordered her.

She sat on the grass while he crept off, quietly following some clue that she couldn't see. He disappeared into some bushes, and returned a few minutes later, triumphantly displaying a small rabbit. Her eyes opened wide. Saliva dribbled from her mouth. She could almost taste it.

As she prepared the rabbit, skinning and disembowelling it, as she'd learned, he built a small fire.

He no longer feared the watchful eyes of the hunters on the ridge, and by now, he was too hungry to care much anyway. They had to eat.

She watched the meat carefully, desperate not to let it burn. This would be the first meal she had cooked for him, and she wanted to get it right.

She wanted to impress him with her skills. She didn't particularly want to taste burnt meat herself anyway, so she was extra careful. Having said that, she was so hungry she felt that she could have even chewed a piece of burnt wood and enjoyed it.

As they threw the gnawed bones into the flames, he leaned back happily onto the grass.

'That was good,' he said, burping happily.

She smiled. It had been good. She'd surprised herself and she'd pleased him.

The next morning, they took up the tracks again. They were fading by now, and it wasn't so easy to follow. They made even slower progress than the day before, and she had to bite her tongue, to keep her impatience from showing.

Eventually, just as the daylight was beginning to fade, he stopped. He put his fingers to his mouth as a sign for her to be quiet, and pointed.

As her eyes followed the direction of his finger, she could see what he had spotted. The faint glow of a fire in the fading light. She smiled happily at him. He had done it. He had followed the family's almost cold tracks, and he had found them. She threw her arms around his neck and squeezed.

'Thank you!' she said.

As they slowly made their approach to the fire, he reminded her of what they needed to say and do. He cautioned her that they would have to be very careful, and remain guarded and vigilant, if they were to stay safe. She nodded her agreement vigorously, all the time wishing he would just hurry up.

The camp was very quiet as they neared. He knew that watchful eyes had been upon them as they approached. She walked a pace or two behind him, as was the tradition.

He paused a few paces from the stockade walls.

'Far-Sight greets the Family!' he called, formally observing the niceties of etiquette.

'I see you, Far-Sight!' a voice from within the stockade returned the formal response. 'You are welcome to sit by my fire.'

The stockade walls parted slightly, allowing them to enter.

She could see from the rigid set of his shoulders that he was tense as they entered. He looked alert, suspicious, careful. Her eyes danced over the group gathered within. Four men stood by one fire. Six women, a couple of girls and a single boy stood by another. No babies.

The fires looked inviting. Her nose caught the aroma of meat cooking and her mouth started to moisten at the same time as her stomach rumbled.

'I am Far-Sight,' he repeated again, as he approached the men's fire. 'And this is my woman. Her name is Stone.'

He had said it so simply, but it startled her all the same. He had given her a name! For the first time in her life, she had a name! She was no longer just a girl with no name. He had announced it to the world, and at the same time he announced that she was *his woman*. The hairs on the back of her neck stood up with excitement and pleasure.

One of the women approached, and discretely took her hand, leading her to the Women's fire. She followed as though it was by old habit, but secretly she was thrilled. The women had accepted her. She was joyful, though the formalities would not yet allow her to smile.

'I am Long-Running. You are welcome to our fire. You are welcome to share our meat,' said the older of the men. He was clearly the Family Father, and was following the etiquette to the hilt.

'I am grateful,' she heard her man reply. 'But we are simply passing by, and wished to greet a neighbour.'

49

Again, formalities and etiquette. She wished they would just get on with it as she was starving, but they weren't finished yet. She knew there would be more. She bit the inside of her lip, to quell her stomach pangs and to hide her impatience.

The women and the girls were all looking at her, obviously amused, as she rolled her eyes pointedly in the direction of the men's fire.

One of the girls stifled a giggle, and the woman who had taken her to their fire offered her the faintest of smiles, her eyes twinkling with merriment.

They were all thinking the same thing, all wishing the men would finally finish with their formalities, so that they could all eat. This was the way it was always done, though, and they all knew it could not be hurried or rushed. To miss even a small part of the etiquette would be a slight to one side or the other, to the visitors or to the Family Father. They would just have to be patient a little while longer.

She listened carefully, as the formalities took their traditional course. There were introductions to the other men around the fire, each one smiling as they raised their spears towards Far-Sight, clashing their forearms against his own.

The invitation to sit by the fire and take meat with them was repeated, together with an invitation to share their stockade for the night. Each invitation was gently and formally declined, and each invitation was repeated again.

Finally, there was the formal acceptance, the formal gripping of elbows, the smiles and the sitting down by the fire. All of them knew the traditions, and all of them knew what the final outcome would be.

She smiled, he had played his part to perfection. One refusal too few and they would all have recognised his inexperience in such matters. One refusal too many, however gentle, would have resulted in the host feeling insulted and would have led to strong words, probably blows, possibly even killings. It had happened before but not this time.

Far-Sight had done it well, she was proud of him and she was glad it was over. They all were.

Everyone was hungry, and the meat was ready.

Now that etiquette had been satisfied, they could eat. And, finally, the women could talk. The formal exchange of news would take place when the men had finished eating, but she knew that by then, she would already know most of it.

Women always knew what was going on, and were always more than willing to share it amongst themselves. Sometimes, she knew the women would add their own embellishments to events, to make them more exciting, but there was always truth at the bottom of it, and anyway, she preferred the way the women told their news to the way the men did. Men's news was always told in a way that made it seem as though they were at the centre of the action, or that their role was far more important than it really was, even if they'd only heard the news second or third hand.

Women were never at the centre of anything, so making themselves seem important didn't come into it. Women told their version much more entertainingly, she thought. She preferred the women's version.

But first, before they could share their news, even before they could share their meat, the women needed to introduce themselves to her.

The older woman introduced herself first. She was called Nut, and as she pointed at the others and shared their names, each of them clapped their hands once.

Stone also clapped her hands together and repeated their names back to them. That was the way it was always done. They would remember each other's names, and next time they met, they would offer the less formal greeting of a discrete smile and a simple side-to-side hand-wave with their hands kept below their shoulders. They revealed their names quickly.

They were all hungry.

It was completely dark by the time they were finally able to bite into their meat. They ate by the bright light of the fire. Stone had to be careful not to take too much into her mouth at once, otherwise she'd have choked.

Other than the small rabbit they'd shared the night before, this was the first decent meat she'd tasted, in she couldn't remember how long. She nearly choked anyway when one of the women asked her how she had come by her name.

'Your name is unusual,' the woman said. 'Stone,' the woman pondered for a moment. 'Is that because you lay like a stone when your man takes his comfort?'

This caused such a fit of giggles from the group that Stone couldn't resist joining in. It felt good to laugh.

'No,' Stone replied, when the laughter had died down. 'I got my name because I picked up a pretty stone before we left the Homeland. I wanted something to remind me of how it was. It's something I can look at as we travel. A piece of Home will always be with me.'

Many of her companions nodded sadly, but not all of them.

'Why would you want to remember that place?' one asked quizzically. 'After all that happened, I would just want to forget it. The further away from it we go, the happier we will be.'

After that, the only discussion that took place, was about their expulsion from the Homeland, and the injustice of it all. They talked about the cliff and the sharp stones, about the boulders, and the children carried away by the landslides, they all lamented about family and friends they hadn't been able to find. There were tears and sighs, and in the end, as the night drew closer around them, a growing resignation.

Finally, just as the men were leaving their fire, stifling yawns, and seeking out their women and their sleeping-skins, Nut took hold of her arm.

'Your kilt is new,' she said. It was a statement, not a question.

Stone hesitated a moment, and then nodded, shyly.

Nut gave her a kindly smile and returned her nod.

As Stone lay down beside Far-Sight, he squeezed her hand.

'You alright?' he asked.

She nodded to him in the shadows, and snuggled into his side. He was warm, and the night was getting cold. It felt good to lay beside him, safe within the stockade.

Finally, they could both sleep at the same time, without one taking watch. As she lay there, staring up at the stars, listening to the quiet but unmistakable sounds of men taking comfort from their women, a thought occurred to her. She dug him in the ribs with her elbow.

'Ough!' he muttered irritably, as quietly as he could. 'What's up with you?'

'Listen!' she hissed into his ear.

'Listen to what?' he hissed back.

'The men taking comfort from their women, stupid!'

'So?'

'So…' she whispered to him, almost inaudibly, 'they're going to start wondering why you're not doing the same!'

'Oh…'

'Is that all you can say? Oh?' she whispered.

'Well, what do you expect me to say?'

'It's not what I expect you to say!' she said. 'It's what they expect you to do!'

'Well, I don't care what they *expect,*' he retorted, defiantly.

'You will care in the morning! They'll laugh at you, and say things about you not wanting your woman!'

He didn't respond, so she continued.

'And the women will tease me about it too! They already think I'm called Stone because I don't please you!'

'Who cares what they think?' he said. 'I don't!'

'Well, I do!' she insisted.

'Anyway, there are formalities. We should keep up traditions,' he told her.

She rolled her eyes, in the darkness.

There were always traditions. There were always formalities. In normal times, after a man had paid the agreed price, the women and girls would take his new woman to a stream or a river, and would wash her and dress her hair with flowers.

More flowers would be woven into a chain and tied around her waist. In the morning, if the chain of flowers was broken or crushed, the women would know that he had taken comfort from her. They would ululate as she joined them, and would tease her around the women's fire as they packed up the camp to move on again.

Right now, though, there was no time for traditions. They had gone a long way past formalities. He had announced to the family all around them that she was his woman. Now they were expecting him to take his comfort.

'I think it's too late for traditions,' she whispered.

He didn't move.

She lay there for a while, waiting, but he didn't move, so she leaned over and pulled him towards her. That didn't work, so she reached down and pulled his leg over her. Eventually, he eased himself on top of her.

'This feels awkward,' he muttered into her ear.

'Why? Haven't you ever thought about doing it?'

'Of course I have,' he admitted, 'but it's not the same as actually doing it!'

'Oh, will you please just get on with it!' she insisted.

Bridie couldn't help but interrupt her mother's narrative.

'So why would she want to pull him on top of her, Mum? That would be really uncomfortable, wouldn't it.'

Hilda looked at her and smiled.

'Why do you think, Bridie? Didn't we talk about all this last year?'

Bridie's eyes widened, as she suddenly realised what her mum was talking about.

'What, you mean she wanted him to...to have sex with her?'

Hilda nodded. Bridie screwed her face up in disgust.

'You mean, like, what, in front of all those people? That's just seriously gross! Eww!'

'Well, not exactly *in front* of them all. It was pitch dark, after all.'

'It's still disgusting!' Bridie told her vehemently.

'And all because she didn't want to get teased by the other girls? Didn't you tell me that I shouldn't feel pressured into doing it just because other girls told me I should? Anyway, she's far too young. He should have respected her more!' she added indignantly.

'Didn't he respect her by not putting pressure on her? He didn't expect anything from her until she was ready. He waited for her to say what she wanted, didn't he?' Hilda affirmed.

'I suppose,' said Bridie, reluctantly.

'And don't forget that all this was a very long time ago,' explained her mother.

'People had different views then, different ways, different traditions. Anyway, lives were short, and difficult. By the time the story started, she had already lived probably more than half her lifetime. She was lucky to have made it that far! And we mustn't judge them by our times and our standards, OK?'

Bridie shrugged.

'I suppose,' she muttered. 'So, anyway, when you said about men "taking their comfort" from women, you were talking about sex, right?'

'Yes, that's right,' her mother confirmed. 'Which is just as well, otherwise we wouldn't be here, would we?'

'So, Stone and Far-Sight made babies then?'

'That's usually what happens when people have sex, Bridie, as we discussed. So may I continue?'

Bridie nodded, but she couldn't help but make one more comment.

'Well, I don't want babies, so I certainly won't be letting boys anywhere near me anytime soon!' she insisted.

'I'm sure you'll change your mind one day,' her mother laughed.

Her mother settled into the story again, brushing biscuit crumbs from her lap.

Afterwards, when he'd taken his comfort, she lay there looking up at the stars again. He'd been right, it had felt strange. It had felt awkward at first, but she found that, once she'd got used to his rhythmic movements, she'd quite enjoyed the intimacy of it.

She wished she had her best friend Berry there to talk to, to tell her what it really felt like. They had spent long hours talking about it, guessing, assuming, giggling, but now that she knew for certain what it was like, she wanted to tell Berry. But Berry wasn't here anymore.

She missed her friend. In some ways, in many ways, she missed her more than she missed her mother. They had been as close as sisters, closer, sometimes.

They had shared everything together, all their hopes and dreams. She'd known that her mother had died on the cliffside. She'd known even before the shock of finding her body. But she didn't feel that way about Berry.

She'd looked in-between the stones. She'd looked for any sign of Berry that she might recognise, but she hadn't seen anything…Nothing.

She guessed her friend might have been buried under the stones, caught in the landslide and hidden forever underneath them. She hadn't sensed her presence, if she wasn't dead on the stones, then she had to look for her. She had to find her.

Beside her, Far-Sight was snoring gently. She reached over and shook his shoulder. He didn't stir, she shook harder. He was still snoring, so she dug her elbow into his side.

Far-Sight sat up instantly, grabbing for his spear.

'What's happening!' he said, loudly.

'Shh!' she whispered. 'You'll wake everybody up!'

She leant on his shoulder, to coax him to lay back down again. As he sank back under the sleeping-skin, he groaned, rubbing his ribs.

'What did you do that for?' he demanded hoarsely.

'I want to find Berry,' she told him.

'What?' he asked, confused. 'Right now? Why?'

'No!' she said. 'Not right this minute! But as soon as we can. I just need to find her, please?'

'Alright,' he replied, holding her hand. 'Then we will, but let's talk about it in the morning.'

When they woke the next morning, she couldn't resist asking.

'Can we go today?'

'No!' he replied sharply.

Stone went very quiet, wishing she hadn't pressed him. He'd been irritable as soon as he'd woken, and she regretted having woken him in the middle of the night.

'I'm sorry,' she said as he left to join the other men at their fire. He glanced over his shoulder, but didn't reply.

Tears stung her eyes…she had irritated him. She didn't like it when he was in this mood. He was usually so calm and was usually so nice to her. Now that he had snapped at her, she wasn't sure what to do, not sure how to make it right. She couldn't talk to him while he was with the men. Women just didn't do that; it wouldn't have been right. She would have to wait until they went to bed that night. That would be her only chance to talk to him today, then she could try to put things right between them.

6

She kept herself busy all day. There was always a lot to do, and she was determined to show that she was pulling her weight.

After they'd eaten, the men left the stockade to go hunting. The family was following a small herd of gazelle. They were difficult to hunt as they were quick and constantly alert, with sensitive noses and ears. The men would have to be very patient indeed, following, creeping ever closer through the long grass, always keeping downwind of the herd. If the herd caught their scent, or heard a suspicious noise, they would instantly stampede and it could be hours before they might catch up with them again.

Hunting gazelle was a long, hot, difficult process, but that was the only option they had at the moment. They had seen no signs of other beasts.

They would not break camp today. Normally, the women would extinguish the fires, pack everything they possessed onto their backs or their heads and follow the men, at a distance. Until it was time to make camp again, as the shadows lengthened.

For once, the herd they were following today wasn't too far away, and their kills would be small enough for the men to carry back to the camp.

The women busied themselves collecting firewood, fetching water and searching for berries and nuts to supplement the meat. Sometimes, if the hunt was unsuccessful, that would be all they had, so they searched diligently. There wasn't much to be found though, and their bags were light when they brought them back to camp.

'Everything's scarce now,' Nut told her as they walked back towards the camp. 'Things were getting bad back in the Homeland, and in many ways, they were worse here. And it's not as though we can rely on berries and nuts like we used to. Even roots are difficult to find now.'

'Is that why the Great Father told us to go?'

Nut nodded sadly.

'It's been getting worse for the last few seasons. It was getting hard to find enough food for everyone. I'd even heard of whole families starving to death, if their men weren't quick enough to get to a herd before everyone else.'

'But I still can't work out why he chose us. It's so unfair!' mumbled Stone.

'It would have been just as unfair for anyone else if he'd held his arms in a different direction.'

Stone just nodded sadly. 'I suppose so,' she answered quietly.

'It could have been worse,' Nut continued, 'he could have just had us all killed there and then. At least this way we have a chance.'

Stone shivered at the thought.

The Great Gathering had always been an exciting place to be.

The families all spent their year separately. They followed the herds, or fished in rivers, or in the Great Water. They looked after themselves, and depended on their own skills as hunters to survive.

Her Family Father was a good provider, and they rarely went hungry. If the hunts failed, if the droughts were longer than usual, or if there weren't enough nuts and berries for the women and girls to gather, they went hungry. It meant that the family might die.

Nobody would help them, nobody could. If the hunting was bad for one, then it was bad for all. If one family helped another, then both families would soon go hungry.

But once a year, on the longest day, the families would all come together in the Family Home. They would fill the valley, all squeezed in beside one another. There were as many fires that lit the darkness as there were stars in the sky.

Each family had to bring their own fire fuel, and their own meat. They would carry it all, on their heads or on their backs, all of them, all but the very smallest children, excitedly following the beaten-down grass that marked the passage of countless feet. All going in the same direction, all going to the same place.

They would find a spot somewhere in the valley and build their fires. There was no room for family stockades, but the Family Fathers would post guards at the perimeter of their spot to guard against predators – though few animals would ever have dared to come amongst such a throng of people.

This year, their family had been lucky enough to find a spot not far from the Great Father's stockade. That was a good place to be. Those camped close to the Great Father were usually considered to be favoured. Every family wanted to be in close to the stockade, but few could.

The first night they had eaten well enough, but sparingly. The meat they had brought would have to last them for three nights, so they had to be careful.

The women had all brought bags of nuts and berries with them, which would help, but those wouldn't have fed a family of so many hungry mouths for more than one sparse meal.

Stone had slept under a skin with the other children. She would normally have slept with the older girls and boys, but she didn't mind for this special time. She wasn't a child anymore. She was now a girl.

61

Children were small. When they grew, if they grew, they would become boys and girls. Size was an important difference between the two groups, there were several important differences.

Younger children, toddlers, were allowed to run around and play as they wished. Once they'd grown enough, boys and girls were given important tasks to do, like gathering nuts and berries, and fetching water. Boys would be taught how to be hunters, and girls would be taught how to be women. She was looking forward to being a woman, then she would be given a kilt to wear. That would show the whole world that she was now a woman.

She was already learning how to skin animals, and how to cook meat. She could already make sleeping skins, and soon she would learn how to slice hide into the thin strips they used to make necklaces and thongs for bags.

Boys would be taught how to make spears, and taught how to use them in a hunt. That was all they had to do, really, but she thought that was probably enough – if they couldn't make good hunters, then their families would go hungry. So, they had probably had the most important things to learn.

But all this learning was frustrating. She was impatient to be a woman. Her mother had told her she would be soon, but only when the time was right. Her mother had already made a kilt for her to wear when that time came. Until then, she would be naked, as she always had been.

At the Great Gathering, when the Family Fathers gave out their family's news for the past year, they would announce that 'so-and-such' a boy had become a man, or that 'so-and-such' a girl had become a woman.

Often, they would also announce which women had been sold to which men, and which of the men had formed a new family of his own. That happened sometimes, when a family had grown too large.

They would also announce who had been given names that year, or that their names had been changed because of something notable they'd done.

She was looking forward to having her announcements made. Then all of the people would know that she had become a woman, and all of the people would know that she had been bought by some man. Most of all, she was looking forward to getting her name. Children were not given names.

It was a waste of time giving children names. Many of them would die before they were old enough to become girls and boys, and lots of girls and boys died before they could become women and men.

Girls and boys could be given names though, if they had special skills, or if they had done something worth remembering. One of her friends was called Berry, because she was so good at finding and gathering berries. She seemed able to find more than many of the women could, that was her special skill, and worth remembering.

Far-Sighted Boy had a very special gift. He was taller than most, about a head taller, and he could see a long way. If he stood on a friend's shoulders, he could see even further. She thought that was very useful, especially when the men were hunting in the long grass, which happened a lot of the time.

She, on the other hand, had no special skills, and hadn't done anything worth remembering. So, she still had no name. She wondered if Far-Sighted Boy would be interested in her, when he became a man. She thought she wouldn't mind if he was.

He was quite good looking, and he was already good with a spear, although he was still unproven in the hunt. Then perhaps, he would be called Far-Sighted Man.

It would be nice if he was interested in her though, because then she would have two sets of beads to wear, and her Family Father would have to choose who could buy her.

She felt the beads gathered at her neck that Short-Spear had given her.

They were pretty, a mixture of shiny stones and animal teeth from kills he had made. She wondered if he had made the beads himself. It would nice if he had, but she didn't think so. His fingers were too stubby for that. He did have good muscles though, and was usually successful in the hunt.

He was called Short-Spear because he preferred to use a short-handled stabbing spear when he was hunting. Most of the others used a long shaft, to stab into the herd from a safer distance. He didn't. He preferred to be almost on top of an animal when he stabbed it. He thought it made him look brave. She thought it would probably get him killed quicker than the others, but it was thrilling to watch.

Men were allowed to give girls beads. It meant that they would be interested in her, when she became a woman. Some of her friends had several sets of beads, and all the girls were jealous of them; she only had one. Maybe that would change if she was given a name. She would have to try to be more interesting, and to practise her skills more.

This year, though, the Great Gathering had not worked out as she had hoped. Her father had made no naming announcement for her. Her mother had not given her a kilt. Instead, the Great Father had walked out of his stockade, making an announcement to all the people.

He began, in his booming voice, to explain that the drought this year had been far worse than ever before. The herds had been depleted far more than anyone could remember. Starvation was imminent – so he had decided that a portion of them would have to be banished into the Nothing.

A huge wail had erupted from the Gathering, as he had spread his arms and told them that all those within his arm-widths would be thrown out of the Homeland. At that moment, for her, and for all those affected, the world, as they knew it, had come to an end.

7

Although there was much to do, their work did not fill every moment. As they sat by the stream, dangling their feet comfortably in the water, Stone asked Nut if she had seen any other people. Nut shook her head.

'It's really strange,' she said, 'but of all those people, countless numbers of people, who were chased over the ridge and into the Nothing, we haven't yet seen any but you and your man. You'd have thought we would, but we haven't.' Nut looked reflective. 'As we came off the cliffside, we saw lots of bodies strewn across the stones. Maybe some of them could have still been alive?'

Stone shook her head quickly.

'No. All those we passed were too broken and battered by the boulders. The vultures…'

Nut took her hand and squeezed it.

'Your family?'

Stone nodded seriously.

'But I didn't see my friend Berry. I couldn't see her anywhere. I hope she's alright. I really have to find her.'

'Tell me about your stone. The one that found you your name.'

Stone smiled, and pulled it from her bag. She held it in her hand, turning it over in her hand. It looked dull, drab, lifeless, nothing like the pretty thing she had seen the evening it had revealed itself to her. She passed it to Nut, who looked at it, she smoothed its surface with her thumb, and handed it back.

'And that reminds you of Home?' Stone nodded, then smiled.

'But you haven't seen the secret yet,' she whispered, dipping the stone carefully into the water.

The misty surface quickly cleared, and Nut stared in amazement as the colours glowed under the water. Blue, red, gold, green, so many sparkling, glowing colours.

'Oh!' she gasped. 'It's beautiful!'

'I'm going to make a bag to keep it in!' Stone said, excitedly. 'I'll hang it round my neck to keep it safe, and I'll have it with me always. It's my piece of home.'

'Would you like me to help you make it? I have a bit of hide I was keeping to make a bag for Long-Running's collection of teeth, but I think it would be better used for your stone. It's a lovely soft piece of gold-coloured hide, the same colour as your skin.'

As daylight began to fade, and as they waited for the men to return from their hunting, Nut helped Stone to make her bag.

Really, it was Nut who did all the work, while Stone watched, enthralled at how quickly Nut fashioned a bag.

Using a tiny antler-horn needle and lengths of sinew she was able to gather the soft hide into just the right size and shape. Last of all, she threaded thin lengths of hide through the top, so that the opening could be drawn tight closed. The hide laces were just long enough to allow Stone to drape it around her neck, so that she could carry it securely.

When she'd finished, she handed it to Stone.

'Thank you so much!' she exclaimed. 'It's perfect!'

'Now that you've seen how it's done, you'll be able to make one yourself, if you need to.'

Stone beamed at her.

'It really is a lovely piece of hide,' she said. 'It must have taken you ages to chew it that soft. Are you sure you really want to give it away?'

Nut shrugged her shoulders.

'I was saving it to make a bag for Long-Running, but he doesn't need it anymore.'

'Why?'

'Because he used all his kill-teeth to buy that stupid piece of laziness,' she said quietly, nodding towards Flower, who was giggling at the other women as they brought in the last of the firewood.

'Oh, sorry, I didn't know,' said Stone. 'I assumed she was your daughter!'

Nut laughed, her laugh came out bitter, Stone thought.

'No,' she said, 'but she might as well be, for all the help she is. No, he bought her at the Gathering. Thought she was young and bright and pretty, like I used to be before I met him!'

'Oh dear…' ventured Stone, regretting having started the conversation.

'I wouldn't mind so much,' Nut continued, 'but now I have to look after her as well! According to Long-Running, she's far too pretty to help with any of the work. So, she just sits on the grass, decorating her hair with flowers and giggling at him.'

'You're the senior woman, can't you just make her work?'

'You're joking!' Nut said. 'I tried that, and all I got was a beating for my efforts!'

'Who beat you? Her? Surely not!'

'No, him. Not the first time he's done it. If anything at all goes wrong, I'm always the one he takes it out on. I thought that might have changed when he took another woman, but it didn't make any difference.'

'That's so unfair!' Stone cried. 'It's not right! You're the senior woman! I don't know him like you do, but I'd never have thought…'

'Don't let appearances fool you, Stone,' Nut replied, almost whispering. 'He's being nice at the moment, but that's only because he's showing off to your man. He's just as lazy as she is. They make a good pair. Usually, he doesn't go hunting at all. He just sends the other men out. Then he stands there and berates them if they haven't brought home enough meat. He really isn't what he seems at all.'

'Goodness!' whispered Stone. 'Why do you put up with him?' She knew it was a stupid question even as she asked it. Women had no say in anything. Their man made all the decisions. His word was law. Women who upset their men ran the risk of being beaten, denied their share of any food, or, if the man was so inclined, of being killed outright.

'Sorry...' she uttered.

Nut shook her head sadly.

'You have a lot to learn,' she said, 'and the first thing you need to learn, is to guard your tongue!

Stone's cheeks heated. She looked down at her feet, ashamed.

'But you are allowed to think, though,' Nut said, smiling at her reaction. 'Just don't tell your man that!'

Still looking at her feet, Stone nodded. Another lesson learned.

'Of course, there are ways a woman can influence her man,' Nut said, 'but it always has to seem like their idea, if you know what I mean. It's a pity your mother isn't here to teach you how.'

'I know,' Stone said. 'I have a lot to learn. Still, I think I've persuaded Far-Sight to help me find Berry. I hope we will leave in the morning.'

Nut looked surprised at that.

'It seemed to me that Long-Running was getting ready to ask him to stay on as one of his hunters,' she said, shrugging her shoulders. 'Still, you never know, if Far-Sight handles it right he might let you go. Etiquette still means something to him. Not much, anymore, but something.'

Their thoughts were interrupted as Flower started ululating. The men had returned. Far-Sight, and one of the other hunters were carrying a couple of small gazelles across their shoulders.

Stone and the other women watched from the entrance, as Flower ran to the tired, sweaty group, she fawned over Long-Running. She had rubbed dirt into her hands and her face, making it look as though she had been working hard all day. Long-Running beamed at her, clearly lapping up the attention.

'See what I mean?' asked Nut, 'scheming little...'

Her comments were cut short, as Long-Running raised his spear and shouted.

'See!' he exclaimed. 'See how I provide for my family!'

Stone caught Far-Sight's sideways glance at him, and wondered what that meant.

Later, as they settled beneath their sleeping-skin, she asked him.

'I just thought it a bit strange that he should claim all the credit for the kills,' he whispered quietly. 'All he did all day was sit on a small hill, and watch the rest of us as we did all the work!'

Stone said nothing, but smiled into the darkness. Maybe, this time, she wouldn't have to say anything.

'On the way back, he asked if I wanted to stay,' he continued.

'What did you say?' Stone asked, cringing silently at the thought that he might have agreed.

'I told him that we wanted to look around,' he said, 'to see if we could find any survivors from our family.'

'Thank you,' she breathed into his ear, relieved.

'I asked his permission to leave in the morning.'

'Whatever you think best, my man!' she whispered happily.

'What are you up to?' he asked, puzzled. 'That doesn't sound like you at all!'

'Oh,' she said, smiling innocently, 'nothing...'

They took their leave early in the morning, straight after a breakfast of leftover meat from the night before. Far-Sight, of course, had to go through the intricate formalities as demanded by etiquette; speeches of thanks for Long-Running's hospitality, for his having allowed them to share his fire and his meat, then the clashing of spear-bearing forearms with all of the men.

Meanwhile, Stone hugged the women and girls and wished them all well.

She hugged Nut the longest and hardest.

'I hope we will meet again,' Nut told her. She was smiling, but Stone noticed the glint of tears hiding in her eyes.

Then she had to run to catch up with Far-Sight. After the formalities had been made, he had simply turned on his heel and walked away out of the stockade. That was how it was, of course. It was the woman's responsibility to keep up as best she could.

She glanced over her shoulder as they mounted a low hill. She could see the small stockade, but she could see no people. They had all gone about their daily business as though they'd never been present.

Far-Sight slowed his pace a little as they started down the other side, giving her a chance to keep up without trotting.

'I saw smoke,' he said.

'What?' she asked, a little confused.

'Yesterday, while we were hunting,' he explained. 'I saw smoke in the distance. It was very thin, high, and very far away, but I saw smoke.'

'There are other people, then?'

'Yes,' he said.

'So, we will go there?'

'Yes, we will go there,' he said, his pace quickening again. 'And we will keep looking, we will keep finding other people, we will keep searching, until we find Berry.'

'Far-Sight?'

'What,' he replied, without looking at her.

'Far? Will you stop for a moment? Please?'

'What now?' he asked. He sounded irritated, but he stopped anyway. As she caught up with him, she threw down her bundles, lifted herself up on tip-toe, and draped her arms around his neck.

'What's this about?' he asked

'Thank you!' she said into his ear. 'Just thank you.'

They walked at a more moderate pace after that, and as the light began to fade, they made a small camp fire and ate some of the meat they'd been given. As they had before they'd met Long-Running and his family, they took turns to sleep, and as the morning sun started to warm them, they set off again towards where Far-Sight had seen the thin trail of smoke a couple of days before.

During the afternoon of the third day, they came across what Far-Sight had hoped they would discover.

Far-Sight called out the usual greeting as they approached the small stockade, in case whoever had built it was still in occupation. There was no answer, and as they drew nearer, they could see from the partially tumbled thorn walls that the place had been deserted for a while. The fire in the centre of the small compound was cold, and animals had already started to gnaw on the few discarded bones that had been strewn around its perimeter.

They tidied the walls enough to deter inquisitive predators, re-lit the fire with some wood that hadn't yet been burned, and finished off their small supply of meat.

Tomorrow's progress would be slower, as Far-Sight would have to spend at least part of the day hunting for the next night's meal. At least tonight they could both sleep at the same time, although she knew that Far-Sight would sleep lightly and warily, just in case.

'Do you think Berry might have slept here, in this compound?' she asked as they lay beneath the sleeping-skin, gazing up at the forest of stars that hung above them in the dark sky.

'I don't know,' he answered truthfully. 'She might have, I suppose, but she could be anywhere.'

'Do you think she's safe?' she asked hopefully.

'If she managed to meet up with a friendly family, I'm sure she will be,' he said, 'but we won't find out until we catch up with whoever built this place.'

'When will that be?'

'How should I know?' he muttered, his voice full of sleep.

'I know,' she said, turning onto her side, so that she could drape her arm over his chest. 'But I know you'll find her for me.'

Another two days passed before they finally found them. As they circled around the foot of a small hill, even she could see a trail of smoke rising up from across the valley.

They headed straight for it, making no attempt to disguise their progress. As Far-Sight had told her, it would be pointless trying to approach stealthily, because there were sure to be guards watching.

As they neared, he called out to the stockade. The usual greeting was returned by a woman's voice. Far-Sight was instantly alert and wary. Women never made the return greeting. That was always a man's prerogative.

There was something very strange and wrong here, but they wouldn't know what until they could enter the stockade, and see for themselves.

As usual, when entering someone else's stockade, he hefted his spear onto his shoulder to indicate that he meant no trouble. Even so, Stone could see that the muscles in his neck and shoulders were tense.

He was wary, and ready to move into a defensive pose the instant he perceived any threat.

As the thorn walls parted to allow them access, they could clearly see that the occupants were all women. There were no men, and only a few children present. The women watched him nervously as he approached, unsure of how to react or what to do or say, now that the formal greetings had been exchanged.

Far-Sight walked to the fire, sat down and placed the two small rabbits he'd managed to catch that day just beyond an arm's length away from him.

Stone understood. He would be much less intimidating that way, and the gift of meat she was certain would be well received.

There seemed to be little evidence of food in the stockade, and although they presented an extra couple of mouths to feed, at least their gift could be shared by all. She took his actions as her cue to greet the women and to introduce herself and her man to them. It was far from the normal way that these things were traditionally done, but these were far from normal circumstances. She explained who they were and why they were here, and she could see the women relax, the more she shared with them.

The older woman, clearly given seniority by the others because of her age and experience, introduced herself as Hide-Woman.

As she prepared the rabbits alongside their tiny rations, Hide-Woman told them their story in a low tone.

'When we came away from the cliffside, we left behind many of our family and friends,' she said. She glanced around at the group assembled behind her.

'We were mostly from different families, but because we found ourselves alone, or nearly alone, we grouped together for safety. There were some men with us also, but one died on the poisoned grass, when he tried to drink from one of the black pools, and another died trying to hunt for meat. He was so weak he couldn't run fast enough and was caught underneath the hooves of the small herd he was hunting. Another one ran off a while ago, saying that there were too many women for him to feed by himself.

So, we were left alone, we women, girls and the few children that were left to us. We have done our best since then.'

'Without men to protect you, you have done well to stay alive this long,' Far-Sight said, nodding slowly.

Hide-Woman shrugged her shoulders. 'Some lone men found us a few days ago. We thought they might stay and help us, but instead they just helped themselves. It would have been better if they had not come.'

'Lone men are always dangerous,' he declared. 'They were in the Homeland, and here, with little promise of retribution, they are probably worse.'

'They came to our stockade as night fell,' continued Hide-Woman. 'They gave the usual greetings, and we opened the stockade to make them welcome. They seemed polite and kindly at first, and we hoped they might stay to help us.'

'You would have been better opening your stockade to a pack of wild dogs,' Far-Sight commented.

Hide-Woman nodded. 'I know you are right, man,' she replied.

'They brought no meat to the fire, but we shared what little we had with them. They took the biggest portions, but we didn't try to stop them. We thought it would be worth a little hunger if they would hunt for us the next day. Then when they had finished eating, one of them grabbed one of the girls and dragged her to his sleeping-skin. We protested, but the others held their spears against us, and we were too afraid to do anything. Then another grabbed a woman and made to drag her off too. Then we all picked up sticks and started to beat them as best we could.

Some of our women were killed by the men, but we inflicted some bruises on them, and they fled. They dragged one of the girls with them. We couldn't get her back.'

Stone was horrified. She knew what would have happened to the poor girl who had been kidnapped. She shuddered at the thought.

'One of the boys followed to try to help her but we haven't seen him since, so I think they have killed him. He never spoke at all, we never knew his name, if he had one. We called him One-Leg Boy.'

'One-Leg Boy?' Far-Sight asked, cocking an eyebrow. 'How could he hope to follow them, if he only had one leg?'

'No,' one of the girls, who was listening at the back of the group, interjected. 'He had two legs, but he limped, so we called him One-Leg. It wasn't very kind of us, I suppose, but he didn't seem to mind.'

'We mean you no harm,' said Far-Sight, truthfully. 'We cannot stay long, but I will hunt for you tomorrow and then we will leave the next morning.'

Hide-Woman nodded. 'We are grateful, man,' she said simply. 'I know it would be difficult for you to provide for so many of us all by yourself.'

'I would try, if I could,' Far-Sight said softly, 'but we have to find Stone's friend, she is called Berry. We need to visit as many stockades as necessary, but we hope to find her eventually. Then, if we can, we will return to help you further.'

'Did you say Berry?' asked one of the women sat further away. 'The girl who was kidnapped said she was called Berry.'

Stone was instantly alert. 'My Berry had a round face and long fingers, and she was always laughing,' she said with warmth, almost not daring to hope.

The woman looked at her carefully. 'Nobody laughs much here,' she said, 'but I remember she did have long fingers.'

'Did she say who her Family Father was?'

'No, she didn't say much at all, not to any of us. Lots of girls and women were too shocked by what had happened, and too grief-stricken by the loss of their families to want to speak of them. It made them cry.'

Stone nodded, understanding. She had felt that way herself many times since the Gathering. But at least she had Far-Sight. That made a big difference.

Far-Sight was asking lots of questions to the women. *Which direction had the lone men taken when they had left? How many days ago did this happen? How many were there?*

As Stone listened to his questions, she watched him churning the answers over in his mind the little information the women could give him. The more he could find out, the quicker he would be able to find the group, and the sooner they could rescue Berry from their grip.

He would find Berry for her. He had promised. And she knew in that moment, he would come back to help these women. She didn't know how, but she knew he would try.

Far-Sight returned three days later, exhausted from carrying Berry.

Once he had rested and had something to eat, he told the women that he had first discovered One-Leg, dead from a spear-thrust to his chest. Later in the day, he had found Berry. She had been discarded by the wayside, dehydrated and covered in bruises and cuts, but alive. He had given her some water, then picked her up and carried her all the way back.

8

Whilst Far-Sight and a couple of the bigger boys hunted. Berry, under the watchful eye of her best friend, Stone, had slowly recovered from her injuries.

Eventually, Far-Sight had announced that it was time for him, Stone and Berry to move on.

Game was becoming increasingly difficult to find, and they needed to find new herds to follow if they were to survive. The others begged him to take them with him as well, and so, Far-Sight became the leader of his now extended Family, and they all began their long journey into undiscovered lands.

Occasionally they would come across other people, usually half-starved couples or small groups mostly of women. Often those people would join Far-Sight's growing band, seeking the security of numbers, and although it meant more work and more responsibility for him, Far-Sight never turned them away.

Over time, as Far-Sight's ad-hoc family grew, so did the number of couples that formed. Inevitably, it followed that several of the women started to produce babies. Stone soon found herself amongst their number, and was very relieved to have women around her, who she could rely on for help and advice.

Some of the women, and many of the babies did not survive. Stone was one of the fortunate ones who survived, and although she suffered the loss of some of her babies, she was able to watch, as three of them, two girls and a boy, grew big enough to help their parents.

The girls learned how to gather nuts and berries, and were taught to find edible roots. The boy learned how to hunt well, and to make the tools that he would need in the future. Stone and Far-Sight were very proud of their children, and very happy with their lives.

One day, as they were walking through a small area of woodland, Stone caught hold of her eldest daughter's arm to stop her.

'What is it, Mother?' her daughter asked.

'Do you hear that noise?' Stone responded. She'd heard a sound that she hadn't heard since she was a girl. She'd heard the quiet, but distinct and recognisable sound of bees buzzing in the distance. They searched the air until they finally caught sight of two or three bees, as they moved from flower to flower in the undergrowth around them. They watched the bees carefully as they flew, and eventually managed to follow them to their nest.

'You know what?' Stone asked. 'One thing I know for sure is that bees make honey. I haven't tasted honey since I was a child, younger than you are now.'

'Is it nice?' her daughter asked, curious.

'It is probably the most delicious thing ever,' her mother informed her. 'I can almost taste it now!'

'How do we get it, then?'

Stone told her what she could remember of watching women gathering honey. They'd made it look easy, even though she remembered that some of the women had been stung while they did it.

'One of the women climbed up the tree to where the nest was, then they hit it with a stick until it fell to the floor. Then some others blew smoke from a fire all over the nest to make the bees quiet, and then they'd made a hole in it and put their hands in to get the honey out. They gave me a finger-full. I'd never tasted anything like it!'

'It's too late in the day now,' Stone continued. 'And anyway, we'll need help. We'll bring some of the other women with us tomorrow. Then we'll all have a taste!'

Early the following morning, they gathered around the tree. Some of the women went to gather firewood, while Stone searched out a long stick.

The fire was lit and liberally covered with grass to make it smoke. Stone called two of the women to ask them the cup their hands together so that she could hoist herself up into the branches. It was a technique they often used when gathering nuts, so they were well practised at it.

Stone climbed towards the nest, though she found it more difficult to climb while holding her long stick than she'd expected.

Eventually, though, she reached the branch and began to crawl along it towards the nest. A few bees buzzed around her, but they were still sluggish in the cool of the early morning.

Once she was sure she could reach the nest with her stick, she called down to her friends to make sure they were ready to deal with it as soon as it hit the ground.

She took aim, and swished her stick at the nest as hard as she could.

It moved the nest, but didn't dislodge it. So she hit it again. This time she saw the nest drop, she dropped her stick and started to crawl back along the branch. By now, though, she found herself surrounded by angry bees.

Bees crawled all over her, on her face, in her hair, in her mouth, over her body. She frantically tried to swat them off as best she could, at the same time she was clinging on to the branch, with one hand.

By now she was screaming with pain from the stings, and her friends watched in horror as she suddenly lost her grip and dropped towards the ground. Her body hit some of the lower branches, and she tried desperately to grab hold of them as she fell. Moments later, she hit the ground heavily and awkwardly, and they all heard a sharp crack as her arm broke.

The women rushed forward to help her, but they had to fight their way through the cloud of bees that still buzzed angrily all over her head and body.

They swatted and swirled their arms to keep them from her and themselves, and eventually the bees seemed to lose interest, and flew away to what was left of their nest.

Stone whimpered as her friends attended to her as best they could. Stone's daughter had run off back to the stockade to get help, and to find her father. He and the other men hadn't yet left for the day's hunt, and he ran with her back to where his wife lay.

He gathered her into his arms, as gently as he could, but even so she screamed as her arm dangled loosely by her side. One of the other women gently moved her arm, so that it lay across her chest, and Far-Sight began the long walk back to the stockade.

As they settled her by the women's fire, Far-Sight went to make sure that everything was secure, and that the camp had enough wood for the fires and enough meat and water to go around.

By the time he returned to check on her, Stone was asleep. Their daughters were sat quietly beside her, ready to help with whatever she might need. Far-Sight sat down with them, near Stone's head. He sat with her for a long time, stroking her hair.

She roused a little as the evening began to draw in but didn't attempt to leave her bed.

One of the women brought her some meat once it was ready, but she didn't want anything to eat. All she would take was a mouthful of water.

Another brought some balm she had made from some of the honey Stone had given them, which she hoped might bring some relief from the stings. The woman started to smear it on Stone's face, as gently as she could, but the more she did, the more Stone gasped in pain. So, she stopped. Instead, she put some honey on her finger and offered it to her.

'Taste this, Stone,' she said. 'It might help your throat.'

Stone opened her mouth a little and licked the woman's finger. It tasted so good, just as she'd remembered, and the liquid did indeed ease the pain, just a bit, in her mouth and throat. She offered a smile of gratitude.

Eventually, as night closed in, and it became dark, Stone looked up at Far-Sight. Firelight sparkled in her eyes.

'It's nice here, nice and warm by the fire,' she whispered.

'Are you feeling any better?' he asked. 'Would you like something to eat now? Something to drink?'

She shook her head.

'I'm just too tired,' she said quietly. 'I hurt all over. I really don't feel well at all. I'm sorry.'

'We will stay here until you are well again. You will have as much time as you need to rest and recover,' he told her quietly. She smiled, but said nothing for a long time.

As the fire began to die down, he felt her stir a little.

'Far-Sight,' she said very quietly. 'Please would you take the Home Stone from my neck? It feels so heavy tonight. Maybe one of the girls could carry it for me? It needs to find a forever home but I can't carry it any further right now.'

He nodded, and gently took the bag holding the stone from her neck and continued carefully stroking her hair. Eventually she closed her eyes.

9

When she opened her eyes again, her mother was sat in front of her, smiling. She smiled back.

'So, my daughter,' her mother said. 'What are you going to do now?'

'I don't know what to do,' Stone told her. 'What should I do?'

'Well, my daughter,' her mother said quietly, 'sometimes I think there is not much that we can do. You are badly hurt. I do not think there is much more you can do.'

'But what about Far-Sight and my children, Mother? They need me. I need to get better so that I can help them into their future.'

'Far-Sight is a good man,' her mother told her, smiling. 'You chose well. Your children are nearly full-grown. You have done well, my daughter. Very well. I am proud of you!'

'But they still need me…'

'Like you needed me, even after the stones…I was not there, but you still got through. You made a good life. Now it is enough.'

'Then I don't know what to do. What should I do, Mother?'

'When you are ready, my daughter, take my hand. Come sit by my fire. We will talk then, and you will feel better.'

Stone reached out and took her mother's hand. She stood, and she smiled as she realised that she felt no pain. She could feel her mother pulling her into her arms, but she resisted momentarily and turned to look at Far-Sight and her daughters.

She felt a sudden lurch of shock as she realised that, laying on the ground beside him, and with her head cradled in his lap, was her own sleeping form. She turned her head again to look at her mother, a questioning look in her eyes.

'Am I dead then, Mother?'

She saw her mother nod gently, and dip her head sympathetically to one side.

'Yes, my daughter, you are. But I will look after you. That's why I am here, to guide you onwards. I will show you the path you need to take.'

'Oh…' Stone said, raising her eyebrows in surprise. 'But I…'

Stone went to turn again towards her husband, but she felt her mother's fingers cup her chin to stop her.

'No, my child, not that way,' she told her. 'You need to look forward now. Look, see…Your grandmothers, all of them, from the beginning, are waiting to meet you.'

'But my daughters need me! And I need them!' she whispered.

'They will be alright,' her mother told her. 'One day, the Home Stone that travelled with you, and now travels with them into the future, will reunite you all. You *will* see them again. But now, look!'

Stone blinked tears away as she gazed in the direction her mother was pointing. As she watched, the colour of the air ahead of her began to change, and she realised that there were colours there. It seemed to her that suddenly everywhere around her had started to glow with colour. All the colours of the rainbow.

She couldn't help but walk towards it.

10

Far-Sight stirred as the very first rays of light appeared in the sky. He shook himself, frowning that he hadn't been strong enough to not doze off during the night.

He looked down at Stone's face, still resting in his lap. It took him a long time to realise that she wasn't breathing anymore.

He sighed deeply and looked over to where his daughters were sleeping. He thought about the Home Stone and how much it had meant to his wife. Although he had never been able to see any value to it at all, and had often teased Stone about her dedication to carrying it everywhere she went, he felt that it was important that he should honour her wish for it to be carried into the future.

He debated in his mind which of the girls he should give that responsibility to, and eventually decided that his eldest daughter would look after it best.

The tribe spent the whole day in mourning for Stone. Usually, when someone died, towards evening, they would carry the body far out onto the plain, and lay it to rest there, knowing that it would not be long before the wild animals that surrounded them would dispose of the body very quickly.

Far-Sight, however, decided that Stone deserved more than that.

Under his guidance, they gathered stones from all around and covered her entire body quite deeply with them to protect it from scavengers as best they could. Even this wasn't enough for Far-Sight, who wanted desperately to pay homage to the woman he had loved for as long as he could remember, the mother of his children.

He thought about it for a whole night, and by dawn, he had decided what he wanted to do. He would erect a tall stone near her grave, to mark the place forever.

While the rest of the tribe hunted, gathered berries and wood for the fires, he and his daughters went out to search for the type of stone he had in mind.

After a few hours of searching, they found one that he felt would be suitable. It was about twice as long as he was tall, roughly as wide as his chest, and, crucially, quite thin. He felt that it would be too difficult to move a much thicker stone, and they would need to move it quite a distance. Before they left, he looked around for landmarks that would help him find it again.

On the way back to camp, they stopped at a small stream to drink. As he scooped the water up to his mouth he froze. There, in the bottom of the stream, were some small stones.

He stared at them for a long time, in wonder. They were small, but they were blue. Blue stones! He couldn't believe what he was seeing. He picked them out from the bottom of the stream, and put them carefully into his bag.

They returned to their stockade just as darkness was falling, and as they ate their meat that evening, he described to the tribe what he wanted them to do. A number of lengths of hide rope would be needed to help them move the stone to the grave, but they would all need to help in the task.

A few of the people frowned and shook their heads, unsure if all this effort was really a useful way to expend their energy but they all had a deep respect for Far-Sight, and there were no dissenting voices. A few days later, and armed with ropes created by the many women in camp, they set off to find the stone that Far-Sight and his daughters had discovered.

It proved difficult to secure the ropes, as the stone had to be lifted every time they needed to wrap a rope around it, but eventually they were ready to begin the task.

With everyone taking part, either pulling ropes or pushing the stone with their hands, it took several days to move the stone into position. They took a rest then, while some went hunting to replenish their rapidly diminishing stock of meat. It was a difficult task for even the best hunters to find enough prey.

They were, by now, a number of days distant from the herds they had been following, and other game was few and far between.

Those not hunting were set the task of digging a hole for the stone to sit in, a short distance from Stone's grave.

Eventually, after a good day of slow digging using antlers discarded from their prey, Far-Sight declared that they were ready to erect the stone. Just before they did, though, he discretely dropped his blue stones into the hole.

He looked towards Stone's grave and sighed.

'I promised, my Stone. I'm sorry I couldn't thread them but I promised.'

More leather ropes were secured to one end of the stone, and almost the entire tribe took part in the effort of pulling the stone towards the hole.

Others were set to prising the stone from its resting place, using long wooden poles, and inch by inch, the stone was dropped into the hole. One last effort was needed to pull it upright, and then the rest of the hole was packed with stones and dirt to lock it into position.

Far-Sight stood back from the stone and gazed at it intently. Finally, smiling, he declared it *perfect*.

He looked around at his people, raised his hands and thanked them profusely for all their effort.

Calling his eldest daughter over to him, he handed her the Home Stone in its little leather bag. As she looped the leather lanyard over her head, he told her. 'It is now your responsibility to carry your mother's stone into your future. Guard it well, and keep it safe until you find a forever home. If you don't find such a place, pass it on to your daughter, and she to theirs until they find it.'

The following morning, they all set off once more to catch up with the distant herds they depended on.

As they filed past the grave, Far-Sight stopped and looked at it.

'A stone for my Stone,' he said. 'There has never been such a marker, and there never will be again. Now the whole world will see how important my Stone was, and she will be remembered always and forever.'

Then, without a further word, he turned and started to walk away.

His children and his people followed him as he made his way towards the receding herds.

He didn't say another word about Stone, but just as he approached a distant hill, he turned to take one last look at the standing stone that marked his wife's grave. He watched as rain began to fall.

He watched as it reached Stone's grave. As soon as it was wettened, the standing stone began to glow with colours he hadn't noticed before, like a rainbow.

He bowed to it, then turned again and walked on.

Hilda glanced over at Bridie. She was looking at her feet again, thoughtful.

'So, there we have it,' Hilda finished. 'That's how the Home Stone was discovered, and that's how it started its long journey here.'

Bridie frowned, still looking at her feet.

'So, he just walked off and left her there?' she scowled.

'What was he supposed to do?' her mother answered, 'he had a load of people still left to feed. She was gone. What was he supposed to do, sit there moping all day?'

'But didn't he miss her?' Bridie asked, thoughtfully.

'Of course he missed her!' Hilda retorted. 'But, in the end, life goes on. It has to!'

Bridie nodded. 'Well, if I've got this right,' Bridie said, 'so Stone gave the Home Stone to her daughter. Then she gave it to her daughter, and she gave it to her daughter, and she gave it to her daughter, and she gave it to her daughter…'

'Alright Bridie, you don't have to overdo it. But yes, you're right. That's more or less the way it went.'

'Until the daughter who finally brought it here? But which one was that? Were there ten daughters then? More?'

'Oh,' her mum said, standing up, 'a lot more than ten. An awful lot more. Thousands of daughters, probably.'

'OK, so before the Romans, then? And you know when he said about there was never going to be another standing stone? Well, we've got loads of them in the top field, so what's that all about?'

'Maybe he started a fashion trend? I dunno. Look Bridie, I need to get your father's dinner ready. You can ask me more questions while I'm doing that, OK?'

Bridie looked at her mum, smiled and rose to her feet, stretching.

'So, bring your book and your cup please, and let's go and get sorted. You can help.'

Bridie rolled her eyes. 'Yes Mum…but I'm not doing the potatoes again.'

Part Two
Bridie's Bridge
Midwinter Solstice

11

Matthew Crawford was certain he could fly.

He hadn't tried yet, but he knew he could do it. With the top button of his raincoat firmly fastened, and with his hands briefly tucked into coat pockets, he would hold out his arms and start running. The rest was inevitable.

His legs were burning; Matthew finally struggled with the last few paces to the top of the impossibly steep track that led from the decrepit wooden hut that served as his form room.

He turned and looked back down the slope, ignoring the other boys as they jostled past on their way to lessons.

Matthew nodded determinedly to himself. This was the place. Right here.

The speed he could get up to if he ran down this slope would surely be more than enough. The wind would gather under his makeshift wings, and just before he reached the bottom, he would jump. He would jump as high as he could, and the wind would lift him. The boys would shout, the masters would grab at his legs, the porters would chase after him but it would do them no good.

He would soar into the air high above them. Up, up, up. Over the walls. Over the streets. Over the river. High over the hills. All the way home.

There was no other way. Despite his pleading, his parents wouldn't come for him. *Only a couple more weeks until the end of term*, they'd told him in their last letter. But the end of his first term as a boarder at Burrell's was still too far away for Matthew. He wasn't allowed out through the gates. So, he would fly over them. All the way home.

Burrell's was an old school. It was a very good school, his father had told him that, on many occasions, and even at twelve years old, Matthew knew he should feel privileged to follow his father and his grandfather through its ancient portals. But he didn't.

In fact, he really didn't like it at all.

Everybody else seemed to know just what to do, how to behave. The masters all seemed so distant and uncaring.

He'd spent much of the term…well, just wandering around, following his classmates, or at least those he sort of recognised, to wherever they were going.

It didn't help that he was tall for his age. People kept mistaking him for a second-year, and sending him to the wrong place.

He was always late. He was always unprepared for his lessons, even when he knew which lessons were coming next. Why did they have to wear brown shoes indoors and black shoes outdoors? He hated his school tie with its light blue diagonal stripes. Boys in the senior years wore ties with darker blue stripes, which in Matthew's opinion, was a nicer colour, he really couldn't stand light blue.

He detested sharing a dormitory with the other boys. Most nights he cried himself to sleep, sobbing secretly into his pillow, hoping that his dorm fellows wouldn't hear him, more than anything hoping and praying, that his mum would come and rescue him from this nightmare. Maybe she'd come tomorrow…

***

'C'mon Mat. You can do it!' he thought to himself, as he stared down the steep track.

He'd delayed only just long enough to give his legs a chance to recover from the climb. He knew he'd have to run faster than ever before, if his plan was to work, and he didn't want to risk a stumble, because his legs were still trembling from the climb.

As he forced himself to wait, his mind ran back over what Mr Pearce had told him at Form Assembly a few minutes before. He knew it had to be now or never.

He'd hardly listened as his Form Master had rattled through the morning prayers and mumbled a couple of notices.

'Rugby will be led today by Mr Skinner, as Mr Thomas is indisposed.'

Mr Thomas always seemed to be 'indisposed', especially after Wales had been playing at the weekend.

Mat hated rugby. He hated Mr Thomas as well. He was Welsh, and was as devoted to rugby. For him, it was almost a religion. For Mat, it was like being thrown to the lions. He hated the way his ears were almost rubbed off during a scrum. He hated the way the other boys would bellow at him when he failed to catch a pass...which was most of the time, because he wasn't allowed to wear his glasses during games, and couldn't even see the stupid ball until it was right in front of him.

The one time he had somehow found it, he'd ran like the wind. Those few moments had been a total release. Free as a bird. Almost flying. Nobody could catch him. He'd ran, as he knew he should, straight towards the double poles of the goal...and then suffered the jeers of his team-mates when he threw the ball over the crossbar. Nobody'd ever bothered to explain that he was supposed to touch the ball onto the ground – actually touch it to the ground – before he could score any points.

As his classmates filed out of the room, Mr Pearce had called him over. He was to go to the headmaster's office at first break.

Mat had never been inside the head's office before. In fact, although he knew who he was from full assemblies, he had never actually spoken to him at all.

Full assemblies took place a couple of times a week. The whole school gathered at eight thirty sharp, in the school chapel. Accompanied by the senior masters, Headmaster Parkes led them in hymns and readings, before giving the important notices of the day. They always looked so stern, though, the masters, like they could frighten learning into their pupils just with a look. Maybe they could. Matthew didn't know. He hadn't learned the secrets yet.

Matthew shivered at the thought of actually meeting the *Head Torturer*. He couldn't think what he might have done, to be in so much trouble. He didn't know of anybody who had been summoned to the Head's office who hadn't been in trouble for something really serious, and he couldn't imagine why he'd been singled out.

Flying seemed a far more attractive idea, and he readied himself for take-off. He balanced on the balls of his feet, and shoved his hands into his coat pockets. Then he reeled backwards in shock, as a voice cut straight through his thoughts.

'Daydreaming, are we Crawford?'

He'd been so lost in thought that he hadn't even noticed Mr Pearce climbing up the steep track towards him.

'Erm...' he muttered, struggling desperately to find the right words.

'Well come on, lad – run!' Mr Pearce said, shooing him towards the school buildings. 'The future won't wait for you, y'know!'

So, Mat did run, just not in the direction he'd planned to.

Now, as he sat in outside the Head's office, Matthew could feel his stomach churning. He wondered if he might have time to quickly run to the toilet block, but decided he wouldn't dare. He had to be there when they called him in. Instead, he just sat there, welded to a small chair in the corridor. By the time the Head's secretary beckoned him in with her finger, he was feeling decidedly unwell.

He was shown through the outer office, past the secretary's tidy desk. There were some feathery-looking potted plants on the window-sill. Through the window he glimpsed fields in the distance. Out in the corridor the place was filled with boys chattering, and the sound of footsteps clattering on the polished floor. It was quiet in here.

The secretary knocked on the Head's office door and waited. A voice from inside rang out in response.

'Come!'

She opened the door and ushered him in. As he entered, his knees shaking, Matron rose from a comfortable-looking chair in the corner behind the door. *Why was Matron here?*

'Ah – Crawford,' the Head started. 'Come in. Yes. I'm afraid we had some bad news last night, concerning your parents.'

Mat wasn't sure if he should say anything, so he didn't.

He wasn't sure that he was all that keen on Mr Parkes. When he'd seen him, high on the stage at full assemblies, Mat had often thought he looked a bit like a strange sort of bird.

Mr Parkes had a long, curvy nose. He was quite thin. Very thin actually. Like he didn't eat much at all. A hawk, maybe. His eyes were as sharp. Stary, scary-looking eyes that never seemed to miss anything. They could focus instantly on somebody, illicitly passing sweets to a neighbour. Just like a hawk.

'BOY!' he'd heard him shout once, at a small chap three rows back from the front. 'SEE ME AFTER!' Somebody had told him later that the boy had put a mint in his mouth while Mr Parkes had his eyes closed, praying.

How did he even do that? No...more a stork, perhaps he was a stork. He was long and thin like that. *Yes, a stork. Maybe a stork-hawk,* thought Mat. Was there such a thing?

'Ah – bad news, I'm afraid,' continued the Head, glancing between Mat and the papers on his desk. 'I'm afraid your parents were involved in quite a nasty car accident yesterday. Well, to cut a long story short, I'm afraid they didn't make it.'

Mat was too stunned to speak. He was confused. He was glad that he wasn't in trouble, but he was having difficulty in understanding what the Head was telling him.

'Rotten luck, I'm afraid, old chap. The rottenest luck.'

'Yes sir,' Mat managed to whisper, his head swimming.

Mr Parkes was speaking again, his elbows resting on the desk in front of him, his fingers pressed against each other just underneath his beak. Matthew watched, distractedly, as Mr. Parkes flexed his hands together as he spoke, as if to emphasise each phrase.

'Now then. I'm afraid that these things happen sometimes. Nothing we can do about it. We just have to be men. You are a man, aren't you? Stand tall, and take it on the chin, eh?'

A diminutive, 'Yes sir,' was all Mat managed to utter.

'Good lad. Now then, pop along with Matron for a bit. She'll look after you. After that, you best go and see Mr Pearce. Mr Pearce will sort everything out. He'll be in his room. Very good. Carry on.'

Mat opened his mouth, but no words came out. All he could think about was his mum. He wanted her to be here, to give him a hug and tell him everything was going to be alright. But nobody was here to give him a hug, and nothing was going to be 'alright,' ever again.

He was determined not to cry. A proper Burrell's boy wouldn't cry. In the strange, unwritten laws of this place, blubbering was simply not allowed.

Matron sat him down in her room, and gave him a cup of very sweet tea. Mat shuddered as he sipped it. He didn't like sugar in his tea, and this was…well, horribly sweet.

Mr Pearce ducked his head around the door and came in when he saw that they were sat there.

Mat quite liked Mr Pearce. He was one of the younger Masters, he taught English. Mat could understand English. He didn't understand most of the other subjects, but Mr Pearce didn't shout like the other Masters. Well, not often, anyway. Sometimes he even smiled.

'Crawford,' he said, tapping him on the shoulder. 'I'm so sorry, old chap, so very sorry. Dreadful thing to happen. Are you alright? Is Matron looking after you?'

'Yes sir.'

'Now look here,' Mr Pearce continued, perching on the edge of Matron's desk. Matron didn't look impressed. 'We're nearly at the end of term. It'll be Christmas before you know it. We'll need to sort out what to do with you, where you'll go. Any relatives who might take you in?'

Mat couldn't think of any. Well, there was one, he supposed. A cousin of his mother's, but she lived in South Africa. He'd never met her.

He just shook his head.

'Right then.' Mr Pearce looked concerned. 'Well, you can't stay here. Whole place closes down, d'you see? Couldn't have you rattling around here by yourself. Nobody here to look after you, anyway.'

He persevered. 'Any friends here, whose parents might be willing?'

Mat shook his head again.

'No,' he thought to himself. 'No, thank you very much.' There were some chaps he talked to, but they weren't really friends. He certainly wouldn't want to go home with any of them.

Mr Pearce thought for a few moments.

'Very well then,' he said, making up his mind.

'Here's what we'll do. It'll do as a plan for now anyway. You'd better come back with me. I'm spending Christmas with my father. It won't be terribly exciting for you, I'm afraid, but it'll have to do. I'll telephone ahead, but I'm sure he won't object, especially under the circumstances.'

'Thank you, sir,' Mat muttered, not really sure if the idea appealed to him or not. He liked Mr Pearce well enough, but he was a 'Sir.'

Worse than that, he was his Form Master. He wasn't at all sure if staying with a 'Sir' was such a great idea…but in the end, he supposed, he didn't really have much choice.

12

The last week of school passed in a haze. Mat cried himself to sleep every night, this time not-so-silently sobbing into his pillow. He didn't care what the others thought. He tried not to think about his parents, especially with what had happened to them, but he couldn't help it.

He was tired all the time. Bad dreams woke him several times every night, and he found himself staring out of the window during lessons. At least the Masters didn't tell him off for it. They all knew, of course, and most of the time they just left him alone.

School finished at lunchtime on the last day of term. The school kitchen gave boarders like him a packed lunch for their journeys home. Mat had packed a small suitcase with what he thought might be needed over the holidays.

All the boys had to wear school uniform when they were travelling, otherwise he would have left it behind.

He would have very much preferred not to have to take any reminders at all of school with him. It was bad enough, he thought, that he was having to spend the holidays with his Form Master...but he'd packed a couple of pairs of jeans, some jumpers and some underwear. He'd also packed his favourite photo of his parents. He couldn't leave them behind. He needed to keep them close to him.

Now he stood in the quad, suitcase in hand, waiting for Mr Pearce.

All around him was bustle. Boys were calling out to each other, excitedly wishing each other 'Happy Christmas', as they climbed aboard the coaches that would take them to the train station, and eventually home. One or two called to him while he waited. He didn't feel like shouting, so he just waved back to them. They smiled at him, encouragingly, as they disappeared into their coach.

Eventually, Mr Pearce jogged over to him. He was running late, and seemed flustered. He was impatient to get started.

They loaded their cases into the boot of the car and climbed in. Mr Pearce had a sports car, a blue MGB. It had a long bonnet, and a top that could be folded down when it was warm and sunny. It looked like it would go very fast. Mat thought that Mr Pearce's car was the best of all the Master's cars and being allowed to ride in it was about the only thing he'd been looking forward to all week.

Mat had never been in a sports car before, but he was excited by the look of them. Now, after getting into Mr Pearce's car, he wasn't so sure.

The seats, he discovered, were hard and uncomfortable and so low to the ground that it felt like they were sat only a couple of inches above the road. With his legs stretched straight out in front of him, the prospect of facing a long journey in it really wasn't quite as appealing as he'd thought.

As they set off, gliding slowly but noisily out of the car park, Mr Pearce glanced at him.

'The reason I was running late Crawford is because I just got off the phone. It seems that my father isn't terribly well at the moment. I'm afraid it won't be quite the celebration it might have been. Still, I'm sure we will muddle through. Mrs Clinton, his housekeeper, is a pretty good cook. At least we won't starve, eh?'

They hadn't spoken much after that. The noise of the engine and the rumble of the tyres on the road made it difficult to hear conversation. Neither of them seemed very much in the mood for talking anyway, and after a while they gave up the effort.

It was late afternoon by the time they arrived. The thin winter sun had already dipped below the horizon. Shadows gathered everywhere, and Mr Pearce had to switch the headlights on for the last few miles. Mat was more than a little relieved when they eventually pulled into a narrow gateway.

Mr Pearce switched off the engine. Mat's first impression of the house was that it looked very lonely, if a house could be lonely that is, or maybe it looked sad perhaps, if a house could look sad. It was set alongside a long, twisty and very narrow lane, and as far as he could see, there were no other houses anywhere close by. They hadn't passed any for ages.

'I was hoping to have got you here before dark,' Mr Pearce said, gazing at the house. 'It looks a lot more inviting in daylight, even at this time of year.'

Mat nodded. He'd have to take Mr Pearce's word on that.

The front door opened as they approached. A comfortable-looking woman smiled at them. Mrs Clinton, Mat assumed.

'Oh, I'm so glad you're here, Mr Pearce!' she said, hugging him heartily. 'Your father's been so looking forward to seeing you!'

She turned her attention on Mat. 'And you must be Master Crawford?'

Mat nodded, not sure whether she would want to be hugging him too. He decided that he wouldn't mind if she did.

'We've really been looking forward to meeting you!' she said, shaking his hand. No hug, then. Mat felt a bit disappointed.

Later, as they sat in the living room, warming themselves in front of the log fire while they waited as patiently as they could for Mrs Clinton to finish preparing dinner, Mr Pearce began to describe how things worked around here.

'Mrs Clinton runs the house,' he started.

'She's a fine woman, and a good organiser. She cares a lot about the family. Let's face it, she's been with us so long, she's as much a part of the family as the rest of us. She's pretty much central to everything, and to be honest I'm not sure we'd manage without her. Despite appearances, though, she can be a bit of a tyrant. She likes things to be *just so,* and gets quite upset if they're not.'

He glanced over his shoulder to make sure he wasn't being overheard. 'So be careful not to upset her!' he said, laughing.

'Yes sir,' said Mat, smiling back.

'Now then. We're rather out in the sticks here, I'm afraid, so not much in the way of social life. As you'll have noticed, we're not exactly surrounded by neighbours. The nearest ones are the Ambrose family, who have the farm further up the lane. They're a nice family, they've been there for ages. They have two boys and a girl. The boys are pretty much grown up now. One of them works in town I think – that's about five miles away, in case you wondered. The girl, Bridie, is more or less your age. Maybe a bit older.'

Mat wasn't really interested much, but he nodded to indicate that he'd been listening.

'We used to have a lot of fun here you know, when I was growing up. I was good friends with Tom Ambrose. His people had a cottage over the fields at the back. He was always over here though. I think he had a soft spot for Bridie's mother even then. He made it pretty obvious. I'm sure that a lot of the time, his coming here was just so he would be a bit closer to Hilda, Bridie's mum. Anyway, it must have worked. They've been married for years now. I was his Best Man.'

'Are there more farms further up the lane, sir?' Mat asked, more for the sake of something to say rather than a need to know.

Mr Pearce shook his head. 'No, that's it really. The lane ends at their place. Nothing beyond that but fields and woods.'

Mrs Clinton called them through for dinner. Mat was sorry to leave the fire behind. He'd noticed a couple of radiators here and there, but they didn't seem to be working very well. The rest of the house felt quite chilly in comparison to the living room.

As they stood, Mr Pearce told him that he would introduce him to his father the next day.

'He's not very good tonight I'm afraid, so he'll be staying in his room. Hopefully he'll be a bit brighter tomorrow. I'm sure you'll like him. He's a great chap. When he's on form, of course.'

Although his room was cold enough to make him get changed under the blankets, by the next morning Mat was surprised to find that he'd slept quite well.

He made his way downstairs for breakfast, and then into the living room to warm up. Mr Pearce was already there, talking quietly to an older man, who Mat guessed was his father.

After introductions, Mr Pearce went to his room to catch up with some homework marking. He left Mat with the old man. Old Mr Pearce had a squarish face, a bit like his son's, but more sort of chiselled. His eyes were blue, but watery, and set deep within the wrinkles that surrounded them. Even his eyebrows were grey, like his hair. Mat liked his smile.

'So, young man,' Mr Pearce Senior began. 'Tell me about yourself. Philip tells me you're interested in boats and such?'

Mat was indeed, and it turned out, so was Mr Pearce.

'I kept a small boat on a river not too far from here, y'know. Had it for years. Great fun! Gone now of course. Nobody here to use it.'

They talked for the majority of the morning. Old Mr Pearce had interesting things to talk about, but he also listened carefully to what Mat had to say. Mat liked him.

Mr Pearce Senior made him feel quite grown up. By lunchtime, though, the old man was tired and retired to his room.

'Pop in for a chat later, eh? Before dinner would be splendid.'

After lunch his teacher returned to his marking, leaving Mat to amuse himself. Not wanting a bored and restless young man on her hands, Mrs Clinton suggested that he might go out for a walk.

'There are some lovely walks around here,' she said, wiping her hands on her apron.

'Better in summer, of course, but still good even in winter.'

As he put on his shoes and overcoat, she called to him from the kitchen.

'Just make sure you look for landmarks, so you can find your way back. I don't want to have to send out search parties, thank you very much! And make sure you're back here before dinner!'

The day was cold, but dry. He was glad to be out in the fresh air. He started to walk up the lane.

Eventually he reached a point where the metalled road surface levelled out. The lane continued in a fairly straight line, but the surface was uneven, partly surfaced with gravel amongst the muddy ruts and tyre tracks.

To one side, a gateway led to an ancient-looking barn, granite-built and roofed with dark slate.

The way to it seemed to have been paved with stone slabs, but long, rough grass had forced its way through the joints between the slabs and seemed almost to be covering the whole surface. The barn's two large wooden doors, which might once have been painted blue if the blistered, weathered surface was anything to go by, were shut firmly, and secured with a heavily rusted chain and padlock hanging from equally rusty metal door handles.

Small plants had infested the guttering and moss and even some grass had somehow managed to find a foothold on the roof.

Mat tried to fathom what the barn might contain, but the cracked windows were dark and obscured by cobwebs, and he really didn't fancy getting close enough to find out what was inside. The whole place seemed forgotten, abandoned, and quite uninviting. He wondered who it might have belonged to.

Glancing back up the lane, he remembered about the Ambrose farm and realising that the barn probably belonged to them, he decided that if the barn was any sort of indicator, they probably wouldn't have been terribly welcoming of strangers.

He wasn't really in the mood to meet any more new people anyway, so he retraced his steps and walked back past the house and further down the valley.

Not wanting to get lost, he stuck to the lane. He walked for what felt like hours, lost in his own thoughts.

He daydreamed about walking with his mum, and swimming and playing beach cricket with his dad. He quite liked beach cricket. They played that with soft balls, not the rock-hard ones they used for proper cricket at school.

Sometimes…a lot of the time, his parents seemed very close and other times, they seemed so far away. There were moments when the realisation hit him that he would never do things with them ever again, it overwhelmed him. Those moments were so powerful that he felt like he'd been kicked in the stomach, and he gasped with the mental pain his daydreams and memories brought him.

He kept his promise, and was back at the house before it grew dark.

Mrs Clinton announced dinner would be another hour or so, so he borrowed a book from the small library in the living room, and settled down to read. After a while, Mrs Clinton popped her head around the door and cleared her throat.

'Don't forget,' she said quietly, 'you promised to go and see Old Mr Pearce before dinner.'

'Oh!' Mat exclaimed. 'I did! I forgot! Sorry, I'll go now. Which is his room?'

Mrs Clinton showed him the way. It was a large and a meandering sort of house, and there seemed to be an awful lot of bedrooms upstairs.

He now knew which one was his, but he had no idea what any of the other rooms contained.

They found Old Mr Pearce in a comfortable chair by a small fire in his bedroom. It was quite a large room, with two windows overlooking the front of the house. His bed dominated the centre of one wall, opposite the fire and there was a range of bedroom furniture on the wall opposite the windows.

The old man smiled as he approached, motioning for him to sit down on one of the easy chairs nearby. They sat and chatted about all sorts of small things. Mat talked about his walk this afternoon and about not liking school, and Old Mr Pearce told him stories of his own schooldays.

'I didn't like school much myself, y'know. Not when I started anyway. It gets better, give it time.'

As dinner-time approached, Mat thought he should go and wash his hands, and tidy up before they ate. The old man thanked him for his company.

'I've enjoyed our chats,' he said. 'Will you come and see me again tomorrow?'

Mat told him that he'd like that.

'Would you do something for me?' Mr Pearce Senior asked. 'Just before you go?'

Mat nodded, and asked what it was.

'Would you look out of the window for me, and tell me what you see?'

Mat stood and walked to the nearest window. He pulled back the curtain a little and peered out.

'I can't see much at all,' he said. 'It's too dark to see far.'

'Can you see the front gate?' the old man asked.

Mat could, just about. There was just enough light shining out from the hallway to allow him to see the gate posts.

'Anybody there?'

'Erm, no…' said Mat. 'Are you expecting someone?'

The old man looked at him sadly. 'Maybe,' he said. 'Probably, although I'd rather he didn't come just yet.'

13

Mat fell into something of a routine. Breakfast, chat with Mr Pearce Senior in the morning, take a walk after lunch, and then talk briefly with the old man again before dinner.

As he grew more familiar with his surroundings, he started to venture over larger areas.

Over the next few days, he found new fields to cross, and a small wood to explore. Sometimes he came across animals, cows and sheep but he wasn't sure that they'd welcome his company, so he gave them a wide berth.

Every evening as he left him to go and get ready for dinner, Mr Pearce Senior always asked the same question. Every night Mat would look, but there was never anybody stood outside, by the gate.

One evening, as their conversation time was drawing to a close, curiosity got the better of him, and Mat decided to ask outright who it was that the old man was watching out for.

'Mr Pearce?' he asked. 'Would you mind if I ask you a question?'

'Ask away, old boy,' Mr Pearce told him. 'I'll tell you, if I know the answer.'

'Who are you looking for every evening?'

'Ah,' said Old Mr Pearce. 'That's a surprisingly difficult question to answer. To tell you the truth, I don't know.'

'Then why are you always wondering if there's somebody out there?'

'Oh, it's only an old wives' tale,' said Mr Pearce Senior. 'I don't know why I even think about it. It just seems to have got stuck in my head, and I can't shake it off.'

'But what is it?' asked Mat, feeling even more curious now.

'Have you ever heard of the "stranger at the gate"?'

'The who?' asked Mat. 'Sorry, no I can't say I have.'

'Well, like I said, it's just an old wives' tale. Nothing for you to worry about.'

'Tell me the story?' Mat pleaded. 'Please?'

Old Mr Pearce thought for a moment.

'Very well, I will but only if you promise not to have nightmares.'

Mat promised, at this point he was thoroughly intrigued.

'It goes like this,' said the old man, and began to recite the rhyme.

'Beware the stranger at the midnight gate.
He hovers near. He won't be late.
So, when you pass, you need not roam,
For he has come to guide you home.'

'But what does it mean?' demanded Mat, impatiently.

'Like I said before, it's just an old story. Just a piece of nonsense. In old times some people thought that a hooded man would appear outside the house of someone who was dying. The hooded man was there to guide their souls on to where they were going. Heaven, or something like that. But it really is only a piece of old nonsense.'

'Do you want me to look now?' asked Mat eagerly.

'I suppose so,' said the old man, laughing. 'You might as well.'

Mat looked. He looked carefully…but there was nobody there. He wasn't sure whether he was disappointed or relieved.

That night, as he made his way up to bed, he thought he'd take just one more peep outside his window.

His bedroom was at the other end of the house to Old Mr Pearce's, but he could still see the gate quite clearly.

He switched off his bedside light and crept gingerly over to the window, careful to avoid stubbing his toes on the furniture. He gently pulled the curtains aside. Looking out, at first, he could see nothing.

As his eyes became more accustomed to the gloom, he was sure he could make out something, a shape of some kind, just outside the gate. The hall light had been switched off, so he couldn't see clearly – but he was sure that something, or somebody was there. It looked very much like a hooded figure.

Mat shivered with the realisation that he might have actually seen something. Did he see something? Were his eyes playing tricks on him?

The thought chilled him to the bone.

He sat on the side of his bed and thought it through. Eventually, he decided that it must have been his imagination, his over-active imagination. Old wives' tales aren't real, and they certainly don't come true.

He threw himself into bed, and under his covers. By now he was too cold to get changed, so he decided to sleep in his day clothes. Just once, nobody would know.

He was just too tired and too cold to be bothered tonight.

Except that he was too excited to sleep. He lay there, tense with anticipation. Could what the old man told him be true?

He was turning his words over in his mind. If this hooded man was some sort of spirit guide, maybe he'd collected Mat's parents too? Somewhere along the way? Maybe he collected them all together and took his parents with him, when he went to collect another one? Maybe?

He had to find out. He had to see his mum and dad again.

Eventually, when the whole house was asleep, and quiet, he decided he just couldn't wait any longer.

He jumped out of bed and gently turned the door handle. With the door slightly ajar, he listened intently. He could hear nothing, just silence and a murmuring of wind against the eaves.

In the darkness, he felt his way to the staircase, descending one step at a time, for fear that one of them would creak under his weight and wake someone. He shivered slightly as the cold night air greeted him, and then he was out the front door, making his way quietly down the path towards the gate.

The lane was empty, and the hooded shape he had seen before was no longer there. He breathed a sigh, of relief and of frustration. If the hooded man wasn't there, maybe the whole thing wasn't true? No…it had to be true. It just had to be! This might be his only chance to see his parents again.

Bundled in his heavy coat, he crouched in the shadows at the side of the lane and waited. He would wait all night, if necessary. He would wait for as long as it took.

He jostled as a cool breeze woke him, and shook him awake. He had no idea what the time was, he must have dozed off, despite trying so hard not to. Annoyed with himself, he screwed his face up in an effort not to drift off again.

Feeling his eyes start to droop, he shook his head to clear the fuzziness away…and then he sensed, rather than saw, what he had been waiting for.

Under the grey, ominous, thick clouds, there was no light from the moon or stars. All he could see were shadows – but there in the distance he was sure he could make out shapes, or at least the hint of shapes and darker shadows.

They were not making any sounds, but as he concentrated and focused his eyes, he was positive he could make out a line of them, a long line of dark shapes in the gloom. There were dozens of them, maybe even hundreds.

The line seemed endless, and they were moving silently through the lane, in front of the house.

Not daring to move, he strained his eyes to catch a glimpse of the individual shapes, hoping to see his parents among them. He imagined them passing before him, holding each other's hands.

He opened his mouth; he was ready to call out as soon as he saw his mum and dad.

He wanted to call them away from this long line of endless marching feet. He wanted desperately to call them back to him.

He made his mind up, in case he couldn't see them, or even if they were not meant to return to him, that he would wait to join the end of the line, following them to wherever they were going.

He got to his feet and dusted off his coat in readiness to join the line...but just at that moment he felt a large hand firmly grip his shoulder! He immediately felt his body go limp, and he almost fainted with fright.

'Please, I'm not dead!' he yelped. 'I'm not dead! Leave me alone!' He was sure he must have dozed off long enough for the hooded man to get him!

'I can see you're not dead!' a man's voice said quietly and firmly from the dark.

Mat felt a rough hand steadying him.

Mat was relieved to see that it wasn't the hooded man in the shadows after all.

The man he did see, however, was almost as frightening.

He had no idea who he was but he was impressively tall, and his hands were massive, like shovels.

'Are you Matthew?' the man continued. 'You must be, I don't know of any other new boys in the area. What on earth are you doing out here? I thought you'd be waiting inside for me. You must be frozen!'

'Who are you?' Mat asked, realising that the man was right, he was bitterly cold. He couldn't control the shivering, which now took over his body.

'Oh, yeah, sorry,' the man replied. 'I'm Tom Ambrose. We live up the lane, up at Home Farm. Philip…Mr Pearce phoned to say that his dad had taken a turn for the worse. He asked if we'd look after you for a while. This isn't a good place for boys at the moment.'

Though Tom didn't let on, Mr Pearce had also explained about Matthew's parents. The boy's world had already been turned upside down. Another death, so close now, might be too much for him to bear.

Mat could hardly walk; his legs and feet were so numb from the cold. Mr Ambrose helped him along the lane. It took a little while before they finally reached the farm.

His first impression of the place was blurred by tiredness and the cold. The narrow lane they had been following ended abruptly at a wooden five-bar field gate directly ahead of them.

The gate creaked in protest as Mr Ambrose swung it open, wide enough for them to pass through, and they stepped into a wide yard, paved initially with huge stone slabs. As they drew nearer to the house, the path turned into rough cobbles.

Matthew was vaguely aware of a tree in the middle of the yard, framed against the bright light of a lamp burning in the low, wide, deeply vestibuled doorway of the house.

Though it was late, Mrs Ambrose insisted that he had a hot bath. He'd been so cold for so long and she knew instinctively they had to warm him up as quickly as they could.

Mat didn't protest. Upstairs, he lay in a bath, hot enough to steam the mirrors and windows of the large bathroom.

Downstairs, Tom told his wife what he'd discovered.

'I found him in the lane outside Philip's house,' he said. 'I asked him some questions on the way home. He didn't say much, though mind you he was shivering so much it was difficult to make out what he was saying. He did tell me that the old man had kept asking him to check out of the window to see if there was a hooded man stood by the gate. He said it was something to do with an old wives' tale. I don't know what he was on about, but it seems to have got to him. He was sure he'd seen this hooded bloke when he went to bed. It played on his mind, and he figured this person might be able to help him see his parents one last time. Bit touched, if you ask me.'

Mrs Ambrose sat and thought about what the boy had said, long after her husband had gone to bed. She made sure Mat was warm and thoroughly dried after his bath, and tucked him into bed. It was a big house, and they had plenty of rooms to spare. One more lad wasn't going to make all that much difference.

She had a house full, with her own kids. She'd hardly notice one more. This one did worry her though. He'd had so many shocks and bad news in such a short time…and for all he was taller than average for his age, he was only a little boy, after all was said and done.

'No,' she decided firmly, 'what this boy needs is a bit of stability, warmth and love. We'll make sure he gets all of that. Even if it is only for a few days.'

***

Bridie's father and brothers were always up early. They had work to do and needed a good, hearty breakfast to start their day well. Bridie knew better than to get in their way but she was up and hungry by the time the kitchen door closed behind the men. 'What was all that about, last night?' she asked her mum, her mouth half full of cereal.

Mrs Ambrose explained what had happened. She didn't spare the details. She needed her daughter to take this seriously.

'I need you to keep an eye on him,' she said. 'You two are more or less the same age. I'm not asking you to mother or smother him, but I really do think he needs a bit of...I don't know...family? Why don't you two watch TV, play games. Show the boy around, whatever. Just be nice, eh? He's been through a lot. Much more than any kid his age – your age – should ever have to. Please? For me?' Hilda chewed her bottom lip and watched her daughter. She knew she'd taken in what she had said. She knew her daughter very well. She thought she could anticipate what her reaction might be. She hoped to herself, she was right. Her daughter chewed more slowly for a few moments. She swallowed the last spoonful of her breakfast, and then smiled up at her.

'Yeah, OK,' she promised. For both of them, that was all that was needed.

Hilda knew that her new charge would be well looked after. Bridie knew that she had a responsibility. She was thirteen now, nearly a woman. It was time she took on bigger responsibilities. She smiled as a thought struck her. For once, she would be older than somebody. She'd be the boss, not just the little sister! She liked that idea...

At the same time...if she screwed up, she'd have her mum to answer. She didn't like that idea nearly as much.

'What's he like?' she asked, her curiosity piqued.

'Well, I haven't seen that much of him or had chance to speak to him much, but as far as I can tell he's a nice lad. Yes, I like him.' Her mother's lips curled into a smile.

That was good enough for Bridie. Like her mum, she could tell whether she liked somebody as soon as she met them.

She could hear Mat's footsteps coming down the stairs. Either way, she was now about to find out for herself.

'Hello,' Mat said as he opened the kitchen door cautiously.

'Morning Mrs Ambrose,' he said, as he noticed her more fully, as he entered the kitchen. Seeing Bridie, he stopped and stood a little straighter, he approached her nervously. He knew a girl his own age lived here, but this was the first time he had met her.

'Morning,' he said, extending his hand, 'I'm Mat.'

As she shook his hand, her eyes ran over him. He was taller than she was. His light brown hair was cut short, like most boys his age, at least the ones who went to *posh schools*.

He had blue eyes, deep blue and sparkly. She loved his eyes, and decided they were his best feature. It was just a shame that he wore glasses, but at least they were clean.

Her middle brother wore glasses; his were never clean. Actually, she was surprised her brother could see through the lenses at all.

Yes, she thought. She was going to like him.

Mat had always been nervous of meeting new people. He always found it difficult to decide if he was going to like them, and whether or not they were going to like him back.

His dad had often told him that one could tell a lot about someone new through their handshake. Bridie's hand was warm in his. She had soft skin. He liked that.

He reminded himself to make eye contact, as his dad had told him, it would show him to be confident and trustworthy.

When Bridie's eyes met his, he found himself feeling less nervous than he had been before. He liked her eyes. They were brown, and they seemed friendly and kind, if eyes could be friendly and kind, and when she smiled at him, he couldn't help but smile back.

Matthew felt himself starting to feel much better about things now that he'd met Bridie.

Bridie had finished her breakfast. She added her dish to the pile in the sink, and called over her shoulder to him, as she rushed out of the kitchen door.

'Come on,' she commanded. 'I'll show you round.'

Matthew hadn't eaten any breakfast yet, but didn't like to ask for any. His stomach rumbled faintly as he followed her into the hallway. He didn't seem to have much choice in the matter. It felt as though her energy was pulling him along in her wake.

She showed him around the house. It was a lot bigger than he'd thought from his brief introduction to the exterior the night before.

There seemed to be corridors and doors everywhere, and after the first couple of turns, he gave up trying to get his bearings.

He knew he'd never be able to find his way through the maze by himself, and after the second corridor, and staircase he couldn't remember whether they'd turned left or right last. Doors were thrown open seemingly at random and closed again just as quickly.

Rooms were quickly shown, before his eyes could even become accustomed to their curtained gloom. Occasionally she would mention that this had been *so-and-so's room*, or had been used for some occasion or other. More often than not, her introduction to the various rooms was simply, 'bedroom!' and 'another bedroom!' This is the 'old sitting room!' and this one, the 'top sewing room!' and such like. There didn't seem to be much difference, between any of them to him. Most of the rooms were large, cold and smelled a bit musty.

She showed him more carefully where her parents' and brothers' bedrooms were and more pointedly, the door to her own.

'I wouldn't want to go in the boys' rooms if I were you,' she said disdainfully. 'They smell, and don't even *think* about opening my door!'

By the time Bridie had finished introducing him to the layout of the house, Mat was feeling really quite overwhelmed. It had felt rather like his introductory tour of the school. He felt now as he had felt then...

He had no idea how on earth he was supposed to remember where anything was. He needed a break!

'Please could you remind me where the bathroom is?' he asked.

Once in the bathroom, as he locked the door, he heard Bridie make her way, noisily, downstairs to the kitchen.

He breathed a sigh of relief as he sat carefully on the edge of the bath. He hadn't really needed to use the bathroom, but he seriously did need to take a breather from Bridie's whirlwind tour.

As he sat there, quietly, he thought again about everything that had happened over the last few weeks. The devastating news about his parents.

He'd really hoped Mrs Clinton might have given him a hug, but she hadn't. Mrs Ambrose was nice, but she hadn't given him a hug either.

He liked Bridie. She was, he reflected, probably the only girl of his age that he knew. But she hadn't given him a hug.

Nobody had. There was nobody else he could turn to for love, even just for a hug. And that's when the tears started streaming down his face.

Bridie was in the kitchen with her mum. She sat at the huge table, but she was staring down at her feet. Hilda noticed. She sensed that something was wrong.

'What's up, Bridie?' she asked quietly. 'Where's Matthew?'

'He went to the bathroom,' Bridie told her.

'So?'

'Just that, well, he's been ages, Mum. Please could you check on him?'

Hilda knocked on the bathroom door.

'Matthew?' she called. 'Mat, are you OK? We were getting worried.'

Matthew gave no reply, but Hilda could hear sobs from the other side of the door.

'Mat, please would you open the door?'

Eventually, after what seemed to be ages, she heard the lock slide back. She turned the door handle.

As she opened the door, Mat just stood in the middle of the room. His eyes and cheeks were reddened. It was obvious to her that he'd been crying.

'Oh my, Mat,' she said. 'Whatever's the matter?'

If she could have bitten her tongue off at that moment, she would have. She quickly realised that her question was ridiculous. For Matthew, everything was the matter.

She walked quickly into the bathroom, took him into her arms and enveloped him as tightly as she could.

He sobbed for a long time, loudly and very wetly.

Eventually, he pulled away.

Out of the corner of his eye, he noticed that Bridie was stood in the doorway. Tears were streaming down her face. Then she turned and ran downstairs.

Hilda held onto Matthews hands.

'Matthew,' she told him as his sobs subsided. 'You've been through so much; I can't begin to understand the pain you're feeling. I know you miss your mum so much. It breaks your heart. I will not even try to take her place…nobody could…but I promise that I will try my best to look after you, as long as you want me to, and to bring you as much comfort as I can. Is that OK with you?'

Matthew sobbed once again, and nodded. Then he took her in his arms and hugged her.

After seeing all the rooms, Matthew decided he liked the sitting room, with its huge fireplace, the wide hearth piled with logs, and its television and comfortable sofas, but it seemed that Bridie had far more interesting things to show him yet. There were more rooms? Surely not, Mat thought to himself.

They made their way through the warm kitchen towards the back door. Matthew wondered if he had the nerve to grab a couple of biscuits as they passed the table, but she was far too quick for him.

'Mum'll kill you if you eat those now! You'll spoil your lunch.'

'But when's lunch? I'm really hungry now!' Mat told her.

'So, you should have had breakfast then!'

'You didn't give me chance!'

'Oh, for goodness' sake!' said Bridie. 'Put a couple in your pocket then. Just shuffle the rest around, so Mum won't know.'

Matthew shoved a couple of biscuits into his pocket.

'Can I just ask?' he said, 'before, with your mum, why were you crying?'

Bridie's cheeks started to redden.

'Well…just because, OK?'

'Because of what?' he pushed.

'Because you're my friend. I was upset that you were upset. That's all.'

'How can I be your friend?' he asked. 'We've only just met.'

She shrugged her shoulders.

'Just because…'

'I like your mum,' he told her.

She looked at him thoughtfully, clearly struggling to know what to say.

'I'm sorry you've lost your mum and dad, Mat,' she said, trying desperately to hide her rapidly moistening eyes.

Mat nodded. 'Me too. I hate it.'

'Well,' she said quietly, 'you can share mine if you want?'

Mat nodded, and smiled at her.

'Thank you,' he said. 'I think I'd like that.'

As they left the house behind and circled into the main yard, Matthew crammed the two biscuits he'd pinched from the kitchen into his mouth. They made little difference. He was still hungry. He glanced at his watch and wished the clock hands would move faster.

'Come on,' she commanded, pulling him along with her energy-force, 'chickens are waiting!'

As his rubber boots splashed across the rough uneven, muddy terrain of the main farmyard, Matthew began to realise how big the farm actually was.

His impression of it so far had been just the front yard, half-seen in the misty darkness of the previous night.

Now, in the broad daylight, he was amazed by the number of out-houses and barns that surrounded the large yard, paved with granite slabs and cobbles.

'This place is huge!' he exclaimed, trying to count the number of doors in the side of one of the out-houses.

'Nah,' she said dismissively over her shoulder. 'This ain't big. I've seen bigger. Still, it does us.'

'What on earth do you do in all these building?' he asked innocently.

She sighed. Patiently, she explained what all the buildings were for. She showed him where the cows were taken for milking, the barns where they kept hay, straw and stacked-high bales of animal feed and eventually opened the door of one of the buildings, to show him where they raised the pigs.

Matthew tilted his head inside to look, and quickly withdrew, as soon as his nose caught the aroma emanating from the sows and their seemingly hundreds of offspring.

'Wow!' he gasped involuntarily, wrinkling his nose and rather hoping that she wouldn't make him go in any further.

Bridie chortled at the expression on his face.

'Yeah, they do rather stink, don't they!' she laughed. 'You get used to it!'

Matthew wasn't at all sure that he wanted to get used to it, and was rather glad when she closed the door and they moved on.

He preferred the chicken coup. It smelled, but nowhere near as strong as the pig-pens. She showed him what to do and he was taught how to feed and water them and how to collect the eggs.

As they took their eggs back into the house, Matthew was relieved to see that Mrs Ambrose had already set the kitchen table, ready for lunch.

They didn't have long to wait before Mr Ambrose and the boys arrived and they were allowed to sit down. Much to his embarrassment, Matthew's stomach growled noisily as he waited for his plate. Bridie giggled as his face turned bright red.

'You hungry, boy?' asked Mr Ambrose. 'Didn't you have any breakfast?'

Mr Ambrose laughed when Matthew shook his head.

'Well, you'll learn soon enough around here, if you don't ask, you don't get!'

Mat looked around the table, while Bridie's mum finished serving their lunch and started passing plates around.

The family were all talking at once, while at the same time helping themselves to bread and butter. Bridie passed him some bread and he smiled his thanks.

He watched all their faces in turn as they talked and laughed and started to fork food into their mouths. Mat was amazed at how at ease they were with each other.

He recalled mealtimes with his own family. They were much quieter affairs, just the odd comment from one or other of his parents while their cutlery clattered quietly against their plates.

He couldn't really remember any proper conversations at their table. Not like here, where there seemed to be at least four conversations going on at the same time.

He'd only been introduced to Bridie's brothers when they sat down at the table for lunch, but they seemed friendly and welcoming.

Of course, he knew Bridie's mum. Mat smiled as he thought of how kind she'd been to him that morning in the bathroom. He'd met Bridie's dad the evening before, and although he'd seemed friendly enough, he didn't really know him properly yet.

Mat reckoned he was one of the biggest men he'd ever met, and he made a mental note to avoid doing anything to make him cross.

Then there was Bridie. She'd made sure he was sat next to her at the table. She'd passed him some bread when everyone else was just leaning over the table and grabbing some for themselves. She'd cried when she'd seen him cry. Best of all, she'd told him she was his friend. That made him feel warm inside.

14

The next morning, after they'd seen to the chickens, they watched television.

As it was Christmas Eve, the good programmes lasted a bit longer than usual, but they were getting bored by lunchtime. Having already shown him around the farm, Bridie wasn't sure what to do with him. She thought hard, then she smiled widely.

'Shall I show you a secret?' she asked.

Before Mat could even answer, he was being pulled out the door.

She led him across misty fields, through gates, past trees, over hills.

Matthew's legs were soon aching, and as he stopped briefly to recover, Bridie turned back to find out what was wrong.

'My legs are aching,' he explained. 'I'll be alright in a minute.'

'You big softy,' she laughed dismissively, as she pivoted to carry on. 'Don't you have hills where you come from?'

There were hills at school but they were short, sharp hills. There was the one that they had to climb from their form-room up to the main body of the school. That was a horrible hill and always made his legs tremble by the time he reached the top.

There were hills around his house too, but they were gentler, easier on his legs.

Thoughts of home brought back an aching emptiness. There was nobody there anymore. It wasn't *home* anymore. He didn't have a home, or know where home was now.

Not wanting to watch her walk further away, he forced his complaining legs to trudge along and follow in her lighter footsteps.

They approached a low hedge of interwoven branches alongside a narrow, muddy track and eventually beside a small stream. On the other side of the stream, some way in the distance and partially obscured by a light, floating mist stood several small mounds of grass-covered earth.

'This is our secret,' she said, whispering into his ear.

'What is?' he whispered back. 'Those mounds?'

'They're part of it, but they came later, along with the circle,' she replied.

'What circle?' he asked, confused.

He couldn't see any circles. He hadn't noticed any circles on the way up either.

'The stone circle,' she said, turning round to point at a couple of granite posts they'd passed through.

'See those? Those are the Summer Stones. They're the main entrance posts. There are loads more, but they are smaller. They're not as easy to see with all the trees and bushes.'

'I thought they were just gate posts,' he said.

Bridie smiled knowingly at him.

'That's what you were supposed to think. I'll show you them another time, they are big, though. Massive!' Bridie's eyes widened.

Matthew gazed around him. He still couldn't see any circles. By now, he was sure she was pulling his leg.

'Yeah right!' he said, sceptically.

Bridie raised an eyebrow in his direction, and shrugged. 'You don't believe me?' she asked innocently.

Mat smiled to himself, convinced by now that she was having him on. 'So...come on then, tell me about it!' he demanded.

'The story goes that a distant tribe got to hear about the secret and they wanted to find out what it was. They'd watched the family gathering here, so they knew more or less where it was but they didn't know what it was. So, they got hold of four giants to help them and they surrounded the whole place.'

Bridie's voice dropped lower, like she was about to reveal the best part.

'Then, just as the ceremony was going to begin, a huge green mist appeared and turned the watching spies to stone – giants and all! That's the story anyway. Its good, isn't it?'

'Oh, come on!' Matthew laughed loudly. 'Even I know that's just plain daft. Tell me a proper story!'

'That was!' Bridie said, looking offended.

'OK, OK...' she paused briefly.

'If you really want to know. So, like I said, over there are the Summer Stones and on the other side of the stream are the Winter Stones. Can't see them today because they're too far away and it's misty out, but they're there.

'Those,' she pointed, 'are the Autumn Stones and the Spring Stones.' She waved and vaguely gestured in different directions.

'I guess they're all the main ones. In between are the Marker Stones. They just sort of fill in the gaps between the main ones. Then there's the secret place, smack in the middle of it all.'

Mat narrowed his eyes at the stones. Bridie watched him closely.

'See?' she said, enthusiastically. 'Told you it was big.'

'So, if you know so much, tell me why they're here – and why is it so big.'

'It's big because there was a lot of people. Back when this was made, it wasn't just one family, it was lots of families. It was like a tribe. There was just a lot of people OK and they all had to fit in. Happy now?' Bridie let out an exasperated huff.

'You didn't say why it was here though…'

'To protect the secret, stupid! Only Family are allowed here, right?' she said, looking frustrated with all his curious questions.

'So, what's the secret, then? You still haven't told me,' he persevered.

She led him down to the edge of the stream.

'Do you see that?' she asked, pointing to a small bridge.

He looked down to where she was pointing. He could see a narrow slab of roughly-cut granite, laid across the stream. It stood a couple of feet above the water.

'That is Bridie's Bridge,' she said reverently.

'Oh,' was all he could say, still not entirely sure if she was making it up.

'It has a long history,' she said, wistfully. 'In fact, this bridge is history. It is the history of this place. It's why we are here.'

He raised his eyebrows in surprise. 'Why who is here?' he asked, 'you mean us?'

'No,' she declared, rolling her eyes, 'not us! but *us*, as in our family!'

'Oh right,' he replied quickly, trying to keep up.

'If you promise to listen properly,' Bridie told him, in a serious tone, 'I'll tell you, then you'll understand.'

She beckoned him to sit with her. The grass was damp, so he laid his raincoat on the ground and they both settled onto it. She spoke in hushed tones.

'I'm Bridie,' she began, 'and my mother is Hilda. My grandmother was Pam. I can't remember what my great-grandmother's name was. Same with her mother, and all my great-grandmothers back as far as time. I don't know any of their names, there are too many of them to recall.

'Anyway, the thing is that the first-born girl has always been the one who knew things that none of the rest of her family knew.

'Mothers would always teach their first-born daughters about the *real* history, not the everyday stuff. They would pass down not so much the things that happened, but the secret history of things that were important, like what made this place so *special*, and why the family is here. The eldest girl is the one who keeps the secrets safe, and then in turn, passes them on to their future daughter. I'm the eldest girl, so it's my job to look after the secrets.'

He was following, as best he could and nodded his interest.

'The thing is, before they came here, and all the way back through our family's history, the eldest daughter of every generation had carried an important heirloom. It was a small stone, about the size and shape of a chicken egg, which the first of our ancestors had discovered in a stream the night before she and her people left their traditional homeland forever.

'She loved how smooth it was, and the way it glowed with flashes of bright blue, pink, yellow and orange, especially when it was wet. It made her happy, and she carried it with her for the remainder of her life.

'She called it her "Home Stone", because it reminded her of where she'd come from. When she was too old to walk any further, she gave it to her daughter and asked her to carry it onwards, until they found a forever home. It was handed from mother to daughter, generation after generation, throughout all the years until it eventually came here.'

'How do you know all this?' he asked, not wishing to interrupt the story, but wanting to understand her history.

'I told you; my mother told me all of this. It's part of the secret that gets passed from mother to daughter, generation after generation. Haven't you been listening at all?'

'Of course I have!' he assured.

'Then may I continue?' she asked, raising her eyebrows in a somewhat sarcastic way.

Matthew nodded at her, and offered an encouraging and apologetic smile. 'So anyway, my people came here first. They were the first ones to settle here. Ever. There had been nobody before them, it was all new.

'There were no roads back then, no tracks, no knowledge of the place. Where they had come from, we have only bits and pieces of memories, but we know that they were hunters, and very good at it. If they hadn't been, they would never have come this far. They had walked and hunted, camped and lived, and they would walk on again, repeating their way of life for generations. They had faced attacks from savage wild beasts, and most of the time fought them off and had hunted them in return. They were a small group, maybe sixty or seventy people and they stuck together...*Family*. They followed one leader, the person who was deemed the strongest of them, and they had to work as a team to survive. It was a wild and treacherous land they travelled through.'

He watched intently as she gathered herself for the next part of her story.

Bridie threw her long brown hair over her shoulders. She had a round sort of face and bright, brown eyes that seemed to look even bigger when she talked about a subject she loved.

He didn't know much about girls, never had much to do with them, but he was becoming more and more comfortable being with her.

He'd been watching and listening to her carefully as she spoke, and was fascinated by how animated her face had become while she was telling her story. He loved the way her eyes widened and sparkled as she talked, and he had started to really look forward to those moments when she flashed a quick look at him, to make sure he was paying attention.

He wasn't at all sure that he entirely believed what she was telling him, but it didn't really matter anyway. He was too enchanted by the sound of her voice and in the way her lips moved as she spoke.

He found her lips, and especially her smile, quite distracting, and every now and then, he had to remind himself to actually listen to her words instead of staring at her face, in case she asked questions later.

One thing he knew for sure, though, was that he wanted her to smile at him always.

'Then they arrived here,' she continued, scanning the field and bridge. 'And they set up camp. They built their homes as they always had, with skins and branches. They lit fires, gathered berries and fetched water from the stream. Some went off to hunt whatever animals they could find. For most of them, it was just another place to camp, to hunt, to stay for a while and then to move on.

'My ancestor, the one who brought the Home Stone here, she came with her friends to this place to fetch water from the stream. It is said that she stopped at the edge of the stream, looked left and looked right.

'She looked ahead and behind her. Then she stood very still, right on this very spot where we are sat and it seemed to her friends that something had changed in her. She just stared into space, into the distance. She took a deep breath and said, "this is a very special place. I can feel power running through it, I can feel it running through me."'

Bridie stirred, jumping to her feet, and looked at the bridge.

'Do you know what ley lines are?' she asked. He shook his head. 'They're lines of power,' she continued. 'They flow through the earth; you can't see them and most people can't feel them or even know they're there. Few people understand them, but they're very special.

'My ancestor felt the power of the ley line that runs through here, across this stream and even though she didn't know what it was or what it meant, she knew that it was special. She came and sat here many times, and she told the tribe's elders that she often felt spirits passing along the line, going somewhere she didn't know.

'They were the spirits of birds and animals mostly, but the most powerful spirits of all, were those that were members of the tribe the spirits of those who had died while they were camped here.'

Bridie remained standing, looking intently at the bridge. 'It seemed to her that the spirits were all pulled through this place, like they'd been caught in a strong wind and blown through. She asked and eventually begged them to help the spirits on their way, by making a bridge so they could get over the stream more easily. She told them what she wanted.

'After searching, they found a huge slab of granite. They cleaned it and chipped pieces away to flatten the top, then they dragged it here. They placed it over the stream, in exactly the place she told them. Before they put it finally into place, she carefully hid the Home Stone under one end of the bridge. It's been here ever since. The family couldn't stay in the same camp all the time, of course. They had to move around to follow the best hunting, but she persuaded them to come back here as often as she could. She felt that it was such an important place.'

He nodded, smiling at her, and whispered, 'She was right, wasn't she?'

She nodded, smiling. 'Yes, she was. This is a very special place. She passed her knowledge on to her daughter. Every generation of women ever since has gained that knowledge, and the more settled the family become in the area, the more my ancestors were able to build on their knowledge.

'Over time, they persuaded the family to build permanent houses alongside the line of force, which is why our house is situated where it is, and to build a village on the other side of the stream for the loved ones who passed on. That's what the mounds are for, over there. They're called barrows, and that's where the dead people live.

'They felt that it was important to have the stream between the two, the living and the dead. The dead passed over the stream to their new homes, to wait until the force was strong enough to carry them further.'

He nodded, looking in the same direction as her. 'That makes sense.'

'They worked out, over time, that the force of the ley line was stronger at certain times of the year. Just like the stream itself. Sometimes it was very weak, and could carry only the smallest of spirits. Sometimes it was amazingly strong, and could not only blow the larger spirits along quickly, but could pull those who were nearly spirits into it as well.'

'Maybe that's what happened to Mr Pearce's father?' he said, thinking out loud.

She shrugged her shoulders. 'Maybe. The ley line passes along the lane in front of his house.'

They sat in silence for a while. Mat thought about everything she'd told him.

'So, when are the strongest times?' he asked.

'Strongest times are usually around the summer and winter solstices, like mid-summer and mid-winter. There are others as well, but not quite as strong. The best of them is called the Solstices and Equinoxes. Solstices are when the days and nights are different lengths, like in summer it's the longest day, and in winter it's the longest night. That was a couple of days ago, but I can still feel the strength of it, even now,' she added.

'Equinoxes are different. That's when the days and nights are the same length, there is one around Easter I think, and another in the autumn. I can't remember when the other strong times are. I don't know everything yet. Those are the most important ones, though. Solstices and Equinoxes.'

'So, what happens to the spirits of people who die outside those times? Do they just hang around, waiting for the force to be enough?' He was thinking about his parents, and wondering if there might still be a chance to talk to them again.

'More or less, I think,' she replied.

'Same as those who die a long way from a ley line. There's not much they can do for a while. They just have to wait patiently, until someone collects them and leads them to the nearest line. Then they wait, until the force is strong enough to carry them on.'

'Right,' he said. 'I get it – so because they can't find their own way, they have to wait for a guide?'

'That's right.'

'So that's what the hooded man does?' he asked. 'The one Old Mr Pierce called the "stranger at the midnight gate"?'

Bridie's eyes widened, at the revelation of his words.

'Mr Pearce told me about the hooded man, we talked a lot,' he clarified.

'Yeah, there are all sorts of names for them but yes, that's what they do. They collect them and bring them together. They make sure they're ready for the force to move them on.'

Matthew sat and thought about all this for a few moments. It all sounded a bit far-fetched but he really didn't want to say so. He liked the story, it sort of made sense. He wanted to believe it, in her words and conviction.

'You said only family is allowed here, didn't you?'

Bridie nodded.

'Then why did you bring me here? I'm not family.'

She gave him a sideways glance, then looked back over the bridge and shrugged. 'Just sort of felt right, I suppose.'

Matthew smiled to himself, feeling the same warm glow as he had felt when she'd called him her friend.

'Thank you for telling me the history,' he told her. 'Will you tell me more stories about it one day?'

'Might do…' she said, smiling, 'but only if you promise to keep my secrets, OK?'

'I will. I promise!' he told her. 'Always and forever.'

15

They camped in the family's sitting room for the rest of the afternoon.

They sat on the floor, leaning back against the comfortable armchairs, eating crisps and mince pies to keep them going until dinner. Bridie told him that she'd made the mince pies herself. He wasn't at all sure he believed her. They watched television and he was happy that they liked the same programmes.

Mat felt comfortable with her, even though she was a girl. He wasn't used to girls. He'd spent most of his life by himself, or in the company of other boys, and he really wasn't at all sure what spending time with girls would entail.

Bridie was different to what he'd imagined girls would be like. She was good company, and a comfortable sort of silence passed between them while they watched their programmes…and he was impressed that she'd wanted to share the secret about her family's history with him.

He thought about everything she'd told him. There was a lot to think about. He wasn't sure what to make of the idea that their Home Stone, as she'd called it, had travelled with her ancestors for so many years.

He shook his head when he considered that. In all that time, over probably thousands and thousands of years, according to her story, how many opportunities would there have been for it to get lost? Probably loads, he reckoned, so that in itself was amazing. Then, why had none of her ancestors thought they'd found a 'forever' home earlier? Somewhere else? Surely a few of them must have thought so. Why hadn't the family settled there, instead of here?

Maybe it was something to do with the ley lines she'd talked about. He'd never heard of them before, but that didn't mean they weren't there. He learnt new things all the time at school, things he'd never heard of, or thought about before. So yes, he thought, maybe it was something to do with that. He could imagine that a powerful earth-force might well have had an influence.

Mat got lost in his thoughts. How strange that the ley line went past Mr Pearce's house? Was it a coincidence that he'd thought he'd seen strange shapes, like shadows, moving up the lane? Had he dreamt them up? Were they really there? Maybe they were…and maybe he'd been right to think his parents might have been following the hooded man.

Mr Pearce had talked about using him as their guide, along the ley line and eventually across Bridie's bridge. And what about those solstices and equinoxes she'd been so keen to talk about. She seemed to know all about them. What was all that about? Was she right? Did they really make any difference to anything?

Or maybe it was all just a load of rubbish, and he was an idiot for even considering it.

The more he thought about it all, the more confused he got. He really wished he was more like Bridie. She always seemed to be so de-cisive, so confident, so self-assured, certainly loads more than he was. And she was fun to be with.

He glanced over in her direction, just to see her burst into laughter over something on the television. Crisp crumbs sprayed from her open mouth and landed on her jumper, and the floor around her.

She took little notice, other than to say 'Oops,' and brush the crumbs away with her hand. She always seemed to be so relaxed about stuff like that. Like it didn't matter, like stuff just happens and you just deal with it. He frowned, wishing he could be more like that. But he knew he really wasn't.

He decided that he really quite liked her, even though she was a girl, and he was a boy. Earlier, she'd told him he was her friend. He hoped that was true. He really liked the idea of that.

Then he noticed that she was looking his way.

'What's that face for?' she asked. 'You look like you lost a pound and found sixpence!'

He laughed in reply.

Then he realised that tears were flowing down his face, dripping off his nose and his chin.

Bridie quickly shuffled across to sit beside him.

'Sorry,' he sobbed 'I didn't…'

'Hey,' she emphasized. 'You don't need to say sorry to me,' she told him as she enveloped him in her arms.

That's when his floodgates really opened, and he found himself sobbing, freely and unstoppably into her shoulder.

She instinctively held him closer and tighter.

'I'm so sorry,' he told her, his voice muffled by her jumper.

'Shh,' she whispered softly into his ear. 'Shh…shh…shh…don't worry, Mat. I've got you. I'll be here for you always. I promise. Always and forever…'

***

Later that same evening, when they'd finished their dinner, Bridie volunteered Mat to help her with the dishes. This was her one regular chore, and she was more than happy to be able to share it for once.

He didn't mind. He thought he liked the kitchen best of all the rooms he'd been in. It was always warm, from the large wood-fired range that sat proudly in the middle of the end wall. The furniture, especially the table, was heavy and solid. He liked the furniture in the house.

When they sat down for meals, the whole family only took up one end of the table.

Matthew wondered how they'd got it into the kitchen in the first place. Perhaps it had always been here, from when the house was built. It certainly looked like it had been there forever. There were a couple of faint burn marks on the surface. He wondered if maybe saucepans had been placed down when they were too hot. The kitchen spanned the whole depth of the house. It had a window that looked out over the front yard, which he'd crossed when he first approached the house with Mr Ambrose.

There was another large window opposite, behind the sink. From that window he could see a corner of the rear garden that encircled the barn. He could see the small gate they passed through in the mornings to collect the eggs and feed the chickens.

There was another larger gate at the opposite end of the garden, from the corner of the house. It was where they let the cows in from the fields at milking times. He guessed his room was more or less right above the kitchen. He had the same sort of view of the surroundings when he peered out of his bedroom window.

If he glanced over his shoulder, at the table, he could see part of the tree. It was a copper beech; Bridie had told him. She'd said that in the spring it was a mass of almost white blossom, and in summer it was covered with beautiful copper-coloured leaves.

At the moment, in the depths of winter, it just looked like a huge skeleton, hauntingly dominating the yard. It was difficult to imagine the tree's beauty and revival in the summer or anything else coming back to life again for that matter, but Bridie said that it would.

Around and around, year after year, a continuous circle. Matthew wished, with all his heart, that people could be like trees and regenerate; despite going through their death cycle, but he knew humans were not like trees. People fell off the world like the dry transitional leaves in autumn. People were not like leaves; you never saw them again. They didn't come back in spring.

Matthew was soon brought out of his reverie of thoughts from the sound of Bridie's voice over the dinner table.

They had finished their dinner and had begun stacking plates and cutlery from the table, preparing for them to be washed in the sink.

'Oh, come *on*,' she whined, exasperated at his lack of speed and skill in washing the dirty plates. 'We haven't got all night, you know!'

'I'm doing my best here!' Mat retorted, not quite sure why she was in such a hurry.

'Oh!' she said, letting out a frustrated huff. 'Here, let me do it, for goodness' sake!'

'Suit yourself!' he muttered resignedly.

He leaned on the draining board as she flashed through washing the last remaining dishes.

'Well don't just stand there!' Bridie said. 'Get that towel working – surely even you can dry dishes?'

He picked up the cloth and started to dry a plate. He was painfully slow, even at that. Bridie rolled her eyes, but for once, held her tongue.

Once she'd finished washing the dishes, she hoisted herself up on the kitchen worktop and perched. She watched as he gradually did the drying-up.

'Do you believe in Father Christmas?' she asked, smiling behind his back.

'Why?' he responded, concentrating on the task in hand. 'Do you?'

'Of course!' she said, in a matter-of-fact tone. 'Why wouldn't I?'

He carried on with the drying.

'You didn't answer the question,' she prompted.

Mat cringed, as he thought about the last time he'd been asked that question. Some of the bigger boys in his House at school had asked him the same thing. He'd hesitated. He couldn't think of the best thing to say to them. They'd teased him about it for days. He'd thought about it later, and had come up with something that he thought sounded really quite clever and grown up. He'd even written it down, so he wouldn't forget. And yet here he was, hesitating again, feeling a bit stupid.

'Well…of course, I used to,' he hedged, remembering the words he'd once thought of, 'but I've grown up now. I don't need to believe in him anymore.'

'So, you think I'm a baby then?' she asked, grinning.

He turned to look at her.

'No, of course not! But well, I'm a chap of course, so I'd probably think differently to a girl,' he said, innocently.

'Oh,' she uttered, in her matter-of-fact voice, as though he'd said something very wise and profound.

'Why didn't I think of that…of course, I'm a girl, so I'd have *girl* sort of thoughts…boys are much more grown up, don't you think?'

'Well,' he shrugged, 'I wouldn't say that, as such.'

She raised her eyebrows.

'It's just, well, girls and boys think about different things.'

She was determined not to let him off the hook just yet.

'Uhumm…' she mumbled under her breath. 'So anyway, do you believe in Father Christmas, honestly?'

He had finally finished drying the dishes. He put the last fork on the counter, and threw the cloth on the draining board as he edged a little closer to where she was sat.

'Ahh…' she said, raising her eyebrows even further. 'Don't just leave it there. Put the cloth on the oven rail, so it'll dry off a bit.'

'Oh, OK, sorry,' he replied, yanking the cloth through the rail on the range.

'Well spread it out a bit,' she said impatiently, 'it'll never dry like that!'

He made a show of spreading the cloth along the rail and smoothing it out. He looked at her with questioning eyebrows.

'Better.' She grinned. 'So, come on, answer the question!'

He shrugged. She obviously wasn't going to let the topic of Father Christmas go.

'You'd like to, right?' she pressed. 'You want to?'

'I, s'pose,' he conceded, in a defeated tone.

She eased herself off the worktop and slid across the room. She leant in close to his ear, and whispered, 'I can prove he exists y'know...'

Matthew shivered at her close proximity.

'What?' he whispered, though he wasn't sure why he asked. 'How can you prove he is real?'

She remained close to the shell of his ear, her face almost touching his. He could smell her. Her scent filled his nose, she smelled of honey and sweetness. It was inviting.

She smelled a bit like his mum. From what he could remember, when she used her special soap ahead of going out for the evening with his dad. As hard as he tried, he couldn't remember the name of it. But the name didn't matter. All that mattered at that moment was that Bridie smelled...well, just lovely. Matthew tried desperately not to blush.

'If you're up for it, I'll show you.'

Mat hesitated. He didn't know what to do, she was right. He actually did want to believe. He wanted desperately to believe in something, in Father Christmas, and, more than anything, in her. He wasn't sure how to answer. Her keen, brown eyes danced under the warm glow of the kitchen bulbs. He felt just a little dizzy. Was she setting him up? Was she trying to make him look stupid?

'Wait until after Mum's tucked you in,' she whispered hoarsely. 'Get dressed quickly, something warm – but be quiet! Dad and the boys would sleep through an earthquake.' She chuckled. 'But Mum hears twigs breaking at twenty paces! Do not make a single sound! Seriously! I'll let you know when it's time.'

'Oh, OK…' he said. By now he was quite unsure about the whole thing. He could imagine her mother's wrath at them sneaking out.

16

He'd done as he'd been told.

He sat on the edge of his bed, fully dressed in his warmest clothes. He waited as patiently as he could muster, or as much as the butterflies would allow him to. His stomach was doing somersaults.

He wasn't sure if it was because she was about to prove Father Christmas was real or just because she wanted to spend more time with him. In some ways, he rather hoped it was because she wanted to be with him. Either way, he certainly knew he wanted to spend more time with her.

At last, just as the bedside clock in his room struck ten pm, just as he was almost about to give up hope and crawl back into his warm covers, he heard a faint rustle in the corridor. He looked up to see a small, pale face appear around the edge of the door.

She motioned for him to follow.

He got to his feet and crept down the staircase, following behind her. They were as quiet as they could manage, careful to avoid any creaky old floorboards that might groan beneath them on the stairs.

They stealthily made their way into the gardens and away up through the fields towards the bridge. There, they very quietly crouched behind the hedge. The stream gurgled nearby. She'd said it was really important that they couldn't be seen, or it would spoil everything.

He crouched as low as he could, trying to make himself invisible.

After a while, his legs started to ache from being scrunched uncomfortably beneath him, and he tried not to shiver from the cold.

She caught hold of his arm.

'Listen!' she hissed, urgently. 'Can you hear that?'

Mat strained his ears, but all he could make out were the faint sounds of the stream, and a breeze that blew in his face as it swirled and rustled the leaves in the hedge behind them.

'I can't hear anything,' he told her.

'Then shut up and listen harder!' she hissed into his ear. 'And keep very still!'

Mat did as he was told. He remained as still as a statue.

Listening intently, he became aware of another rustling sound in the distance. Maybe it was the same breeze that froze him, or the sound of a bird beating its wings through a garden.

They remained crouching, their limbs aching with the effort of keeping still. Mat felt his throat tighten with anticipation. As the sound rapidly approached, the air around them started to lighten, then it began to hum with a faint glow.

That's when he felt it, he felt something pass nearby. It hovered in the air above them. Mat felt as though his hair was being ruffled by unseen fingers. He glanced upwards toward the pitch-black sky, there was a scattering of twinkling stars, but he couldn't see anything. He certainly sensed something, though. Something or someone was definitely there...

The glow pulsated around them; it was bright enough to make the frost glisten on individual blades of grass. He couldn't work out what colour the glow was. There was a distinctly golden aura, or was it silver?

The colours changed and blended into a rainbow of colours, he could see blue, emerald green and flecks of crimson red. It was confusing, although, beautiful.

Behind them, the sound of rustling seemed to stop and the air prickled and shifted. Mat's senses heightened uncomfortably. If he could have made himself smaller, even more invisible, he would have.

He really didn't understand quite what was going on around him, but right at that moment he fervently wished he'd stayed in bed!

He could feel his right leg twitching, as if preparing himself to run or even fly. He looked at the night sky, and towards the stars, far up and far away. He imagined himself up there.

But he didn't want that, not really. He wanted to be here, to be here with Bridie, by her side. He wanted this. All of it.

Behind the hedge, a cloved foot stomped and he could make out an animal snorting.

It was right behind them!

Mat flinched, his hands clamping harder together in his lap. He gritted his teeth together in the hope that they'd stop chattering as hard. He could feel a sense of increasing dread rising from deep within him.

Whatever the animal was, it would surely sink its teeth into his neck. Its mouth would clamp down and drag him into that lonely hedge. He could almost feel its hot breath. He could almost smell the stink of it. It would be horrible. It would hurt. It would be a painful death…He wanted to tell Bridie to run and hide, or run back into the house.

A hand landed gently on Mat's shoulder from behind. It wasn't Bridie's. No, this hand was much bigger than hers. He turned around, half expecting Bridie's father! He had surely caught them sneaking out into the middle of the cold night. He braced himself for a telling-off, for being out so late. He was surely done for.

He sensed her father's voice, but the voice that spoke, it wasn't her father's. It was a deep and a calming command, and it resonated through him.

'Matthew.' The hand pulled him up. 'Bridie,' his voice said, in a low rumble, 'you too.'

Bridie silently got to her feet.

They stood on the track, standing before a figure who was easily the biggest man Mat had ever encountered. He was much bigger than Bridie's father, this man was huge. He was taller than Mr Parkes, taller than anyone he'd ever seen.

He wore a long cloak of what might have been a russet colour, maybe metallic brown. Nothing like the bright red outfit that Mat would have expected, like he had seen in pictures in the media depicting Father Christmas.

The hood, arms and hem of the cloak had a thick trim of white fur. The man had a white snowy beard, which matched his long hair.

The sleigh he stood beside looked ancient. The wood was worn, but every inch was covered with deeply carved designs. He could see trees, deer, faces, holly leaves, mistletoe, so many different intricate designs, he couldn't register it all.

Matthew looked into the giant's eyes; his kind eyes mesmerised him the most. They were unusually bright, and sparkled with cheer and laughter.

The glow surrounding them was the same aura emitting from the giant.

The colours sparkled and shimmered, lighting up the very air around them. As he breathed in the glowing lights, Mat could almost smell it too, almost taste it. It was a faint taste, he struggled to name it. Mint chocolate? Pine on a winter's day? Ginger and cinnamon perhaps? He didn't know, but he liked it. It made him feel happy, a sense of elation. That dreaded feeling he'd had before left his body entirely

'You know who I am,' the man said, smiling warmly. It was the type of smile that made his eyes crinkle in the corners.

The voice echoed through his mind, filling his ears with warmth. It wasn't a question; it was a statement.

To his surprise, Mat found himself able to nod.

He glanced over at Bridie, who appeared to be lost for words. Her eyes shone, a smile lit up her moon white face, staring at the vision in front of her.

The figure looked down upon them both, and smiled. His sapphire-blue eyes gleamed.

'I have brought a message from your parents, Matthew, and a gift.'

Mat's throat was too tight. He couldn't speak.

'They are sorry that they can't be with you this Christmas,' the huge man told him. 'But they want you to know that they are watching over you. Their thoughts, their hopes and their dreams are all around you. Though you can't see or feel them, their arms are encircling you, holding you tight.'

Mat finally found his voice to speak. His words came out strangled. Each one hurting his throat.

'I wanted to see them. I wanted to be with them,' he said sadly.

The giant figure placed a hand on Mat's shoulder.

'That can't happen, no matter how much you want to see them again,' he said gently. 'They have already passed over the bridge. They are gone from this world. They stand now in the sunshine and starlight, beside another stream, a beautiful stream, but it is one which they cannot cross again. You will see them when the time is right, but it is not now. Be patient, there is so much for you yet to accomplish on this side of the stream.'

Mat felt tears welling in his eyes, they began to sting. He couldn't speak. He felt Bridie take his hand and squeeze it gently.

The giant of a man took a deep booming breath. The air around him shone even brighter.

'Bridie will look after you. Let her guide you, she knows the way.'

Bridie's face beamed with pride as her smile grew wider.

He encircled them in his arms, drawing them both closer to him, hugging them gently.

He is real, thought Mat, *he feels real, not a vision.*

'Stay close to each other, always,' he said before releasing them. 'Now I have work to do!'

He threw his head back and laughed, an enormous, joyful, comforting laugh.

The sound stirred the glow again, brightening the colour and his laughter filled their ears. The trees around them trembled, and the frost on the branches glinted like stars.

Mat was sure he felt the ground beneath his feet rumble faintly.

'Oh!' the figure said, raising his snowy eyebrows. 'Goodness! I almost forgot your gift! That would never do, would it?'

He turned to reach into his bag, chuckling merrily to himself as he did.

'Here it is,' he said, smiling warmly. 'The gift from your parents.'

'What is it?' asked Mat, as he received a small, shining globe from the jolly giant's outstretched hand.

'This is your parents' love. It will stay with you wherever you go. It will be with you always, no matter what. May it keep you safe and warm and happy all your life.'

Mat held the globe gently, staring in wonder, as it began to melt into his hand. The glow of it travelled up his arm.

He watched as his skin began to shimmer with its light. Slowly, gradually, he felt it move through him, and although the light eventually faded into him, as it worked its way deeper, he could feel the magic from his ears to his toes. It warmed his whole body, his whole being, with its enchanting joy. He couldn't help but smile.

As he climbed into the sleigh and seized the reins, the giant figure looked down at them one last time.

'Happy Christmas, Matthew! Happy Christmas, Bridie!' he bellowed. 'Goodnight!'

Then he was gone, leaving a trail of shimmering light and two open-mouthed children behind him.

They stood together in the gathering darkness, holding hands, straining to see the last remnants of the cheerful glow as it disappeared into the distance.

Eventually, when the sleigh disappeared into the night sky, and all there was to see was moonlight and shadows, Bridie squeezed his hand and whispered, shakily, 'Time to go home.'

They walked quietly, side by side, not daring to speak of what they'd seen, in case they might wake up and find it was all just a dream. Eventually, Mat just had to ask.

'How did you know he'd be there?'

'I didn't, really.' Bridie shrugged.

'So, you were playing tricks on me? I did wonder…'

'To start with I was,' Bridie said truthfully. 'Sorry, I didn't mean any harm. Not really, but my grandma had told me stories about her mum seeing him, and the glow. I didn't really believe her. I was as surprised as you were when he appeared!'

As they followed the track through the last field before the house, Bridie stopped and giggled excitedly.

'What?' Mat asked, stopping beside her. 'What's so funny?'

She continued to giggle, punching his arm playfully,

'See?' she whispered loudly. 'I told you Bridie's Bridge was a special place…'

He turned towards her and gripped her hands. He had to take a couple of breaths before he could speak.

'And you were right,' he whispered. 'It really is!'

'Your hands are hot,' she told him quietly. 'Are you alright?'

'I don't know,' he said. 'I'm not sure I'll ever be *alright* again...but to feel my mum and dad's love flowing into me like that was...was...just amazing! I've never felt anything like it before! I can still feel it inside me now!'

'Maybe that's why your hands are so hot!' she said.

'I'm glad you can feel it too,' he told her. 'If there's one person in the whole world I'd want to share this feeling with, it's you!'

She pulled him into a hug.

'Thank you,' she whispered. Then she looked up into his face and smiled broadly.

He would have liked to stay like that forever, with her pressed against him in his arms.

'But now,' she sighed, as she broke away, 'all we've got to do, is to get back in the house without anybody knowing!'

17

Three sharp raps at the door. Three sharp, desperate raps. Mat counted them.

Eight o'clock in the morning. It could only be her! Only Bridie would be hammering on his door at this time on Christmas Morning.

Her mother had told them before they went to bed, that they weren't allowed to go downstairs before eight o'clock. Not a moment before. Bridie had probably been awake for ages, watching the clock diligently.

'Are you up?' she whispered urgently through the door, but she was far too excited to wait for a reply. 'Decent or not, I'm coming in!'

As the door opened, she could see him standing by the window.

'Mat!' she hissed at him urgently. 'What are you doing! Come ON!'

Mat's mind had been too full of the night's events to sleep.

He'd laid on his bed for a while, but was too restless to stay there, so he'd opened the curtains to look out into the early morning gloom. It was still too dark to see properly, but he could hear leaves being blown around in the yard below. He imagined them being picked off the tree in the front garden, and carried by the breeze, swirling around the house, dropping and being pushed on again by the winter wind, until they finally got stuck in some sheltered corner.

'What are you staring at?' she demanded.

She was wearing a dress. Mat had never seen her in anything but jeans.

She looked different, and he liked it.

Her dress was red, with arms that reached between her elbows and her wrists. The skirt ended just below her knees. And he noticed a delicate silver bracelet on her wrist. He thought she looked just stunning. 'You look…you have knees!' he said.

'Matthew Crawford!' she retorted, rolling her eyes. 'Of course I've got knees! Everybody's got knees!'

She tried her best to look cross, but Matthew noticed she blushed instead. Matthew later learned that same afternoon that Bridie's mother had asked her sister-in-law Brenda to make it for Bridie especially to wear today. It was fashioned from dark red velvet with a cowl neck.

Mat thought it fitted her perfectly, and Bridie looked and clearly felt so grown up. It was her special Christmas dress, she reliably informed him. She loved it.

'Come *on*!' she protested louder, tugging at the hem of her skirt. 'You KNOW we can't go in the front room until everybody's downstairs! Hurry up! Please?'

As she rushed from the room, a sudden thought occurred to him. Like the leaves outside, he had been caught up by forces stronger than he ever was.

Forces which had picked him up, swirled him around, dropped him and drawn him on again. Like all the other lost souls, all the way here, all the way to Bridie's Bridge.

He listened, and smiled, as she made her way noisily through the corridor, banging excitedly on doors.

She was waking the house up, calling them all out, drawing the family with her, a force as insistent and as irresistible as the ley line in the lane outside.

Mat glanced back over his shoulder, through the window at the brightening sky. He knew that eventually whatever had pulled him here would weaken, and that the wind would come and blow him all the way back to school. He didn't want to go back, but he knew he'd have to one day. The breeze would collect him, and the forces which seemed heightened here at the farm would carry him away like a leaf.

The thought saddened him, but he was certain he would come back.

He would always find a way to get back. The forces would always pull him back. He wouldn't resist it. He would never wish to resist it

Matthew really hadn't been looking forward to today. It would be his first Christmas day ever without his parents, and he seriously hated the prospect.

He'd always loved Christmas. For him it had always been a magical time.

His mum always made sure of that. They'd put the tree up a couple of weeks before Christmas, and as he got older and big enough, he'd help to decorate it. He'd always loved the lights especially.

He recalled that there was one set of lights that looked like fruit. He'd particularly liked one light that looked like a grape. It was all sorts of shades of purple and green, and he'd been so upset when his dad had tested the lights and his favourite set just wouldn't work, no matter how hard he'd tried.

Matthew had cried all that evening. He hated when things got broken and wouldn't work. He still did. It didn't matter what it was, cups, plates, glasses…but that broken set of lights had really, really upset him.

He recalled that, by the time he'd got downstairs the morning after, the grape light had magically started to work again. None of the other fruit lights, just that one. Matthew remembered being completely amazed that it was there. He hadn't been able to take his eyes off it. He'd later learned that his dad had patiently hacksawed the glass cover away from the original light, and had somehow managed to cellotape it to a plain white bulb.

It was still his favourite grape light, though. It was still there, and he loved it.

That particular Christmas was the one engrained in his memory the most. He had actually spoken to Father Christmas up the chimney. It had been truly thrilling to hear his slightly muffled voice from the rooftop, and to hear his replies to his excited questions. The only frustrating thing was, that his dad had always been in the bathroom when Father Christmas called! Despite Matthew's very vocal encouragement, shouting to him up the stairs, he'd always arrived in the front room just after Father Christmas had had to leave!

This year, he realised, things were going to be different.

Bridie's dad had brought their Christmas tree in just the evening before, after they'd eaten dinner. They'd spent a couple of hours decorating it, and then it was lit for the first time. Matthew had looked, of course, but there had been no purple grape light. He hadn't really expected it to be there, but he'd looked all the same. It had still been exciting, and the overall effect, he had to admit, was really beautiful.

Of course, Father Christmas hadn't called down the chimney to them. He hadn't really expected that he would. But in the end, it hadn't mattered. He'd met him later, up at the bridge. Matthew almost had to pinch himself to realise that he had. With Bridie's help he had really spoken to him! Face to face! And he'd held his hand and everything!

It was a shame that he hadn't been able to stroke the reindeers, but Father Christmas had said that they were a bit skittish and might kick, so best not touch them.

So, it was going to be a different Christmas, Mat thought. But it would still be lovely.

Matthew realised that he wouldn't have any presents waiting for him this year, but he'd already received so much from Bridie's family, that he seriously didn't mind.

They'd already given him warmth and kindness, consolation and hugs…but most of all, he'd found Bridie.

He remembered holding her hand, almost all the way back from the bridge the night before, and the thought of it sent a tingle down his spine.

Her friendship had become the most important thing in his life. She lit up his world like a Christmas tree, and he never, ever, wanted that to stop.

Spring Equinox

18

Mat was relieved by the time he finally turned his car into the lane that would lead him to Home Farm.

He always made the same journey, at this time of the year, driving the same road back to the farm, during the festivities, looking forward to being greeted by the familiar face and those beautiful brown eyes that he always so looked forward to seeing.

He was tired. It had been a long, cold drive and he was glad it was almost over.

He was home and it was nearly Christmas. It was nearly his tenth Christmas with Bridie.

He was almost at the end of his course at university. Just one more term of lectures and coursework, then some final exams and then that would be that.

In some ways, he was glad to be almost done with it all. He would finally be able to get a job, and be able get on with the rest of his life, without the pressure of endless university deadlines.

He'd made some good friends at university, and he knew that he had learned a lot. He felt that he'd grown as a person. Mr Pearce had been right to encourage him to apply to Lancaster. The lecturers in the English Department were excellent, and their research interests were fascinating and inspiring. He really had enjoyed his time there. Mat exhaled and let out a sigh of relief. Now it was nearly all over. All those years of study and application, nearly done and dusted.

The first term back at Burrell's, after his parents had died, had been traumatic. He really, really hadn't wanted to go back there after the Christmas holidays. Mr Pearce and Mrs Ambrose had talked some sense into him though, and so, reluctantly he had gone.

Things had settled down a bit over the next few months, and though he had still struggled with the unwritten laws that made the place work, with Mr Pearce's encouragement, he had eventually managed to make some progress with his schoolwork.

Mr Pearce had been his first Form Master. He'd been kind to Mat following the death of his parents, and had patiently acted as his unofficial mentor and guide throughout his years at Burrell's and beyond. If Mat had a problem Mr Pearce would help him sort it out. Most of the time that meant coaching and talking, helping him to find his own solutions.

Sometimes, if it was something that a boy of his age simply couldn't manage, he would actively intervene to sort things out. He'd talked him through decisions about staying on, to complete his A-levels. He'd helped him sieve through the various options available to him when it came to choosing the right course, the right university, to get a good degree.

He felt that Mr Pearce had certainly been right to recommend Lancaster, and Mat had no regrets about his decision to attend there.

He hadn't realised until much later, though, just how active Mr Pearce was, in terms of looking after his interests during the months following his parents' deaths.

His parents' financial affairs had been complicated and it had taken solicitors a good while to sort out.

Mr Parkes, the headmaster, had been rather concerned that Mat's school fees were not being paid on the normal termly basis. Mr Pearce had felt it vital that Mat's life should be as settled as possible, especially while his grief was still so raw.

He had offered to put Mr Parkes's mind at rest by paying the fees out of his own pocket. Eventually, Mr Parkes reluctantly agreed that the school would waiver Mat's fees, until his own funds could be drawn upon. To ensure that the process would be handled efficiently and as quickly as possible, Mr Pearce had acted on Mat's behalf in negotiations with banks and solicitors.

He had eventually arranged that his inheritance should be held in a Trust Fund until Mat was old enough to take responsibility for it himself. In the meantime, the Trust would pay his school fees, living costs, and a small allowance for pocket money and travel expenses.

His allowance increased when he went to university. There was enough, just enough, to buy a cheap car and still have a little left over to supplement his scholarship grant. It wasn't much but it helped to make life a bit more comfortable.

Mat didn't know much about Mr Pearce's involvement. At the time, he'd been too young to know the details and was simply too young to ask. In his twelve-year-old mind, he'd simply assumed that things, well, just sort of happened.

It was only until a chance conversation took place last summer, between himself and Bridie's father, did it dawn on Mat how important Mr Pearce's influence had been to his life, and the realisation occurred to him that actually he hadn't really known all that much about Mr Pearce, throughout the years at all.

The strange forces that had brought him here in the first place had always pulled him back, throughout all of the intervening years, to Home Farm, to the family and to Bridie. Matthew knew in his heart it always would.

***

When they'd talked about him having to go back to school after their first Christmas, Bridie had simply shrugged.

'I can't see the point,' she'd said. 'Why go all the way back there? You could go to my school, then you can come home every night.'

Bridie didn't have a high regard for school. Unlike Mat, who was struggling to fit in at a school he didn't like, and where the boys didn't seem to like him much either.

Bridie just didn't seem to care about schools generally. She went, but only because she had to. She learned, but only because she'd be bored if she didn't have something to do while she was there. She didn't see the point of it all, and if it hadn't been for her parents' insistence, she would much rather have stayed at home and looked after the chickens.

She reckoned, as she quite happily told anybody who'd listen, that there were more important things in her life than school. To her, it was just a waste of time and she couldn't wait until the day arrived where she would no longer have to go.

Once the decision was made about Matthew's schooling she accepted it, on the condition that Mat came home every holiday. As long as he did, she decided she would be happy.

So, he had. He'd come back for every holiday, and by now he felt, as they did, that he was just part of the family. He wrote to them, through Bridie, every week.

He told her about his lessons, about the marks he got for his homework, and how much he hated rugby. He wrote about cricket and how the cricket ball had nearly taken his nose off because he hadn't seen it coming his way. He wasn't allowed to wear his glasses while playing sports of any kind. He posted his letters on a Friday, so that they would receive them Saturday.

She would leave his letters on the kitchen table, and her mother would read them out loud on Sunday mornings, over breakfast. Bridie liked that. It was like he was there, with them, in the room, telling them all about his week.

Sometimes, she would write back, but not very often. Usually, she only wrote when there was something important to tell him, like when her brother Bill finished his apprenticeship at the blacksmiths, or when she had the flu. She'd written two pages that time. She didn't like writing letters much, she felt she was better at talking.

She didn't think Mat minded that much. They would catch up properly next time they saw each other. She would have lots to tell him. She was his best friend, his Bridie, he once told her. And he would always listen to her.

Whenever they could, the family planned events so that he could be there with them. It just wouldn't have seemed right if he wasn't there, involved and a part of everything. He'd asked if they would be able to come and see him graduate next summer. There was no hesitation.

'Of course we'll be there!' Mr Ambrose had said. 'We'll have to get somebody to see to the animals, but of course we'll be there! We'll make a proper do of it – we'll stay in a hotel!'

They had to have a family conference about it. There was plenty of time – nearly a year – but there was a lot to plan. New clothes were a high priority for her and her mother. That alone, had taken up most of the evening.

19

During dinner the following evening, Mr Ambrose had asked Mat what his plans were after graduation. They'd talked about it many times over the years, but Mat had never really made his mind up what sort of a job he'd really like to do.

'You're going to have to decide soon though, aren't you?' Mr Ambrose had insisted. 'No point drifting into something you might hate.'

'Actually,' started Mat, 'I've been thinking seriously about becoming a teacher, that is something I'd like to do.'

Bridie had nearly choked on her potato. She was laughing so much, she had to spit it out, before she choked any further.

'Bridie!' her mother had hissed. 'Manners!'

'Mat Crawford!' Bridie had said, when she'd recovered enough to speak. 'A teacher! Really? How on earth do you think you'd ever be a teacher? You have enough trouble stringing two sensible words together when it's important. Honestly! I would have been less surprised if you'd said you wanted to be a farmer – and you'd be rubbish at that too!'

'I do my best!' Mat had retorted, trying his best to not look wounded. He was used to being teased about not being as fast as the others at hay-making time, and his overall nervousness being around the animals. Chickens were OK. He could deal with them, it was the cows he wasn't so keen on. They had horns.

'I think she might have a point though, dear,' Mrs Ambrose had said, supressing a chuckle. 'You do struggle a bit sometimes, trying to find the right words, don't you.'

'But I think it would be good,' Mat had responded, struggling to make his point, 'you know, teaching people about what I love, like reading and writing.'

'No, no,' Mr Ambrose had interjected. 'I think if that's what he wants, he should try it. The boy has got ambition. He certainly has the knowledge. If he really wants to do it, he will. And I'm sure he'll do his best.'

'Thank you, Mr Ambrose!' Mat had said, almost triumphantly, trying to ignore the laughter all around him.

'That's just what Mr Pearce said too.'

'Well,' Mr Ambrose had continued. 'If Philip Pearce said that, it must be true. He's not often wrong about important stuff.'

'Well, he did alright, didn't he?' Mrs Ambrose added.

'Philip used to have trouble himself, talking about important things too. But he came good in the end though.'

'That's what I mean,' Mr Ambrose had continued. 'If Philip could do it, so can Mat.'

'I can't imagine Mr Pearce ever having trouble talking,' Mat had said. 'He can talk the hind legs off a donkey when he wants to, and he always makes sense.'

'Well, I can assure you,' Mrs Ambrose had replied, 'he certainly wasn't always like that. He didn't do that good a job when it came to asking me to marry him!'

Bridie let out a gasp. 'What?' she'd said, shocked. 'Mr Pearce? You mean *our* Mr Pearce?'

'Yes,' her mother had confirmed. 'Our Mr Pearce, and you needn't look that surprised either, young lady. I'll have you know I was quite a looker back in the day. I had a string of boys hanging from my every word, I did!'

'Mr Pearce?' Bridie had insisted, clearly aghast. 'Was this before Dad asked you? How did he make a mess of it, then?'

'Your dad hadn't asked me then,' her mother had continued, smoothing down her apron and settling into the story. 'Though, I thought he might. I thought Philip might, too. I liked them both well enough. Handsome boys, they were.'

Bridie's eyes widened. 'What happened, then?'

'Well, I'd been going out with Philip for a while, off and on, but then he went to university. Big deal that was, back then. Not many people went to university. Anyway, while he was away, your dad came calling. So, I thought I'd go out with him too, you know, just to see if I liked him as much as I liked Philip.'

'Go on, then!'

'Trouble was, I did. I liked him every bit as much as Philip,' she said, smiling across the table at her husband. 'So, then Philip came back on holiday, and came calling again. Anyway, your grandma said it wasn't right to keep stringing them both along, so I told Phil about your dad.'

She'd stopped to pour some more tea. Bridie had managed to get to the pot before she did, and topped up her mother's cup.

She knew from previous occasions, that if her mother poured the tea, she'd go on to pour everyone else a cup. Then the pot would be empty, so she'd go and make some more. While she was doing that, she'd find something else that needed doing, and then she'd get distracted, and would never get round to finishing the story. It happened nearly every time her mother started to tell them something interesting. It was very irritating.

'You can't stop now, Mum! Come on, spill the beans!' Hilda let out a small sigh of defeat and continued.

'So, the next thing I know, Phil is coming round, banging on our door. I agreed to talk to him. We went out for a walk, up towards the bridge. Philip is muttering away to himself about things not being right, about it not being fair. In the end, I got fed up with it, so I stopped and told him if he had something to say, to just spit it out.'

'And did he?' Bridie interjected.

'Well, no, not really. That was the problem. He was always the same, even from way back. It was never quite the right time for Philip. He could never quite find the right words. He would always just end up red in the face and looking confused. That's the trouble with people like him…you know…brainy people. They seem to live inside their heads too much, and sometimes I think they sort of get stuck there.'

'And?'

'So, I told him to go home and come back when he'd made his mind up about what he wanted to say. Then I might listen, but I wasn't listening to any more of his muttering and stuttering. So off he went. Didn't see him for a week. In the meantime, your dad had come round and asked me straight out, no fuss, no bother, words all in the right order and everything. So, I said yes! Why wouldn't I? He was lovely and handsome, and he knew just what I wanted to hear. I do like a straightforward man!'

Bridie had looked, wide-eyed, from her mother to her father and back again.

'Aww!' she'd said.

'Crikey!' Mat had joined, smiling. 'So if Mr Pearce had managed to get his words out, he might be Bridie's dad? Can't imagine it…'

'All water under the bridge now, though,' Mr Ambrose added, laughing. 'Mind you,' he'd said, looking straight at Bridie, 'I reckon Philip had a lucky escape. Look what I got lumbered with!'

Bridie's punch had landed square on his shoulder. He was still laughing after she'd left the room rubbing her hand.

'Seriously, though, Mat,' Mr Ambrose had continued, 'Phil's a nice chap. He really is, and he's one of my best friends. I think it would be best not to say anything about all of this when you see him, eh? He'd be really hurt if he thought we'd been making fun of him.'

Mat had agreed. He was still struggling with the thought that Mr Pearce might have been Bridie's dad. If he'd got his act together, things would have been different. If Bridie's mum had actually wanted him. Even so…*Mr Pearce? Surely not…*

He wasn't sure quite how such a thing would ever come up in conversation with Mr Pearce, but he certainly wasn't going to mention it anyway.

'Yeah…my best friend,' Mr Ambrose had continued. 'And my Best Man, as it turned out.'

Mrs Ambrose had looked at her husband, and raised her eyebrows.

'He didn't do such a great job of his speech, though, did he?'

'Well, he wasn't that used to talking in public back then. Things have changed.'

'I do know I made the right decision, though,' Mrs Ambrose had said. In return, her husband had given her a look that Mat could only describe as pure devotion.

'Anyway, he's done alright for himself, has Philip,' Mr Ambrose declared warmly, 'and he's done a fine job of looking after your interests too.'

After the conversation, Mat was left stunned. Mr Pearce had done all that for him? *For him.* He hadn't known a thing about it until now. Why would he have bothered? He was only one of his pupils, after all. He was going to have to say 'thank you,' in a big way. Mr Pearce would still be at home for a few days. He'd have to go over there tomorrow, or at least before he went back to university. He couldn't not say something now.

'You knew about all this?' he'd asked Mr Ambrose.

'Yes, I did,' Mr Ambrose had confirmed, seriously. 'Philip could see that we were fond of you, so he reckoned we'd want the best for you, like he did. As things progressed, he could see the way things were going.

There were delays, then more delays, then there would be decisions to be made. You had nobody to make those decisions for you. He was the only one who could really, other than the solicitors or your Headmaster. He wanted better than that for you. I suppose it meant more to him, after having just lost his dad. He knew what you were going through, what you were facing. So…he took the weight on his own shoulders. He muscled in, gently of course, that's what he's like…even though his help wasn't exactly welcomed by the banks and solicitors. He felt he had a responsibility for you, as your Form Master. There wasn't anybody else. I think he was right.'

'I never knew anything about this…'

'Why should you? You were only what, twelve? What sort of decisions would you have made, even if you'd been allowed to make them? No. Phil reckoned you needed somebody in your corner, fighting for your best interests. He came and talked to us a few times when he was home for weekends. There wasn't anybody else really. He couldn't ask his father of course, so we were the next best thing. We talked, we discussed, we figured things out. In the end, we decided between the three of us what he should try to do.'

'What was that?'

'Well, we reckoned if it was left to the solicitors, they'd take the easiest option. They'd just hand over your assets to the school, expecting that the headmaster would look after your best interests.'

'Mr Parkes?'

'Mmm. Well, we reckoned that if the school was given control, Mr Parkes would probably have had authority over things like this. So yes, we guessed he would have taken control of your money. We were sure that he would have done his best, but Phil wasn't convinced that Mr Parkes would have had the time to do it, as well as Phil.

'So, we decided to try to take it on ourselves. We took legal advice on what to do and how to do it. We decided to have a go. We had to go to court and everything. In the end, we won. We were allowed to look after your interests. Phil managed most of it, but he always talked to us about any big decisions.'

Mat had looked between Bridie's parents. As far as he was concerned, they were like his parents too, or as good as. He didn't know what to say.

'Listen,' Bridie's mum had initiated softly, reaching over to take his hand. 'Mat, listen to me. There's a lot of love here for you. Us, the boys, Mr Pearce and especially Bridie. We all love you and we want the best for you, whatever it takes. Always.' Mat smiled at her words.

Mr Ambrose hadn't finished talking yet.

'Phil said the court had granted us an order of,' he paused, trying to recall the words, 'Ah that was it, yes – *In Loco Parentis*. It was French, or something. I don't know. Anyway, he said it meant *in place of a parent*. We took that seriously.'

Mat had noticed that Bridie's dad had his serious face on. He knew that face very well. It was the one he'd always worn, when one of his kids had needed a telling off. Mat had been the focus of that look himself a few times over the years, and he knew that Mr Ambrose had something profound to say.

'He took it very seriously, did Philip. Very seriously. I think he must have reckoned that it was as close as he was ever going to get to being a proper dad, and he wasn't going to make a mess of it.'

'Wow…' Mat had whispered, stunned. 'I never knew…I never realised…'

'I tell you what, though,' Mr Ambrose had said, looking uncharacteristically emotional, 'I know Phil would agree – for all the worry, for all the responsibility, it has been worth the effort. You've been worth the effort. We're so proud of you, son. All of us are. Very proud.'

***

Mat switched off the engine, and breathed a sigh of relief, smiling to himself about the memory of his own reaction after he'd heard about what the Ambroses, and Mr Pearce had done for him. He reflected that Bridie had been right about the fact that he always stumbled to find the right words to express his feelings about anything important. And that in the end, he'd just reached across the table to seize Bridie's mum and dad's hands, and had whispered, 'Thank you…'

He eased his back, cramped from the long drive, and opened the car door to let a few more of the engine fumes out.

As he climbed out of the car, Bridie slammed into him like a tidal wave. She wrapped her arms around him and squeezed as hard as she could.

'You're home! I'm so glad you're home!'

So was Mat. This was home and he was very glad indeed.

20

The next morning, Mat decided that he'd better have a look at the engine, to see if he could find where the oil was leaking from. He realised, as soon as he raised the bonnet, that it was a bigger problem than he'd anticipated. He wouldn't be able to fix it himself.

There was oil all over the engine, and when he checked the levels, it was easy to see that there was very little left in the engine. He'd have to ask Bill, Bridie's brother, to have a look at it for him. Although it wasn't his job, Bill was pretty good at fixing cars. He just seemed to have a natural talent for fixing things.

Mat closed the bonnet, and frowned sadly at the car. It was his first car, an old Cortina, and though it was nearly as old as he was, he was really quite fond of it. Although, there was almost as much rust as paintwork, and though it had always smelled of hot oil as soon as the engine got warm enough, he was still proud of it.

So far, it had always got him to where he wanted to go, but even Mat realised that it was never going to get him back to university in this state.

He sighed. If Bill couldn't fix it, he'd just have to take the train back after the holidays.

He heard a crunching on the gravel of the yard. Bridie stood by his side, hugging her cardigan around her, against the chill.

'Dead?' she asked.

'Probably,' replied Mat. 'I think it might be, shame, though. I really liked that car.'

'No point mooning over that old rust-bucket!' Bridie laughed. 'Why don't you get something half decent?'

'I might have to now,' he replied. 'I'll ask Bill if he can save it.'

'OK,' she said, 'but if Bill can't do anything, I'm sure John will do you a good deal on a car, if I ask him nicely.'

'John who?' Mat asked.

'My friend John. He sells cars from a place along the road from Aunty Brenda.'

Mat had met Bridie's aunt a few times. Bridie had helped her dad's sister in her children's clothes shop quite often when she was a teenager. Once she'd left school, she'd gone to work there more or less full time.

Aunty Brenda made really good clothes in a little room behind the shop, and she'd taught Bridie how to do it. Mat had been in that room once. It was terribly overcrowded he'd thought, with sewing machines of all types and sizes, and an almost overwhelming amount of fabric. Most of it was filed, like in a library, on shelves along two walls.

There was so much of it that he'd wondered how they could even remember what was there. There were rolls of fabric stacked up and leaning against walls, or folded up in great piles that seemed to fill every spare bit of space.

There was so much stuff crowded into the little room, that Mat had wondered how they ever managed to find the space to work.

Bridie was totally besotted with the whole thing. She loved it, and was always boasting about how wonderful the outfits they made were. Mat had never seen anything she'd made but if the look on her face was anything to go by, he could well believe it. He liked Aunty Brenda. She was always happy.

She always seemed to leave trails of cotton wherever she went but that didn't matter. She was a warm and comfortable person to be with. Bridie loved her and that was enough for Mat.

'I've asked John to come for New Year's Eve,' Bridie said. 'Then he can meet the whole family. You'll love him!'

Mat wasn't so sure he would. He wasn't at all sure he liked the idea of a 'John' at all. He'd meet him, of course. He didn't have much choice, but the thought of Bridie even thinking about other males....it just wasn't right.

'What's that look for?' Bridie asked sharply.

'What look?' Mat replied innocently

'I know that look, Matthew Crawford. You get that look every time I say something you don't like.'

'Sorry, it's just that…well…you know…'

'No, I do not *know*,' she rounded on him. 'Just because I mention that I've got a friend, what's wrong with that? Am I not allowed friends of my own now?'

'No, I mean yes,' he stumbled, 'I mean…'

'Just what do you mean then? Am I not allowed a boyfriend? Well, if that's your attitude,' she scowled. 'I'm not going to listen anymore.'

She stormed into the house, leaving Mat feeling foolish and confused.

They'd had arguments over the years, but only over silly things. He didn't know why, but this didn't feel like a *silly thing*.

He really was not comfortable with the thought of her having a boyfriend. It had never come up in conversation, not even the possibility of it. In his imagination, there was only ever supposed to be him and Bridie.

They were supposed to stay close to each other always. He'd always felt that they had, but now? How were they supposed to stay close to each other now? She wouldn't think of him anymore, if she had a boyfriend. She wouldn't want to stay close.

The thought of not being close to Bridie stung him painfully, deep inside.

What could he do? What could he say that would make it alright? He didn't know.

He couldn't think about it. He hurt too much to think.

For the first time, he realised what he'd always known. He loved Bridie. Not as a friend, not as a brother. He just loved her. It was as simple as that. And just as complicated.

And there was no way he would ever buy a car from anybody called 'John'. No way. Not ever. He'd rather walk.

21

Bill couldn't fix the car. He said it would cost more than the car's scrap value to repair. So, Mat had taken a train back to Lancaster.

Though it was nice not to have to breathe hot oil fumes all the way back, Mat would have preferred the drive. Sitting in a train carriage, staring out of the window, gave him too much time to think. He'd tried reading, but he couldn't concentrate.

He didn't feel like writing.

He tried to think about the essay he was supposed to have written over the holidays but that didn't last long either. He really wasn't in the mood for 'Green Knights,' 'Knights Tales', or anything else really.

Despite his best efforts to concentrate, all he could really think of was how distant Bridie had been over Christmas. It really hadn't felt 'normal' at all. All she'd talked about, it had seemed to Mat, was this John guy.

His mind drifted back to Christmas Eve, when at sunset, they'd taken their traditional walk up to the bridge. As always, they'd reminisced about the events of their first encounter there, ten years before, and something of the magic they'd felt then.

Every year it felt like the same magic. But it was different this time. Bridie had seemed preoccupied, a little too impatient to get back to the house. It didn't seem to matter much what Mat said to her that night. She was waiting for John to call.

Mat had dreaded New Year's Eve. The more he'd thought about it, the more agitated he'd become. John had arrived, sweeping into the yard in his silver, almost new VW Golf. He'd parked on the other side of the tree, several feet away from Mat's rusting, hulk of a Cortina, and Bridie, excited and flushed, had rushed out to meet him. Mat couldn't watch as she hugged him.

Bridie had proudly escorted John around the room, her arm entwined affectionately in his as she introduced him, one by one, to her family.

It was a crowded room, with most of her extended family present for the celebrations.

It took a little while before they arrived to where Mat was standing.

Mat had wondered how she would introduce him, and what he thought he might say in return. He'd promised himself that he wouldn't make a scene. He knew how important the New Year gathering was to the family, and he didn't want to spoil it for them.

'And this is Mat,' she'd said. There were no lengthy explanations of who he was, or why he was there. It was all very straightforward. He just 'was'. He was part of the furniture, just part of the natural order of things and the dynamics that made them a family.

In the end, after all his practising inside his head, he hadn't actually said anything at all. He'd just shaken hands and offered what he'd hoped would pass as a smile. He'd hoped it hadn't looked too much like the sneer he'd felt like delivering instead.

Mat had spent an uncomfortable evening trying to sound sensible whenever people involved him in conversation. Bridie's brothers and their girlfriends were always good fun to talk to, but tonight, he was struggling to keep a fake smile on his face, let alone join in with their banter.

He hoped nobody had noticed him continually glancing over to wherever Bridie was.

Beth did though. Beth was Bill's fiancée. Mat liked her a lot. She was fun, and she clearly adored Bill. They weren't planning to get married for another year or so, but Beth had become so close to them all that it felt like she was already part of the family.

'Mat,' she'd whispered to him conspiratorially, 'you're staring at her again.'

'What?'

'I said you're staring at Bridie again. She'll notice in a minute, if you're not careful!'

'Sorry,' he whispered, 'I didn't realise I was staring.'

'Well, you were. And not very subtly, either! What's going on with you two, anyway? You've hardly spoken to each other all Christmas. You're usually inseparable!'

'Nothing,' he'd said bleakly.

'Rubbish!' Beth had retorted. 'Look, if something's happened, get it sorted. Everybody's noticed there is an atmosphere between you. Everybody's worried.'

'Sorry,' he'd repeated, staring at the floor.

'One-word answers aren't going to cut it, Mat! If you won't tell me what's going on, I'll ask Bridie!'

'No!' Mat had hissed back at her. 'Don't do that. She'll be cross at me again. It's just me being stupid as usual.'

'It's the fact that he is her boyfriend, isn't it!' Beth had said, her eyes widening in realisation. 'It is, isn't it! You're jealous!'

'No, I am *not jealous*!' Mat had lied. 'I just don't like him. He's not right for her. End of story.'

'Yes, you are jealous! I know you, Mat. You are an open book. You love her, and you're definitely jealous.' Beth crossed her arms and smiled knowingly at him.

'Just leave it, eh?' Mat had pleaded. 'Can't do anything about it. No point upsetting her.'

'Well,' she'd huffed. 'If you do love her, you're going to have to do something about it, aren't you! And soon, too, otherwise you'll miss the boat. She's been seeing him for a while now, and watching how they are together, I'd say it's getting serious.'

Mat had nodded, resignedly, knowing she was right.

He'd tried to apologise to Bridie before he left. He'd tried to explain, to make things right but it had come out in a jumble of confusion.

They were out in the yard, waiting for Bridie's mum to bring the car around.

'I'm sorry Bridie,' he'd started. She glanced at him, her eyebrows arched.

'For what?' she'd said. 'For being a prat? For blanking John at New Years. For not talking to me?'

'For everything,' he'd said, his head down. 'All of it. He seemed like a nice enough bloke, I suppose.'

'How would you know? You hardly said two words to him. You hardly spoke to me all Christmas, for goodness' sake! And that look...don't think for one moment I didn't notice...'

'I'm sorry,' he'd said. 'Really sorry, for everything.'

'Doesn't matter,' she'd said flatly.

'Yes, it does. I don't know...'

Mat's voice trailed off.

'Don't know what? You always start saying something, and then don't finish it. God!' she cursed, frustratedly.

'No, I mean, I don't know. I really don't know. I know how I feel, but I don't know if I should say. I don't know how to fix it all.'

'What?' she'd asked, exasperated. 'Just spit it out! For goodness' sake, Mat! For once, will you just say what you mean.'

'Well, see, it's just that I always thought of us, well, like John Donne's compasses.'

Bridie's eyes knit in confusion. 'What? Who on earth is John Donne?'

'I told you about him ages ago. He's one of the metaphysical poets I was studying…'

'I don't remember,' she'd continued. 'How am I supposed to remember? The stuff you're learning is just so boring…'

'He wrote about lovers, being like the two legs of a compass, so they'd always be joined somehow, no matter how far apart they were…'

'I have no idea what you're talking about!' she'd said, rolling her eyes. 'Mat Crawford, you really are an idiot sometimes! Sod your meta-whatsits! For once in your life, will you *PLEASE* just say what you mean!'

Mat had tried, but he hadn't been able to find the words.

'Look,' she'd said in a sympathetic tone. 'I'm sorry I'm thick. I just wish you would say stuff straight. Never mind all the flap and fluster – just say it!'

'You're not thick!' he'd said, sombrely. 'Please! I'm doing my best here!'

She'd given him an exasperated sigh.

'Look, what I'm trying to say is…'

But it was too late. The car was here.

She'd let out a frustrated yelp, as she turned to run into the house. She'd glanced back at him as she yanked the door open.

'Do you know what, Matthew Crawford!' she'd shouted, her voice breaking. 'You can be a real idiot sometimes.'

'I love you, Bridie…' Mat called after her, but not loudly enough. The door had already slammed hard, behind her.

The car journey was a silent one as Bridie's mum had driven him to the station. He'd felt more lost, more alone, than he had ever been, since that first Christmas when he lost his parents. He tried not to think about when he had first met Bridie, and their encounter with Father Christmas…when Bridie had saved him…That was when he had stopped feeling lost, being by her side.

He didn't know what to do about it all, how to put things back to the way they once were. Him and Bridie, Bridie and him. It just didn't seem to make any sense, them being apart.

In Mat's mind, it had always been that way, it made sense to be together. It should always be that way. He just didn't know what to do, to make it so.

He felt so frustrated.

Why could he never just say the right words.

22

Spring Term was busy. He'd known it would be. A couple more essays, and his dissertation to hand in, then that would be that. He had some last-minute cramming over the Easter vacation, then straight into a few short weeks of exams. His final exams. It was his last chance to earn himself a good degree.

He knew what he had to do, but he couldn't concentrate. He did his best, but every time he sat down to write something really profound for his dissertation, Bridie sprang into his mind. She was always there, dangling off John's arm, mocking him, sneering at him. She filled his every waking thought. She glared at him over his cornflakes.

She smiled at him through the spring sunshine, as he ate his sandwiches at lunchtime. She laughed at him late at night while he tried to read through his notes.

Though he'd written home regularly, as he always had, he'd received no letters back from Bridie. She obviously didn't want to talk to him. He felt disappointed and distraught.

Stuck in the middle of the busiest term, just when everything hung in the balance, he felt trapped. With the work and the pressure he was under, he couldn't go home. Even though he was desperate to, he just couldn't. The next few weeks would decide his entire future. He had to stay at university. Why could she not write at least? Surely, she could see how much difference that would make? Even just a page, to say she was OK. That they were, OK?

Finally, a letter arrived in the post.

He didn't recognise the writing on the envelope, and was dreading what the letter contained, and who the writer may be. Cautiously, he opened the letter.

It was addressed from Beth. He was surprised. She'd never written to him before.

She started by telling him all the family news, how the farm was doing, and gave an update on Bill, now that he'd completed his apprenticeship. He'd done well and the blacksmith he'd been training with had decided to keep him on. Beth was relieved, as it meant a substantial rise in Bill's earnings. Enough, she hoped, to make it possible for them to get married sooner rather than later.

She ended with some news of Bridie. It wasn't the sort of news he wanted to hear. Beth was great friends with Bridie. Mat knew they obviously talked and shared things. After their conversation at New Year, Beth wrote she'd felt it best to let him know that John had asked Bridie to marry him. She said that Bridie had told him that she'd have to think about it, but knowing Bridie, Beth didn't think she would keep him dangling on a string for too long.

Mat was lost for words again.

He was more lost than he'd ever been. It wasn't fair – how was he supposed to cope with news like that? How was he supposed to concentrate now? This was the most important few weeks of his life. How well he performed in his exams now would make the difference. It would shape his whole future. It would shape their whole future. How could she do this to him.

***

It wasn't the dissertation he'd wanted to hand in. He was hoping to produce something masterful, succinct, insightful and well researched, but he'd run out of time. It wasn't the quality he'd wanted to achieve in his writing, but in the end, it was the best he could do.

He was walking slowly down the steps into Alexandra Square, intent on returning the last of his books to the library, when he heard a familiar voice call out his name.

His tutor, Professor Pattison, shouted at him from her office window.

'Matthew! I want to see you!' she hollered. 'Now please!'

Mat made his way sheepishly back into Bowland College, and down the corridor to the professor's door. He knocked, and waited.

'Enter!'

He heard echoes of Mr Parkes' voice, as he gripped the door handle.

'What on earth is this?' she demanded, throwing his dissertation at him across her desk.

Mat had always got on well with Professor Pattison. She was Head of Medieval Studies, which was the course Mat had elected to focus on. She had been really helpful to him throughout his course, and he'd always appreciated the amount of extra time she'd given him over and above her seminars. At the same time, she could be rather frightening, when the mood called for it.

Clearly, she was in that mood today. Mat cringed inwardly. He'd seen her like this before. Never aimed at him, but frightening all the same.

'This is rubbish,' she shouted, '*RUBBISH*. What were you thinking! Where on earth was your *BRAIN*. I know you've got one! Why did you not think to use it now, at this critical point.'

Mat wilted. Tears began to sting his eyes but he blinked them back. There was nothing he could say. Deep down he'd known it was rubbish.

'Mat,' she said, in a slightly calmer tone. 'This is nothing at all like I've come to expect from you. It's always been a pleasure to read your essays. You've always, always been amongst the tier for top marks. What is this all about?'

Mat didn't know what to say. He was as disappointed in himself, as she was.

'So, what's your problem?' she started again. 'There must be something. I really did wonder whether somebody else had put your name to this dissertation before handing it in. It is a good job I know your style. So, what is going on with you?'

Mat felt that he could only tell her the truth. He told her everything, about Bridie and her bridge, about Father Christmas, the family, John, and lastly, how he felt about Bridie.

He expected her to laugh, to mock and to ridicule him, for allowing himself to get so distracted but to his surprise, she didn't.

Professor Pattison sat quietly at her desk and looked at him, her fingers entwined under her chin. It was still frightening.

She always looked intimidating.

'Right,' she said, decisively. 'Get yourself sorted out. You have a week until the end of term. As soon as the vacation begins, get yourself home. Tell this girl how you feel. *Do not* flap about. No flowery stuff, just say it straight. Tell her how you feel honestly, and get it off your chest. You might still be disappointed, but at least you can say you tried and you'll know where you stand.'

Mat nodded, not daring to say anything.

'Then get yourself back here. Get stuck into your revision. You only have a couple of weeks to get your brain straight – and this time, I expect you to use it!'

Mat nodded again.

'As for this?' she said, pointing dramatically, and with exaggerated distaste, at the dissertation on her desk. 'I'm giving you three days to submit something that reflects at least...at least...something of the talent I know you have.'

'Thank you,' Mat breathed.

She shrugged.

'I have a little influence with my colleagues,' she said. 'Hopefully I can persuade them that this was the right thing to do. Mitigating circumstances, or something,' she mumbled. 'You'll still lose marks on it because it's late but...well to be honest, this isn't worth anything.'

Mat telephoned Mr Pearce. He knew there wasn't enough in his bank account to cover it, but he really, really needed to buy a new car. Mr Pearce was his only hope, as the chief executor of his Trust account.

He breathed a long sigh of relief when eventually Mr Pearce agreed to the extra funds. He'd arranged a transfer into Mat's bank account. It should arrive just in time to allow him to purchase something inexpensive but reasonable. At least it would be something that would get him home at the end of the week.

He bought several pizzas, a couple of sandwiches and some chocolate from the shop in Alexandra Square, and took the bus back to his room in town. For the next couple of days, he did nothing but write. He slept little, relying on increasingly strong coffee to help keep his eyes open for as long as possible.

He'd run out of everything but biscuits the day before, but hadn't allowed himself to stop. He was as close to exhaustion as he could imagine by the time the deadline was up.

At two minutes to nine, on the third day, and with a deep sigh of relief, he dropped his new dissertation into the professor's college mailbox. Just in time.

At least he was happier with his work. He just hoped that he hadn't let the professor down again. He didn't think he had.

He took the bus back into town. He'd arranged to meet a flatmate who knew about such things and he was relying on his expert advice to choose a new, and hopefully more reliable, car.

He was pleased with his purchase. It wasn't quite the VW Golf that his rival had sported, but at least his second-hand Ford Escort would get him home and hopefully back again.

It was going to be close to the wire. He called into a local insurance broker to obtain the necessary insurance documents, and then into the Post Office to get a tax disc. Then he went back to his flat to sleep. He'd arranged that his flatmate would wake him in time to leave for home.

Then he slept, for a solid twenty-four hours.

***

It was late by the time Mat got home. Having heard a car pull up, Mrs Ambrose met him at the door. She'd been in bed for a while but had come downstairs for a drink of water. Mat was the last person she'd expected to see.

'Mat! What are you doing here?' she whispered loudly to him, pulling her dressing gown around her, against the drizzle. 'We didn't expect to see you until after your exams!'

Mat was too tired to feel hungry but she insisted.

'What do you want?' she asked. 'A bacon sandwich? An omelette or something?'

Mat settled for a piece of cake. He didn't really want anything at all, but she wasn't going to let him get away with just a cup of tea. He struggled to eat his cake as she brought him up to date with family news.

'Did you know that John has asked Bridie to marry him?'

He was having difficulty swallowing his bite of cake and couldn't answer.

'I don't know,' she continued, not noticing his distress, 'she's been in a strange mood lately. She said she was excited when he asked her but then she told him she'd think about it. Well, you know as well as I do, how contrary she can be.'

Mat was only able to nod. He was struggling to swallow, the cake, his emotions.

'I don't know,' she continued, 'I always imagined it would be you she'd choose.'

Mat was still doing his best not to cough crumbs all over the table. He gulped down some tea, hoping that might help.

'You two were always so close!' she said. 'I really can't understand how she took up with somebody like him. Ah well, her choice, I suppose.'

He finally managed to clear his throat and took another long sip of tea.

'I don't understand her at all, sometimes,' Mrs Ambrose confirmed, distractedly. 'Why she would want to keep him dangling for so long is beyond me.'

Mat sighed. He'd finally recovered from his coughing enough, to speak.

'To be honest,' he said, dejectedly, 'I always thought it would be us too.'

Mrs Ambrose raised her eyebrows. Having started, Mat felt obliged to say more.

'I think I've been in love with Bridie for…well…for I don't know how long. I just didn't realise it, not like that.'

'Well, if you've realised it now, why haven't you done something about it?'

'I tried,' he said plaintively. 'I did try. It just sort of all came out wrong.'

She listened quietly while he explained what had happened at Christmas, about the torture he'd been through over the Spring Term, and about Beth's letter.

'So, Beth wrote to you, did she?' she commented, looking at him quizzically. 'Did she, indeed?'

'I think she guessed how I felt, at the New Year's party. I think she just wanted to help.'

'Mmm,' she muttered. 'Well, at least it finally woke you up. Maybe Beth's meddling will give you a chance to make things right with Bridie.'

'If I can think of what to say. And if she'll even listen.'

'Lord help us, Mat! I love you, but you can be so frustrating sometimes!'

'I know…I'm sorry.'

'Well, there's no point sitting there feeling sorry for yourself. Look where that's got you so far!'

She sat back in her chair, her arms folded, glaring at him. It felt like the time he was fourteen, and had been caught trying out Nick's new motorbike. Nick, Bridie's brother, loved bikes. She'd glared at him then. He felt decidedly uncomfortable.

'Right,' she said, leaning towards him decisively. 'First thing tomorrow, here's what you do. You take her out for a walk, and you tell her how you feel. You tell her straight, mind, no faffing about, OK? Might not do any good, but at least you'll have tried. Like I've always told you, if you don't ask, you don't get.'

'That's more or less what Professor Pattison said.'

'Well, she was right. Now get yourself to bed, otherwise you'll be like a wet rag tomorrow. And for goodness' sake, stop looking so mournful! If there's anything that'd definitely put her off, it's you looking so damned miserable all the time!'

23

Mat was up and waiting in the kitchen, watching Mrs Ambrose fussing with the breakfast things. He just couldn't stay in bed any longer. He was too on edge. He stood up as Bridie entered the room.

'Mat!' she said, clearly surprised. 'What are you doing here?'

Her mother answered for him. 'Mat needs to talk to you now. Go for a walk, and for once, listen to what he has to say. You can have breakfast when you get back.'

'But I need to get to work!' Bridie retorted. 'We've got to finish off orders for Easter. I can't just "go for a walk", for goodness' sake! I haven't got time. I'll be late!'

'I'll call Brenda and explain, OK? Go on, the two of you. Mat hasn't got time to wait until it's convenient for you. He's got to get back to university. He's got his finals to get ready for, don't forget. Hurry up!'

They walked in silence for a while. They meandered along the ley line track, hiking up through the fields.

He could sense that she was getting agitated but he really wanted to get to the bridge before he said anything.

It was their special place.

He wouldn't feel comfortable saying what he had to say to her in the middle of a field. Especially with curious cows following them. They had horns and everything.

'So? What do you want to say?' she asked him, breaking the silence.

'Not yet. In a minute.' He replied. She grunted impatiently.

It was raining by the time they made it to the bridge. Bridie had opened her umbrella. She hid under it, hugging her coat around with her spare hand.

She gave him a stern, impatient look.

'Right!' she snapped, tight lipped. 'We're here. I'm cold, I'm wet and I'm late for work. Say what you want to say and say it quickly or I'm going back.'

He wiped the worst of the raindrops from his glasses, he could imagine her foot tapping impatiently in her rubber boot. He knew it would be.

He took the umbrella from her, tucking it between his arm and his body, so that it sheltered them both, leaving his hands free. It felt awkward, but he was determined to do this as planned.

'Well?' she demanded.

He took a deep breath, took both of her hands in his own and launched into the phrase he'd figured would be a good place to start.

'See, it's like this,' he said nervously, 'I don't want you to marry him.'

'Excuse me?' she asked, snatching her hands away.

'You mustn't marry John,' he said, desperately trying to make it clear.

'Why on earth shouldn't I?' she asked, edginess crept into her voice.

'Because...' he stammered.

'Because what?' she demanded. 'Because you said so? What do you think gives you the right?'

'Because...' he tried again, frustrated that he couldn't get it out.

She gave him a withering look.

'Right, so you get to choose who I can marry and who I can't now, do you?' she demanded angrily. 'What are you, my owner or something?'

'No!' he said. 'No! Of course not! I just meant that…'

Why was she always so awkward? She wasn't listening at all. Could she not understand what he was telling her? Professor Pattison's voice echoed in his head. 'Don't faff about. Tell her straight!'

'Bridie…'

'Don't you *Bridie* me, Matthew Crawford,' she shouted, grabbing the umbrella and pivoting away from him.

'I'll marry who I damned well like,' she snapped over her shoulder. 'You can just keep your big nose out of my business from now on, thank you very much'

'No!' he said desperately. 'Please Bridie! You've got to listen!'

'So far, all you've done is tell me what I can't do. Why should I listen to anything you've got to say?'

'Because…' Mat hesitated.

'Oh, for goodness' sake, will you stop flapping and get on with it? *WHAT!*

'Because you should be marrying me!' he shouted back at her.

Bridie stilled.

'What?'

'You heard,' he said. 'There, I said it.'

'Why on earth would I want to marry you, of all people?' she smirked, 'just because you said.'

'No! Oh, please Bridie!' he pleaded. 'Please give me a chance here!'

'No!' she snapped. 'I can't! Even if I wanted to, I can't'

'Why not?' he demanded, taken aback.

'Because, you idiot, I've already sort of promised John.'

'Then unsay it!' he said. 'Un-promise!'

'And what if I don't want to *un-promise*,' she glowered.

'But you must! Please! You have to! It was always supposed to be the two of us! Not anybody else. Just us. We were supposed to "stay close always!"' he said, desperately.

'But that's not enough, is it? Not nearly enough. Why would I want to be saddled with an idiot like you anyway. Just because we were "supposed to stay close forever",' she asked sarcastically.

'No! Because I love you. I love you, Bridie!'

She stood silently for a long moment; her head tilted to one side. Rain splattered on her umbrella. It ran down his glasses, dripping off his nose. He didn't care.

'Finally.'

'What?' he asked, confused.

'Finally, you said it.'

'Yes. So?'

'Took you long enough, didn't it,' she grinned.

'What do you mean?'

'I mean, I've known you loved me for years. You were just too much of an idiot to realise it,' she said smugly.

'I don't understand,' he said. 'How could you know I loved you when I didn't myself? Why didn't you say something before?'

'I knew, because I know you, Matthew. I know you better than you know yourself and I was waiting.'

'For what?'

'For you to realise. For you to tell me yourself.'

'Oh,' was all he could find to say.

'So?' she asked

'So what?'

'So now you can ask me properly.'

'Oh…right!' he said, a light dawning inside his head. 'Will you marry me, Bridie?'

'No.'

'Pardon?' asked Mat, now totally confused. 'But I thought you said…I thought you meant…'

She shook her head. Tiny drops of water flew from her hair. They looked like stardust, he thought.

'Oh no, my boy. You don't get away with that. If you're going to ask me, you have to do it properly. On your knee. With a ring and everything.'

'But it's pouring with rain, Bridie. The grass is soaking wet! And I haven't got a ring anyway…'

She looked at him defiantly.

'I don't care if you have to kneel in the stream, Matthew Crawford. If you're going to ask me to marry you, that's how it'll be, OK?'

'I still don't have a ring,' he muttered, as his knee squelched into the muddy grass.

'Oh, that's alright,' she said, fishing in her jeans pocket. 'I knew you wouldn't think of that. I brought the engagement ring my grandma left me, just in case. So, come on then. Get on with it. I'm getting wet.'

Mat looked up into Bridie's face, he was drenched through, as he said the words she wanted to hear.

'Will you marry me, Bridie? Please.'

She beamed down at him.

'Yes, of course I will, Matthew. You only had to ask!'

He took her hand in his, placing Grandma Pam's ring on her finger.

She had always loved that ring ever since she was a little girl and her grandma had shown it to her. She thought the cluster of tiny blue sapphires was just so pretty.

It felt right. It felt perfect.

They looked down at their hands, joined together. Her hand felt warm in his. They both caught their breath as a faint glow passed from his hand to hers. It was just like they had seen, when he'd held the globe that first Christmas.

They both stared, as the glow that warmed their hands moved gently through their fingers.

They watched, fascinated and grateful, as his love flowed like shining liquid. They could feel it everywhere, wrapping itself around them. It felt so good. Deep within them, they felt their souls kiss.

When he climbed gratefully to his feet, squeezing some of the muddy water out of his jeans, she tapped him on the shoulder.

He looked up and she kissed him lightly on the lips. It felt as though he'd had an electric shock. He liked it, though. It made him happy. Very happy.

'There,' he heard her giggle. 'Sealed with a kiss. I've always wanted to say that!'

24

As they started their long walk back down to the farm, hand in hand, he just had to ask.

'Bridie?'

'Yes?'

'Do you always have your grandma's ring with you?'

'No, of course not! Don't be daft, I'd probably lose it somewhere!'

'Then why did you have it with you today? Did you have this all planned or something?'

'Yep!' she said, triumphantly.

'How?'

'Since before Christmas,' she said, in a matter-of-fact tone. 'Beth and I were talking about her wedding plans, and she asked if I thought we'd ever get married.'

'Oh, OK.'

'Anyway, I said that if it was left to you, you'd flap and fluster around for years, before you even realised that you loved me, let alone actually ask me to marry you. So, we came up with this plan to…well…sort of nudge things along! I say *we* but it was mostly Beth's idea really.'

'So, all that stuff with John?'

'All part of the plan.' She nodded. 'Worked though, didn't it?'

'Yeah,' he said, still trying to get his head around it all. 'I suppose it did.'

'And John? Won't he be upset?'

'John? Nah. He'll be fine. Beth told him what to do. He is her cousin. He was happy enough to go along with anything, as long as there was plenty of food involved. Nice enough chap. Bit of a prat though, if you know what I mean. All he ever talked about was cars. On and on, and on…Bill liked him, of course, but who cares what he thinks anyway.'

'Beth does?' Mat suggested, tentatively.

'Don't be daft…she tells him what to think…'

'So how did you know? When did you know?'

'When did I know I loved you? I've always loved you, Mat. For years. Everybody knew. Except you, of course.'

'Crikey,' he said, 'I wish I'd realised sooner.'

'Me too,' she said, 'it would have saved a lot of irritation. Still, never mind. You weren't ready, and that was that. You can be very frustrating, you know. I just had to be patient.'

Mat was impressed. She was probably the least patient person he knew.

'Like I said, you just needed a bit of a push.' She smiled, punching his arm playfully.

'You really are an amazing woman, Bridie Ambrose!'

'Not for much longer, I won't be.'

'You'll always be amazing!'

'No, silly,' she said, smugly, 'I meant I won't be Bridie Ambrose much longer. I'll be Bridie Crawford!'

Mat just couldn't help but smile.

'Bridie Crawford!' he shouted, punching the air. *YES!'*

His Bridie. At last, she was his Bridie.

As they passed the courtyard tree, Mat noticed for the first time the tree's blossom flowers. They had decorated his new car. He stopped to look at Bridie under its boughs, and pulled her close.

'So, you really do love me then?' he asked, just to be sure. Just to be finally, irrevocably sure.

'Yes, Mat,' she laughed, rolling her eyes at him. 'I really do.'

Then she curled her arms around his neck, and raised herself on her tiptoes.

'I love you, Matthew Crawford. I love you with all my heart,' she uttered breathlessly, just before their lips met.

'Do you know what day this is?' she asked as they reached the door.

'I don't know, I've lost track. Saturday, maybe,' he asked. 'Why?'

'It's the Spring Equinox,' she whispered, smiling. 'It's a special day.'

'More of your plotting and planning?' he smiled shaking his head.

'Not everything in life can be planned, Mat. You know that. You of all people should know that. Sometimes you've just got to trust in nature and go with the flow.' She looked around, wistfully at the trees.

'Told you it was a special place though, didn't I?' she smiled coyly, gently punching his arm again.

Summer Solstice

25

Mat grinned as he turned into the yard that night. After a long winter, it was a relief to find that there was still just enough daylight for him to see across the valley.

For once it wasn't raining.

He could see the first glimpses of greenery beginning to erupt in the trees and bushes down the road. He nodded absently to himself, knowing that from this point on, daylight would slowly begin to linger later, and last well into the evening. It was spring which meant new beginnings. The promise of long, warm summer days ahead.

It had been a year of new beginnings. A year full of promise. The best year of his life. He was happy. Happier than he could ever remember.

He remembered that it had been raining that day, this very day, exactly a year ago. That was the day that he'd realised, with Bridie's help, that he loved her and he just had to spend the rest of his life with her.

That was the day, with Bridie's help, that he'd proposed to her. And that's when he'd started, for the first time in his life, to feel truly happy.

He remembered the feeling of intense relief as the last day of his final exams had drawn to an end. Then the feeling of intense dread when they'd informed him that he was a borderline case.

He would have to undergo a Viva Voce examination to decide what sort of degree he would be awarded. He'd done so much work, put so much time, effort and dedication into his studies, that he dreaded the prospect of slipping below the upper second degree that he so desperately wanted. The thought of letting down so many people, seeing the disappointment in their faces, made him wince.

By the time the oral component of his examination was over, he'd been emotionally and physically drained. The examiners had grilled him for what had seemed hours. They had drilled into his brain, picked at his answers, in every minute detail, and left him feeling that he'd forgotten even the most basic knowledge he'd so carefully acquired over the last three years.

Finally, they'd dismissed him. By the time he'd left the room, the back of his shirt had been uncomfortably wet. He leant against the corridor wall for a few minutes, before he could summon the energy to walk into the college bar for a consolation pint.

Mat didn't particularly like drinking, but that afternoon the cold, soothing liquid had been very welcome indeed.

He hadn't been looking forward to learning his fate, but he'd known he'd have to find out in the end.

As always, the college had displayed the finalist's results on one of the office windows. He'd waited until the crowd thinned before approaching the window. There were a lot of names, all listed under the various degrees that had been awarded.

The list of names who had been awarded upper-seconds was enormous, but he'd worked steadily through, searching for his name. It wasn't there. He'd checked the list again, but no amount of searching would make his name appear.

His heart sank as he forced his eyes down, to examine the lower-second class awards. Again, he worked methodically through it, he imagined how on earth he was going to tell everyone. Mr Pearce, he knew, would be terribly disappointed. After all his coaching and encouragement, he would finally find out that Mat hadn't been worth any of his time and effort.

Mat blinked back the tears at the thought of that interview. He was determined to face up to his fate, like a man. Echoes of Mr Parkes rang through his brain. 'Be a man,' he'd been told when his parents had died. 'Be a man.'

He'd have to face the family as well, of course. They'd be sympathetic, but of course they would be disappointed. It would show on their faces when he told them. They'd probably think it through about attending his graduation.

Bridie, of course, didn't care at all for education. For her, it was just something that had to be got through, and then left joyfully behind as soon as you were allowed to do so. She was proud to be making children's clothes that people wanted to buy. That was her job.

She was proud to be making *practice dinners,* that her soon-to-be husband would come home to.

Admittedly, he didn't usually want seconds, and sometimes he didn't finish it all, but he always had as much as he wanted, he always enjoyed it. Most of the time anyway. Sometimes he dropped hints that…well, maybe what she'd served wasn't necessarily to his taste…so then she'd quietly remove it from her list – but even so, he always ate well. That was enough for her. As long as he was happy, she was happy. Same with his education. If that was what made him happy, that was fine with her.

Bridie had dropped hints about jobs in town but he'd set his sights on teaching. She wasn't totally convinced that he'd be very good at it, but if her dad and Mr Pearce reckoned he could do it, that was good enough for her.

All the same, Mat could just imagine her voice, 'I told you so,' when she found out that he hadn't made the grade after all. That just couldn't happen. He really just couldn't go home, if he'd have to face her disappointment in him. She wouldn't be able to disguise it. He couldn't bear the thought of seeing it unravel.

So, he checked again. Very carefully. His name wasn't there. He couldn't bring himself to check the third-class degree list. He just couldn't.

Despondent, he wandered sullenly, over to where Professor Pattison was helping the office staff serving strawberries and cream to the finalists. He'd apologise, of course. She'd be disappointed. He hoped she'd be kind, but he wasn't too hopeful.

'So, Mat,' she began, frowning. 'By the skin of your teeth, eh?'

'I know,' he said, 'I feel sick. I'm so sorry.'

He might as well get used to saying it.

'I really am surprised at you Mat,' she continued. 'If only your last term had been better. Your marks for the rest of the course, well, if only you'd kept that up.'

Mat just sighed, welling up. Enough was enough. He just wanted to go home. Of course, he would then have to explain himself, all over again, probably several times. And he wouldn't be able to escape.

'Still,' Professor Pattison continued. 'A first is a first, even if it is only by a squeak.'

'Pardon?'

'Pardon?' she asked. 'Surely, you've looked at the degree notice?'

'Yeah,' he replied, 'but I couldn't find my name.'

'You obviously didn't look properly,' his professor insisted. 'Look – I'll show you.'

She pointed straight at his name. First Class Honours. The shortest list and one of the few. The only list he hadn't even thought of checking. It had never occurred to him,

Mat was speechless.

Professor Pattison was beaming with pride.

She'd hugged him. Mat had been surprised, this wasn't the Professor Pattison he knew.

'Now then,' she'd said, still beaming widely at him and unnervingly. 'Go on to do great things, Mat. Go on and make me even more proud of you.'

Mat was still smiling as he climbed gratefully out of the car. He stretched his back, then pulled a suitcase out of the boot, and stood for a few moments looking at the house. 'That's it!' he said out loud. 'I'm finally home for good!' *I've done it!*

As he opened the front door, he put his suitcase at the bottom of the stairs and shouted to let them know he was home.

There was no answer, which he thought was strange. It was late afternoon, and he'd imagined that Bridie's mum would have been preparing dinner.

He glanced at his wristwatch. Surely Bridie should have been home by now? *Oh well* he thought, feeling a little deflated. *Cup of tea it is...*

As he pushed open the kitchen door, though, he was confronted by balloons, bunting, a table full of party food and, best of all, all his favourite people.

Bridie was the first to rush towards him, and as she hugged and kissed him repeatedly, everybody else crowded in to greet him.

They were all there, Bridie's mum and dad, her brothers Bill and Nick, Beth and Nick's new girlfriend, who he hadn't been introduced to yet, all beaming with smiles.

Hanging at the back, was Mr Pearce. Mat smiled. Mr Pearce, grinned with an almost imperceptible smile. He nodded at him, and winked.

It had always been the same with Mr Pearce. Most of the time, he'd been in the background, as Mat progressed through school.

Mat understood that it wouldn't have been right for him to have shown any favouritism, so as signs of approval he'd had to put up with a nod, perhaps a small smile, and, if he'd excelled at something, the occasional wink of the eye across the room. Those small gestures had always been enough for him, and he'd appreciated them greatly.

Today, though, as the celebrations began to ebb, he found Mr Pearce standing by his side.

Mat smiled, and told Mr Pearce, 'Thank you so much for pushing me on. I wouldn't have done anything like as well, if it was just left to me!'

Mr Pearce, in return, offered him a full smile and then, very much to Mat's surprise, placed an arm around Mat's shoulder and said simply, 'Matthew, you will never know how proud I am of you! Well done!'

Later, after they'd waved off those who had to go home, Mat and Bridie sat down on the front doorstep, gazing up at a sky full of stars.

'So, did you have a good time?' she asked him.

'Pretty much,' he assured her. 'Yep, a pretty much perfect day.'

'Only *pretty much*?' she asked him.

He looked down at her upturned face, leant over and kissed her on the lips.

'Now it's perfect,' he said, as she giggled and snuggled her head deeper into his shoulder.

26

When his graduation day arrived, Bridie had been really proud of him. He'd hoped she would be. He'd prayed she would be and she was.

Mr Pearce had stood up as he received his diploma. He'd been clapping so hard that even Mat could hear him from the stage. Mr and Mrs Ambrose had stood and clapped too.

They'd smiled broadly at him. They were obviously proud. Bridie hadn't clapped. She'd stood, but she hadn't clapped like the others. She'd just stood there, smiling proudly at him, her hands clasped in front of her. He could almost see her knuckles whitening.

Even from the stage, he could see tears glistening down her cheeks. At that moment, Mat had found it hard to hold back his own emotions. Her approval was all he really needed. It was all he'd ever wanted, and now he knew he had it.

That was enough for him. Right then, at that moment, he felt proud of himself.

Later, as he'd emerged from the ceremony, she'd hugged him tightly. Tears continued to stream down her face again, before anyone else could get nearby. Then, and only then, had she allowed anyone else close enough to shake his hand, slap his back, and congratulate him. They'd all stood there in the sunshine, happy, proud and relieved.

Not least Bridie, even though she'd muttered something about the cheers making her jump, and how long the ceremony had taken to complete.

'There were a lot of graduates this year,' Mat had explained, placating. 'Everyone's earned their moment. Everyone deserves their moment. It takes a while.'

'As far I was concerned,' she'd smiled adoringly, 'there was only one.'

As they'd walked down to the Lancaster House Hotel, where the family was staying, she'd hung on his arm, proud and protective, her body-language clearly stating 'this is my man – don't even think about it!' She hadn't needed to. For Mat, it was only she who existed. Everyone else, her family included, intruded only momentarily in his thoughts and attention.

'So, what did Princess Alexandra say to you?'

'I can't remember. Something about how hot and boring it all was?'

Bridie had punched his arm, but a bit more gently than she normally did.

'Don't be silly!' she'd said. 'She didn't speak to many people, just a few. What did she say to you?'

'I think she asked about what I was going to do next?'

'So?'

'So what?' he asked, teasing her, as she normally teased him.

'So, what did you say, idiot?'

'Oh,' he said, as if the Chancellor's question had been simply conversational, 'I think I said something about wanting to teach…'

Bridie laughed. He braced himself, expected her usual comment about his being the least likely teacher she'd ever met, but he was surprised.

She'd hugged his arm even tighter.

'Mat, if that's what you want to do, you'll do it, no question,' she'd said proudly. 'I don't really care what it is, but whatever you end up doing, I'll be right here, by your side. And I'll be proud.'

Mat had hardly been able to breathe, let alone reply.

***

Their wedding had followed shortly after. Mat hated clichés, but he really did feel, looking back on events, as though he'd been in the middle of whirlwind. It was one thing after another. Home after graduation…a few days respite…then straight into wedding planning. That really wasn't his thing at all, and he was very happy to let Bridie, Beth and Mrs Ambrose make all the decisions. As long as he was there to say 'I do,' he really couldn't have cared less about the details.

Yes, those flowers would be lovely. Yes, those hymns would be great. Colours? Perfect! Maybe we could include…no? OK, no problem. Just a suggestion.

The ladies were in full wedding flow, and Mat had spent the first week or so in the vortex of their energy.

Gradually, he had managed to manoeuvre himself, as gently and as invisibly as he could, to the slightly less disturbed air of Mr Pearce's living room.

Mr Pearce had been a true friend throughout everything. He'd taken care of him when his parents had passed away. He'd introduced him to the Ambroses.

Mat thought a great deal of Mr Pearce. He valued his opinion, and for the most part, took his advice.

'So,' Mat had said one mid-summer afternoon, while they enjoyed tea on Mr Pearce's lawn, 'now I just need to get a job!'

Philip Pearce placed his cup into the saucer on the patio table and looked thoughtfully at Mat.

'Well,' he said, 'if you're still set on teaching?'

Mat nodded.

'Well, in my early days it was fairly simple. If you managed to get a decent degree from a decent university, you'd have been pretty well set. Schools were always keen to take graduates in subjects they needed.

'Nowadays it's a bit different. Now, you not only need a decent degree but qualifications to say that you're able to teach. As far as I'm concerned, if you can teach, you can teach. If you can't, you can't. You'd know in the first few days or weeks whether it was for you or not, and so would the school.

'Then there'd either be a job, or a polite parting of the ways. There was none of this namby-pamby *theoretical* stuff when I started out.

'Different now. Rules are rules, or at least the new rules are the new rules! So, what do you do? If you're intent on being a teacher, you need to get a teaching qualification. Another year at university. That will be one of the new universities, one of the old teacher training colleges. I never needed to bother with them but I've heard they're pretty good.'

'To be honest, I'm not sure I could stand another year at university,' Mat responded as gently as he could, 'and I'm not sure Bridie would put up with it either!'

'Well, maybe she won't have to,' said Mr Pearce. 'I've heard of a new scheme to encourage graduates into teaching by offering "on the job" training.'

Mat's ears perked up. Mr Pearce giggled.

'Actually,' he said, 'it looks very much like the sort of training I did when I first started out. Strange how fashions keep re-emerging, eh?'

With Mr Pearce's active encouragement and mentoring, Mat had eventually applied for a vacancy at the local Grammar School.

It wasn't Burrell's, but he didn't want Burrell's. He wanted ordinary. He wanted normal. He wanted a job that would allow him to get home every evening. That was important to Mat. He didn't want to be separated from his family, he wanted inclusion. He didn't want his students to feel separated from their families, as he had felt. He also didn't want them to feel separated from their communities, as he once was.

He wanted his students to feel absorbed, nurtured, loved.

He felt very strongly about that. Burrell's had never given him any of that. He wanted better for his pupils, and he wanted better for his family. If that meant a lower salary, so be it. It didn't matter. For Mat, some things were more valuable than money.

***

His interview had been scheduled for the afternoon. He'd planned a lazy morning. He'd planned to stay in bed until he was good and ready to get up, then he'd make himself a light breakfast.

Perhaps he would take a short stroll in the fresh air, to steady his nerves. Afterwards, he'd get changed and allow himself plenty of time to find a parking spot, driving into town for his interview.

Bridie, it seemed, had different plans for him. She'd woken him early and insisted he help her with the chickens. Then she'd made him an enormous breakfast of eggs, bacon, beans and hash browns. After that, she'd pressed his suit and informed him, in no uncertain terms, that he needed a haircut. She wasn't going to have him turn up at an important interview with hair that looked like a hillbilly. Absolutely no way.

She'd cut his hair for years, whenever he was home, and he thought she made a pretty decent job of it. It also saved him the cost of the barber's shop in town, which was useful.

Unfortunately, this time, somewhere between the clipping, the combing and the scissoring, her hand had slipped. All he'd heard was a slight gasp, and a whisper of 'Oh no! Oh Mat, I'm so sorry!'

Mrs Ambrose had been horrified when she'd walked into the kitchen to find Bridie crying and Mat holding the side of his head.

There were no cuts or bleeding, but Bridie had somehow managed to take a large chunk of his hair off, right down to the scalp. It was pretty obvious, and no amount of judicious combing was ever going to cover it up.

Bridie was distraught. She didn't know what to do with herself, and Mat had spent the rest of the morning consoling her. It had certainly taken his mind off his interview, and he'd been relieved, rather than nervous, when he'd set off for town.

He'd almost been tempted at one point during the morning to call and tell them he was ill or something. In the end he'd decided that if he was going to stand any chance at all of getting the job he wanted, he would just have to go. Come what may. It might be his only chance.

Once the school secretary had shown him into the room, he'd spent much of his time distractedly trying to keep his head slightly turned away from the panel. In the end, nobody seemed to have noticed, so he was hopeful that he'd got away with it.

The interview, he felt, had gone reasonably well.

He thought he'd answered all of their questions quite sensibly and thoroughly, and although he knew he would have been up against strong opposition, he felt as confident as anyone, under the circumstances. He felt, at least, that he'd given himself a good shot at it. He would have another few days to wait until he would learn the outcome.

After the interview, the headmaster, who was chairing the panel, showed him out to the car park. They made small talk as they made their way through the myriad of corridors and down the main staircase.

Once he'd opened the door to let Mat out, the Head had looked straight at him.

'Just out of curiosity Matthew, who cut your hair?' he'd asked, without a hint of a humour.

Once Mat had somewhat reluctantly explained what had happened, the Head allowed himself a small smile.

'I thought it might be something like that,' he'd replied. 'It's usually either the girlfriend, the wife or the mother. Happens surprisingly often, you know.'

Then, smoothing his own receding hairline, he'd laughed. 'I'm afraid I have the scars to prove it!'

In the end, Bridie's disastrous haircut hadn't mattered. It was his values, enthusiasm and knowledge that had made the difference, and it was those that had got him the job.

27

Matthew and Bridie were to be wedded in the summer. Just as Bridie had planned.

It hadn't mattered to Mat when it was. He'd have married her in a snowstorm if she'd wanted, or stood chest-high in flood water. He had to agree, though, that the summer was by far the best time to get married.

They'd agreed on a fairly quiet wedding, in the company of just family and a few close friends.

He knew from the New Year gatherings that her family was quite large, but what he hadn't anticipated was that not all of her family could get to their house for New Year. A number of them did, but even so, a few lived too far away to make it. They'd all decided to make a special effort to come to Bridie's wedding though. They were all determined not to miss it, and only a couple of family members who were unable to attend due to the distance didn't make it in the end.

Mat had lost touch with most of his acquaintances at Burrell's, but he had invited a few people from university. He'd never been that good at making friends, and even less good at keeping in touch with them. Bridie, on the other hand, knew lots of people, she had many friends, and kept in touch with them.

On the day of the wedding, both sides of the church were pretty much full, even though Mat had never met a few of them. It didn't matter.

Nearly all of them knew him, or knew about him, and if he was good enough for Bridie, he was good enough for them. Just greeting them all, he calculated, was going to take a large chunk of the afternoon.

The day dawned bright and sunny. Even in the early morning it was warm, so he and Mr Pearce had sat out in Mr Pearce's garden to drink their tea.

Mat had spent the night at Mr Pearce's, sleeping in his old room for the first time since his first Christmas spent at the farm. He'd had little choice in the matter back then, and even less choice now – Bridie had told him quite categorically, that he wasn't allowed to see her before she arrived at the church. It was traditional.

That was the end of the matter. So, he could either stay at Mr Pearce's or sleep in a hedge somewhere. It was up to him; she didn't care which. She'd packed him off, with an overnight bag and his graduation suit, with strict instructions about hanging it up properly.

'I haven't spent an hour pressing it and picking bits of fluff to have you turn up looking like a rag bag,' she'd told him. So, he'd carefully lodged it in the wardrobe, where it hung, waiting in preparation for the hour to arrive when he would put it on.

As the morning progressed, Mat had become increasingly nervous.

He could scarcely talk, stammering in conversation instead. Mr Pearce had maintained a lengthy monologue for most of the morning, in an effort to calm him down to sensible proportions. He'd kept it up all through breakfast, in the car, and he was still talking as he stood by Mat's side in the church.

Although he could hear his voice, Mat didn't have a clue what Mr Pearce was talking about. He'd stopped listening some time ago. He'd even given up trying to smile. Like everyone else there, he was just waiting for Bridie.

A hush had descended over the whole church, as the wedding car arrived. He could only see the white-ribboned bonnet.

He saw the car rock, almost imperceptibly, and heard its doors closing. Beth and Mrs Ambrose were stood in the doorway, waiting to check her over. They were there to smooth wrinkles, fluff whatever needed fluffing, and check her make-up before she made her entrance.

Mat turned away, looking nervously from the vicar to Mr Pearce and back again. She'd told him he wasn't allowed to look. He was to wait until he heard the music, then count slowly to eight. Then he could turn around to see her.

'And Mat,' she'd said firmly as he'd left the house the previous evening, 'Don't you dare mess up your lines tomorrow! Listen, breath and speak clearly. And don't forget to breathe!'

Breathe. One. Listen clearly. Breathe. Two.

He heard Mrs Ambrose taking her place.

Breathe. Three. Breathe. Speak carefully. Four.

He made it to five, and turned around.

Mr Ambrose, smiling happily, though clearly uncomfortable in his new suit, was already halfway down the aisle. Hanging gracefully on his arm was the most beautiful woman he'd ever seen. White. Flowers. Smiling. Looking at him and walking towards him.

As she saw him turn to look at her, she raised her eyebrows and cocked her head very slightly to one side.

'Five,' she'd mouthed, beaming triumphantly.

The rest of the day had been a joyful blur of handshaking, laughing, stolen glances between him and his beautiful Bridie, and of heart-stopping moments when she looked his way and smiled.

His Bridie. Always and forever. She'd promised, and she meant it.

28

Spring again! Matthew thought, as he drove through the lanes on his way home.

Spring was almost his favourite time of the year, after Christmas and summer. Christmas was probably his favourite, he reckoned, with all its jollity and lights, but it was at the same time cold and very short.

Then it was just the dreary misery of winter.

Winter, he thought, just had to be got through…cold, wet and often icy.

The only thing that brightened winter at all, for Mat, was spending the long evenings snuggled up by the fire with his new wife. Summer, he thought on reflection, was most definitely his favourite season. Long, warm days, sunshine, sitting out in the garden, picnics…he loved it all.

Spring, though, was different. It was always so full of promise!

As he drove, he couldn't help but notice the increasing number of tiny green buds on the bushes and trees. In a few weeks, maybe even just a few days, the tiny leaves would appear, that would soon transform the lanes with so much lush growth.

As he parked his car beneath the still bare branches of the copper beech, he glanced up and wondered if he could see even the first hints of new growth. *Not yet*, he thought, *but it won't be long!*

'Matthew Crawford! Are you going to stand there daydreaming all night? Your dinner is on the table – come ON!' Mat smiled, and followed her indoors.

'What do you think you're doing, Mr Crawford?' she laughed, as he reached from behind her to stroke her tummy. 'We're perfectly fine thanks, but Beth is coming over in a minute to work out what else I need to do before the baby arrives! I want these dishes out of the way before she gets here. So, get that tea towel moving, please!'

Mat plodded through the drying-up, while she went to answer the doorbell. Three more months. It seemed like forever. Mat wasn't sure he could wait until July, but if Bridie could be patient, so could he. As if they even had a choice in the matter anyway.

She'd told him the news she was pregnant after Bill and Beth's wedding reception, last October.

She'd told him just after they'd arrived home, tired but happy. It had been a great wedding, and this time they'd been able to properly enjoy Beth and Bill's wedding bliss. This time they could just watch and laugh as the happy couple faced the whirlwind.

They'd even managed to enjoy some of the buffet this time. At their wedding, Mat hadn't even seen it until it was nearly all gone. He hadn't cared. He hadn't even realised that he was hungry, until there were only a few curled-up sandwiches and cold sausage rolls left.

She'd told him as they sat down for a cup of tea. She'd sat forward excitedly in her chair and giggled at him.

'What's up with you?' he'd asked, amused by her antics.

'I didn't want to tell you before the wedding,' she'd started, 'I know you. You'd have blurted it out to everyone.'

She'd looked so excited as she'd told him. She'd looked so proud of herself. Tears of joy had trickled down her face as she'd said the words. His own tears soon joined hers, as he kissed her, hugged her, spun her around the room.

'Careful!' she'd giggled.

'It's alright, Mat!' she'd said, laughing at the mortified look on his face, 'I'm not going to break! It's just that you nearly knocked my tea off the table!'

Mat had hardly stopped smiling since the news. He hadn't known that anybody could be as happy as he felt in that exact moment.

Beth popped her head around the kitchen door.

Mat smiled at how radiant she looked.

Pregnancy certainly suited her, he thought. It was early days yet for her, but she'd been so excited to tell Bridie as soon she'd found out. Bridie and Mat had decided that they'd wait a year or so before trying for a baby, so as to let Mat settle into his new job. Beth hadn't wanted to wait, and she'd fallen pregnant shortly after their honeymoon.

'Hi Mat!' she said, smiling. Then she chuckled and yelled. 'Bye Mat!' as she followed Bridie's voice up the stairs.

'Come on Beth! We've got loads to do.'

***

The nurse who had done the scan had asked if they wanted to know if the baby was a boy or a girl, but Bridie had shaken her head, as she hadn't wanted to know.

'I want to do it the old-fashioned way,' she'd said. 'We'll find out when it's born.'

Then she'd given Mat a worried look and asked him if that was alright.

'As long as it's one or the other,' he'd told her, 'I really don't mind!'

Of course, that had meant they didn't know what colour to decorate the nursery. If they'd known, the choices might have been much simpler.

'Neutral, then?' Mat had suggested. 'Maybe yellow or something?'

'Oh Mat,' she'd muttered. 'You can be so predictable. No, I want something a bit more exciting than *yellow*.

They'd talked about it, on and off for weeks, but still hadn't reached a decision.

'This is ridiculous,' she'd said eventually. 'I'll ask Beth. You're no help at all!'

Mat finished tidying the kitchen. He knew she'd do it again when she came down. She always did. Mat was always sure he'd known where to put the plates, where to hang the cups, how to stack the saucepans, but she inevitably seemed to be able to spot something out of place. Then she'd fuss about it, tutting and clicking her tongue, moving bits and pieces to where they should have gone in the first place.

Sometimes, increasingly often, Mat thought the kitchen ended up very much as it was when she'd started, but whatever. It made her happy to be the expert. He wasn't going to make a fuss.

He sat at the table, trying to concentrate on his marking but the regular peals of laughter he could hear from upstairs kept interrupting his thoughts. Never mind. He'd plod on as best he could and finish it off when it was quieter.

He was really enjoying his job and despite Bridie's reservations, he thought he was pretty good at it. He was only a trainee, so the school didn't really expect perfection from him at this stage, but the feedback he'd had so far seemed to be favourable, so he thought must be doing something right.

Mat thought this new scheme was much more to his liking than having to spend another year miles away, attending a full-time post-graduate training course. This way he was in school most of the time, though he did need to attend the teacher training college for a week every term. He felt much more like a proper teacher this way. It also meant that he was able to come home every night, which was important to him. Now that Bridie seemed to be getting bigger every day.

She looked so radiant, so beautiful and so full of joy and anticipation, that he didn't want to miss any of it.

Another year's training after this one, and then he could look for a proper job. Then he really would be a proper teacher. It would be perfect if that job was at the Grammar School…but he hardly dared to dream that.

29

Mat looked up from the papers that were spread across the table and looked around the familiar kitchen. Nothing had changed much since his first visit here, back when he a boy.

Tea-towels were still hung to dry along the handle of the range. Saucepans were stacked in the same corner of the worktop. Cutlery was still kept in same drawer, and plates were still stacked in the same cupboard.

Bridie hadn't wanted to change anything. It was just as she'd always known it. She liked it that way. Continuity and tradition were important to her.

The only thing that had changed since they got married was that her mother was no longer in charge of the kitchen.

That still seemed strange to Mat.

He missed her mum bustling around, doing the washing, setting the table, preparing dinners. He certainly missed her dinners. She was an excellent cook, and the memory of the smells and flavours she created wafted back to him like a warm blanket.

Bridie was a good cook too, and getting better at it all the time. It was just a case of practice, he guessed, like with his teaching. They'd both get better at it with time and patience. The trouble was, though, Bridie wasn't particularly good at patience. She claimed she was, but he wasn't so sure. Or maybe, she just got impatient with him?

Mat pulled a face, maybe her mother was right, after all. Maybe he did live inside his head too much. Maybe he did get stuck there sometimes.

He did need a nudge every now and then. Bridie was very good at that. She was a good *nudger*. She'd had plenty of practice, after all. And she was usually right. No, she was nearly always right. As he'd been told that first Christmas. She really did know the way.

It still seemed odd not to see Mr and Mrs Ambrose sat there at the table though. Apart from the odd dinner, they hadn't sat there since his and Bridie's wedding.

'No,' Mrs Ambrose had told them. 'Your father and I will be perfectly comfortable at the small end.'

The *small end*, as they called it, was situated at the other end of the house. Home Farm was a big, rambling house. When he was small, Mat had often wondered if it went on forever. There always seemed so much of it. He'd tried exploring it when he was younger, but even so, it had taken several attempts to look inside every room. He didn't go into the ones that were occupied because they were private.

He hadn't dared go into Bill's and Nick's rooms, Bridie's brothers. They were bigger than he was, for one thing, and he didn't think he'd be able to run fast enough to escape their wrath. Bridie had told him what she'd do to him, in graphic detail, if he'd dared to even open the door to her room. So, he hadn't.

He had managed to visit all of the empty rooms eventually, so he knew where the small end was. It was almost like a self-contained apartment, with its own kitchen and living room and everything. It was small, but certainly big enough for two people to live in quite comfortably.

They'd moved in while he and Bridie were away on honeymoon. They'd greeted them in the kitchen when they'd returned, and then had left them to it.

Bridie had told her parents that they really didn't need to move out to the small end at all, but her mother had insisted.

'I know what it's like,' she'd told them, in a decisive tone. 'I had to share this kitchen with my mum for long enough after we got married. At first it was nice to have her company and advice, but after a while we started to get on each other's nerves…especially here in the kitchen.'

She'd sat there, in her usual place at the table, telling them horror stories about the problems that she'd encountered while she and her mother tried to share the same kitchen.

'At first it was little things,' she'd said, 'like her moving things I'd put down, or the rows we had when I wanted to put something in a different place. The worst part was over meals.

'"Roll that pastry thinner, Hilda," she used to say, "your father likes thin pastry." Then I'd reply. "But my Tom likes his pastry thicker!" No, it really doesn't work. And anyway, we'll only be a shout away.'

So that's how it came to be. Mr and Mrs Ambrose had moved into small end. He and Bridie had taken over the rest of the house. Or more accurately Bridie had, and Mat didn't get in her way.

It had worked out quite well…but it still seemed strange to Mat that the family weren't all here, together anymore. It had seemed even stranger when he and Bridie had moved into her parents' bedroom. Mat still didn't feel entirely comfortable about that.

Nick, Bridie's brother, had stayed in his old room, and ate his meals alternately with his parents or with Bridie and Mat.

Now that his father was getting older, he had taken on more and more responsibility for running the farm. He had a long-term girl-friend, but he didn't seem to be in any rush to get married. At the moment it suited him to stay in the house. He could run the farm much easier from there.

Mat eased himself up from the table, as soon as he heard the girls coming down the stairs.

He put the kettle on to boil and assembled three cups on the work-top. As they sat having a cup of tea before Beth went home, the girls had shown him the list of things they needed to buy. They'd decided on yellow for the nursery, which both of them had agreed was by far the most suitable colour. Mat almost said something, but thought better of it.

'This is great!' Beth exclaimed as she put her coat on. 'We can do yours now, and then we get to do it all again soon for mine!'

It was still very early days yet for Beth. She was hardly showing at all, but she was so excited. Bridie had been overjoyed for her too, for both of them. The babies would be more or less the same age, and would be able to play together.

Beth and Bill had a small house in town, adjacent to his workshop. In the years since Bill had completed his apprenticeship, his boss had decided that it was time for him to retire. He'd offered the business to Bill, if he could raise the money, otherwise he'd put it on the market.

Their parents had both given them some money as their wedding gift, and they'd used that as a deposit. Now Bill was working all hours to pay off the business loan he'd had to take out to cover the rest.

Mat had talked to Bridie at one point about possibly investing in the business from his inheritance. It would take some of the weight off Bill's shoulders, but she'd thought that Bill would probably refuse. He was a proud man and would want to prove that he could do it by himself.

Mat could always offer later on, if things looked like they might be getting too difficult. Bridie had promised that she would keep an eye on things through Beth and suggested they'd talk about it if the occasion ever arose.

30

The weeks of spring passed quickly.

Most of Mat's weekends were devoted to decorating the nursery. Most of Bridie's weekends were devoted to supervising him, which usually involved a good deal of telling him what he was doing wrong. Eventually, though, they were able to stand back and admire what they'd achieved.

Mat was very pleased with it. So was Bridie, though, as she pointed out, the room was far from finished yet.

'There's a list a mile long,' she told him. 'There are curtains to hang, the cot to paint, all sorts of things to do.'

Bridie's bump was getting bigger with every passing week, and Mat could tell that she was beginning to worry that they wouldn't finish everything before the baby arrived.

To move things along a bit quicker, while he was instructed to paint the cot, Beth had been enlisted to help Bridie with the rest.

'Those bits are far too fiddly for you,' she told him firmly, 'you'd only make a mess of it.'

He was quite surprised that she'd trusted him to paint the cot all by himself. His painting must have improved with practice.

The nursery was the room next to theirs. It was small but cosy, and being next door to the main bedroom, Bridie would be able to hear the baby in the night. She'd have the baby in a crib next to their bed for the first few weeks or months but eventually the baby would inevitably grow out of the tiny crib.

The nursery was steeped in family history, which Bridie liked. It had been hers before she was big enough to have her own bedroom. Before her it had held her brothers, and before that, it had been her mother's nursery and even her grandmother's. There was a continuity to it, which appealed to Bridie's love of tradition.

Bridie held her breath as he opened the tin of paint. She bit her lip as he dipped the paintbrush. She couldn't watch, as the brush approached the cot.

'Right,' she said. 'That's you sorted. See you downstairs.'

It had taken a lot of will-power for her to resist hovering, giving advice, telling him how to do it but she knew she had to let him do it for himself. He'd be fine. She was sure he'd be fine. He'd done a pretty good job on the door and the skirting boards. Not perfect, but OK.

Mat knew, secretly, that she would probably rub it down tomorrow, if he did make a mess of it, and just do it again herself without telling him.

***

The next day, she'd only spotted a couple of runs in the paintwork when she checked it over after he'd gone to work. Actually, not too bad at all.

It would, she hoped, get past even Aunty Brenda's critical eye. If it didn't, she'd just have to tell her not to mention it in Mat's earshot. She wouldn't have her husband belittled, not under any circumstances. That was her job, if she felt so inclined.

Aunty Brenda was coming over this afternoon. She'd made her a new cover for the cot and another one for the pram. She was looking forward to seeing them.

Aunty Brenda always made such lovely things. Bridie had cleaned up her mum's old Silver Cross pram.

Now it was lovely and shiny, and really quite new-looking. She knew that her mum had bought it new when she was a baby. It had been bought just for her. That made it special and she'd looked forward to being able to use it for her own baby.

The boys had used the pram her grandma had given to her mum, but by the time Bridie had arrived, the old one was pretty much wrecked. The boys had eventually used the wheels to make buggies with. What was left of it was still in the barn.

'They're all white!' Mat said as she showed him the things Aunty Brenda had given her.

'I know, aren't they beautiful?' The covers were made from white broderie anglaise, lightly padded and trimmed with a different pattern of broderie anglaise around the sides and hem.

Bridie thought they were stunning. She knew that she could have made them herself, she'd made enough of them for customers in the past but it wouldn't have been the same. These were special. Aunty Brenda had made them especially, just for her, and that meant a great deal to her.

They fitted the cot and pram perfectly. She was so pleased and couldn't wait to see her baby tucked up underneath them – and more importantly she was eager to wheel it around the town, to show it off to her friends and customers. She was really, really looking forward to that!

'But they're white!' Mat said again.

'I know – I can see what colour they are!' His habit of stating the obvious could really grind sometimes.

'But you said you didn't want white,' he tried to explain. 'You know, when we were choosing colours for the nursery.'

'Oh, that's different,' she replied, in her matter-of-fact voice. 'Anyway, Aunty Brenda's going to add some ribbon to the edging when we know whether it's a boy or a girl. It'll be pink for a girl, or blue for a boy.'

'Oh, right,' Mat muttered, wondering, not for the first time what the fascination was with all this fussy stuff.

'Wouldn't it have been easier just to wait and see what comes?' he suggested, logically. 'Then you could have had all pink or all blue covers.'

'Oh, for goodness' sake!' Bridie hissed, rolling her eyes. 'What's the point? Just go and wash your hands ready for dinner!'

31

Spring evolved into summer, and Mat grew increasingly excited at the prospect of finally seeing their new baby.

Bridie, on the other hand, just wanted it all to be over and done. She'd be overjoyed to hold her baby, but she was looking forward to seeing her feet again.

It felt as though her body didn't belong to her anymore. Her movements were restricted by her enormous tummy. She'd long since given up trying to drive the car – she just couldn't squeeze in behind the steering wheel. She found it difficult to reach across the kitchen worktops. She couldn't stand for long, and sitting was desperately uncomfortable.

July simply couldn't arrive quick enough for Bridie.

The remaining weeks were an array of moans and groans, as Bridie soldiered on, with all the aches and discomfort that is expected in a third trimester.

'Mat, please would you dry my feet? I can't reach properly.'

'You carry on. I need to go to the bathroom again.'

'I know you're trying to help, Mat, but it really is easier if I sit sideways to the table, OK?'

'Please would you rub my back again? No! Not THAT hard!'

'If you make me go through this again, Matthew Crawford, I will literally kill you. Seriously!'

Mat felt awkward and uneasy. There really wasn't very much he could do to help, or to make her feel better. There were times when he wished he could undo it all…but as Bridie told him, it was rather too late for that now.

'I'll cook dinner tonight, OK? Then you can put your feet up for a while.' Bridie cringed at the thought of the mess her kitchen would end up in.

'Thank you, darling, that would be lovely. What are you thinking of doing?'

'I thought fish fingers and mashed potatoes, if you'd like that?'

Bridie breathed again. Surely, even Mat couldn't go wrong with that?

Bridie was quite pleasantly surprised. The mashed potato was a little coarse for her liking, but it was edible as long as she put plenty of butter on it. The peas were OK. A little cold, but OK. The fish fingers weren't too bad either. Some of them were hardly even singed.

'That was lovely. It made a nice change to be waited on!'

'Only a pleasure.' Mat beamed in response to her unexpected compliment. 'I'll try something different tomorrow night, if you like? Maybe egg and chips?'

Bridie sighed. She knew he was doing his best. She knew he was trying to please. She was concerned, though, that hot oil and Matthew just didn't seem like a great combination.

'We'll see…' Bridie muttered, as he went to the kitchen, to do the dishes.

***

Bridie was bored. Her ankles ached, her back ached, but most of all she was bored. The early summer days were gloriously warm and sunny.

From her bedroom window, she could see wild flowers adorning the fields. The scent of freshly cut grass floated tantalisingly through the door, as she made her way out into the yard.

She needed to be outside for a while. She wasn't used to being cooped up indoors.

She just needed to breathe some fresh, clean air for a change.

She sat for a while, on a picnic chair under the shade of the heavily-leafed copper beech tree in the front courtyard.

Then she meandered over to the main farmyard, talking to the chickens that skittered around trying to avoid her feet. She spoke to the cows on the other side of the hedge. She leaned against walls and gates occasionally, to rest, even though she felt fine. It just felt so good to be outdoors again.

She knew he'd be worried if she told him that she'd been wandering around outside, so she kept it to herself. It was her secret. She wouldn't tell anyone at all, because she didn't want them to make a big thing of it, and try to keep her locked up in the house again.

On the morning of the mid-summer solstice, as the sun rose higher in the clear, blue sky, she made her way once more out into the fresh air.

Mat had gone to work as usual. Everything was quiet.

There was the ever-present sound of hens clucking and scratching for food in the yard, and the occasional cow calling to its friends in a distant field. It was a perfect, calm, quiet summer day.

Bridie was exhilarated to be outdoors, and free again. She wandered around the yard, and then decided to venture a little bit further. She promised herself that she wouldn't go further than she felt able to, and certainly no further than she'd be able to get back again, under her own steam. There was still more than a couple of weeks to go before the birth, and she was finally feeling a bit better.

Bridie opened the yard gate and set off across the field. It was only a short way to the next gate. She could make it that far, at least. She would rest there for a minute, she decided, and then make her way back.

She leant her back against the gate, and gazed toward the house.

Then she turned and folded her arms on top of the wood. It felt quite comfortable. She smiled, contentedly proud of her achievement. She gazed over the next field for a while and giggled as she opened the gate. She felt like a schoolgirl, sloping off lessons.

32

The school secretary knocked quietly on the door and entered the classroom. She approached his desk and leaned down to whisper into his ear.

'Sorry to disturb you, Mr Crawford. There's been a phone call. Some kind of problem at home. Please would you call them back?'

This was one of his assessment days, when another teacher would sit in class and observe him teaching. They'd take notes, and they'd talk through any issues later in the staffroom.

'Mr White, would you mind please?'

As he made his way to the office, his mind was racing. He'd never had a phone call from home before. They knew he'd be teaching, and that it wasn't possible for him to drop everything. It was lucky Mr White was at hand and could cover the class, otherwise…

As the secretary reached for the door handle, he heard Mr Parkes' voice ringing in his head. 'Come!'

No. Please…

That ancient echo again, reminding him of when he was summoned to his office and was delivered the news about his parents, he tried not to panic, he tried to steady his breathing.

He shakily picked up the phone, Mrs Ambrose sounded worried.

'I can't find Bridie,' she said in a worried tone. 'Was somebody going to take her somewhere today?'

Mat didn't think twice, he simply left the school in a blind haze of racing thoughts and uncertainty, and drove home as quickly as he could.

The secretary had told him that she would explain to the headmaster. It would be fine. Everything would be fine.

'Just go, Mr Crawford. We'll take care of things here.'

He'd have to apologise to the head tomorrow. Today, he just needed to find out what was going on. He had to find his wife.

The tyres of his car came to a screeching halt on the gravelled driveway.

'She's not here, Mat,' Mrs Ambrose informed him, as he hurried into the house. 'I popped up to check that she was OK, but she wasn't here! I've looked everywhere. I can't find her anywhere!'

Mat threw his briefcase into an armchair.

'I'm sure nobody was coming over today. She'd have told me. She didn't leave any notes or anything?'

Mrs Ambrose shook her head quickly, looking around the room.

'OK,' he said, forcing himself to breathe. 'I bet I know where she's gone. I can only think of one place.'

Mrs Ambrose grabbed her handbag, and followed Mat as quickly as she could out the front door. He was already sprinting across the field.

'Bridie!'

He spotted her as he ran through the last gate. She was sitting quietly on the grass, gazing across the bridge. She was leaning back on her hands, her legs stretched comfortably in front of her. She turned as he approached.

'Bridie!' he called again as he came closer. 'What on earth are you doing all the way out here? We were worried!'

'Sorry,' she said quietly, 'I went for a walk.'

'Obviously!' he said, the panic subsiding.

'Bridie!' her mother shouted as she caught up with them. 'You stupid girl! Anything could have happened!'

'Sorry Mum,' she replied, looking sheepish, 'I didn't think.'

'What are we going to do with you...?'

'It was such a lovely day; I just needed some fresh air. I had a lovely walk. I'm fine, honestly.'

'How are we going to get you back?' her mother asked. 'It's a long walk.'

'I know!' Bridie said, brightening. 'But I'll be fine, honestly. I'll just take it slow.'

'No,' her mother said, firmly. 'I'll stay here with you. Mat can run back and ask Nick to bring the trailer up. It'll be a bit bumpy, but you can't walk back all that way.'

Mat turned to make his way back.

'Are you OK, sweetheart?'

'Yeah, I'm fine,' she uttered. 'Sorry Mat. I really didn't mean to come this far. Just once I'd started, I sort of had to keep going.'

'OK, then. You stay here with your mum. I'll be back in a min...'

Bridie had let out a startled 'Oooh!'

'What's the matter?' asked Mat, feeling panicked again.

'I dunno...' she mumbled, slightly breathless, 'but it hurt!'

Mat could see that Mrs Ambrose was holding her breath.

'Oooh!'

'Another one?' asked her mother, concerned.

'Yesss!' Bridie hissed, now breathing shallowly.

'I know what this is then,' confirmed Mrs Ambrose, with a hint of resignation. 'You're having contractions.'

'What?' asked Mat, startled.

'Contractions,' repeated Mrs Ambrose. 'Baby is coming.'

Mat tried not to look like a startled rabbit, caught in headlights. 'But the baby is not due for another two weeks!'

'Sorry to disappoint you, Mat, but babies come when babies come. That's just the way it is.'

Mrs Ambrose sat down on the grass next to her daughter. She frowned and raised her eyebrows.

'And that walk wouldn't have helped either. That was just plain silly, my girl.'

'I'm sorry Mum. I just felt so well. I didn't think it would hurt.'

'Well,' said Mrs Ambrose firmly. 'Can't be helped now.'

She turned to Mat. 'Right!' she said sharply. 'Run and call an ambulance, Mat. Now please!'

'No!' Bridie protested loudly. 'I want him here with me! Please don't send him aw…Oooh!'

She eased herself onto her back, raising her legs and rubbing her stomach, seeking comfort, trying to find relief.

Mat really didn't know what to do for the best.

'Can't you hold on for me to get an ambulance?' he said, alarmed at the sudden turn of events.

Bridie glanced at him briefly, rolled her eyes and let out an exasperated sigh.

'Matthew Crawford,' she said. 'For someone who is meant to be a clever man, you do say the stupidest things sometimes!'

Then she looked up at him again and smiled.

'Look. This baby just will not wait any longer. She wants to be born right here, by the bridge.'

'She?' he asked, by now thoroughly flustered and confused. 'How do you know it's a girl?

'Because if it was a boy,' she said, trying not to wince at the pain of the growing contractions. 'If it was a boy,' she repeated, 'he'd be just like you. He'd dither like there's no tomorrow!'

She let out a short humourless laugh, waiting for another contraction to pass.

'He'd probably want to put the whole thing off until September or something!'

'Are you sure you don't want me to run and call an ambulance?' he asked.

'No!' she shouted. 'No! Stay here! I want you here! There's no time!'

Mat knew in his heart that she was right. He was sure he wouldn't have time to reach the first gate, let alone wait for an ambulance, before the baby was born.

And he was right. Labour was that quick. Even Bridie's mother was surprised. No sooner had he sat down beside his wife, she'd gripped his hand hard, groaning loudly. After that it was all over very quick.

Bridie's mum leapt into action, Mat heard a baby's cry, and their daughter was born.

As gently as he could, Mat helped Bridie to lay down, while her mum checked the baby over.

'She's fine,' Hilda told them. 'At least, as far as I can tell. We'll have to get an ambulance to take you both to the hospital to make sure, though. Mat, will you run and call one please?'

Mat nodded and went to stand up, but Bridie held onto his hand. 'In a minute, please Mum? Please can he at least meet his new daughter?'

After she'd recovered a bit from the exertion, Bridie wrapped their daughter in Mat's shirt, and held her close for the first time.

'Would it be alright with you if we call her Brenda, after my favourite aunty?' she asked, looking pleadingly into Matthew's eyes.

Mat couldn't contain his happiness. He couldn't speak, so he just nodded his agreement and beamed until his face ached. He couldn't quite believe it – he was a father!

Bridie smiled gently into her daughter's face, gazed fondly up at Mat and back to her daughter.

'Hello, my Brenda,' she whispered, almost inaudibly, while gently combing the baby's mob of thick chestnut hair with her fingers.

She smiled when the baby opened her eyes momentarily and looked up at her.

Mat thought Brenda was the most enchanting thing he had ever seen.

Her hair was the same colour as her mother's, and he guessed, though he hadn't yet seen them, that her eyes would be the same shade of brown as hers too. If they turned out to be blue, like his own, then that would be perfectly fine too.

He really didn't care. It didn't matter. She was healthy, Bridie was healthy, and that's all that mattered to him. She was his baby, and he had already lost his heart to her.

He swore to himself that he would protect and look after her always. Always and forever.

'Thank you,' he whispered into Bridie's ear. 'Thank you for making this beautiful thing.'

Bridie beamed up at him proudly. 'She really is, isn't she?'

Then he saw it, felt it. A glow had gently surrounded them. It glistened and hovered in the air. Mat knew instantly what it was. He'd seen it before. Here, with Bridie, he'd seen it that one Christmas he would always remember.

He watched amazed as his baby, their daughter, breathed it in. The smells and feelings were the same. They were the same exquisite, sparkling, shimmering colours he remembered. The intriguing, elusive scents that had comforted and enchanted them both when they were children. It had found her, their newborn, and found them in this special moment that would change their lives forever.

She consumed it. As they all did, joyfully.

His daughter, Brenda, nestled contently in her mother's arms. Mat remembered Father Christmas's words to them, 'stay together,' and they had, only now they were a family of three.

Peaceful. Found. Not lost.

33

Hilda watched the ambulance pull out of the yard, carrying her daughter, her son-in-law and her new granddaughter away. They'd be back again soon, she was sure. She'd given birth herself enough times, and had seen enough new babies to know that they were alright. There was nothing wrong. The doctors would need to check that everything was as it should be, and then they'd be home.

She stood in the kitchen. Her kitchen. *No, not anymore*, she corrected herself. Her daughter's kitchen, Bridie's.

She looked around. Everything looked like it did before, nearly a year before. There were only a few things that were different…but things change. Time moves on. Still, she was glad that Bridie hadn't wanted to change things too much. She could sense the continuity. She knew that was as important to Bridie as it was to her. She was content. She was tired, but she was overjoyed. It had been an eventful day.

As she sat down in her old familiar seat at the kitchen table, she went over in her mind everything that had happened that day.

She thought about the alarming moment she was not able to locate Bridie. It was a surprise, and a relief to discover her daughter sat on the grass beside the bridge, right where Mat had thought she would be.

In that moment she was glad she found her, and when Bridie had gone into labour, her joy at delivering the baby, Bridie's daughter, her granddaughter; and the glow – that delightful, unexpected, peaceful glow that had surrounded them, warmed her and filled her with a sense of joy.

She had never seen it herself, until today. She had heard about it from her mother and her grandmother but she had never experienced it.

She remembered the sense of anticipation when her mother had described it to her, and the sense of disappointment years later, when she'd realised that she had never seen it for herself, and was probably never likely to. Her mother had told her that not everyone would witness it, and that sometimes several generations might pass until it was ever seen again.

She remembered arguing with her mother about the subject, and being told that it was only ever seen when the ley line was at its most powerful, and even then, only when those present were particularly emotional. It was emotion that made the difference her mother had told her. She recalled her mother telling her she was probably just too practical to see it with her own eyes, too good at hiding her emotions to be able to properly see it.

Her mother had been right, she supposed. She was a practical person. She could get things done. She liked things to be straightforward and she liked straightforward people.

Tom was a straightforward man, and she'd fallen in love with him because of it. But she'd never really been a terribly emotional person. She couldn't help it, she just wasn't. She loved people and her family especially, she felt joy, happiness and sadness, just like everyone else…but she just wasn't the sort of person to let emotions run away with her.

She'd always thought that Bridie took after her, in that respect. She was a good, practical girl. She was great at getting things done. At the same time, she had to admit, Bridie was different. She was passionate, very passionate at times. Bridie could be just as stubborn and as patient as she was, when it suited her but there again Bridie had a dreadfully impatient side too. Not to mention, impetuous and opinionated.

Mat was certainly emotional. He was probably the most emotional person she knew. Probably too emotional for his own good sometimes. Not for the first time, she pondered how on earth they'd ever got together. Something about opposites attracting, she supposed. Or maybe it was just that they complemented each other so perfectly. They fitted together, body and soul, like two sides of the same coin.

Whatever it was that made them work, it was their emotions this morning that had allowed her a glimpse of the glow. Even if it was second-hand. Bridie had explained that she and Mat had seen it before, when they were little. She'd told her about their first experience of it, all those years ago, and she'd told her about them meeting Father Christmas.

If her grandmother hadn't told her something similar, she wouldn't have believed her daughter. How could she have done so? She hadn't believed her grandmother then, and had dismissed it as just another of Grandma's stories. The old lady could certainly spin a tale, she remembered with a smile…but now she wondered if she'd been telling the truth all along. She remembered the conversation vividly, as though it was only yesterday.

'And sometimes,' her grandmother had said, 'just sometimes, the energy of the place is so strong that when it mixes with your own emotions, if they're powerful enough, then it can show you figures. Real people, and let you see them, touch them and talk. It's really wonderful!'

Her grandmother had ignored the look of disbelief on her face.

'Happened to me when I was a girl,' she'd continued, 'I'd just lost my dad. Farming accident, very sudden. I can't remember how old I was, maybe eleven, or twelve? Anyhow. It was just before Christmas.

I couldn't stand another moment of being locked up in the house, not with all that crying and bawling going on. I just couldn't stand to see my mother so upset.

'So, I took myself off for a walk, to clear my head. I found myself up by the bridge, thinking about my dad and my poor mum being so upset. I remember just squatting down on the grass and bursting into tears. Thought I'd never stop. Then the glow appeared, and slowly, over the bridge, appeared a figure – Father Christmas. He put his arm around me and made me feel better.'

Hilda sighed, thinking about her grandmother, and how she would sit right here, at this very same table, having to listen to her granddaughter's practical explanation of what she thought had really happened.

'No, girl,' she'd been told. 'You don't understand. At times like this, around the solstices especially, such a powerful mix of energy and emotion can cause the glow to create the very person you wish to see, the person you need consolation from.'

She remembered laughing it off, but she also remembered very clearly, the last thing her grandmother had ever said to her on the topic.

'Well, my girl,' she'd said, in an endearing tone, but with an impatient edge to her voice, 'I really do hope that you never have to go through pain yourself. If you do, I hope that the glow will send the right person to help you through it.'

After what Bridie had told her this morning, and seeing it with her own eyes, she began to wish she'd listened a bit better to what her gran had been trying to tell her.

She'd only ever half believed any of the stories that her mother and grandmother had told her, but she had kept her promise to pass them on to her own daughter, when the time was right. She'd done that.

Maybe half-heartedly but she had done it. She was comfortable she kept her promise.

She was less comfortable with the mess the kitchen was in. She knew that Mat had been doing his best to look after things, to look after his wife but this? This was a complete mess.

She sighed. Why hadn't Bridie called her? She'd have been happy to help. Of course she would.

In her heart, she knew why Bridie hadn't. She knew that Bridie had felt very strongly that Mat needed to do this. Bridie had known that this was his chance. She'd known that he'd had to do whatever he could to help his wife, to make her comfortable, to look after her.

Hilda nodded to herself.

She knew Mat very well. She loved him like a son. In many ways, he might as well be. Fair enough, he'd been away at school, he'd been away at university…but in all the important ways, she'd brought him up. She'd advised him, nurtured him, consoled him, lectured him.

She was incredibly proud of him, but he could be so frustrating at times.

She knew that Bridie had been right though. Her daughter had turned out to be a very wise woman. He had tried hard. He had done his best. He really had.

Matthew had finally learnt to be less inside his head. He had found a way not to be stuck there, isolated from reality.

Mat could be frustrating in this sense. He could be difficult to fathom. He was certainly complicated but she'd done her best. In the end, she had to admit, Bridie had done the better job. Bridie had for once and for all found Mat. He wasn't lost anymore. But this kitchen was still a bloody mess!

She sincerely hoped this would be the last time she would clear up after him. She would do it for her daughter. She knew just how much it meant to Bridie to have her kitchen tidied and clean. Things in their place, the range warming the room, tea-towels drying on the rail. She would have something ready to eat, warm and tasty, for when they got home. She would do this for Bridie, for them both and for her new granddaughter.

Then she would retire into the background again.

She would stand by to help, if asked. She would forever be the presence to watch, observe, advise when asked but the future was all about them. This was their time and she hoped they were wise enough to realise it.

She felt a sense of contentment wash over her.

She was satisfied in the knowledge that she would help from the side-lines, from the shadows. Nurture her granddaughter and watch her grow. There was now another female in a very long line of women. Another woman to watch over the bridge and to maintain and keep the knowledge and the traditions alive.

There had been so many already, the line stretching back in time beyond all rhyme and reason. Another to take the line forward into the future.

Continuity. Hope. Love. Always and forever.

'Grandma Hilda,' she uttered.

'Yes, I like that.' She smiled to herself. 'That'll do for me.'

Autumn Equinox

34

Mat leant back on his elbows, watching his daughter playing with her cousin down near the stream.

It was a beautiful, warm, summer's day. It was perfect. This was his favourite time of year, other than Christmas. He loved Christmas, with its bright lights, warm fires, and the joy of sharing time with a loving, happy, and growing family. The trouble with Christmas, though, was that it was inevitably followed by long months of winter, with its dreary darkness, rain and cold. No, he decided, summer was his favourite. Definitely his favourite.

Warm sunny days like this, followed by more warm sunny days, followed, hopefully, by even warmer, even sunnier days. That was his idea of perfect.

This was his very favourite of all the summer days, though. Today was Brenda's birthday, and they were spending it here, like they had every year since she'd been born. Right here, on this spot, next to Bridie's Bridge, thirteen years before.

Every year since, on her birthday, they'd brought a picnic up here, and all of them, the whole family, had relaxed and played games beside the stream.

Almost every year, anyway.

There had been a couple of times when it had rained. Then they'd had their picnic on the floor in the living room, but those times had been rare. Even on those days, though, they'd always come here. Even if only for a few minutes, they'd come. In rubber boots, carrying umbrellas, they'd always come. This was the special place. Bridie's special place. They had to come.

Toby was just a few months younger than Brenda. He was tall and stocky, like his father, Bill.

He towered over Brenda, who was small like her mother. It didn't matter – they were great friends. Or at least they were, as long as he did what Brenda told him. Brenda may be small in comparison but she was certainly the boss. Toby didn't seem to mind. He just tagged along. He'd follow Brenda anywhere...

Mat looked around and smiled. All the family were here.

Mr Pearce, who was sprawled in a deckchair and sat near Bridie's parents, was snoozing beneath what Bridie had christened *that awful hat*. Stained and scruffy, the wide-brimmed monstrosity was his pride and joy, the hat he had worn for years as a cricket umpire at school and for the county.

Unlike Matthew, Mr Pearce was passionate about cricket, and since his retirement he'd indulged himself by following the England team on several of their international tours. He'd been all over the world, and over the past few years, they'd received postcards from him, from all sorts of romantic places. The furthest he'd been was Australia and New Zealand, and his hat bore shiny Kangaroo and Kiwi badges to prove it. India, Pakistan and the West Indies had followed.

He'd picked up a nasty stomach bug during one of the Asian visits, having made the mistake of enjoying a salad dish from a roadside vendor. He'd been laid up in his hotel room for a week, but hadn't told them about it until he'd got home. After that, Bridie had made him promise that he would stick to watching home matches.

Mr Pearce had argued and pleaded, but in the end Bridie had prevailed. She could be an irresistible force when she wanted to be, and even Mr Pearce wasn't immune to that. She'd persuaded him that he was far too important to the family to risk losing him, just because of his love of cricket.

Bridie couldn't stand his cricket hat though, and Matthew recalled her instructions when he'd left for Mr Pearce's house the night before their wedding. 'And you can tell him NOT to bring that awful hat tomorrow!'

Mr Pearce had laughed quietly to himself as he'd propped it on the dashboard of his car just before they walked into the church. 'Just to let her know that she doesn't always get her own way!' he'd said meaningfully.

Bill was laid on the grass with his wife, Beth, playing with Toby's baby sister, Amy, who had been born the previous autumn.

Bridie's middle brother, Nick, was sat on a deckchair, talking to his parents. Nick had pretty much taken over running the farm now. His father was finding it a struggle to let go of the reins entirely, and Mat watched as Nick listened carefully to whatever advice his father imparted to him.

Mat smiled. He knew that Nick always listened, despite the fact that he usually ended up doing things his way in the end. So far, he seemed to be doing a pretty good job of managing the farm. Miranda, Nick's wife, was laid on the grass beside her husband. Her bump seemed to be getting bigger every day.

Nick and Miranda seemed to have been going out with each other for years before there was any mention of marriage, and Mat had started to wonder if they'd ever manage to tie the knot. Bridie and Miranda were great friends, and from what Bridie had told him, Mat knew that Miranda was more than keen to settle down and start a family.

Nick, on the other hand, had always dragged his feet. It was never quite the right time for Nick. The farm always came first. If he wasn't rushing to get the hay harvested before the rain came, he was busy planting potatoes or shearing the sheep to talk seriously about getting married.

'We'll get to it one day,' was all they could ever get out of him, and Miranda had started to wonder if that day would ever actually come.

Farmers were always busy, and now with his father playing an increasingly smaller part, Nick was busier than ever.

There would never be a perfect time, so Bridie and Miranda had taken it upon themselves to arrange everything. They'd worked secretly, giggling and conspiring until finally, just before Christmas, they'd drawn a huge line through the Saturday in Nick's day-to-day diary. Beside that line they'd written, 'Town with Mat.' That was that.

Mat wasn't very keen on deception. He was actually a terrible liar. Everybody knew when he was trying to pull the wool over their eyes. Especially Bridie. Somehow, she knew whether or not he was telling the truth as soon as he opened his mouth.

Mat had no idea how she did it but she knew right enough. In the end, he'd found it simpler just to tell her the truth. It was so much better than the consequences. But, despite his reservations, Mat had agreed to play his part. His task was to drive Nick into town and to make a big thing about Nick dressing in something reasonably smart. Bridie had made him practice the lines – he was instructed on what to say. They'd be popping into the pub afterwards for a pint with some of Mat's friends from school.

Nick had been surprised when they'd arrived at the Registry office, and confused when he realised that most of his friends, and all of his family were there, every one of them in their Sunday Best.

When he'd seen Miranda waiting for him at the end of the room, he'd been too astounded to think of any more excuses…and so, a few months later, Miranda's second wish inevitably came true, and she was soon expecting her own little one.

Mat gazed admiringly at his wonderful, resourceful, wife. She never failed to amaze him.

Bridie was sat on the grass, her arms wrapped around her legs, gazing dreamily across the stream.

Mat smiled at her. 'Are you OK hun?' he said, softly.

Bridie turned and smiled at him, nodding.

'You were miles away,' he said. 'What were you thinking about?'

She turned her gaze back toward the stream.

'I was just thinking,' she said, quietly. 'That's my family over there, in the barrows. I've no idea who they were or what they were like, but they're my family.'

Mat smiled as he watched her face. He loved the dreamy, far-away look in her eyes.

'Then I got to thinking about all the women before me,' she continued. 'I was imagining them here, sat like we are, looking over the bridge. There have been so many of them, all through the years. Hundreds of them.'

'Too many to count, I'd imagine,' he replied, nodding.

'And then I got to thinking. One day I'll meet them all. Probably here, by the bridge.'

Mat didn't say anything, he was imagining too.

'Can you imagine what that will be like?' Bridie said, quietly. 'Hundreds of them, waiting here to meet me? I'd know some of them, like my gran and my great-gran. I can just about remember her. But I never met the rest.'

'Mmm,' he said. 'I guess that would have been difficult.'

Bridie turned and laughed at him.

'No, I mean, they'd all want to say hello. Can you imagine, hundreds of people waiting to talk to me, to welcome me?'

'Well, if it's anything like your family,' Mat said, smiling, 'it'll be bloody noisy!'

Bridie looked straight into his face, she let out a chuckle, and rolled her eyes.

'Idiot!' she snorted, punching him playfully on the arm.

Bridie glanced up at her approaching daughter.

'You alright sweetheart?' she asked. 'Enjoying your birthday?'

Brenda nodded in response, and sat down on the grass close to her mother.

'Mum, you know you said to me this morning that I was all grown up, now I'm thirteen?'

Bridie nodded, wondering where this conversation was heading.

'Well, I was thinking maybe now you could tell me about the first lady, the one who found the Home Stone? You always said you would when I was old enough? Well now you said yourself I'm grown up, so...'

Bridie sighed. 'Well, it's really a long story, so maybe not today. We have company. We can't just ignore them. It wouldn't be fair...'

'Please Mum?'

Bridie turned her head questioningly towards her husband. Mat returned her look with a smile, and raised his eyebrows.

She sighed again. 'Oh, alright,' she said. 'Settle yourself down then and pay attention. I will be asking questions later!'

Brenda laid down on the grass and rested her head in her mother's lap. Bridie smiled at her and ran her fingers through her daughter's hair.

'So, it begins with a girl with no name. They were moving fast.'

'Mum?'

'What?'

'Why doesn't she have a name?'

'I'll explain in a minute.'

'It just seems daft, that somebody wouldn't have a name. Everybody has a name.'

'Well, if you listen to the story, you'll find out.'

'Mum?'

'What now? Look, if you're going to interrupt all the time…'

'Sorry Mum…' Brenda sighed.

'So,' Bridie continued. 'They were moving very fast…'

After a while, Bridie glanced down at her daughter. Brenda was fast asleep. Bridie smiled at Matthew, and they both laughed quietly.

'Seems I'll be finishing the story another time.'

35

By the time school broke up a few weeks later, Mat was more than ready for a break.

It had been a long, hard year, and his new responsibilities as Head of English had taken time to get used to.

The unusually hot and humid summer term had made the boys irritable and impatient to be outside. He couldn't blame them. It felt the same way for him and the other staff.

All the same, there had been exams to get through, and it had taken a lot of patience and hard work to keep the boys focussed. O-levels first, then the all-important A-levels. They had some really bright lads in the upper-sixth this year, lads who could easily get places at the top universities…if only they could be persuaded to concentrate for a few more weeks. Somehow, he hoped they had succeeded.

They'd managed to pull even the most reluctant of their students through the last days of term.

Now Mat stood in the quad, watching the last of them running for their buses home. Results wouldn't be out for a while yet, but he was sure they'd have at least some decent successes amongst this excited, relieved, white-shirted crowd.

He peeled off his black master's gown as he made his way slowly back up the long, curving steps of the main stairwell, glad to be free of the weight of it all, at last. He enjoyed most of the traditions that went with working at the Grammar School, and was proud to wear the gown that marked him out as a teacher…but it really wasn't a comfortable tradition in summer heat like this, and he would be glad to see the back of it for a while. Thankfully, gowns were not compulsory attire for staff meetings.

As he made his way along the corridor towards the staff room, he reflected upon his first year as Head of English. He was still surprised that they'd given it to him. He knew he was terribly young for such seniority. Indeed, many of his team were quite a bit older and he was sure every bit as capable for the role. Probably more so, he imagined.

He'd been reluctant to put his name forward for it when the post was first advertised, and even when he wrote his application, he hadn't really been sure if he had enough experience.

Bridie had eventually persuaded him to try. He smiled. She'd done a lot more than just persuade. She had pushed, pulled, argued, cajoled and teased him for days. Every night when he'd got home, he would find the application forms in his place on the dinner table, with a pen at the ready. 'You always dither and dather,' she'd told him. 'But not this time, Matthew Crawford. This time I *will* make sure you do something about it.'

Eventually he had picked up the pen. She'd been right of course, and he'd later realised that many aspects of his life would have been a lot simpler if he'd just done as he was told in the first place.

In fact, Bridie had taken great joy in telling him just that. Several times.

Mat enjoyed the drive home that evening. It was warm as he drove with the sunroof open. He loved the scent of the country, especially in the summer. The smell of freshly cut grass reminded him that Nick would soon need his help with hay-making. He enjoyed that, and although he knew he would ache from head to foot for the first few days, he relished the opportunity to get outdoors and do something other than marking papers.

That was still a few weeks away though, and they had booked a short family holiday by the sea first.

Bridie and their daughter had talked of very little else for the last few weeks.

New clothes had been bought, and on Sunday mornings he'd been treated to fashion shows of the things they'd shopped for the previous day. He knew that whatever encouraging comments he might make, most of it would be taken back the following weekend, and exchanged for something else. He couldn't see the pleasure in it himself but the girls were thoroughly enjoying themselves.

***

The smells of cooking met his nose before he made it to the kitchen. He loved Bridie's cooking and his appetite was thoroughly awake by the time he opened the door.

'Hi sweetheart,' he called across the room. 'How was your day?'

While they ate, his daughter's running commentary on her last day at school disguised the fact that his wife had hardly spoken a word since he'd got home. She'd returned his kiss and had asked how his day had gone but hadn't had much to say since then. Not that she'd had much chance, given the constant chattering from the other side of the table.

Dinner was finished and Mat sat back in his chair, satisfied. He looked from Bridie to Brenda.

'Thanks, sweetheart, that was lovely.' Then he closed his eyes, as the two most important women in his life began their usual evening routine.

'Brenda. Dishes please?'

'Why is it always me?' his daughter asked, rolling her eyes.

'Erm…because I asked you?'

'Why is it always my job? I didn't ask for it…'

'I don't see why it's *such* an inconvenience. I don't ask you to do much else, do I?' Bridie told her.

'Huh!' the usual retort. 'You make me tidy my room, don't you?'

'So? It's your room! Who else should do it?'

'OK, girls,' Mat interjected.

'Do we have to do this every ni—'

'And I have to look after Beth's baby!'

'What's that got to do with anything?' his wife gasped.

'Oh, per…lease! *YOU* make me do it!'

'Actually, no I don't. They pick you up, they pay you to babysit.'

'So?'

'Look, you two,' Mat tried again, 'it's the end of term. I don't mind doing the dishes, just this once?'

His daughter opened her eyes widely and accusingly at her mother.

'No, Mat,' his wife said, folding her arms decisively. 'The dishes are Brenda's job.'

'And anyway,' she continued, facing her daughter down, not letting the argument go. 'It's only every couple of months, and you do get to watch TV with Toby, even on a school night.'

'That doesn't even count? Like, it's homework? We *have* to watch it!'

Mat wasn't at all sure about this counter-point. His daughter now looked at him, anticipating his questions.

'It's "drama" Dad – we have to watch *Neighbours* and *Eastenders*, so we can talk about, well, how they did stuff.'

Mat still had his doubts, but thought better of it in expressing them.

'Right!' he said in his best teacher's voice. 'Enough is enough! Brenda – dishes! Bridie – front room!'

And that was the end of that.

While Brenda reluctantly and noisily attacked the washing up, he gazed at his wife's face while she watched the television.

'Are you OK, sweetheart?'

'Yeah,' she said, keeping her eyes fixed on the programme. 'Yeah, I'm OK. Just a bit tired, is all.'

'You need a holiday,' he said. 'Only a couple more days.'

Bridie smiled.

'Yes,' she said. 'I think that's just what I need. I think that's what we all need. It'll do us all the world of good.'

Holidays for Bridie and Mat were special times.

They'd honeymooned in Cornwall. Bridie had loved it. They'd spent their days on the beach at Hayle, and it hadn't really mattered much whether it was sunny or not.

They used Mat's big university umbrella wherever they went. They'd sat under it, while it shielded Bridie's fair skin from the strong rays of the sun; they'd hung onto it and while it protected them from being sand-blasted by the gusty onshore wind, and they'd giggled under it as the rain dripped off its edges and scattered the sand all around them.

They'd travelled to Paris one Easter, towing their tiny daughter with them. She'd learned to walk on a grassy bank, bathed in sunshine, by a lake in a park near Montmartre. The artists in the shadow of the ancient church at Notre Dame had impressed Bridie greatly and she'd proudly hung one of their charcoal portraits of her over their bed when they'd got home.

Mat's over-riding memories of that time were the colours of the sunshine, gold and amber, and of Bridie laughing as they'd almost fallen down some steps. They were walking down from Montmartre towards the river at the time.

Most of their summers, though, were spent at home. They would picnic at the bridge. They'd take their little girl to the park in town, or to open days at nearby gardens. Sometimes they went to the zoo, a couple of hour's drive away, though Bridie wasn't really keen on that. She didn't enjoy seeing the animals so caged up. It just didn't seem right to her. But they'd loved those times. They were family times, just for them, and they were enough.

This year, though, they'd decided to travel further. They'd be adventurous. Mat's increased salary had made a difference, and since Christmas, Bridie had spent hours poring through travel brochures. In the end, they'd chosen Malta.

'It's just what we need,' she'd said. 'Warm and sunny and they speak English!'

'And we get to fly in an aeroplane!' Mat had said enthusiastically. They'd never flown before and the thought of it added an extra layer of excitement for him.

Bridie hadn't thought about how they'd get there.

'Oh, yes…thrilling…' she'd said, unenthusiastically.

36

'Isn't this great?' Mat asked, addressing no one in particular. He was really enjoying their visit to Valletta.

They'd just finished what they'd both agreed was the best lemon cheesecake ever.

Mat leaned back comfortably in his chair, stretched his legs out in front of him and waited for his coffee to cool. As far as he was concerned, it was a perfect day.

The sun poured down on them from a startlingly blue sky, a warm breeze played against the bare skin of their legs and arms, and their neighbours who were sat at the outdoor tables were relaxed and happy, grateful for the shade offered by the café's enormous parasols.

His daughter grinned at him and nodded enthusiastically, her mouth full of ice-cream.

He glanced over at Bridie. She looked better now than she had when they arrived, but she still seemed tired and drawn, he thought.

'Are you OK, sweetheart?' he asked, concerned.

She'd been a lot quieter than normal before they'd left home. Mat had put it down to her fear of flying, and she had clearly not enjoyed the journey. She'd sat between them on the aeroplane.

Brenda had taken the window seat, and supplied them with an animated commentary all the way. Bridie had closed her eyes tightly during the take-off, gripping his and their daughters' hands, until Brenda had complained. Then she had sat, tense and nervous, for the whole journey. Landing had been another exquisite torture for her, and she had descended the stairs to the tarmac gratefully, but shakily.

'Do you want me to find out about trains and ferries for the trip back?' he asked, peripherally noticing his daughter's shoulders slump with disappointment at the prospect. She'd loved flying, and their coach transfer from the airport to St Paul's Bay had been filled with her ideas about becoming an air hostess.

Bridie glanced over at him and shook her head.

'No,' she said. 'Honestly, I'll be fine. It would take ages. Anyway, it would cost a fortune.'

'It'd be worth it, to save you worrying about flying home,' he suggested. 'Then you might start to enjoy the holiday properly?'

She shook her head again, but didn't reply.

Mat decided he would look into it anyway, just to find out what the options were. Their hotel wasn't up to much, a bit more basic than they might have hoped, but the food was acceptable and the staff were friendly. He was sure they'd help him find out.

If there was a way to get home that didn't involve flying, it had to be better than having her holiday spoiled. They'd been in Malta for four days, just over half-way through their stay. There was still time for her to enjoy it without having to worry about the trip home.

They'd spent the first couple of days exploring the area around the hotel. They'd found some nice cafés and bars and had spent the long, warm evenings listening to some good live entertainers at outdoors venues along the sea front.

The hotel had organised a coach trip around the island, which had given them a chance to glimpse some of the places they might not have found otherwise. They'd stopped for lunch in Marsaxlokk, a little fishing village in the south of the island.

They only had an hour or so, but Bridie had managed to buy a pretty embroidered table cloth from the open-air market there. They just had time to enjoy a lunch of fresh sea salmon, bony but tasty, in one of the harbour-side restaurants. They decided they'd like to come back for a longer visit, under their own steam, if there was time later in the week.

Mat sipped his coffee, distractedly watching tourists meander past them down Republic Street. Waiters, carrying trays of drinks and enormous ice-creams, emerged from the Caffe Cordina opposite. They dodged expertly through the crowds to deliver heavy loads to the tables where they were sitting in the Piazza Regina.

As the door opened, he caught a glimpse inside the café. Heavy chrome and plate glass display cases. There was a huge, old-fashioned coffee machine. An immense, decorated mirror behind the long counter. It looked traditional. Bridie loved traditional things.

He glanced over to tell her about it. She was massaging her temples. She looked back at him.

'What?' she asked, irritably.

'Are you sure you're OK?'

'Mat! Will you stop?' she snapped. 'I'm fine! Honestly! Just a stupid headache, OK?'

'How long have you had it? Why didn't you say?'

'Look, it's just a headache, alright? I've had it a few days. Probably just the heat. Happy now?'

'OK,' he muttered. 'Have you taken something for it?'

'No,' she said, frowning at him. 'I forgot to pack anything.'

'Right then,' he replied, decisively. 'We'll find a pharmacy on the way back to the bus and get something. If you'd said something earlier, we could have sorted it.'

Bridie just frowned, and pulled a sarcastic face at him.

Between them, their daughter looked from one to the other.

'God!' she sighed, wiping ice-cream from her face with the back of her hand. 'You two are SO embarrassing sometimes!'

***

Bridie was still asleep when he awoke, so he sat on the small balcony to read for a while. She was still sleeping when his daughter awoke, so they left her in bed while they went to find some breakfast.

She was up, showered and dressed by the time they got back. She smiled as they entered. She seemed brighter this morning.

'Sorry darling,' he said, 'Brenda was hungry. We didn't want to disturb you.'

'That's fine,' she replied. 'I'll get a cake or something later. I feel much better now. I think the sleep must have done me good.'

'Even so,' Mat said. 'We'll have a quiet day today. If you're still alright tomorrow, we can do something.'

They went for coffee and cake in one of the local cafés, then for a quiet walk along the sea front. They sat on a bench for a while, watching boats coming and going.

Children were swimming off the rocky shore. When Brenda made it clear that she was getting bored and irritable, they went back to the hotel, so that she could go and swim in the pool.

She played for a while with her new best friend Petra, a girl who was the same age as Brenda, and who was staying in an apartment a few doors down the corridor from them.

'Do you know what?' Bridie asked, stirring herself.

'What?' he asked in reply.

'This is getting pretty boring now,' she said. 'Let's do something.'

Mat put his book down. 'If you're feeling up to it?' he said. 'What would you like to do?'

'Let's go out somewhere, we'll find one of those cranky old buses you like so much, and we'll go wherever it takes us.'

'Suits me!' he said, pushing his chair back.

'Come on Brenda,' she called to her daughter, 'your father's taking us out to lunch!'

Mat was fascinated by the yellow buses they'd seen all over the island. Most of the service buses were reasonably modern but some were really quite unusual. The ones he was most interested in seemed ancient in comparison with the others. They had no doors, just openings with steps and rails to help passengers climb aboard. Some seemed to have no windows either, or perhaps they'd been wound down so far, they couldn't be seen. Mat reckoned that was probably quite sensible, given the climate.

All of them had been highly decorated and personalised by their drivers.

The cabs were like shrines, with photos of family, pictures of religious figures, beads and crucifixes all carefully displayed on every spare surface. On many, the bodywork had been covered with intricate designs over the standard yellow, while on the inside, the bench seats were of ancient slatted wood, rather than upholstered.

So far on their excursions, they'd been ferried around on the more standard buses, but Mat really wanted to ride in one of the old-fashioned ones, if he could before they went home.

As they reached the bus depot, they spotted what they were looking for. The driver, well used to the attention his bus usually received from tourists, proudly posed beside it for photographs, and then they were off.

They had no idea where it would take them, or what time it would arrive, or indeed whether they'd be able to find anything to eat when they got there.

'Doesn't matter,' Bridie told her daughter, in answer to her many questions, 'we're on holiday. What we do, where we go and when we get there doesn't matter. We're going on an adventure!'

By the time the bus stopped at Medina, they were all quite grateful to get off. It definitely had been an adventure, not a particularly comfortable one, and Bridie made it clear that they'd be waiting for a bus with upholstered seats for the journey home. Mat was quite happy to agree. His curiosity had been satisfied.

As they made their way into the ancient city, they were all struck by the atmosphere. It certainly lived up to the name the driver had given it – 'The Silent City'. Even Brenda spoke in unusually hushed tones.

'How come it's so quiet?' she whispered, as they walked across a cobbled square.

'They probably don't let noisy little girls live here!' her mother retorted gleefully.

'Really?' asked her daughter seriously. Bridie just gave her a despairing look.

They looked for a café or a restaurant where they could get a late lunch, and found one perched high on the city walls. At their daughter's insistence, they shared a pizza. The view was outstanding.

They could see for miles, across villages and towns, churches and hotels, all the way to the shining blue Mediterranean in the distance. While they ate, Mat spotted what looked like runways on the flat plain far below them.

A waiter told them that it was an old war-time aerodrome, part of which had been converted into a shopping centre. They'd re-used many of the old huts and buildings as shops and workshops.

'This is Malta's unofficial motto,' he told them. Waste not, want not. We don't throw much away!'

Every now and then, aeroplanes climbed from the new airport, slightly to one side. Mat and his daughter were fascinated to watch them pass so close. They were almost able to make out the passengers inside them.

Bridie didn't look. She really didn't need reminding that soon she'd be a passenger on one of those planes.

Mat caught her look, and explained what the hotel staff had told him about ferries and trains. He showed her a piece of paper they'd written out for him, detailing the journey.

'I thought it might be possible to do it overland,' he said. 'And I was right. It's a bit complicated, with a few changes along the way but it could certainly be done, if it would make you feel more comfortable?'

Bridie's eyes glanced through the notes, widening markedly when they found the cost.

'How much?' she hissed, in alarm. 'You must be joking, Mat! We couldn't possibly afford all that! And even if we could, look how long it would take!'

'Might be better than flying?'

She knew as well as he did, that they could afford it. He could easily have used his inheritance money for it, but Bridie had always resisted any attempt to use that for anything short of a full-scale emergency. She always referred to it as their 'rainy day' fund, and firmly maintained that if they couldn't afford something out of their salaries, then they would just have to make do without. Mat had come to consider that it would have to be a rainy day of biblical proportions before she'd even think about breaking into their savings.

'No,' she said, 'definitely not. No way! Anyway, the thought of spending that much time with Brenda sulking at me all the way because I'd stopped her getting on a plane is just not bearable. No, honestly. I'll be fine.'

'You sure?' he asked, tentatively.

'I'll fly, OK?' She held her hand up to stop him responding. 'Just don't make me watch them, that's all. Let's leave it at that.'

'How much was it, Dad?' Brenda piped up.

'Never you mind!' her mother answered for him sharply, giving her daughter a withering look. 'A lot more than you've got in your savings anyway, young lady.'

'Oh…' said Brenda quietly, wishing she hadn't asked. She wasn't very good at saving money.

***

They had an early dinner on the last evening of their holiday. They'd decided to eat at an Italian restaurant they'd found a few minutes' walk away from their hotel. Bridie had already packed most of their suitcases, keeping out only what they needed for the evening and for the journey home. She'd planned to enjoy a relaxing evening on the balcony, so she was a bit surprised when Mat asked if they fancied a walk, once they'd finished eating. He wanted to go and explore the red fortified tower they'd noticed whilst on a sightseeing coach the day before.

'It doesn't look like it's too far along the coast-road,' he told them. 'Maybe an hour or so's walk there and back.'

Neither of the girls seemed at all enthusiastic at the idea. Both just wanted to sit on the balcony and relax, so he elected to go by himself.

When they had made themselves comfortable, Brenda surprised her mother by asking if she'd tell her some more of the story, she'd shared on her birthday. Bridie agreed, as long as Brenda promised not to fall asleep again this time. After some debate about where the story should begin again from, Bridie settled to the task.

'So, you remember that they had arrived at a stockade with a few people inside?'

Brenda nodded.

'And you remember that he'd introduced them both to the man who seemed to be the leader of the group by saying, "I am Far-Sight," as he approached the men's fire. "And this is my woman, her name is Stone…"'

Matthew arrived at the apartment just in time to hear the last few words of the story, and to hear Bridie tell her daughter that she'd have to stop there.

'Sorry darling, I really can't tell you any more tonight. My head is absolutely splitting now. I need to get to bed. We've got a busy day tomorrow.'

Brenda got up and kissed her mother on the forehead.

'Sorry Mum, but thanks for telling me the story so far. It's really fascinating. And it's important for me to know how our family started.'

37

His exam papers had arrived shortly after they'd got home. The dead-line for their return was always a tight one, and from past experience, he knew that to get the task done in time, he was going to have to concentrate hard.

He'd marked exam papers every summer for the last few years. His family knew how much hard work went into getting them completed, and made a point of leaving him alone to get on with it. They saw him at mealtimes but that was about it.

This year was no exception, and once the papers had arrived, he rarely emerged from his tiny study. Bridie would take him cups of tea and coffee occasionally, but other than that, she didn't disturb him.

One evening, as she knocked on his study door to call him for din-ner, his daughter waited for him to come out. She looked worried.

'What's up, sweetheart?' he asked, wondering how much it was going to cost him this time.

'Do you think Mum's OK, Dad?' she asked.

'Why? Is something the matter?'

'It's just that she seems so tired all the time,' she explained. 'Even more than when we were on holiday. And she's always taking tablets for her headaches.' Mat promised her he'd look into it.

After dinner, he decided that he'd take the rest of the evening off. He was ahead of schedule for a change, and only had a few papers left to mark. One evening off wouldn't hurt.

As they settled into the living room and while Brenda began the washing up, for once without the usual protest, he asked his wife how she was feeling.

'Oh,' she said, 'I'm fine. Why do you ask?'

He explained about their daughter's concern but she waved them away.

'No, just a bit tired, that's all. Nothing to worry about.'

'Still,' he persevered, 'I don't think it would do any harm to get it checked out, eh? You've been like this for a few weeks now. Probably just need a tonic or something?'

Eventually, Bridie promised she would make an appointment with the doctor. Then she looked at him, quizzically.

'Is this why you're taking the evening off?'

'We worry about you. I worry about you. I just wanted to make sure you're OK.'

'In that case, Matthew Crawford, you had better get back to your marking. The sooner you're finished, the sooner we can get on with the rest of the summer.'

As he settled back at his desk, he couldn't help but think about her.

The fee he received for marking the exam papers was good, and would certainly help towards the inevitable costs of Christmas but sometimes he wondered if it was worth the amount of time he had to spend locked away from his family. Maybe he'd think twice before agreeing to do it next year.

Bridie couldn't get an appointment at the surgery for several days. It was always difficult to get appointments there but during the summer with so many of their staff taking leave, it was even more so.

'I'll be alright again by then, seemed hardly worth the bother,' she'd said when he asked. 'I'll leave it a week or so and call them again, if I don't feel any better.'

***

Before Mat knew it, the hay-making season was upon them. Nick always needed as much help as he could get at this time of year, and Mat was happy to lend a hand. He wasn't terribly expert at it, and was always being teased for being so slow, but it was all light-hearted and he just plodded on, doing his best.

They started early and finished late during hay-making. It was hard work, and as he'd predicted, he ached all over for the first few days. By the time he got home, late in the evening, just about all he was fit for was a shower, something to eat and bed. Bridie always insisted that he showered first, before sitting to the table. The hard work and fresh air always made him feel hungrier than usual, and he would very much have preferred to eat first, but she wouldn't have any of it.

'It's bad enough trying to keep this place clean without you spreading grass seed and dirt everywhere,' she told him. 'And anyway, you stink. Get in the shower before I hose you down in the yard!'

Mat smiled. She said the same thing every year. It was exactly what her mother used to say when she ran the kitchen. No doubt his daughter would say the same thing when it was her turn. He quite liked that, the continuity of it all, traditions upheld and reestablished, year after year, and he played his part to perfection, groaning as he made his way upstairs, usually after stealing a bit of something from the table as he passed.

He was never sure if she'd put something there for him to grab. He wouldn't have been surprised. It was the sort of thing she would do. He smiled as he walked up the stairs, her voice ringing in his ears.

'I saw that! That's one less for you, mister!'

While the hot water soothed his aches away, Mat thought back over the day. For all his aches and pains, for all the sunburn and blisters, he'd thoroughly enjoyed it. It had been a classic hay-making day.

They'd started early, as they always did. Mat had stood with the others at the edge of the first field. He never grew tired of days like this. Despite the early hour, it was already warm.

The sun rose above the hedges, into a crystal-blue sky. Hardly a breeze, just enough to occasionally rustle the dry seed-heads of the hay before them. Watching the eddies echoing across the field, he was reminded of their honeymoon in Cornwall, and the hours they'd spent watching the waves gathering in the ocean, eventually petering out high up on the sands where they sat, just out of their reach.

Unlike many farms, they still made hay here in the traditional way, with scythes and rakes, forks and haystacks.

Nick had been keen to try new ways but given the steepness of some of the fields and the rough, undulating ground of the rest, his options had been limited.

He'd have liked to have brought in one of the enormous combine harvesters that some of the neighbouring farms used, but they really weren't suited to places like Home Farm, with its hills and small fields.

Last year, he'd tried using a petrol-driven grass mower, but that hadn't worked as well as he'd hoped either. The metre-wide cutting blades at the front of the machine had cut the hay well enough, but keeping the machine on a straight even track, especially over some of the steeper places, had been difficult.

He'd persevered for a morning, but by lunchtime the thing had been loaded back onto the trailer. Fair enough, it had cut the hay a bit quicker than they would have managed by hand, but when he'd stooped down to smell the hay, even Nick had had to proclaim it a failed experiment.

'Stinks of petrol and exhaust fumes,' he'd announced, with a look of distaste on his face. 'Cows won't eat this. A waste of time. Glad I only hired the stupid thing!' So, it was back to scything the fields by hand. They'd left the mower-cut hay where it was. Nick was cross about the waste, but spoiled hay was no good for winter silage. Nothing but the best would do for Nick's cows.

Mat had been glad that Mr Ambrose had managed to persuade Nick to hire the machine first, before buying one, just to make sure it was going to work as well as Nick had hoped.

He knew full well that, if the experiment had failed, the hay-cutter would have been left out in the fields for weeks, gently rusting, eventually to be consigned to the Old Barn to join the host of other disused machinery that the family had tried out over the years.

The Old Barn, down by the end of the unmade section of the lane that led to Home Farm, had once stored hay and animal feed. It had become a general storage place for all sorts, what Mat could only describe as rubbish mainly, but various members of the family had decided the rubbish might be useful one day.

He'd tentatively suggested, shortly after marrying Bridie, that it might make a good garage for their growing fleet of cars. That suggestion was met with general disapproval, on the grounds that the present contents were far too valuable just to throw away.

Everyone knew that it would never get used, but it didn't seem to matter at all. They couldn't bring themselves to throw anything away.

There was even an ancient steam tractor stored in the barn, a relic of a time, nearly a century before, when a previous moderniser had reckoned that mechanisation was the way forward. Now it had become one of the many reconstruction projects that Bill had promised himself he would tackle, as soon as he had the time.

Mat wasn't about to hold his breath until that great day dawned, though.

As Mat had stood at the edge of the field, he couldn't help but smile. Nick noticed, and smiled back at him.

'Beautiful, eh?'

Mat had nodded happily. It was indeed, a beautiful sight. They'd picked the perfect moment to start hay-making. The long grass was dry. Its brown seed heads waved and rustled at them gently in the light breeze, inviting their attention. In amongst the dry grass there was a riot of colour. Wild flowers, self-seeded, or introduced by birds. Red, blue, gold and pink flower heads danced happily in the early morning sunshine.

Perhaps sensing the hay-makers' presence and intention, bees panicked to gather as much pollen from the flower-heads as they could, before they were mown down. They'd have to be quick. Mowing was about to start. Mat knew that other wildlife inhabited the hay-fields. Rabbits, field mice, sometimes the occasional hare, had all revelled in the long grass, left peaceful and undisturbed since last season.

He couldn't see any this morning, though. It was as if some ancient memory, instilled across the countless generations that had inhabited these fields, had warned them that their home was about to be dismantled. They would have to move on to what would become next year's hayfields, while Nick's cows would take over from them in these, to enjoy the fresh new growth of grass left in the wake of the scythes.

Nick glanced around at his team. His father and his brother stood ready. Mat was still daydreaming, of course. Nick cleared his throat to garner his attention.

'Ready boys?' he asked simply, and seeing that they were, started the day with a swift sweep of his scythe to give himself a bit of working room. 'Off we go then.'

As he had every year since his father had given him the lead, Nick broke into the song that would give the team their rhythm.

'*One man went to mow, went to mow a meadow. One man and his dog went to mow a meadow.*'

With each song word, Nick's scythe slid smoothly through the long hay before him, depositing the cut hay in a small pile at the end of each scythe-stroke.

Mat smiled as he heard the familiar, rhythmic '*Shhwwp. Shhwwp*' of the first scythe.

He spat on his hands, and readied them on the wooden handles of his own. He lifted the scythe comfortably in front of him, judging its balance and position for his first sweep.

Once Nick had moved forward a few paces, his father picked up the song and sang his own line, it was designed to overlap Nick's, knowing that the few paces separating them would mean that there was little danger of accidentally scything Nick's feet off as he went.

'*Two men went to mow, went to mow a meadow. Two men, one man and his dog went to mow a meadow.*'

Mat was always 'four men'. He was always the last in the line. His lack of skill and speed dictated that he had to be. Otherwise, he'd be a danger to himself and to everyone else. Mat didn't mind. He knew his limitations. He was just happy he was included at all.

They moved gently, rhythmically, and surprisingly quickly across the field. Every now and then Mat spotted the tell-tale signs of a small animal, obviously reluctant to leave home until the last possible moment, scurrying away through the uncut grass. By the time Mat reached them, the others were stood waiting for him to catch up. As he joined them, Nick called over to him, teasingly.

'Still with us then, Crawford?'

Mat laughed. It was the same every year. He was used to their teasing.

Nick cast an expert eye down the windrow lines, the natural deposit of cut hay left behind at the end of every stroke of the scythe.

Later in the day these long lines of hay would be gathered up, raked and rolled into huge balls, to be left at one end of the field. Then, just before they finished for the night, the piles of cut hay would be brought together and stacked on drying racks, the outer surface carefully combed downwards to allow any rain that might fall overnight to run off without soaking the hay inside.

Only at the end of the hay-making season would the racked hay be gathered onto a trailer and taken to the yard for baling and storage. If they'd judged the weather right, all of the hay would be dry and sweet, and would stay that way all through the winter.

Looking back over the area they'd cut, Mat watched a small flock of birds land, keen to take advantage of the worms and insects exposed by the newly low-cut grass. He smiled as a couple of magpies made an ungainly landing, skidding to a halt a pace or two from their initial touch-down. They picked themselves up and strutted to and fro, proud and erect, as if trying desperately to pretend that their crash-landing wasn't entirely their fault.

They didn't stay long, perhaps too embarrassed to remain under his watchful, knowing gaze.

Checking the windrows, Nick raised an eyebrow and nodded his head.

'Pretty straight,' he said. 'Even yours, Mat! Not too many divots either, surprisingly. We might make a half-decent hay-maker of you yet!'

That had pleased Mat. He was used to being the 'fourth man', and being teased about his lack of prowess, but this year he'd really, really wanted to make a good impression.

Most evenings for a week or so before hay-making was due to start, he'd secretly borrowed a scythe from the barn and practised his swing. It had helped to build up his shoulder muscles, wasted after a year of sitting at a desk, and the practice had certainly helped to improve his swing. The trick, he'd found over the years, was getting just the right balance.

Mr Ambrose, who had coached Mat years before, had always re-ferred to the practised action as 'getting in the swing.' The swing had to be about a quarter turn, with hips and shoulders in line, while at the same time making sure that the blade of the scythe was kept just an inch or so above the ground. It wasn't easy to achieve, but this year's practice had helped.

Hopefully nobody would notice the scratches on the blade he'd borrowed. It would probably take ages to grind them out, but it was only an old scythe, so hopefully nobody would bother about them.

'Right lads!' Nick commanded. 'Move down, sharpen up, and move on!'

And so, the process started again, and would continue all day until the field was cleared.

Matthew didn't wear a watch while hay-making. None of them did. Inevitably, sweat and dust would gather under the strap and soon create an irritating sore that would take ages to heal. Instead, they judged the time by the sun. They set off for the fields just after the sun rose, and would finish work just as it set again in the evening. They'd stop for lunch as the sun was at its highest.

The routine at lunchtime was also part of tradition. There wasn't time for the men to come down from the fields, to wash, and to eat at the table, so Bridie would always bring something up to where they were working. It was nearly always the same. Cheese sandwiches, maybe some biscuits, or an apple, a bottle of water and a flask of tea.

They'd collapse gratefully onto the ground to eat, surrounded by dust motes and small flying things, leaning back against the tractor tyres and hedges. They'd set to work again, and work solidly until it was almost too dark to see.

Today, though, it was his daughter who brought their lunch. Mat was instantly worried.

'Is Mum OK?' he asked, concerned.

'Mum's asleep,' she told him.

'She's been taking a nap in the mornings, and sometimes going to bed in the afternoons, but today she was in a deep sleep, I didn't want to wake her up. So I brought lunch.' She smiled.

'Was that OK?' She was clearly nervous that she'd done something wrong.

'No, it's fine sweetheart,' he reassured her. 'Thank you. I was just worried that Mum might be poorly.'

As she turned to leave them to eat, he called her back.

'Please tell Mum that she's to ring the surgery this afternoon, to make an appointment. Say I said so.'

Brenda looked almost close to tears. Was this what she'd feared all along? Did she think he hadn't listened?

'Don't worry, sweetheart,' he continued quietly. 'I'm sure every-thing will be OK. Like Mum said, she'll be back to her normal self in no time. Just that I'd feel better if she had a tonic or something.'

38

Bridie had asked him to be there. Or had he insisted on it? He couldn't quite remember. It didn't matter, he wanted to be there.

All he could hear were the bells ringing in his ears. Church bells, like the ones they could hear sometimes up at Home Farm, if the wind was in the right direction. Church bells calling the faithful to prayer.

'Nothing we can do. Nothing we can do. Nothing we can do. Nothing we can do...'

On and on and on, the words struck him, just like the bells.

It wasn't fair. He couldn't get away from it all. Those bells wouldn't stop echoing around his head.

Then he heard his wife's breathless, whispered question.

'How long?'

Those words pierced him straight in the middle of his forehead. For a moment, the bells froze, and clattered. Shattering his world.

If he'd been at school, he would have planned a strategy to get them through. He would have written lesson plans. He would have persuaded his students, cajoled them, perhaps ridiculed them for their lack of application, but eventually, he would have inspired them to achieve greatness, and to soar to heights they never thought they could achieve.

How was he supposed to manage this? How was he supposed to help his family through this? More importantly, how was he supposed to help Bridie through it all? What were the milestones, the markers?

What was success? As far as he could see, there was no success. He could inspire nobody. He didn't want the sort of success the doctors had spoken of.

He could think of nothing, nothing at all, but the prospect of losing his Bridie.

He'd spoken to the Head, of course. He'd had no choice. He felt useless to the school in his present state.

He was twelve years old again, waiting nervously for his interview with Mr Parkes.

'Look here…rotten luck old chap…all gone…be a man…Matron will sort you out…Mr Pearce…'

Those bloody stupid bells again, he could hear them in the distance. Please would somebody stop those bells.

He waited until the Head had finished shuffling his papers, then he'd delivered the news, poured it all out.

'Oh, dear me…' the Head had started. 'My dear chap, I'm so sorry. Please take as much time as you need. Come and go as you please. We'll fill in the gaps. You need to look after Mrs Crawford now and your daughter, of course. Please let me know if there's anything you need. Anything at all.'

He'd had to stop the car on the way home. He couldn't see where he was going. Those stupid bells, he could have sworn he could still hear them…

***

'Mat?'

'Yes sweetheart?'

'Come to bed?'

'In a minute.'

He wanted to go with her. He wanted to be with her, to love her always, forever. He knew he wouldn't be able to sleep. He knew if he climbed into bed, she wouldn't sleep because he couldn't sleep. She needed rest. She needed normal and ordinary. He couldn't relax. How was he supposed to do that?

She'd asked him for normal, ordinary. But what did that mean now? Nothing was ordinary. Nothing would ever be normal again. How could it be, if she wasn't here.

She was the centre of his world. Everything spun around her. Everything, and how could his world turn, if she wasn't there to make it happen.

She wanted him to hold her. She needed him to hold her. He needed to hold her forever in his arms. Always and forever, just like they'd always said. Like they'd always promised.

The world was spinning too fast. He couldn't keep up. Running. Breathless.

'I'll just put this cup in the sink.'

Ordinary. Normal.

'OK, see you in a moment.'

Bridie didn't want any breakfast. Mat made her some toast anyway. As he spread butter on it, she went and sat in her usual place at the kitchen table.

Mat glanced over at her, noting that she'd worn the jumper she usually put on to do housework. She'd bought it to wear at Christmas years before. It had originally been bright red, her favourite colour, though now it was looking faded and dull. The hem had always been loose fitting, but over time the collar and sleeves had become stretched and baggy, which only served to emphasise how much weight she'd lost from her neck and arms over the past few months.

Mat felt as though she was fading away before his eyes.

As he reached for the jar of marmalade, his eyes dropped momen-tarily to her legs, and he wondered to himself why he hadn't noticed before how baggy her jeans had become.

He'd always loved the way she'd had to stretch her jeans over her thighs to pull them up. He thought she had lovely legs, but she'd moaned about them periodically, claiming that she'd have to go on a diet before long.

Now, he reflected, her legs were about as thin as they had been when he'd first met her, when they were both in their early teens.

Realising that he'd been holding his breath, he had to force himself to breathe properly again. It was something that he'd caught himself doing more and more lately.

Mat placed Bridie's toast on the table in front of her, and went back to fetch their cups of tea.

Bridie glanced down at the plate before her and thanked him. Mat noticed that, while she sipped her tea, she left the toast untouched.

They sat in silence for a while. Then she reached across the table and seized his hand.

'OK,' she said. 'We need to be practical.'

Mat was amazed at how calm she was. His insides were in turmoil. His mind was seizing up from the swirling, gnawing emotions he was feeling. She was as calm as he had ever seen her.

'First up,' she said, 'Brenda gets the house. I know everybody lives here. I know it's Mum's house at the moment, on paper, but she'd have left it to me eventually. It's always passed down to the eldest daughter. Not the eldest boy, not the husband. Always the daughter. So I won't be here, that doesn't matter. That just means that my Brenda is the next in line. OK?'

'Doesn't your mum already know this?' he asked.

'Yes, of course she does. There's no question about it. Never has been. Never will be. I just need to be sure. I just need it…you know…written down somewhere, so that I know it will happen the way I want it.'

Mat understood. 'Then that, my darling, will be the way it will be. Just as you want it. Don't worry.'

'You'll write it down for me? Please, I just need to know that it will happen that way. I know it will, but I need you to make sure it will. Will you write it down for me? Please. Please,' she implored.

Mat couldn't bear the look on her face. She was so desperate, in so much need of reassurance, that it hurt him, physically. He would have agreed to anything, absolutely anything, if it would have given her comfort.

'Would you take Brenda out for a walk, please Mat? I'm starting to worry about her a bit now. She hasn't left the house for days. She hasn't seen her friends for ages. I know she's worried…you know, about everything, but I think she needs a bit of normality back in her life. She'll be back at school soon, which will help, but she needs to be out for a change, getting some fresh air. Maybe you could take her to look for blackberries or something? She's always loved doing that.'

Neither Mat nor Brenda wanted to go out and leave her alone, but Bridie insisted. As they pulled on boots and coats, and made their way resignedly towards the back door, Bridie called after them.

'And don't forget to take carrier bags with you!'

As they walked through the front gate and out into the lane, Mat looked at Brenda and said, 'Right! Mum said you were the expert at finding blackberries. Where should we start looking?'

'Up here Dad,' she told him. 'Me and Mum found loads last year. Look! There's some already!'

It didn't take long before their fingers started to turn purple with dye from the blackberries. As their carrier bag grew heavier, Mat found himself really rather enjoying the experience. Brenda proved to be adept at finding the sometimes quite elusive fruit, but she often needed help to harvest the higher ones.

Mat was enlisted to reach up to the highest places, and into the deeper recesses. He did his best to get as many as he could, but it was a slow process. Thorns grabbed his coat sleeves and scratched his arms and hands, quite painfully at times, and he wasn't at all impressed by the number of spider webs he had to push through. But he kept going.

Eventually, they realised that juice was beginning to seep through the bottom of the carrier bag from fruit squashed by the weight of the crop on top of them, so they stopped picking. Mat found a low tree branch a little further up the lane, and tied the bag there so that they could collect it later. Then they carried on walking.

'Which way do you want to go now?' he asked her.

'Let's go this way, Dad,' she told him. 'It's nice up there.'

As they walked, Brenda kept up a constant stream of chatter. She pointed out various things to him, in case he'd missed seeing the biggest cobweb in the world, or hadn't realised that those are Guernsey cows in that field, not Jerseys, or that he'd failed to hear a particular bird singing.

'Listen Dad! That's a blackbird! Hear it?' When he mentioned that he hadn't, she chastised him.

'Then you're not listening properly! Stop a minute, and just *listen*!'

They walked on, and Mat started to realise how much he'd missed simply breathing in the fresh air of the countryside he was so familiar with, and how much he'd missed feeling the sun on his skin.

He started to appreciate also how much he'd missed by simply not paying attention to the passing seasons.

His year was so dictated by the academic cycle, the constant grind of lesson planning, homework marking and exams, that it was easy to miss the passing subtleties of the natural year, which were actually happening all around him.

He hardly registered the transition from winter into spring, not noticing those moments when the days started to feel a little longer, and the air around him began to feel a little less chilly. The change from spring into summer completely passed him by.

Generally, the onset of autumn went quite unnoticed, until the weather turned frosty, and the trees were pretty much bare of their leaves.

Today, though, he felt that he could smell the subtle change in the air that occurred as the summer's heat started to dissipate, and when early morning sunshine started to give way to the early morning mist that would soon enough turn to ice on his car windscreen.

Today he was just beginning to feel a real and growing connection to the natural world around him, and he suddenly realised that this was because, through his daughter's constant chatter, she was introducing him to her world.

He felt that he knew these lanes, fields, hedgerows, and trees very well…but he didn't know them in the same way as she did.

'Me and Mum came this way in the spring,' she was telling him. 'And you'd never guess what we saw! The biggest falcon ever! Mum said she'd never seen one like it! It was right there, up in that tree. It's not there now, though. Oh well.'

'Mum doesn't like going down that lane, Dad. Last time we tried, she said it was too slippery with dead leaves. They fall off the trees and just sort of sit there. They're lovely when they're nice and dry. Then you can crunch through them. They make a sort of crackly sound. But when they get wet, they just get slippery. So, we don't go down there.'

As she spoke of dead leaves, Matthew saw, for the first time today, that one or two leaves had already fallen from the trees around them. Not many, just a few. They'd been there, on the ground beneath their feet, the whole time they'd been walking.

He had hardly noticed them. He could feel the air around them was still quite warm, not really chilly at all, but still these leaves had fallen. It was their turn to fall, and they had.

Brenda held his hand as they walked back down the lane to retrieve their bag of blackberries from the tree branch, and as they approached the house it occurred to him that Bridie and her daughter had a very special relationship, one that he had only really observed, rather than joined in with.

He loved his daughter with his whole heart, but he knew that he had missed so much, so many little details,

He realised, with an almost physical pain, that he knew so little about his daughter, but he also knew that that was going to have to change.

Soon, he realised, he was going to have to step up and take Bridie's place in Brenda's life, to offer what guidance he could, to keep her safe, to make her happy if he could.

He knew that he was facing an almost impossible job, but he was determined to do it as well as he could.

I have so much to learn, he thought to himself, *and so little time to learn it in.*

And he still had Bridie to look after, to make comfortable, and to love. He hoped it would never end. But he knew it would.

'That's too wet. Strain it off a bit more.'

'A bit more butter…no.too much. Too late. Never mind. Don't worry. It'll be fine.'

'Three minutes, no more, OK? Otherwise, they'll be hard as nails.'

'Don't mix colours and whites. That's why everything's blue.'

'Brenda's growing so fast. You'll need to take her shopping on Saturday.'

Ordinary. Normal.

He made life as ordinary as possible, but life was in the fast lane and he was running. Breathless.

39

They sat by Bridie's bed.

He wasn't running anymore. He had eventually managed to catch his breath. Life was certainly not ordinary, and it certainly was not normal. But it was calm.

The family had all been to see her, one after the other, at intervals throughout the afternoon. None had stayed long. They didn't want to tire her. Some had sat and talked quietly with her for a while. Some had kissed her cheek, and left hurriedly, not wanting her to see them upset.

Her mother had stayed the longest, smoothing her daughter's hair, and whispering to her so quietly that he couldn't make out the words, just the sound of her voice over the rhythmic whirring of the fan that stirred the air around her.

Bridie had closed her eyes while she listened to her mother's calming, soothing voice. Mat could hear the sound of it, rising and falling, melodic and gentle, as he watched her mouth move and her eyes study every inch of Bridie's face, every eyelash, every pore of her skin, soaking up every detail and engraining them deep into her memory.

Eventually she had kissed her sleeping daughter's forehead, whispered to her one last time, and eased herself, regretfully, from the bedside chair.

As she crossed the room, circling the bed, she stopped to kiss her granddaughter's head.

'Do you want to come home with me, or go back with Aunty Beth?' she asked quietly.

Brenda looked at her, confused. 'I want to stay here, with Mum,' she said, her eyes moving pleadingly between Mat and her grandmother.

'I'm not sure that's a good idea, darling,' her grandma said, stooping down to look deep into her eyes and holding her hands. 'Mummy is asleep. You haven't had any tea. She wouldn't want you to be hungry.'

'But I'm not hungry, Grandma, and anyway there's plenty of biscuits,' Brenda said, pointing at a plate on the table next to her. 'The nurses brought them.'

Grandma Hilda tried one last time. 'Are you really sure you wouldn't rather remember Mummy like she was, when she wasn't poorly? I think I would have, when I was your age.'

'But I have to stay with Mummy. I promised,' Brenda answered, 'she needs me. Daddy needs me.'

They both looked over to where Mat was sitting, by the bedside. 'Daddy? Please?'

Mat couldn't bring himself to send her away. He knew his daughter very well. She was like her mother, just as strong-willed, and just as determined. In the end, it had to be her decision. He knew that she would need to know, afterwards, that she had stayed close to her mother, for as long as her mother had been able to stay close to her.

And she was right, he did need her nearby.

Mr Pearce had crept into the room later in the evening. Stirred by the slightest sound, Matthew glanced up to see his old friend standing hesitantly in the doorway.

He looked distraught, and Matthew wondered if he'd been weeping. His faithful old cricket hat was screwed tightly in his shaking hands, and despite his best efforts, he couldn't return Matthew's welcoming smile. Eventually, he moved towards Bridie's bedside. She was sleeping. Mr Pearce touched her arm very gently, and then pulled himself away.

As he turned to leave, he reached over to squeeze Matthew's shoulder before leaving the room as quickly and as quietly as he could. Matthew realised that, for the first time since he'd known him, Mr Pearce was lost for words.

Mat watched as Bridie drifted in and out of sleep, her hand in his. He didn't want to count the seconds, minutes, hours. He wanted this night to last forever.

He watched his daughter, she was asleep, curled up on a couch in the corner of the room. She'd fallen asleep shortly after midnight.

He smiled to himself, realising how like her mother she was when she was asleep. The same dark hair cascading over her face, gently moving as she breathed in and out. The same pale, round comforting, moon face. The same hands, curled under her cheek.

He was glad she hadn't struggled to stay awake. He didn't want her tired, and tense, through staying awake through so many long hours.

He sensed Bridie watching him, studying his face.

'You were miles away,' she said quietly.

'I was watching Brenda sleeping. She looks so much like you when she sleeps.'

'She stayed then? I thought she would.'

'She said she'd promised.'

Bridie nodded her head faintly.

'She told me she would look after me while I was poorly.' She smiled. 'I told her she didn't have to, but she said, "Yes I do, Mum, I've promised now".'

Mat smiled. 'You girls always do keep your promises, don't you.'

'Always.' She nodded again.

'Do you know what tomorrow is?' she asked.

'Sunday?' he suggested.

'No, silly, what day is it?'

'Oh,' he replied, realising. 'Autumn Equinox. Sorry. I'd forgotten.'

'Special day,' she said.

'Give my love to Mum and Dad, eh?' he asked, finally accepting the inevitable. She smiled.

'You still miss them, don't you?'

'Every day,' he said, truthfully. 'But it doesn't hurt so much now, not like it used to.' She squeezed his hand.

'I'll do better than that,' she said. 'I'll give them a hug from you. Just like they gave you that Christmas when you first came to stay.'

'Thank you,' he uttered breathlessly, remembering that night, and the feeling of his parents' love flowing into him.

'Don't worry,' she whispered. 'I'll be there waiting for you, when it's your time.'

'Thank you,' he said, struggling to speak. 'I know you will. I will look forward to that moment with all my heart.'

'But that won't be yet,' she said. 'Not until it's your time. Not until it's properly your time, promise me! Like Father Christmas told you. You have too much to do yet.'

'It's just not fair,' he whispered. 'How am I supposed to live without you?'

'No,' she told him, as firmly as she could muster. 'I need you to promise me, you'll be there for Brenda. Our Brenda. She needs you.'

Mat nodded, sorrowfully.

'Promise me,' she repeated. 'I need you to see her grow. I need you to make sure she's happy.'

'I promise,' he said, almost inaudibly. 'I promise.'

'Will you do something for me?' she asked quietly.

'Whatever you want,' he said. 'Anything, always.'

'You and Brenda have to stay close together, always. And you have to listen to her. She knows the way.'

'What am I going to do without you?' he questioned, trying desperately not to sob, and staying brave for her.

Bridie smiled faintly at him.

'You can get Brenda to sort your sock drawer out, for a start,' she whispered. 'If it was left to you, you'd wear odd socks every day.'

'It's OK,' he whispered back, smiling weakly, 'I've got another pair like that for tomorrow.'

'Matthew Crawford,' she said, almost inaudibly. 'You can be such an idiot sometimes.'

Mat felt her hand twitch, almost squeezing his hand but not quite. He longed to feel her punch his arm. He could almost imagine it.

'But I do love you,' she whispered.

'Always and forever.'

Just before dawn broke, their daughter woke with a start. She rushed to her mother's bedside, and urgently seized her hand.

'Mum?' she said, with a hint of hope to her voice.

Mat thought he saw Bridie's mouth move. He was sure she was trying to smile.

They heard her sigh. They felt her hands and her face relax.

Seconds passed. Long drawn-out moments. Still, they held her hands.

His daughter took a deep breath. He realised that they'd both been holding their breath, hoping, willing, wishing.

She reached over and grasped his hand. She gripped his hand strongly, it reminded him of how hard Bridie had gripped his hand the moment Brenda was born. He looked at her, confused. Then realisation dawned. The inevitable and painful realisation had dawned on them both.

She looked into his eyes.

'Oh, Dad,' she said in a loud whisper, tears streaming silently down her face.

40

It was still the early hours of the morning, just after daybreak, as they pulled into the driveway. Mat opened the car door, and breathed in the early autumnal air. Crisp, fresh, and scented slightly with the tang of manure. Home.

Chickens scurried around in their pen, waiting for their morning grain and release. Small, dry, copper-coloured leaves were beginning to gather in odd corners of the yard. One flew past his face as he stood from the car, making him flinch involuntarily. He turned to watch it fly away. The circle was turning again.

As he opened the kitchen door, he could see that they were all there.

His parents-in-law sat at the table, mugs of tea cooling in front of them. Miranda, who was close to her due date by now, was sat in an easy chair near the wood-fired range.

A tea towel was spread along the rail. Just like Bridie had showed him. Beth was standing near Miranda, delivering her a cup of tea. Bill and Nick stood from the table, as Mat and Brenda entered.

Mat couldn't think of the right words. Why could he never think of the words when he needed them? If he could write the words down, they'd be perfect. They'd be eloquent, thoughtful, comforting.

Instead, he stood there like a fool. An idiot. Bridie's idiot.

He didn't need to say anything. They all knew. They just knew.

'Cuppa?' asked Beth, as practical as ever.

Mat breathed out, the moment of trepidation passing.

'Please,' he replied. 'But no sugar, thanks.'

He couldn't stand sweet tea. They all knew that. Matron had forced sweet tea into him after his parents...he really couldn't have stomached sweet tea on top of everything else. Not today.

He had to go into town. There were formalities. Bill offered to drive, but he felt that he really needed some time alone.

He'd been up all night. He hadn't slept for days.

Nick informed him, quite gently, if he went to town looking like he did right now, he'd probably get arrested for vagrancy. Mat smiled at that. That would never do. Bridie would have killed him if he'd gone out looking rough. She'd have killed him twice if he'd got arrested for it. What would people have thought?

He washed, shaved and changed, and waited for his breakfast to cool down.

Leaving his daughter nestled quietly in her grandma's lap, staring emptily, he left for town.

Grandma Hilda always knew what to say, what to do. He knew Brenda felt lost and lonely, and she needed her grandma just as much as he needed his wife. They would help each other find a way through, in the next few days.

Before he could get lost in his sad thoughts once more, he left, just as the warm, early morning day began, and a chorus of birdsong greeted him. He could hear Bridie's voice clearly.

'Good morning, my darling,' she said. He looked up at the blue sky above him.

'I brought you a beautiful summer morning,' she continued, 'just to show how much I love you.'

He walked silently through a silent town, and she walked silently beside him. He could feel her hand in his, comforting, familiar.

They had walked down the aisle. They had pushed Brenda's pram. They had carried birthday cards and Christmas gifts.

They walked together as they always had. He could hardly remember a time when she had not walked beside him.

Then she was gone, as suddenly as the thought had arrived.

The solitude was quiet at first, but soon it felt overwhelming.

Angelic voices shaped words that he could almost, but not quite make out, in the distance. The tones were both as unavoidable as grief, and as fulfilling as their love had been. Their requiem grew until it occupied every one of his senses. It consumed his world at that moment. He welcomed it, embraced it.

It was both sad and joyful.

It made him smile; it made him tear up. Beautiful, irritating, familiar, insistent, comforting. Whatever the meaning of the words may be, he didn't understand, but they lifted his spirit and hushed the panic in his mind.

It was the song of their love, and it was as beautiful as the angels who sang it. They were calling her home.

***

His daughter wanted to go to the bridge.

They stood on the bank of the stream, looking over the solid, earthly, timeless granite slab, towards the field of barrows beyond.

Bridie's bridge. Bridie's family. All together. Watching and waiting. Waiting for her.

The sun settled gradually behind the hills, casting silhouettes of the trees. Birds fluttered and swooped, seeking a last meal of gnats and overlooked seeds. The warm, glorious, awful day was passing.

Mat and his daughter stood together, he encircled his arm with hers, it was comforting to both. They stood quietly. There were no words. No words were needed. Each was lost in their own thoughts, their own private memories. Lost souls, waiting. It had been a strange day.

They needed to be quiet, but together, in this special place. They were in no rush for the day to end.

Grandma Hilda would be preparing supper for them, but she'd understand.

Here they would stay, caught between sunset and moonrise, until Brenda was ready to leave her mother to the bridge.

He wasn't sure that he'd ever reach that moment himself, but when Brenda was ready, that would do for him.

Mat reflected on all the things that had happened.

Christmas miracles, proposals, births, picnics.

All were part of her. All were part of him. All were part of this place. This was Bridie's secret. Her special place, just like she'd told him all those years ago. She'd been right. This was a special place.

As the day turned to twilight, bats swooped around them, harvesting the last flying things above the water, they started to see the air lighten.

At first it was faint; perhaps a last glimmer from the dying sun, but after a few moments it grew stronger, until it illuminated everything around them.

Mat recognised it and smiled. He knew what it was. He had first seen it that first Christmas Eve with Bridie, many years ago, when he was Toby's age. They had waited to watch Father Christmas cross the sky above them.

He had seen the same glow again, that mid-summer morning, when his daughter had been born.

The glow had always brought him consolation. It had always brought him joy. He welcomed it with all his heart.

He heard his daughter gasp as she watched the colours pulsating and changing around her.

She grasped his hand tight, and he saw her smile as she seemed to recall the forgotten smells and tastes it had given her on the morning she had first breathed it in. Her very first breaths as a newborn. She wasn't sure why she recognised it, but she knew it. It was part of her. She welcomed it, and it welcomed her.

Mat smiled. This place was special to her by now. It had always been her favourite place, but now it was different. Now it really did mean something. He was glad of it.

As the glow embraced, and danced around them, and moved within, Mat saw a figure approach.

He could make out she was a woman, but couldn't quite see her face, she had a look of joy and a demeanour that seemed to resonate with power.

She moved towards them. He hoped, with all his heart that it was Bridie, that he had been allowed to see his Bridie again, one last time.

As the figure appeared more clearly, he could see that it wasn't her. She moved with the same graceful fluidity as his Bridie, but it wasn't her. His heart sank a little. She was small, light-skinned and dark-haired like her.

When his eyes were able to focus on her face, he could see that she wasn't his Bridie, it wasn't his wife.

The woman watched them, as the glow continued to dance and surround them. She moved to the edge of the bridge and stopped. She held her arms out wide, as if summoning their presence closer.

'Brenda,' she said, in a warm, comforting tone. 'Come to me.'

Brenda approached, and the figure took her hands in hers, she looked back toward him. She looked straight into his eyes, and it seemed to him she was looking deeper, beyond him physically, and into his very soul.

'Matthew,' she said, in tones that were soft and comforting, but her voice was so quiet to his ears that he could hardly hear it, and she spoke in a language he had never heard before.

In his ears, she sounded like the angelic voices he had heard earlier in the morning.

Her voice was beautiful, but he couldn't understand what she said. In his mind, though, while she still spoke comfortingly, liltingly, almost musically, he could hear her very clearly and understand every word.

'I want you to know,' she continued, 'your Bridie is safe. She has been found. She is content.'

Mat felt a wave of relief. The worry that she might not have found her guide dissipated with her message.

The woman smiled. 'There was no question of that,' clearly reading his thoughts.

'She was one of ours and we would have found her. She has joined me, just as all the others joined, when it was their time.'

Turning to look at his daughter, the woman gazed at her intently.

'You are the one now. You are taking your mother's place on your side of the bridge. Watch over it well.'

Brenda studied her, transfixed, a smile spread across her face.

The woman spoke again, holding Brenda's hands firmly.

'Your mother wants you to know, she is sorry that she can't be with you now. She knows that you will be happy. Although you cannot feel them, her arms are embracing you, loving you, protecting you. They will be there always. Always and forever.' She looked adoringly at Brenda's face.

'Your mother sent you a gift.'

Matthew watched, as a pale, shining orb of light appeared in the woman's palms. It flowed into Brenda's small, delicate hands. It travelled along her arms, it shimmered and sparkled, and slowly faded, as it disappeared deep within his daughter.

'Her love will stay with you always. It will go wherever you go. It will always be there, deep within you. May it keep you happy and safe, for the rest of your life.'

Mat exchanged smiles with the woman, then she unclasped her hand from Brenda's. She turned towards him.

'Matthew – you know that Bridie's love is always with you. It always will be, deep within you, wrapped up safely with your parents' love. Hold it close. Never let it go. When it is time for you to join her, she will be here, at the bridge, to take you into her arms. When it is your time, you will fully understand how rooted and powerful her love for you is, and has always been.'

The woman slowly withdrew across the bridge, fading gradually, as she reached the barrows. Just as she started to dissipate from their view, she turned towards Mat one last time.

'You were right, by the way,' she said, knowingly. 'It is pretty noisy.' She smiled once more, and then vanished.

Brenda tugged on his sleeve, and looked up at his face. She was happy. He could see it, her happiness radiated from her very core.

Together, they walked back down to the house. They walked in silence, through the many gates and fields.

As they approached the house, Brenda stopped and faced him.

'I always knew Bridie's Bridge was special,' she said, with a smile tugging the corner of her mouth.

Mat smiled back; all he could do was nod his agreement.

'Well now I know why!' she beamed, and punched him on the arm.

She felt a little bit more reassured. She knew who she was. She was Bridie's daughter, and she wasn't lost anymore.

Epilogue

41

If there was one saving grace about getting older, it was being able to have a nap when he wanted, without anybody making funny comments.

Anyway, old people dropped off after lunch, didn't they? It was expected. It was allowed.

That didn't apply, of course, to Brenda's brood, his grandchildren. They were still young. Very young.

As soon as they'd eaten, they were up and looking noisily for something to do. He should have been used to it by now, and most of the time he didn't mind at all.

He welcomed it in fact, enjoyed it. He loved being around his grandchildren, playing and telling them stories. He cherished watching them invent new games to play, and watching them grow.

Petra was the eldest. She was thirteen, the same age her grandmother had been when he'd first met her. Then there was Martha, who was eleven, then the four-year-old twins, Chris and Paul. They were by far the most boisterous of them all. Always in some sort of trouble, but always laughing and happy.

Mat was very proud of them all, and especially proud of how his daughter and her husband, Gerald, were raising them. They were good kids. They'd done a good job.

He liked Gerald. He was a nice lad. Him and Brenda had met when he'd come to help Nick out on the farm one summer and he'd just sort of stayed. They'd married when Brenda was nineteen, and he'd done a good job of looking after her ever since.

When Nick had retired, Gerald had taken on the farm, alongside Nick's boy Joe. They got on well, and though he was no judge of anything much to do with farming, it looked to Mat like they were making a pretty good fist of it between them.

Mat sighed.

Just one more year, and I'll retire too. Just one more year.

He was more than ready for it. He was tired of it all now. He was tired of pretty much everything nowadays.

He loved Brenda and her family, but he was tired of feeling like he was in the way. When she'd married, he'd got his things together, ready to move down to Small End in the house but she wouldn't hear of it. She said she still wanted him around, not tidied away into some obscure corner, like a piece of discarded furniture.

He'd appreciated her words, but now he wished he'd gone anyway. The kids were lovely, but as they grew, he felt more and more as though he was in the way. Apart from anything else, their energy made him feel more tired than he probably really was. Most of all, he was tired of feeling lost and lonely.

He had done his very best not to let his feelings show, but he was pretty sure his daughter knew. He just missed her mother so much, his Bridie. Even after all these years, he missed her so much.

'Come on, you lot,' Brenda had called to them as soon as the dishes had been dried. With Christmas just around the corner, the children were getting increasingly excitable with every passing day. She knew her kids.

Outside was the best place for them when they were in this sort of mood.

'Let's go for a walk. Give your poor old granddad a few minutes peace to enjoy his nap.'

From his seat at the ancient table, he watched as they skipped past, shouting and excited to be out in the fresh air.

As his daughter danced by the window with them, she stopped briefly, to blow him an extravagant kiss with both hands. He laughed and returned the gesture gratefully. She beamed and then she was off, like the gusty wind.

She rounded up her energetic brood.

He knew where they'd end up. It was the same place they always ended up on special days. She'd walk them all over the farm, through its woods and fields, climbing gates and splashing through mud, gradually wearing down the children's energy, until they were a bit more manageable.

They would end up at the bridge. It was a tradition that they could never break. High days and holidays, and always without fail, on the solstice and equinox days. It was a magnet, and they couldn't resist its pull.

Mat would normally have gone with them, but his feet weren't so good these days, and he worried that they might have to fetch the tractor to carry him back. That would be embarrassing. No, he'd just wait for them here, in the kitchen, in the warmth. He remembered the special things that had happened to him and his Bridie in that special place.

He glanced through the window at the huge copper beech in the courtyard. As always at this time of year, a few leaves still clung desperately to its sleeping branches, unwilling to finally let go.

As he watched, a gust plucked them at last, they swirled and got carried away to some unseen corner of the yard. He nodded. That was the way of it. That was always the way. The great tree would sleep through the mid-winter storms, then spring would come, bringing blossom and the promise of new life.

In the summer, the leaves matured and the tree grew stronger and autumn would inevitably follow. Old, decaying leaves would be blown away forever, and the tree could sleep again. Around and around. A continuous circle, just like it had always been, and always will be.

Picking up his almost empty coffee cup, he made his way to the comfortable seat by the range. Glancing around the kitchen, his eyes rested briefly upon the map hanging proudly on the chimney breast. He'd drawn it many years before, to record the positions of the stone circle that surrounded the bridge.

His daughter had found it, screwed up at the back of a desk drawer, while she was tidying his study. She'd ironed out as many of the crinkles as she could, and had framed it, proudly presenting it to him on his birthday a few years ago, along with a watercolour painting of the bridge that his niece Amy had created especially for him.

He really liked the watercolour, which he thought had caught the very essence of the place. The childishness of the map, however, still embarrassed him, but he'd been grateful for the girls' efforts all the same. It brought back so many memories.

On the day she'd told him about it, Bridie had half promised to show him the circle one day. She'd never got round to it, so one summer he'd decided to find it for himself. He'd been what, maybe sixteen at the time?

He'd just finished his O-level exams, and hadn't yet started his A-level course, so he had no reading or revision to do.

Bridie was spending most of her time working at Aunty Brenda's that summer, and he was bored. He'd borrowed one of Bill's tape measures, and had spent a fortnight poking through undergrowth, pulling apart brambles, peering through ferns and gorse, locating each and every one of the stones. Some were clear and obvious, just like the Summer Stones.

Two taller stones, almost side by side, for each of the two solstices, and two slightly shorter stones for each of the two equinoxes. Summer, winter, spring and autumn.

Most of the others were quite small, easily overlooked, easily mistaken for natural boulders, but there they were, recognisable in the right places, once you knew where to look. As he'd found them, he'd recorded their position on a sheet of paper.

Once he'd finished his search, he'd persuaded a very reluctant Bridie to walk round the circle with him. She'd been right, it was enormous. She'd been right about the bridge being smack in the middle of it.

Actually, if his reckoning was right, the centre of the circle was more at one end of the bridge, than the other. He remembered being puzzled by that. It would have made more sense if it had been at the centre of the bridge, but no matter how he did his calculations, it always turned out the same.

The centre of the circle was always at the Summer Stones edge of the stream, just a short step onto the bridge. Mat had wondered if that was where Bridie's ancestor had hidden her Home Stone so many years before, and whether the colours of the glow they had seen that first Christmas Eve had been caused by the vibrant colours in the stone.

When he'd pointed out his observation, Bridie had just shrugged it off. Maybe his amateurish drawing wasn't as accurate as it might have been. Maths had never been his strong point.

She was usually right about his short-falls.

It had taken the best part of an hour for them to complete the circuit, by the end, she'd been hot, tired and fractious. She'd told him quite firmly, she would most certainly not be walking round them again.

He remembered being a bit disappointed that she hadn't been more excited about his discoveries, but he'd persevered, and had finished off the map anyway. Just for the sake of completing something. She'd said it was a waste of time mapping something that they all knew was there, but it would have irritated him not to have finished it.

Even though it really didn't mean anything to anybody else.

The task done, he'd stuffed it away in his room, out of sight and out of mind, and had forgotten about it. It had stayed hidden for all the intervening years until his daughter had brought it to light again.

After the effort she'd gone to in order to make it look half presentable, he hadn't had the heart to hide it away again, so it had stayed where she'd put it, on the chimney breast. Matthew knew that the stones had all been overgrown again.

They were hidden. Maybe that's how they should have stayed. It was enough to know that they were there, still protecting the secret.

He reflected for a moment, as his gaze was drawn upon the simple, scruffy, off-white umpire's hat that had occupied pride of place on a peg, behind the hallway door. It was placed there after Mr Pearce had passed away. It had once been pristine white. Now, it was stained and crumpled, almost beyond recognition.

He smiled, remembering the wise old head that had worn it so proudly, and so stubbornly, for so many years.

He missed his old friend, just as he missed all the others who had left him behind.

Most of all, he missed his Bridie, but that absence in his heart was different. The others, he felt, had just gone. They had moved on and left. He missed Bridie.

He missed all sorts of things about her. He missed being able to reach out and stroke her face or her hair. He missed her smell. She'd always smelled nice, fresh and clean, like that the clear brown pear soap she had always used.

He missed holding her hand. The comforting feel of her palm against his. He even missed her playful punches on his arm.

But in other ways, in important ways, she was still with him. She was always just on the edge of his consciousness, only just out of sight. He could sense her around him.

Like the stones, she was hidden but not far from him. Like the stones, he knew she was there. Everywhere. Always. Forever. She'd promised.

He yawned, he had his daughter and her family and he was comforted by them. They were the future, and he was glad he was present to watch them grow. Even now, at mid-winter, they were reminders of spring and summer, and he was grateful to bask in the warmth of their energy and love.

He stretched his legs before him, enjoying the warmth of the range. Just as it had done so for years, whenever he closed his eyes, the angelic choir began, unbidden, their familiar requiem.

Quietly at first, but soon overwhelming, the voices shaped words that he could almost, but not quite, make out. It washed over him. Beautiful, irritating, consistent, insistent, comforting. He had long since given up trying to decipher the words, simply accepting that, whatever their meaning, the music of their sound lifted his spirit while they comforted his thoughts.

Bridie was smiling at him. She always smiled at him whenever he dreamed about her, which was often. In his dreams she was as lovely as she'd been when they married. Sometimes he could hear her voice. It made him happy to see her, happier still to hear her, even just for a few short minutes. He always woke up smiling. She always made him smile.

Sometimes he would see her in the kitchen, sat at the table, or stood in front of the range. Sometimes he would watch her sleeping, her dark hair streaming across her face, gently moving as she breathed in and out.

Today she was stood where he saw her most often, on the bridge. Their special bridge. Bridie's bridge. And she was smiling at him again.

'Mat?' she was calling. 'Matthew!'

He was smiling back at her.

'Well?' she said. 'Are you going to stand there dithering about all day?'

'Pardon?'

'You were always the same,' she laughed, rolling her eyes at him. "Never do today what you can put off until tomorrow". Will you come *on*!'

Her hands were stretching out to him, beckoning. She was still smiling, beaming.

He would wake up any minute, but he knew he would wake up with a smile. He always did when he dreamed of her.

'Mat!' she said, more sharply. 'Will you *PLEASE* hurry up?'

'What do you mean…' he uttered back.

'Come *on*, haven't I waited long enough?'

'You mean…'

The gusty wind at his back propelled him, but he could feel something stronger than the wind pulling him forward, forcing his feet to move, slowly at first, then more hastily towards her, along the ley line, and onto the bridge.

'You mean, this is the time? It's my time? Really?' he asked.

As she folded him in her arms, he was enveloped in her warmth. It felt good. So good. It made him happy.

'Matthew Crawford,' she whispered into his ear. 'For a clever man, you do say the stupidest things sometimes.'

'I love you so much,' was all he could find to say.

She punched him gently on the arm, smiling into his face.

'I love you too, you idiot…' she said tenderly. 'I always have. I promised, didn't I. Always and forever.'

Brenda watched her eldest daughter. She was standing very still, staring at the bridge.

Beyond her, Brenda could just make out a sparkling glow, fading quickly as it moved away through the barrows.

She remembered that glow. It was the same glow she had seen after her mother had passed away. It was the same one that had sparkled and shimmered all around her, the moment she had been born. She remembered the scent.

Brenda sensed what was happening. The glow had always made her feel content, comforted.

Today, though, she wasn't entirely sure how it made her feel. Consolation, perhaps.

She was happy for her father, and for her mother. But, if she was to be honest with herself, she felt unspeakably sad.

She walked over and put her arm around her daughter's shoulders.

'Did you see the lovely colours, Mum?' her daughter whispered, in awe. 'What are they for?'

'I think…' Brenda whispered low, and smiled sadly, 'I think…I think it may mean that Granddad isn't lost anymore,' Brenda sighed. 'I think Grandma Bridie has found him again. She'll look after him. She promised she would, and she will.'

Always and forever.

Part Three

The Road from Bridie's Bridge

42

As she watched her train disappear out of view, Petra stamped her foot so hard on the platform that it echoed off the walls of the station building.

'Aargh!' she growled. 'Damn! Damn! Damn!'

Michael flinched as she turned sharply on her heel and glared into his face.

'This is all your fault!' she shouted. 'Why did you have to be late, today of all days?'

'Sorry,' he said, raising his hands in surrender, 'I was only a few minutes late. I honestly thought it would be OK!'

'Well, it's bloody well NOT, is it!'

She stomped across the platform and flopped down heavily onto a bench.

'Look,' he said, 'I'll go and find out what time the next train is, OK? Then I'll buy you a coffee while we wait. I won't be a minute.'

She glared after him, as he walked through the door of the ticket office, cursing under her breath that she had accepted his offer of a lift to the station. She didn't know him all that well, and now she wasn't at all sure that she even liked him much. He was a friend of a friend, who'd just happened to be in the same club as her and a group of friends. They were celebrating the end of their exams.

He'd been at an adjacent table to theirs, and had overheard her tell her friends that she needed to catch the eight o'clock train the next day, but that she hadn't been able to book a cab yet. He'd leant over and suggested that he could drive her, if she wanted. She'd been grateful at the time. Now, she certainly wasn't.

He looked a bit sheepish when he emerged from the ticket office.

'Sorry babe,' he said. 'Seems the next train will be Monday morning.'

'Well,' she muttered. 'Could this day get any better? And do *not* call me *babe!* I hate it.'

'Sorry,' he said again. 'I'll take you back to your house then, shall I?'

She pursed her lips. 'I don't have any other choice, do I? Thanks to you, I'll have to ring my mum and apologise for missing her birthday party. She'll be so disappointed!'

He watched her thoughtfully, while she sat there seething.

'Tell you what,' he said, 'you missing the train is my fault. I'll hold my hands up to that. I can do something to make sure you don't miss your mum's party, though. How about I drive you home?'

She thought about it for a moment, then agreed.

'Thanks,' she told him, begrudgingly.

It was a long drive, certainly a lot longer than he'd bargained for, and it wasn't a particularly pleasant one either. Hardly a word passed between them all the way there. It was mid-afternoon by the time they arrived at Home Farm.

Michael unloaded her bags from the boot of his car and dragged them up to the front porch.

'I suppose you'd better come in for a cup of tea before you go,' she said, instantly regretting having suggested it. 'My mum will be wondering whose car it is.'

He smiled ingratiatingly as she introduced him, and once seated at the huge table, gazed around the kitchen appreciatively.

'My word, what a wonderful home you have here Mrs Morris,' he observed. 'And what a fascinating house this is!'

Brenda beamed, enjoying the compliment. 'Thanks, we like it…'

'I noticed while we were unpacking the car that the house seems to have been extended and adapted several times,' he continued, 'I bet there's quite some history here. Have you been here long?'

Petra slumped deeper into her chair, resigned to the fact that her mum would soon launch into pretty much the whole family history.

Thankfully, her mother only gave him a potted version, but even that had taken half an hour or more.

Michael had leant forward in his chair, attentively listening, offering encouraging little interjections here and there.

'My word…goodness me, who would have believed it…' amongst others.

Petra had sat quietly throughout, her arms firmly folded, squirming inwardly at his very obvious fawning.

Eventually, and just before her mum started pulling out her baby photo albums, she stood and hinted that he perhaps might need to be setting off soon, to avoid arriving home too late at night, in the dark.

'Oh Petra!' her mum had said. 'I won't hear of it! After bringing you all the way home, surely you can't expect him to drive back straight away? No, I won't hear of it. He must stay until the morning. I'll go and make up a bed.'

Petra sighed resignedly, while Michael eased himself back into his chair, smiling triumphantly in her direction.

'Well, he seems like a nice enough boy,' her mother cajoled, as they drank their first cup of tea of the morning. 'It was really good of him to drive you all the way home, wasn't it?'

Petra shrugged her shoulders.

'Oh, he's alright, I suppose,' she condescended. 'He can be quite good company when he wants to be. I was just so cross with him yesterday. If he hadn't been late picking me up, I wouldn't have missed my train.'

'Oh, it was pretty obvious when you got home last night that you two had had a falling out. Dinner was a bit tense to say the least!'

'Well, you didn't have to invite him to stay, did you?'

'Actually,' her mother said, 'yes, I did. You really couldn't expect him to turn straight round and just drive all that way back now, could you. It just wouldn't have been right.'

Petra shrugged her shoulders again, and leant against the back of the chair.

'Well, he's certainly making the most of your hospitality,' she said, glancing at her wristwatch. 'If he stays in bed much longer, he'll think he's staying another night!'

'Oh, he's alright, leave him be,' her mother said. 'Though I'm amazed he slept through the noise when the others got up.'

Petra smiled and nodded.

'I know what you mean,' she said. 'I thought they'd be quieter when they grew up. Some hope!'

'So, what does he do then, your Michael? Is he your boyfriend?'

'First of all, he is certainly not my boyfriend!' Petra replied curtly.

'But he'd like to be?' her mother interjected. 'He clearly likes you…'

'No, definitely not. He hangs around with us sometimes, and as far as I'm concerned that's all there is to it.'

'Even so,' said her mother, raising her eyebrows pointedly, 'not many *just mates* would volunteer to drive you all the way home at the drop of a hat, would they?'

Petra laughed, and changed the subject.

'So, he is studying archaeology. He's just finished his Masters. Just about as boring as you could get.'

Her mother smiled, and got up to boil the kettle again.

Petra looked around the familiar kitchen. Nothing had changed much since the Easter holidays, when she'd last sat there at the huge kitchen table. Nothing ever really changed here.

Through the front window she could see the huge copper beech, glorious in full leaf at this time of year. Turning her head, she scanned the towels drying, as always, on the rail of the range. Above the range was the map her grandfather had made years before, along with some of the pictures she and her siblings had drawn while they were at primary school.

'Oh, my goodness,' she gasped, 'you still have the pictures!'

Her mother glanced at them and smiled.

'Of course!' she said. 'Why wouldn't I? They make me happy. They remind me of the wonderful kids I created. They're as much of the history of this place as everything else.'

Petra smiled back at her.

'Aren't we still your wonderful kids?'

This time it was her mother's turn to shrug.

'Of course you are, but things change. You've all changed, and so have I. That's why it's nice to keep memories alive. The good ones, anyway.'

By the time Michael came downstairs, Petra and her mother were washing and drying the breakfast dishes.

They turned as he walked through the kitchen door.

'Good morning, good morning!' he exclaimed brightly, rubbing his hands together. 'Anything I can do to help?'

'No thanks,' replied Petra, rolling her eyes at her mother. 'We're nearly done. Seems there are some benefits to always being late, eh?'

'Sorry,' Michael said with a sly smile, as Brenda set a cup of tea on the table for him.

'Would you like some breakfast? she asked.

He refused, but before he could protest, a plate of bacon and eggs was placed on the table, and he looked at it with obvious relish.

Once he'd eaten, Petra brought him another cup of tea while Brenda quickly washed his plate.

Michael smiled as his eyes wandered around the room. Petra watched him and laughed.

'Casing the joint?' she asked.

'No,' he laughed. 'I was just thinking what a lovely comfortable room this is. You can't help but feel a sense of family everywhere you look.'

Petra smiled in response. 'We like it.'

Michael's eyes opened more widely as he spotted a map. She watched him studying it, his head slightly to one side.

'That's interesting,' he said at last. 'What's that all about?'

Petra explained that her grandfather had drawn it, many years before on his school holidays, and that they'd found it again and kept it on display in his memory.

'Well, it looks like he put a lot of time and effort into it,' Michael said. 'It's really quite good. Does it show anything close by?'

'Well,' announced Petra, 'not just close by, but nearby. Actually, it's on part of our land.'

Michael's eyes widened in surprise, as he sat forward attentively.

'May I see it?' he asked.

Petra shrugged, wishing fervently that she hadn't told him where it was.

'Seriously, you wouldn't be able to see much. Nobody goes there now, it's rather overgrown. Anyway, you'll need to get away in a minute, if you want to get back before dark.'

'I'm not in that much of a hurry, and I really couldn't miss the opportunity to have a look. It's not a site I'm aware of. Please? It would be seriously interesting!' he said, tapping the side of his nose. 'I have a nose for these things, you see.'

'It'd be seriously boring, you mean!' replied Petra.

He tilted his head to one side, grinning widely. 'Please...Please nicely? Pretty ple...'

Petra frowned at him, folded her arms and sat back in her chair.

'Seriously, no,' she sighed. 'Sorry. It's just that it's a family thing. We don't want strangers trampling all over it.'

'But that's just silly!' he retorted abruptly. 'If I'm right, and the site is unknown to archaeologists, then you really need to have it written up properly.'

'Absolutely not!' she retaliated. 'It's private to the family and it's going to stay that way!' Petra looked over to her mum, appreciating some back up. 'Mum? Will you tell him please!'

However, far from backing her daughter up, Brenda shook her head and shrugged her shoulders.

'Look, I really don't mind if he has a quick look. It won't do any harm.'

Petra threw her mother an exasperated look.

'Oh, alright then!' she said sharply. 'You can have a quick look, but don't say I didn't warn you...it's really not that interesting.'

'It's a fair old walk from your house, isn't it! And that hill is a killer!' Michael said, as they reached the hedge that surrounded the stones.

'Is it?' Petra responded nonchalantly. 'I'm so used to it; I don't really notice.'

They approached and made their way over to the stones.

'Here you are then,' she said, waving her hand and pointing to the area in front of them.

Petra was quite surprised to find that large areas of the circle were now almost completely overgrown with tall, uncut grass, bushes and gorse.

There had been hardly any overgrowth last time she'd been up here at Christmas time.

She felt that it was almost as though the stones were trying to hide themselves from prying eyes. The thought made her feel quite uncomfortable.

'OK,' Michael commented quietly, his eyes already scanning and assessing. 'Ah!' he said suddenly. 'Found one!'

He sauntered off to examine the stones more closely.

He was fully alert, his head twitching from side to side, and his eyes darting all over the place.

'Wow! This is brilliant!' he exclaimed repeatedly, as he made his way slowly around the ring of stones. The bigger stones were easier to see than others, but it wasn't long before he'd completed the full circuit.

Finally, he crossed over to the centre of the circle.

'Ah, yes!' he gasped, staring at the bridge. 'This is the centre of everything. And if I'm not mistaken, the reason for everything! I wonder why…I wonder why the centre of the circle is…'

'Right!' Petra called over, interrupting him. 'Seen enough? Can we go now?'

'Just a few more minutes,' he pleaded.

'No, that's enough,' she said firmly. 'Time to go.'

Michael was buzzing with excitement on the long walk back to the house. His mind drumming a thousand miles an hour, Petra could hear him muttering to himself. He was clearly trying to work out why the centre of the stone circle was positioned one end of the bridge, rather than in the middle. And why it was a bridge at all, rather than a taller standing stone, or an alter stone.

As far as Petra was concerned, one thing was certain. She wasn't about to tell him.

***

'Are you OK Petra?' her mother asked, while they were tidying up after the picnic.

Petra yawned. It had been a long day, and she was quite glad it was nearly bedtime.

'Yeah, I'm alright,' she replied. 'Just it's been a really busy term. I'm glad that's all over now, and I must admit I'm really looking forward to getting away for a while.'

'After all your hard work the last three years, I think it'll do you good to just kick back and relax somewhere sunny and warm. Last I heard you were thinking of somewhere in Greece. Did you decide where?'

'Andrea didn't care where we went, just somewhere hot and sunny. Roxy's parents went to a place in Corfu last year. A little village up in the north of the island. They said it was lovely. Great beach, friendly locals and not too frantic in the evenings. Enough to do, but relaxing, if you know what I mean. So, we thought we'd try it. We did a bit of research and booked an apartment that looks nice.'

Roxy and Andrea had been Petra's housemates at university, and they all got on really well.

'How long are you going for?' Brenda asked.

'Two weeks. We'll fly out on Saturday morning, so we should have a decent amount of time left to explore. Andrea planned it so we can be back in time for graduation, though, to be honest, at the moment I wouldn't particularly mind if I missed it.'

Brenda blinked in amazement.

'What? Why would you want to miss one of the most important days of your life?'

'Well, I'd enjoy celebrating with my friends, I'd really rather not risk crossing paths with Michael again.'

'Why on earth not?' her mother questioned.

'I'd just prefer to avoid him, OK?'

'He seemed such a nice chap,' Brenda persisted. 'Why would you want to avoid him that much?'

Petra pulled a face. She thought about telling her that Michael had called and texted her several times since leaving for home. Every time it had been to plead for permission to come back and investigate the circle for scientific purposes.

'Just not my type,' she shrugged, 'though he thinks he is.'

Brenda laughed. 'Oh well, hopefully he'll get the message eventually, eh?'

43

After an early flight and an hour's transfer by taxi, they arrived in the village just in time for a late lunch. The taxi driver stopped in a narrow road right outside a restaurant.

At first, they were confused, as they were not able to assess that their apartment was a short walk down a lane that ran beside the restaurant.

Even before they'd paid their driver, one of the waiters from the restaurant had pulled one of their suitcases under the wide, vine-covered eaves of the restaurant, whilst another had grabbed hold of two of their cases and was beckoning them to follow him down the lane.

'Leave the other case here,' he instructed over his shoulder. 'I will fetch it. Just bring your small bags.'

He talked non-stop as they walked past the kitchens at the side of the restaurant and on towards the long white walls of a pleasant-looking apartment complex.

'You had a good flight, yes? Is hot, eh? Good sunshine today. Will be good for your holidays. You will eat at the restaurant tonight, eh?' he said with a thick accent. 'I will reserve a table for you. What time you like. No problem. You are in number three, Christina told me. Here, the key is in the door, OK? Yes. Is a good place.'

He lifted the cases up onto a low balustraded walkway in front of their apartment, that clearly served as a balcony as well, and left immediately to fetch the third case.

As he expertly hoisted the last case onto the walkway, Andrea was the first to reach for her purse, trying to work out what tip might be appropriate. He was already walking away.

'But wait,' called Andrea, pulling a note out of her bag, 'I haven't given you a tip.'

He waved it away. 'No, no need. Oh, and Christina will be here tomorrow, I think. Maybe.'

As he walked away, he called over his shoulder, 'OK, see you later. When you want.'

They'd travelled in jeans and thin jumpers. It had been an early start, and the air was cool. Now, after a couple of hours of sunshine, they couldn't wait to change into something more weather appropriate. Petra contemplated taking a quick shower, but they were all too hungry to wait.

As they walked back up the lane towards the road, they were surprised to find that the restaurant was very quiet. They stepped inside and looked around. There were no customers, no sign of anyone working, and the tables weren't set. Petra glanced at Roxy and pulled a surprised face.

'This doesn't look good, does it!' she said. 'Where is everyone?'

There was no sign of the waiters who had met them just a few minutes before. Just then they heard the noise of crockery clinking somewhere in one of the rooms behind the main floor. Andrea called out to whoever was there, and a few moments later, a face appeared in the doorway.

'Hello?' he announced, clearly surprised to see anyone in the restaurant.

'Hi,' Andrea spoke, 'could we get some lunch please?'

The man in the doorway shrugged his shoulders.

'Restaurant is closed now,' he informed them. 'Nobody here. Come back tonight, OK?'

'Is anywhere open at lunchtime?' Andrea asked. 'We're new here. We don't know anywhere.'

'Sure, sure,' said the man, approaching them closer. He was wearing what appeared to be chef's trousers, an apron, and a stained T-shirt. 'Sure, is plenty of places. Walk to the village, OK?'

They thanked him, and made their way out to the road. There was a field just opposite, it was full of dry, long grass and dotted by a couple of olive trees. To the right they could make out a more sizeable road. And to the left, opposite to where they stood, was a small shop with a sign that read, 'Supermarket' over a door and another sign that read 'Cava.' A couple of ice-cream freezers stood outside between the open doors, together with a small stand of what looked like beach parasols and bottles of sun cream.

Further down the road, they could see a couple of shops and a taverna, all of which looked closed, and in the distance, what might have been a souvenir shop.

'So,' asked Roxy. 'Which way should we go? Left, or right?'

'To be honest,' stated Petra, 'I'm too hungry to care. Let's see what the shop has to offer. We can eat something at the apartment and explore later?'

The shop was actually much bigger inside than it had appeared from outside.

It didn't take them long to find some cakes and biscuits to satisfy their hunger.

As they paid for their goods, Andrea thought she'd do a little research. She asked for directions to the beach, and whether it was normal for all the restaurants to be closed at lunchtime.

The man behind the small counter was very helpful, and they soon discovered, if they'd explored a bit further up or down the road, they would have found everything they needed.

'The beach is maybe a five-minute walk down there,' he said, pointing. 'And there are lots of good tavernas and cafes on the beach road, they stay open all day. There are more restaurants down the main strip, just round the corner in the other direction, but probably the best restaurants are the two behind you. They only open in the evening though.' They hadn't even noticed the other restaurant, which was on the other side of the lane that led to their apartment.

He asked if they wanted some water to take back to the apartment. 'The water is OK here, but not as nice as bottled water. It's heavy to carry, though. Shall I bring it later? You are in Christina Apartments, no? I saw you come from there…' They thanked him for his help, and made their way back to the apartment.

After their light lunch, lulled by the growing heat, they fell asleep in the shade of the balcony. By the time they stirred from their nap, it was far too late to do much exploring.

So they took turns to shower, eventually dressing for dinner and made their way to the restaurant.

As they emerged from the lane and turned to enter through the side entrance, they were amazed to see that the restaurant had been transformed.

It was already busy with customers. Smart in white shirts, black trousers and shoes, waiters were threading between tables with trays laden with drinks, and some very enticing aromas were emerging from the kitchens hidden in the background.

They very quickly caught the eye of one of the older waiters, who waved and called over to them.

'Ladies, welcome! Kalispera! Here is your table. I am Constantinos. This is my restaurant. You already met my sons Matthaios and Antonis earlier I think?' Pulling out a chair he motioned to them to sit, he called over to his eldest son, and told him to take their drinks order.

'Matthaios will bring menus. I will come back soon to take your order for dinner. Welcome to our restaurant!' he beamed. Before they could reply, he was scampering away to entice in a young couple who were hanging around the main doorway, clearly unsure whether they should wait or walk in.

'Please, please,' he was saying to them.

'I will find a nice table for two. Please sit. The Special tonight is…'

Meanwhile, the girls were distracted by Matthaios asking what they'd like to drink. When they clearly couldn't make up their minds on what to have, he quickly told them he would be back in a moment, before rushing over to another table to take their order.

Matthaios was soon back at their table, presenting them with menus and asking if they had made their minds up about drinks. They clearly hadn't still.

'Don't worry,' he told them. 'I will bring some wine while you think. Do you like red or white? I will bring both…'

Moments later he returned with a half-carafe of red wine, a half-carafe of white and three glasses. In the balmy warmth of the evening, the outside of the chilled carafe of white wine was already running with condensation.

As Roxy began to pour their wine, Constantinos, the owner, returned, and sat in the vacant chair at their table, notepad in hand. Despite the warmth of the evening and the bustle of the restaurant, he was smiling and clearly unflustered.

'Busy tonight,' he stated. 'So, what would you like to eat? Tonight's special is fresh sea bass. Delicious. Or maybe you prefer something from the menu?'

The girls had hardly had time to glimpse at the menu yet, and what they had seen looked unfamiliar.

'What's this?' Andrea asked him, pointing at the long list of choices.

'Ah yes,' replied Constantinos. 'Stifado. Beef stew with onions. Superb. I'll be back.'

He had rushed away to draw in yet another group of people. He glanced round the restaurant. There was hardly space left for a table of five people, but he called to Antonis, his younger son, to help him move the last couple of smaller tables together, the guests sat down.

By the time he returned, the girls had decided what they'd like. Constantinos quickly scribbled on his pad, ripped the page out, and rushed the slip of paper back towards the kitchen.

As he passed their table again, he smiled at the girls and told them their order wouldn't be long.

'It's all fresh,' he called back at them, as he moved on to take another order. 'Everything is fresh. Fresh takes time! Yammas!'

The girls sipped their glasses of wine as they sat waiting for their meals. Roxy preferred the red.

Petra and Andrea were enjoying the white, and soon their carafe was quickly empty. Andrea managed to catch the eye of one of the other waiters and asked for some more.

Matthaios arrived shortly with a fresh carafe, and asked if they'd like some bread and butter while they waited. Petra thought that would be a good idea, as she could imagine that Andrea, who was not used to drinking very much, especially in this heat, might soon not be in a fit state to enjoy her meal.

Petra heard Andrea sigh, and she muttered something under her breath that Petra couldn't make out.

'What?' Petra said, knowingly.

'I was just saying how gorgeous he looks,' she replied.

'Who, Matthaios?' Petra probed, thinking that Andrea was probably right.

She thought Matthaios was rather good looking, with his swarthy, tanned complexion and trim figure. He was a few inches taller than his father, had short dark hair and a wonderfully friendly, pearl-white smile.

She smiled, as she watched him navigate between tables.

'No,' said Andrea, with a wistful look in her eye. 'Adonis.'

Petra followed the direction of her gaze.

'His name is Antonis,' she corrected.

'Are you sure?' asked Andrea. 'He looks like Adonis to me…'

'Andrea, please would you put your tongue back in your mouth? You're drooling!'

Later, after they'd finished their meals, Constantinos came and sat down at their table.

'So,' he asked. 'How were your meals? Good?'

They all agreed that the food was delicious, and Constantinos pulled out his notepad to work out their bill. As he wrote down their orders again, he quickly jotted down what each of their meals had cost and muttering to himself in Greek, he mentally added it all up.

In turn, the girls divided the total in three and pulled some notes out from their wallets.

When he brought their change, which they refused, Constantinos also brought with him a small tray with some drinks on.

'I thought you might want to try this,' he said. 'Metaxa. Greek brandy. It's on me, to say welcome to your holidays. Enjoy!'

None of them were great drinkers of spirits, but they each took a sip, to be polite. To their surprise, they found themselves enjoying the taste.

As the restaurant quietened and the last of the guests' dishes had been cleared away, Matthaios came and joined their table, just as his father had done earlier.

'You had nice dinners? I like this time of the evening. We can relax a bit and get to know our guests. What are your names?'

Andrea and Roxy introduced themselves. Petra didn't, despite prompting. After an excellent meal, and after a couple of alcoholic drinks, she was feeling rather playful.

'No,' she teased. 'You'll have to guess!'

Matthaios was a bit taken aback, but decided to have some fun with her. He tilted his head to one side, and stared thoughtfully into her eyes. He rubbed his chin.

'Mmmm,' he said after a few moments. 'To me, you look like an Anne.'

The girls giggled, as Petra shook her head.

'Nope,' she said, raising her eyebrows. 'You're wrong. You'll have to keep guessing!'

She did her best to stifle a yawn. 'I'm sorry, maybe another night though, it's been a long day and we need to get some sleep.'

Matthaios chuckled, he stood up, ready to go back to work.

'In that case, you will have to come back and give me another chance!'

***

The following morning, they set off to explore the village. They wandered down what they later learned was the 'old village' road, past a quiet, white church and the souvenir shop they'd spotted the previous day.

At the end of the road, they could finally see the sea sparkling through a gap between two buildings.

There seemed to be more shops along the road to the right, so they followed that route.

They wandered past several of them selling olive-wood souvenirs, leather goods, summer clothes and beach accessories, until they passed a couple of restaurants, both of which were already busy with customers who were enjoying breakfast in the rays of the sunshine.

They decided to stop for drinks at a friendly-looking place with lots of tables outside, all shaded from the already warm sunshine by large umbrellas.

As they settled at one of the tables, they were approached by a young English lady who asked what they'd like to order. She was about their age, with a very welcoming smile. Petra liked her straight away.

None of the girls were in the mood for hot drinks, so they asked the waitress what else might be available.

'Well, do you like coffee?' asked the girl, and when they all nodded, she continued. 'Why don't you try a frappe? It's like a sort of iced coffee. Very popular in Greece. Very refreshing.'

The waitress brought their drinks, and she chattered whilst they were sipping them appreciatively. She introduced herself as Lisa.

The taverna was still fairly quiet, but she constantly scanned the tables while she talked. She asked when they'd arrived, where they were staying, and whether they'd been to Corfu before.

As they were finishing their frappes, Roxy was already casting her eyes around to see where they might find to sunbathe. Lisa noticed, and waved her hand over the stretch of sand between the sea and the tables where the girls were sat.

'We have loads of places here if you want to lay on the sand.' Noticing Roxy's expression, she continued, 'Or just along the way, there's Layla. She has sunbeds.'

As they left the taverna, following Lisa's directions, she called after them. 'If you want somewhere a bit different for your evening meal, you might want to try our upstairs restaurant. Great for watching the sunset and the food is good too!'

They waved back at her. 'Sounds great! We'll be there!' Lisa put her thumb up in response.

Layla, as they soon discovered, was a middle-aged Greek lady. She had a small patch of sand just a short distance away from the tavernas. She had a dozen sunbeds and large parasols for shade. She was sat on a folding chair, sheltered from the hot sun by a large parasol. Next to her was a stack of folded sunbeds. She quickly put down her knitting as they arrived.

'Hello my ladies!' she said, smiling broadly. 'You want sunbeds? Three? OK, OK! You want shade? One, two? No problem!'

Petra and Andrea shared a parasol. Roxy decided she didn't need one, and laid out in the full sun.

'What is the point,' she said, oiling herself with her newly acquired carrot-infused sun-oil, 'of coming all the way here, and going home as white as we came?'

The other girls shrugged, and hoped she wouldn't regret exposing herself to that extent.

44

The following day, as the girls emerged from the apartment, cups in hand, they couldn't miss seeing a relaxed-looking lady of comfortable proportions in a flowing white kaftan, perched on a chair just down the walkway from them.

She had a small laptop and a bottle of water on a small table next to her.

The lady looked up as the girls took their seats.

As soon as she saw them, she stood and approached the balcony.

'Hello, hello my ladies! I am Christina! Welcome, welcome! How are you, well? How is your apartment, good? It is clean, yes? You have everything, yes?'

The girls could hardly get a word in, but nodded vigorously and smiled.

'I am very sorry I was not here when you arrived,' Christina continued, shrugging her shoulders occasionally.

'I live in Corfu Town. My husband has a business. Very busy. Very busy. Obviously, I have to look after him. I have three sons. They have businesses as well. I must always keep an eye, to make sure they are alright. I cannot always be here. It is a long drive, you understand?'

By now she was leaning, arms folded, on the blue-painted balcony railing.

'Tell me, tell me. You are young ladies. You don't have boyfriends? You are students? What?'

Petra laughed. '*We were students!*' she offered, during a small break in Christina's monologue.

'What, they throw you out?'

'No, no,' Petra reassured her. 'We have finished now. We will graduate soon.'

'Ahh,' said Christina, nodding decisively. 'Ah yes, I understand. You like your apartment? We have everything! Come, I will show you.'

She launched herself at the step to the balcony. It was a high step, so she used the balcony rail to pull herself up.

'Oh my God,' she muttered to herself. 'That step! Come, come. I will show you.'

The girls bundled out of her way as she made for the apartment door.

'See, see!' she called behind her. 'Look the kitchen. Everything is there. Cooker, dishwasher, washing machine, fridge, everything. You cook? No, you are young girls. Young girls don't like to cook. Me, I love to cook. See the shower. It is hot enough? I don't like this shower. When we close for winter, I will throw it down. Make a new one. It will be better…'

She meandered through the whole apartment, pointing out details here and there. The girls were all very relieved they had tidied their bedrooms.

Before they'd arrived, they'd expected to find themselves in far less luxurious surroundings.

Their apartment was well decorated, with lots of colourful paintings on the walls and ornaments on practically every shelf. They'd found standard crockery in the kitchen cupboards, but there was also a tall glass cabinet in the dining area, it was full to the brim with what looked like antique crockery and glass. They had decided to give that cupboard a wide berth, to avoid being responsible for any breakages.

'So, you see? Everything!' said Christina, as she made her way out again onto the balcony. 'Look the glass cabinet. Look! Nice things, yes? Use these things, OK? Use everything. You want anything, tell me. Tell me! I will fix. No problem.'

Christina had to almost jump from the step, holding tight to the balcony rail to stop herself falling.

'Argh, this step!' she muttered frustrated. 'I will fix this in the winter. So, my ladies, tonight I will stay here. I have one empty apartment. I will stay there tonight. There is a customer arriving tomorrow morning. She is an old friend. I want to talk with her. Then I will go to Corfu Town. I will return...sometime. Maybe. I will see. If you have questions or need something, talk to Constantinos. You know him? From the restaurant? Yes, of course. He is a good friend. He will fix for you, OK?'

The girls all nodded, she flopped back into her chair. She waved to the girls. 'OK, my ladies. Have a nice day! Enjoy! Enjoy!'

Later that morning, they made their way to the beach.

As they reached Layla's patch, Andrea noticed how much her knitting had grown.

Layla had already laid out their usual three sunbeds, and a large parasol in anticipation of their arrival, but instead of joining the other two, Andrea went over to chat with Layla about her knitting. She found it fascinating to see how quickly the needles worked, and they soon fell into an easy conversation about the skills involved.

Layla asked her if she'd like to try, and the two of them spent the next few hours sat under Layla's parasol while she taught Andrea the rudiments. The other two could hear them chatting and laughing at Andrea's many stumbling attempts to get it right.

It became their routine for the next few days – frappes and chats with Lisa, sunbeds and knitting with Layla, and then dinner either at Lisa's restaurant or Constantinos'.

They loved every minute of it, although Roxy moaning about her sunburn did detract from it just a bit.

Just after their first weekend in the village, Petra's phone rang. They'd arrived at Lisa's and had just started sipping their usual frappes.

Petra jumped when she heard the strident ring of her phone, and fumbled around in her bag until she found it. It rang off just as she did.

'Oh God,' she whispered, looking at the screen, 'it's my mum.'

She sighed, her shoulders sagging. 'She's such a scatter-brain, my mum. She probably sat on her phone or something.'

Then she thought for a moment. 'I'd better call her back anyway,' she said, resignedly.

It seemed to take forever for the phone to connect.

'Hello?'

'Hello Mum? You called me?'

Petra could sense an edge in her mother's voice. 'I did! Yes, I did! You didn't answer.'

'Mum, sorry. I couldn't find my phone, what's up?' In a sudden moment of panic, she added, 'Is it Dad? Is something wrong with Dad?'

Her mother dismissed her concerns instantly.

'No, he's fine! No, it's Michael!'

'Michael? What on earth has he got to do with anything?'

'He's the problem!' said her mother, her voice raising as she spoke. 'He won't go away!'

'What?' Petra thought quickly, lowering her voice just enough, to try and calm her mum down. 'What do you mean, he won't go away?'

'Him and his mates,' her mum continued. 'They've been camping in the top field. I asked them to go away, but they just won't! I don't know what to do, Petra! Please, please, what do I do?'

Petra drew a deep breath.

'OK Mum,' she said quietly. 'So what's going on? Start from the beginning. How on earth didn't you know he's camping in the top field? They'd have to go past the house to get there, surely. Didn't you see them?'

'He called me and asked if he and some friends could come and camp up there for a week or two. I thought it would be alright. He's a friend of yours, and he seemed really nice.'

'Oh, so you *LET* them camp there? I told you he was trouble!'

'I'm sorry, Petra. I'm so sorry! I thought he was really your boyfriend, but that you'd fallen out or something. I thought I was helping. I didn't know they were going to start digging around the stones, and flying drones all over the place!'

'*WHAT?* Petra shouted. 'What! Digging...Drones, what do you mean, he has drones? You can tell them to stop straight away! Threaten them with injunctions or something! Do something Mum, can't Dad do something!'

Her mum was quiet for a moment.

'I'm sure he would, but...'

'But what?'

'I'm sure he would, but he's in hospital...'

'Huh? Why is he in hospital? Why didn't I know? You just said he was alright. What's wrong with him?'

She heard her mum sigh. 'He had a ruptured appendix...'

Petra bristled. 'Is he alright?'

'Yes, he's on the mend now. I had to call an ambulance for him. They took him in on Saturday...'

'Oh my God, Mum,' Petra said, exasperated. 'Why on earth didn't you let me know? That's why I got you your mobile phone! So, you could call me if there was something wrong.'

'Sorry, darling,' came her reply. 'I just didn't want to spoil your holiday. It's your first holiday abroad, and you've worked so hard to get your degree. There wasn't anything you could do, and I just didn't want to spoil it for you.'

Petra took a couple of breaths, trying to calm her nerves.

'You're right, I can't do anything about Dad. He's in the right place. But I *can* do something about Michael! I'll get home as soon as I can...somehow...and I'll get him sorted for once and for all!'

She could almost sense her mum's relief. She didn't have to say anything.

'Right,' Petra said. 'I'll let you know what I'm doing. And make sure your bloody phone is switched on and has plenty of charge!'

Petra's friends were horrified when she explained what had happened. Both of her friends offered to accompany her home.

'OK!' Roxy had told her. 'I'll be right there by your side. I actually never did like Michael anyway!'

But Petra had already made up her mind that, although she might have to cut her holiday short, there was no reason why they should.

Eventually, they settled on helping her pack her things, while Petra spent most of the afternoon scanning her laptop and making calls to various airlines trying to find the earliest possible flight home.

The best she could find was a flight very early the next morning, but it meant landing at an airport quite far from her home.

'Better than nothing,' she told her friends. 'But with Dad in hospital, I'll just have to hire a car to drive home myself.'

She booked and paid for the flight, then booked a hire car to be picked up from the airport. It was a one-way hire, so at least she wouldn't have to worry about driving it back again.

She winced as she totalled up the numbers. It would be a fair old hit on her credit card, but she resigned herself to it.

She was usually extremely careful about her finances, but sometimes she realised, she just needed to spend. She just had to get home, and quickly.

The next problem was arranging a taxi to the airport. She rang several numbers, but to no avail.

In desperation, she walked up to the restaurant to ask for advice. As it was quite late in the afternoon, the family and their staff were gathered for their meal. Apologising for the interruption, she explained her predicament.

Without hesitation, Constantinos informed her it wasn't a problem.

'Don't worry. It's fine. You will need to be at the airport for maybe four o'clock? So, you will have to leave here about three. We will still be working, so me or Matthaios will drive you to the airport. No problem. Seriously. Now – you will have dinner tonight? We will reserve a table for you.'

She really couldn't refuse.

45

Matthaios came and very quietly collected her bags from the apartment, just before three o'clock. His father's pickup truck was already parked outside of the restaurant.

He offered an apology that he couldn't provide something more luxurious, as he loaded her bag straight into the open back of the truck.

It was a long, very dark drive to the airport, and as they made their way along the twisting mountain roads and through sleeping villages, he tried several times to start up a conversation. Petra, on the other hand, was too tired and worried to make much of an effort, so for most of the journey they travelled in silence.

As they finally approached the airport, she asked how many euros she could give him to compensate for the fuel and his time.

Matthaios shook his head. 'Listen,' he told her. 'We are friends. Friends help friends when they need it. Maybe you can buy me dinner when you come back?'

In the streetlights of the airport, she caught a flash of his white teeth, as he grinned at her. She smiled back.

'I would like to come back one day,' she said. 'But right now I don't know. I have no plans.'

He nodded. 'One day, maybe. I hope so.'

A few minutes later, as the airport doors came into view, he turned toward her. 'When we stop, you should give me a hug and a kiss.

Right? Like we are old friends. Otherwise taxi drivers will think I am stealing their fares by bringing you to the airport. OK?'

Petra shrugged. 'OK, I guess you know best.'

As he pulled her bags out of the back of the truck, he took her into his arms and kissed her cheek gently.

'I hope you have a good flight, and that your father is soon well.'

She offered him a tired smile and thanked him for his kindness.

She waved, as he pulled away, wondering if he would look back. She hoped he would. But then, why would he?

For him, she was probably just another customer, another English girl on holiday. Another girl he could flirt with. Another girl he could have a laugh with, and then wave goodbye to. Why should he even think twice about her?

But then again, she thought, maybe he wasn't like that. Maybe he could see something in her that might be worth more than just a 'summer' thing? She rather hoped he might.

She rather hoped that he might be a man she could trust, someone she could wrap her arms around, and keep forever, given half a chance. Maybe even someone she could fall in love with…given half a chance.

After all, she thought, *he is just, well, drop-dead gorgeous…*

She watched as he reached the end of the drive in front of the airport and circled back towards the main road.

Only the lights of his pick-up were visible, behind the coach park. She waved again.

She couldn't see inside the cab. She waved anyway, hoping, imagining that she could see his unforgettable smile, and his eager wave.

She sighed, tilting her head to one side as she watched his tail-lights recede into the night.

'Oh well,' she muttered under her breath. 'I guess we'll never know now, will we…'

Then she sighed, and turned to walk into the airport.

Thanks so much Michael, she thought to herself, as she walked through the doors. *You've managed to screw my life up yet again...just you wait 'til I see you!*

***

It was late in the afternoon by the time she pulled up outside of the house.

She was already tired from her early start, it had been a long drive from the airport, and her eyes felt prickly as she wheeled her cases into the hallway.

She was a bit disappointed to find that nobody was home.

There was a note from her mother on the kitchen table, explaining that she had driven to the hospital to bring her father home.

'Right,' she muttered to herself, setting off up the hill towards the bridge, 'no time like the present!'

She walked at a fast pace, despite the steepness of the hill, talking to herself, and by the time she reached the stone circle she was so angry at Michael that she no longer felt the ache in her legs.

From her mum's brief description, she knew she wasn't going to like what she saw, as she strode past a Land Rover parked outside of the circle. As soon as she saw the sight for herself, her hopes that her mum had been exaggerating were completely dashed.

She paused briefly to stare, and her eyes widened as she took in the pitched tents, the roped-off areas, the signs of trenches being dug and worst of all, the sight of a hastily-erected winch and pulley system above the bridge itself.

Ropes had been suspended from the scaffolding, wrapped around one end of the bridge, and she could see Michael and a couple other men pulling at ropes, to try and lift the end of the bridge.

Petra let out a horrified scream as she ran towards them.

350

'Stop!' she yelled, *'STOP!'*

The men dropped the ropes as they turned towards her.

Michael raised his hands, trying to keep her away from the bridge. 'No, Petra,' he shouted. 'Keep away! You can't stop us now!'

'Yes, I can!' Petra screamed into his face angrily, struggling to avoid his flailing arms.

'You have no right to do this! Get away! Get out!'

She ducked under his arms, and swerved to avoid the grasp of one of the other men. She jumped onto the bridge.

Taking hold of one of the ropes, trying desperately to pull it free from the scaffolding. It was stuck and she couldn't shift it.

Michael hastily approached her, trying to take hold of her arms, in her blind anger she was stronger than him. She lashed out at his face with one of her hands, still stubbornly holding onto the rope with the other. She winced as she felt her hand hit his face.

He recoiled, clutching his nose. Blood started to pour.

'Go away!' she let out a bitter cry. *'I will not let you do this!'*

As one of the other men tried to wrap his arm around her waist to pull her away, she gave one last strong tug on the rope.

She felt the bridge shift from beneath her feet, it tipped slightly to one side. She hung onto the rope with all her strength, to avoid losing her balance.

The bridge finally broke free from the bank and rose a few inches into the air. It shifted from its spot, a place that had been its home for thousands of years.

Petra screamed in frustration. *'No! Put it back! Please put it back!'*

Michael and his friends backed away, staring intently at the bridge.

Petra looked down to see what they were staring at.

A light mist slowly enveloped her feet.

As she watched, amazed, it rose up her legs and started to change colour.

Within seconds, she was completely immersed in a brightly coloured, misty rainbow. She forced herself not to panic.

She glanced over at the men, who had now stopped halfway between the bridge and the stone circle.

Through the rainbow mist, she could just make out Michael. He was still gripping his nose; his hair was caught in a strong wind.

She looked at the other men, all caught up in the rainbow whirlwind.

All three men were bent over, towards her, tangled in the force of the wind gust.

Petra could feel no wind at all.

She could make out a low humming noise that increasingly got louder. As the noise began to crescendo, the men were blown backwards, rolling over and over, until they hit some of the stones in the circle. They were being forced through the gaps in the stones, and out into the gorse in the fields around the circle.

Petra's attention diverted to the rest of the stone circle, tents were being ripped from their moorings, and flung high into the sky, they were jettisoned in the gorse field along with the men's equipment. Ropes, spades, scaffolding, winches and pulleys soon joined them.

In the distance, a Land Rover drove away at speed down the hill, and towards the road.

She was jolted heavily to the ground as she felt the bridge drop suddenly, and back into its usual resting place.

Instantly, the wind stopped and the mist cleared.

She could hear birds singing somewhere in the distance, she felt her legs begin to shake as she collapsed to her knees on the bridge. She was too dizzy to stand, so she sat. Tears streamed unheeded down her face.

Petra finally got to her feet, and stumbled shakily all the way home, to find her mum and dad sat in the kitchen.

Her mum looked up as she came through the door,

'What on earth have you done to your hair!' she shrieked, while Petra's dad sat at the table staring at her open-mouthed.

'What?' asked Petra, confused. 'I haven't done anything to it, why?'

'Just go and look in the mirror! Look!' her mother demanded, pointing at the mirror on the wall opposite.

Petra stared at her reflection, dumbfounded.

Her reflection didn't have the usual light brown hair.

She stared, with an open-mouthed expression. She recognised her blue eyes, the same small mouth, but the girl who stared back at her, had hair with all the colours of a rainbow. She had rainbow-coloured hair!

Petra's knees gave way again, and she collapsed in a heap on the floor.

As she'd helped her daughter stumble up to her room that evening, Brenda had managed to extract some of the details about what had happened up at the bridge. Though she'd wracked her brain to come up with some plausible explanation for what might have gone on that afternoon, and especially to her hair, she had failed miserably to do so.

There didn't seem to be any reasonable explanation for any of it. She'd planted a very shaken up Petra on her bed, with the promise of a nice cup of tea.

'No sugar, though Mum. Can't stand sweet tea,' Petra said in a low voice.

'I know, my darling,' came her mother's reply, as she pulled the door to behind her. She wondered why Petra would have to remind her not to add sugar to her tea.

She knew full well that Petra never took sugar in anything.

Since the unexplained events of the afternoon, Petra had hardly left the house. She'd stayed in her room most of the time, appearing only for occasional meals. Brenda was getting increasingly worried about her.

She knew that Petra had heard from her friends, Andrea and Roxy. Petra had shown her their texts. They'd asked if she'd got home OK, after she'd left Corfu, and then they'd both let her know that they'd got home safely from their holiday. She'd seen Petra's short, and occasionally one-word replies.

46

A week had passed.

Petra's hair had remained unchanged.

Brenda sat at the kitchen table and waited for her daughter to appear for breakfast. It was a bright morning, sunny and warm, and Brenda sighed. It seemed such a shame to waste it. It would be autumn soon. The days would get shorter, the rain would come, and the frost would set in. Summer, for Brenda, never lasted long enough.

She glanced up as Petra entered the room. She smiled, then got up to switch the kettle on.

'I've been thinking,' she said, as the kettle gradually started to whistle to a boil. 'It's such a lovely morning. It seems a shame to waste it. Do you fancy a walk?' She watched her daughter closely as she sipped her tea.

'OK,' Petra eventually muttered, 'why not.'

They walked for what felt like ages, eventually they ended up at the top field.

Brenda sensed Petra's hesitation as they approached the circle, and caught hold of her hand.

She knew full well that Petra had been avoiding going anywhere near here, but she knew in her heart, that her daughter needed to get over it. Petra's dad, Gerald, had been there a few times in the meantime, and had gradually found and removed whatever evidence he could find of Michael's camp.

'Well,' she said. 'We're here now. Might as well get it over and done with, eh?'

Petra just shrugged her shoulders. They walked forward, through the Summer Stones.

They stood there for a while. Brenda looked all around the circle and over to the bridge. Petra spent most of the time staring down at her feet, looking thoughtful.

'You OK?' Brenda asked.

Petra was silent for a moment. She glanced over at the bridge, and directly into her mother's face. She took a deep breath before she said anything.

'Can you feel it, Mum?' she asked.

'What darling?'

'Can you feel any of the magic? I used to feel it all the time, and I'm sure you did too…like a sort of, I dunno, an atmosphere. A buzz. Can you feel it now?' she said, looking at her mum hopefully. Brenda took a deep breath.

'Can you?' she asked in return.

Petra took a long time to answer, but eventually she shook her head slowly.

'I can't,' Petra whispered sombrely. 'I can't feel anything. I'm so sorry, Mum, but it just feels so empty now. Like it's gone, all the magic, just…gone.'

Petra felt tears begin to sting her eyes and she started to weep. Brenda gathered into her arms and wept with her.

Brenda looked around at the stones.

'Yes, it's strange,' she started. 'I know what you mean. The stones just feel cold now. I mean, they were always cold, but like you said, there was always something, a feeling. I can't describe it…it's changed.'

She sighed, looking finally at the bridge.

'The worst bit is, I don't feel anything from the bridge. Nothing at all. I always used to. I was always able to look at it and at least imagine I could see the colours. Even though they weren't there. I always hoped to see them anyway. It felt like a connection to my mum, and then my dad. Your grandparents. It always comforted me.'

'I'm so sorry, Mum,' Petra whispered. 'I wish, I wish I'd never brought him here, Michael, I mean. He's spoiled everything, hasn't he?'

She hugged her daughter close.

'Yes, I think he has,' she said sadly, 'but if I hadn't been so stupid as to let him camp here it would have been different.'

Petra looked into her mother's eyes.

'So, what do we do now? Can we get it back, the magic?'

'I guess we'll just have to wait and see,' her mum said decisively. 'Come on, let's go back and have a nice cup of tea, eh?'

That was always her mum's solution to any problem.

Petra reflected as she sat on her bed. A nice cup of tea always made things feel better.

Except that it hadn't made her feel better at all. In fact, she wasn't sure she'd ever really feel better ever again.

Petra leant forward on the side of the bed, and stared at her feet, deep in thought. How on earth could a cup of tea make better what had happened? It couldn't. How could a cup of tea make her feel better? It couldn't, because it was all her fault.

Everything was her fault. It was her who had brought Michael here in the first place. It was her who had shown him the stone circle. It was her who had shown him the bridge.

Worst of all, it was her who had caused the bridge to move. *Fair enough*, she thought to herself, it had been Michael and his mates who had tied the bridge up in ropes, but it had been her who had actually pulled the rope that had lifted it.

Petra felt completely despondent. She recalled that the last time she'd felt this bad was when she was little, when her pet rabbit had died. That had been her fault too, she remembered.

She'd forgotten to pull the blanket down over the front of the cage, and it had caught a cold and died. None of the other rabbits in the cage had died, just hers, because it was her fault. Her mum had told her it wasn't her fault, that rabbits sometimes die unexpectedly, but Petra knew better.

The cup of tea her mum had made to make her feel better hadn't helped then either.

But this was far worse than losing the rabbit. This time, it wasn't just her who'd suffer, but the whole family.

The bridge was the whole point of them being here.

It was their link to the past, to their ancestors, not just for her and her mum's generations, but for all those yet to come. And then she thought of the countless generations of women stuck on the other side, with no way to get through to them…and the countless generations of women to come, who would never get the chance to cross the bridge and meet their ancestors.

The link was broken. She couldn't fix it. The only remnant of the magic that had been there in the bridge was now her weird hair. She hated it. It was her punishment. It was all her fault, and she felt so guilty.

'There's nothing I can do. Nothing I can do. Nothing I can do…'

Tears flowed down her face unheeded, until she finally surrendered to the solace of sleep.

***

Andrea had texted to ask if she would be going to the Graduation ceremony, she told Petra she missed her and would love to see her there. It wouldn't have been the same without her.

Petra had decided not to go. She didn't want to risk bumping into Michael, so instead, she'd wait to get her degree in the post.

Brenda had been a bit disappointed about that. She'd already bought a new outfit, but more importantly she felt that it would have done Petra the world of good to attend with her friends. Petra was determined to not go however, so that was that.

As the weeks went by, Brenda's concerns grew stronger, and she started hinting that maybe it might be a good idea to get some medical advice.

'No Mum,' her daughter insisted. 'I don't want anybody to see me like this.'

'Like what darling?' she'd asked, gently.

'Like THIS!' Petra had told her, pointing to her hair. 'I just want it to go back to normal again.'

They'd talked about it for a while.

Brenda had suggested that it might grow out in time, or that they could go to the hairdressers and get it dyed, but Petra was obsessed with the notion that her new hair colour was permanent and that nothing could be done about it.

'If I go out, people will stare at me. I'd hate that!' she'd said.

In desperation, Brenda had persuaded her to take a photo of her hair and send it to Andrea and Roxy, to see what they thought. If they thought it looked stupid then Brenda would help her dye her hair at home.

Brenda had taken the photo, and Petra had sent it to her friends with a simple question: 'What do you think?'

Their replies had been almost immediate.

Oh WOW! Andrea had texted back. *I love it! You look amazing! It really suits you!*

Roxy had been even more forthright and supportive with her response. *I'm so jealous! Where did you get it done? Must have taken ages!*

For the first time in weeks, Petra smiled to herself and over the next few days, she seemed to slowly get back to her usual, confidant self.

One morning, as Petra sat on her bed, brushing her colourful, bright hair, the phone rang.

'Petra?' a woman asked in a distinctly Greek accent 'This is Christina. You know me? Yes, yes, from the apartments! Yes, my darling. How are you, well?'

Petra was surprised to hear from her. 'Yes, thank you Christina. I am well. How are you?'

'Listen, my darling, listen. I have been thinking about you. Yes. It was a shame you had to go home. You have missed your Corfu sun? I know this, my darling. Is your father OK now? Good, good.'

Petra could hardly get a word in.

'So, I am thinking, my darling. You will come back now. Now it is quiet months. Your apartment is very cheap now. I wait for you! You will find cheap flight and you will come to your Christina. Yes, good, good. I want you to be happy. I will make sure of this. Let me know your flight. I will pick you from the airport. Excellent! Bye Bye!'

'Thanks Christina, but I…' Petra's voice trailed off, as the phone line went dead.

Over breakfast, she told her mother about her strange phone call.

'Wow, actually that sounds like a great idea!' her mother replied, enthusiastically.

Petra was quite taken aback. She hadn't expected her mum to be at all pleased at the suggestion.

'But I couldn't possibly go, Mum!' For one thing I can't afford it. Coming back from Corfu last time completely maxed out my credit card!'

'Oh, don't be silly,' her mum said, dismissing the argument with a wave of her hand. 'Your father and I will work something out. Just go and enjoy yourself.'

Petra tried to protest; her mum interjected.

'So, grab your laptop and find a flight!'

Petra did as she was told. She searched all the websites she could think of, and eventually found flights that she felt weren't overly expensive. Even so, she felt guilty to be spending so much money.

When she summoned up the courage to show the cost of the flight to her mother, she just glanced at the details and told her to add to the cart and buy. She slapped her bank card on the table, and told her to use it.

'No excuses, Petra,' she told her. 'Just go!'

Although she didn't say it, she was just relieved that her daughter had something to look forward to.

She'd been so worried about her in the last few weeks, and this seemed like a very positive move forward.

47

As she'd promised, Christina met her at the airport.

She ran to her, arms outstretched, as soon as Petra emerged through the doors from the baggage collection area.

'Oh my God!' she screamed, right into Petra's ear, as they dragged the luggage towards her car 'Oh my God! I am happy you are here! I love your hair! It must have taken a long time, yes? Maybe I should do this…'

'It didn't take long, really…' Petra began, but Christina wasn't really listening. She was shouting at an airport official, and gesticulating that he should load Petra's case into the boot of her car.

He looked quite reluctant, but Christina shouted even louder, until he did as he was told.

'These men!' she said, as they settled themselves into their seats. 'These men think they rule the world. Hah! Then they meet Christina! Then they do as they are told…so tell me, your parents, they are well?'

And so began a long monologue, about Christina's family, and all the latest gossip and goings-on in the village. They finally drew to a halt outside the lane, beside the restaurant.

Before she was even out of the car, Christina was shouting at whoever might be working in the restaurant, to help with Petra's bags.

It sprang to Petra's mind that it wouldn't have mattered much if it was someone from the restaurant or just a passing member of the public. They would still have done as Christina had told them.

'You came back!'

Constantinos smiled broadly at her as he grabbed her bags from the boot of Christina's car.

'I am very happy!' he said. 'Christina was worried about you. Matthaios has been worried that you wouldn't return. Me, I knew you would come back! Some people say they will, but they don't. I just knew we would see you again. I know these things, welcome!'

Petra couldn't quite believe the reception she received; she knew immediately she really was *welcome*.

As Constantinos dragged her bag down the lane to the apartments he kept up a constant dialogue in Greek, with the trailing Christina behind them. She followed as quickly as she could as he marched ahead of her.

Christina's voice boomed from behind, so he could hear.

She gestured, and called at the top of her voice, telling him he should take the bags into the apartment. He shrugged, and shouted back to her, hoisting the bags up onto the landing and into the apartment.

He rolled his eyes, looking sideways towards the vocal Christina.

'Nobody argues with that one!' he said quietly, smiling. 'Seriously, as if I don't know where you are going! By the way, your hair is lovely!'

Petra smiled to herself.

Later that evening, everyone turned to look at her as she walked into the familiar restaurant.

Inwardly, she winced, hating the attention. Outwardly, she smiled with as much confidence as she could muster, and quickly sat down at the nearest available table.

Matthaios smiled broadly, as he brought her a menu. 'I am happy to see you again, Vivienne!' he said as quietly as he could, above the music and nearby conversation.

Despite Christina's claim that the village was very quiet, there now seemed to be a flurry of tourists for this time of year, and it seemed to Petra that the majority of them must have gathered here.

'Still wrong!' Petra answered with a giggle.

As she studied the menu, she glanced up momentarily as a customer entered the room. It was an older lady, and she recognised her as someone who was staying at the apartments. She'd seen her earlier while she was sitting on her balcony, enjoying the warm Corfu sunshine. She didn't know her name, but she smiled at her as the lady approached her table.

'Sorry to interrupt,' the lady announced, 'but it's getting a bit crowded now. It looks like we're both here on our own, so would you mind if we shared a table?'

Petra welcomed her to the table instantly, secretly glad for the company.

Earlier that afternoon, she realised that she missed the company of her friends. The older lady looked friendly, and Petra decided that it would be nice to get to know her.

The lady had only just made herself comfortable when Matthaios approached carrying another menu.

'Maureen!' he said merrily to the older lady. 'Good to see you. How are you, well?'

The two of them exchanged a few words, and it was obvious to Petra that they were well acquainted. He turned to Petra and explained.

'Maureen has been coming to the village every year, for as long as I can remember. She is like family now. I have known her since I was this big,' he said, his hand hovering around his knee level.

'Maureen,' he said, his dark eyes never leaving Petra's. 'I would like to introduce you to this beautiful young lady...but I don't know her name,' he grinned. 'She won't tell me!'

Petra laughed, and explained to Maureen about their name game. 'We started it a while ago,' she said, 'when I was here last. So far, he's guessed and offered a hundred names, but he still hasn't got it right!'

'It is very irritating,' said Matthaios, putting on his best serious face. 'Still, I keep trying. I will find out one day. Now, ladies, what would you like to order?'

Maureen proved to be great company, and the evening went by quicker than Petra would have liked.

As usual, Constantinos sat at their table to work out their bills. As they were leaving the restaurant, Matthaios waved and called over to them.

'Goodnight Maureen!' he said. 'Goodnight, Barbara! Sleep well, see you tomorrow.'

'You've tried that one before!' Petra called back to him, laughing.

From across the restaurant Matthaios held his hands out in an exaggerated expression of frustration.

'I'm running out of ideas now!' he laughed. 'You will have to tell me soon!'

'Maybe, but not yet,' laughed Petra as she and Maureen turned into the lane. As they walked, arm in arm towards the apartments, Maureen suddenly stopped and looked up.

'Kalinihta Tigris!' she said quietly.

'What?' asked Petra, bewildered.

'You've not seen Christina's tiger? Up there, on the balcony to number four?'

Petra looked up. 'I can't see a tiger,' she said. 'Where?'

'Up there, on the balcony, see?'

'In this light, all I can see is a white thing by the balustrade,' Petra replied.

'Well, it's faded a lot now.' Maureen told her. 'But five or six years ago Christina put a big stuffed tiger up there. Of course, then it had all its colours in full glory. Frightened me to death when I first saw it, I tell you! Over the years, with all the sunshine, it's bleached most of the colours out. But I still look up every night and say goodnight to it. It's just one of those little things you do. Christina has very much her own style, I think.'

'She certainly does!' Petra told her. 'You really love it here, don't you!'

Maureen looked her in the eye. 'Yes, I really do. I love it here. It's like home from home…but warmer! And I love Christina. She's really quite unique. You should see her house in Corfu Town. To call it distinctive would be an understatement! Have you seen her dressed up?'

'No, not really,' Petra replied.

'Look next time she is going out with her husband, if she goes from here. She really can be quite stunning!'

'I certainly will, then!' said Petra, as they hugged each other good-night.

It didn't take long for Petra to fall back into the same routine she and her friends had followed during their last holiday here. She would have a light breakfast on the balcony, sometimes exchanging greetings with Maureen if they were both up at the same time.

Christina was often there as well, perched on her usual chair in the main walkway through to the other apartments. They would have a chat while Christina gave usually very vocal instructions to the cleaner. Then Petra would stroll down to the beach for a frappe with Lisa, and sometimes a bit of sunbathing if she was in the mood.

One day she was a little late returning from the beach, and it coincided with the time Matthaios was due to start preparing the restaurant for their evening service.

He waved to catch her attention, and walked over towards her.

'So, Joanne, are you well?'

She laughed. 'Still not right!'

'Now, if I remember, my lady, you promised me dinner? From when I took you to the airport?'

'Oh yes, I'm so sorry,' she replied slowly, her mind whirring. 'I'd forgotten about that. Yes, of course. I do owe you dinner.'

'Are you free tonight?' he asked, eyes hopeful. 'My dad has given me the evening off. That doesn't happen very often, and I'd like to spend it with you. Would that be OK?'

Petra was caught quite off guard. She had imagined they wouldn't be dining together so soon.

'Well, yes, that would be good. Where, here?'

'No, no,' he said. 'That wouldn't be a night off at all! I know a place, though, I think you will like it. What time would be good?'

Petra walked slowly back to her apartment.

She hadn't forgotten her promise at all, of course, but she hadn't wanted to seem forward by reminding him of it.

She hadn't thought that she'd ever come back here, really, let alone that he'd take her offer at the airport seriously.

But he had remembered. He really had. He'd asked her out! He'd actually, really asked her out! Maybe he'd heard her thoughts as he'd driven away from the airport that time? Maybe he really had missed her? She didn't know what to think.

She threw herself into the chair outside her apartment, and took several deep breaths.

Was this real? Had he really, truly, asked her out? *Me?* She thought, *Me? Really? Seriously? Why me? I mean, he's seriously gorgeous. Why would somebody as gorgeous as him, ask somebody as ordinary as me?*

She curled her arms around herself and squeezed herself hard, her mind started racing a million miles an hour.

Make-up…shoes…dresses.

'Oh my *God!*' she muttered under her breath, wishing Andrea or Roxy were there with her. '*I need help!*'

48

Matthaios pressed the doorbell for her apartment, he was on time.

Petra had spent ages deciding on a dress. She had eventually called Christina to help with her dilemma. When Christina walked into her bedroom, she was confronted with Petra in her underwear, and an array of dresses laid out across the bed.

'Oh my God!' Christina muttered. 'What are you doing?'

'I'm trying to decide on what would look best for dinner with Matthaios tonight,' Petra responded, more than a little flustered.

'Short, Long, mid-length? I really can't decide! What colour? Yellow? Or maybe this orange one? I don't know! I'm too nervous to think.'

Petra studied all of the dresses.

'Hmm…this one,' Christina said enthusiastically. 'OK, yes definitely this one. It suits your complexion. Especially your new hair colour!'

Christina held up a pretty blue floral sun dress to Petra's frame, nodding cheerily.

'Oh God!' Petra responded. 'I forgot about my hair!'

Petra thought about her make-up.

'I think, my darling, it is best to keep it simple. Not too much. Just enough. Be yourself, not a painted thing. He will like that better.'

Petra hugged her, and said, 'What would I do without you?'

Before Matthaios was due to collect her, Petra sat on the bed and looked at her reflection in the mirror.

She leapt up, quickly ripped off her dress and threw on another. An off-white one this time, with mid-length sleeves and gold leaf detail near the hem and neckline. She sat down again, more than a bit flustered, just as the doorbell rang.

'Come in,' Petra called, as nonchalantly as she could, her heartbeat quickening. As Matthaios entered the apartment, his eyes went wide, taking in her appearance.

'Wow!' he exclaimed. 'May I say, you look absolutely lovely!'

'Well thank you, kind sir!' she replied. 'One does one's best…'

'Well, you certainly succeeded,' he told her.

Petra smiled, observing his smart, light blue trousers, his brilliant white T-shirt and the soft brown-leather jacket he had draped casually over his arm.

As he leaned in to kiss her cheek, she caught the scent of his aftershave. She couldn't quite place which one it was, 'L'eau D'Issey' maybe? Whatever, it was lovely, heady, and he smelled as gorgeous as he looked.

'Look, now you must tell me your name,' he said, raising his chin in a proud manner. 'I refuse to go to dinner with a girl with no name,' he grinned

She laughed teasingly. 'Well, you must try one last time.'

'OK,' he replied, with a thoughtful expression. He tapped his forehead. 'My last guess, Bridie?'

'Wow!' she gasped, very surprised. 'Actually, you are very close. That is not my first name, but Bridie is my middle name, after my grandmother! How on earth did you guess that? It is not a common name.'

'Well,' he said simply, shrugging his shoulders. 'I have run out of other names, but I remembered a young girl who came to the restaurant last year. I don't remember much about her, but the name was unusual and stayed in the back of my mind.

'You must tell me your first name, before we go home. OK?'

She agreed, and they walked slowly up the lane towards the road, where a taxi was waiting for them in front of the restaurant.

They both waved to Constantinos and Antonis, as the taxi pulled away. Constantinos smiled and waved back, wishing them a good meal.

'OK,' she said, as they seated themselves in the taxi. 'Now you at least know my middle name. Do you have a middle name, or are you just Matthaios?'

He leant his head to one side, and pulled a face.

'Well, to be honest, Matthaios is really my middle name. My first name is Alexandros, but I don't really like it. I prefer to be called Matthaios.'

Petra raised her eyebrows.

'Well, this is weird,' she uttered, a thoughtful expression on her face. 'My grandparents were called Matthew and Bridie.'

'The names go together well I think,' he said confidently, his smile sparkled in the passing streetlights. 'Like your middle name and mine...'

Petra's back stiffened a little. Surely, it must be just a coincidence, their middle names being the same as her grandparent's first names? *Just coincidence*, she thought. *but strange, though.* She wondered if her grandparents' middle names were the same as hers and Matthaios's first names, 'Petra' and 'Alexander.'

No, surely not. She'd never heard of her grandparents having middle names at all, but if they turned out to be the same as their names...that would be just too weird. She'd have to ask her mum, next time she called her.

The restaurant he'd chosen was a traditional Greek one.

Hard, straight-backed chairs, painted blue. White tables with blue tablecloths. White walls, with blue painted windows and doorframes, comfortable, warm and inviting. It was quiet, and not overcrowded either, with guests or cramped with furniture.

'This is a very good place,' he told her, as they took their seats. 'Excellent food, mostly for Greek locals. You will enjoy, I think.'

A waitress approached and greeted them with a huge smile. She obviously knew Matthaios, who kissed her cheek and spoke rapidly to her in Greek. The waitress grinned broadly at her, then turned to Matthaios and said something that sounded like 'Brava, Matthaios, Brava!'. Then she shook her head and was laughing heartily, as she made her way to the kitchen. Petra had no idea what was said, but smiled to be polite.

'You are friends?' she asked.

'She is my cousin, Eleni, her husband Kostis is the chef. This is their restaurant.'

'She seems very kind,' Petra replied. 'I love her laugh!'

Matthaios returned her smile.

'She is good fun. Kostis is an excellent chef. Now, I have ordered for you a Meze. I hope you will like it. It is sort of a selection of different Greek food. Like samples, if that is the right word?'

'I'll certainly give it a try,' Petra told him. 'It sounds like it might be an interesting evening!'

Their wine arrived, and they chatted about all sorts, while they waited for their food to be served. He was good company, and Petra felt relaxed when she was with him.

While they picked their way through what seemed to be an impossibly large selection of dishes for just two people, they told each other about their families.

Petra spoke about the farm, and what she remembered of her grandfather's stories about mowing hay. Matthaios exchanged his tales about the family's olive groves, and how important they were to them.

'Some of our trees are very, very old. My father thinks maybe more than two thousand years, but they still give olives. They are amazing trees. We make enough olive oil from them to use in the restaurant all year.'

He made her laugh with wild stories about the antics some of their customers got up to while they were at the restaurant, especially during their 'Greek Nights,' which Petra had seen for herself could be great fun. Matthaios and his family always seemed to go out of their way to make sure their customers joined in, if they could, or at the very least, laugh and tap their feet to the music.

As the evening drew on, Petra had to reluctantly admit she really couldn't eat any more of the delicious food.

Eleni returned to ask, through Matthaios, if she would care for a dessert. Petra declined, saying that they had been spoiled with the quantity and quality of the mezes, at which Eleni seemed satisfied that the restaurant had done their job well.

She motioned for them to stay at the table while she bustled off once more to the kitchen, quickly returning with a tray of drinks to conclude their evening.

Matthaios thanked her, and pointed to the tray.

'She doesn't know what you prefer, so she has brought both ouzo and Metaxa. Do you like ouzo?' he asked.

'Is that the one that smells like aniseed?' she asked, and when he nodded, she said, 'sorry, I really don't like aniseed at all. Anyway, I think I've really had quite enough to drink for one night.'

Matthaios passed her a glass of Metaxa, and took another for himself.

'Eleni would be insulted if we don't take something,' he glanced at Eleni who was busy with another table.

'I like ouzo very much,' he continued, 'but it does stay on the breath afterwards. So, I will enjoy a Metaxa with you.'

Petra felt really rather flattered he considered her like that, and raised her glass to him.

'Thank you so much for a wonderful evening. I can't remember the last time I enjoyed myself this much.'

'It's my pleasure.' He nodded. 'I feel the same.'

After a few moments of quiet, she looked at him and smiled.

'So,' she said, 'after such a lovely evening, it would seem silly to go on with our game.'

'Ah…the game,' he said, leaning back in his chair, smiling. 'You're finally ready to tell me your name?'

'Yes,' she admitted, giggling quietly to herself. 'It's been fun, though, hasn't it?'

'It's been fun' he repeated, 'but very irritating at the same time!'

'I'm sure,' she said, smiling back at him.

He leant towards her. 'So, are you going to tell me or not?'

'My name is Petra.'

'You have a Greek name!' he announced, forgetting that the few people left at the surrounding tables could overhear.

'Is it?' she asked, surprised. 'I had no idea! My mum told me she'd made a friend while she was on holiday in Malta once with my grandparents. Her friend was called Petra. Mum really liked it, and always wanted it for her daughter if she ever had one.'

Matthaios smiled, nodding.

'You know that most Greek names have a meaning?' he asked.

'I wouldn't know,' she said.

'Well, your name, Petra, in Greek this means stone. It's a good name!'

Then he noticed that Petra had suddenly paled.

'What's the matter?' he asked concerned, he sat forward in his chair. He really hoped he hadn't ruined their lovely evening with a stupid remark, though he couldn't for the life of him work out what he said wrong.

Petra shook her head slowly.

'No, it's OK,' she said, stroking her rainbow hair distractedly. 'It just took me by surprise. Sorry.'

This time it was his turn to shake his head, and leaning towards her, he reached out to take her hand in his.

'I'm so sorry,' he uttered. 'I don't know what I said that upset you.'

'Stone is such an important name to our family.'

'I'm sorry, I didn't know. Tell me?'

'It's a long story,' came her quick reply, 'I wouldn't want to bore you…'

'We have all the time you need. Now, do you want a taxi home, or maybe you would like to walk? It's a nice walk, along the beach road. It's not too cold yet, I think.

'Actually, that sounds rather nice. It'll walk off some of that excellent food, and if you really want, I'll tell you the story.'

Matthaios caught Eleni's eye, and asked for the bill. Petra bent down to pick up her clutch bag. She rustled through it for her purse.

'What are you doing?' Matthaios asked as she started pulling out some notes.

'Paying the bill, of course,' she said, 'it's the dinner I owe you. Remember?'

'Oh, no, no, no!' he whispered loudly. 'Would you show me up? What man does not pay for the bill when he has a beautiful lady with him. People would laugh at me. This will not happen!'

'Oh, sorry…' she said simply. 'I hadn't thought of that.'

'I don't know about it in your country,' he whispered quietly, 'this is Greece. Here the man pays, if he is a man. OK?'

'Fine,' she said, smiling. 'So, if I'm not allowed to pay for the meal I owe you, I'll just have to cook one for you instead. Would that suit your ego?'

Matthaios beamed at her. 'That will do nicely,' he said, nodding happily.

Then she realised that he'd won. He'd managed to secure another date with her. She sank back into her chair feeling content.

'You are too clever for your own good,' she laughed.

A smile tugged at the corner of Matthaios lips; he raised his eyebrows.

'Is good, eh?' he questioned. She just nodded slowly; her cheeks ached from smiling all evening.

As they stood to leave, Eleni walked them to the door, she turned and gave Petra a brief hug.

'Is good to see Matthaios happy,' Eleni told her. 'You are good for him, I think. Thank you. I hope you will come again soon.'

As they emerged from the restaurant a while later, Petra shivered a little.

'You are cold?' asked Matthaios. 'You want my jacket? Or would you prefer a taxi?'

'No, no,' Petra reassured him, 'but I'm glad I brought my cardigan!'

The night was dark and cloudless, as they began their walk. There were no streetlights on this section of the road. Petra looked up to see a night sky full of stars.

'Absolutely beautiful,' she whispered, just loud enough for him to hear.

Matthaios smiled at her in the darkness. 'It's good when there are no lights and you can see such a big sky over the water. I guess we can see it anytime. I sometimes forget to look.'

'You really are very lucky to live in such a lovely place.'

He nodded in the darkness. 'I know,' he said, 'but it's just home to us. We don't even think about it. But yes, you're right, we are very lucky.'

They walked in silence for a while, until Matthaios cleared his throat and asked, 'Would you like to hold my hand? The road is dark, and you might trip...'

'Only if you insist!' she giggled, and squeezed his hand gently in hers.

Squeezing her hand in return, Matthaios asked if she was ready to tell her story. She sighed.

'So,' she began, 'it all starts with a girl with no name...'

'Ah!' he interrupted, rolling his hand over hers, 'that's just like you! You were *"the girl with no name"* until tonight!'

'That was only because I was teasing you,' she laughed.

It was a long walk back to the village; she still hadn't quite finished the story by the time they reached the lane to her apartment.

As they approached, he put his fingers to his lips.

'Shh,' he said, reaching the corner between the restaurant and the lane. 'They'll still be working. If they see me, I'll have to go and help close.'

They crept into the lane, trying to be invisible.

Petra heard Constantinos's voice in the dark.

'Matthaios!' he spoke some words in Greek that she didn't understand.

Matthaios's shoulders sank in disappointment, as he answered.

He rolled his eyes. 'I told my dad I'll be there in a minute,' he said.

As they reached Petra's apartment, he motioned that they should sit on the steps to the balcony.

'So, what happened next?' he asked quietly, sounding intrigued for the rest of the story.

'So, I was so angry that Michael could have done such an awful thing, after I specifically told him not to.

'I made my way up to the bridge as soon as I got home. What I saw there…well, it was just terrible! Michael and his friends had set up camp on the grass right inside the stone circle.

'They had set up all sorts of equipment and it looked like they were getting ready to dig holes around some of the stones. But the worst thing was, and what had frightened me most of all, was that they had built a sort of crane over the bridge. There were ropes from it, and underneath the bridge. They were getting ready to lift it! My bridge!

'Well, I can tell you, I had never been so angry in my life. I completely flipped out. I screamed at them, at the top of my voice and ran at the bridge.

'I kept screaming and tried to unravel the ropes, but I couldn't shift them. Michael ran up to me and tried to calm me down. He kept trying to tell me how important it was for them to investigate. I shouted at him that I didn't care about archaeology, but he didn't listen, and he tried to stop me untying the ropes.

'In the end I found myself stood on the bridge with him trying to drag me off. I started jumping up and down.

'Then the strangest thing happened. I started to hear a sort of humming noise. It was coming from the bridge itself. I looked down, and I could see a sort of mist around my feet. It changed colour, and was creeping higher and higher up my legs. As it reached my stomach, a wind started to blow across the bridge.

'It got stronger as the mist grew higher and higher. Then…I dunno…the world sort of exploded around me. I was completely covered in the mist, but surrounding me was this enormous wind.

'I couldn't see much because of the mist, but I got glimpses of people running away screaming, and of tents and equipment bring lifted high in the air and tossed all over the place. I was really scared; I can tell you!

'Then suddenly everything stopped. The wind was gone, and so was the mist, and I was left standing there on top of the bridge.

'As I looked around, the whole circle of stones was empty and calm. Outside, though, all sorts of bits of rubbish were caught up in the gorse and against the field walls, further away. I couldn't see any people there at all. Michael wasn't there, and nor were his friends. The strangest thing was that the bridge felt different. I'd always felt…like a sort of buzz, I suppose. Not something I can describe, but there was always something, like an atmosphere. It wasn't there now. It felt different, empty.

'Once I'd stopped shaking, I made my way back down to the house. As I opened the kitchen door, my mum shrieked at me. *Oh my God, Petra! What happened to your hair?*

'I just stood there and said nothing.

'Then she told me to look in the mirror. My hair turned to this. Like a rainbow! I've no idea what happened exactly.

'I didn't sleep hardly at all that night, and the next morning I went back up to the bridge. It looked the same as it had always been…but it was like there was nothing there. There was no buzz. No atmosphere. It just wasn't there anymore.

'After that, I really didn't want to leave the house. I stayed in my room most of the time. Mum was really worried. She was so apologetic. It was her who'd let Michael and his mates up there, and she felt awful about what had happened.

'I stayed in my room for weeks, but my hair didn't change back.

'That's when I got a call from Christina. Mum encouraged me to come back here, to Corfu. So here we are.'

By now she was fighting back the tears at the recollection of the ordeal.

Matthaios had put his arm around her and drawn her close. Eventually the tears subsided. She wiped her face on her arm and looked up at him.

'I bet you think I'm crazy now.'

He only smiled; the same warm smile she was starting to grow rather fond of.

'You don't believe a word of it, do you?' she sobbed again.

'Well,' he said, 'I'll remember not to make you angry; that's for sure!'

She laughed, relieved to have got it all off her chest.

She sighed. 'Got any questions then?'

He looked at her thoughtfully. 'Plenty, actually,' he said, 'but my questions will wait until tomorrow. Come to the restaurant in the morning. Maybe about eleven? I will be there. I will make breakfast for you. Just for you, we will sit at the family table. No guests, no family, just us. Then we can talk some more.'

She looked up at him, tears welling in her eyes again. She nodded.

'Thank you.'

'What for?' he asked

'For listening, and for tonight. It was very special.'

'I hoped it would be,' he said, 'and for me it was too. I'm happy you thought so.'

Then he leant towards her and kissed her, very gently, on the cheek.

'Sleep well,' he said, rising from the step. 'I'd better get back there and help my father out.'

She stood, leant against the balcony railing and stretched her back.

'See you in the morning,' she called after him very quietly, conscious of the other guests. Then she turned and walked towards the door, but glanced back in his direction.

He reached the end of the lane, and she could see his smile as he blew her a kiss.

She smiled and blew a kiss back, as she stepped into the apartment, closing and locking the door behind her.

She reflected on the evening's events as she turned out the lights in the lounge and made her way into her bedroom.

It had been, she thought, a lovely evening. She'd learned a lot about him during their meal, and she'd shared with him more, much more than she'd imagined she might ever be able to share with anyone else.

She certainly hadn't planned to, by any means, and she wondered, sleepily, if she'd been right to do so. Towards the end of the evening, though, whether it was right or wrong, she'd come to feel that she could trust him with her secrets.

And to her surprise, he hadn't laughed at her.

He'd smiled, and squeezed her hand encouragingly every now and then. That was important to her, very important.

As she dropped into bed, turned out the bedside light and pulled the quilt up over her shoulders, she wondered what he was doing now. Washing the dishes probably, she thought, and maybe preparing tomorrow night's meals. She wondered if he was thinking about her, she was certainly thinking about him.

She hoped he would sleep well, once he got home, and that he might dream about her. She knew beyond doubt that she'd dream about him.

More than anything, she wished he was still here with her. Talking, if he wanted to, or maybe just holding her.

She smiled to herself as she closed her eyes, and she could feel something stir deep within her soul, as she drifted off to sleep.

49

When she arrived at the restaurant in the morning, Matthaios was nowhere to be seen.

Petra frowned, thinking he'd either overslept or forgotten.

She heard a faint clatter of utensils behind the scenes, so she knew he was there. Relieved, she sat down at the family table and waited.

What they called 'the family table' was just outside the entrance to the kitchens and the room they prepared the drinks in. It was big enough for maybe a dozen people, but it was only used for guests when there really wasn't anywhere else to seat them. Most of the time the table was used as a brief retreat for those who were working in the restaurant, whether family or not.

She had noticed it before, on any given afternoon, this was where they all gathered to share a meal before the evening service began.

They would sit, eat, have a couple of drinks and chat. Then they'd go off to their various stations to begin their evening's work. The 'family table' was important to them, as a place to relax, to unwind. Although there was only herself and Matthaios in the restaurant, she felt as though she was intruding on their family privacy, and she felt a little uncomfortable at being somewhere she didn't really belong.

Matthaios's face soon appeared in the doorway.

'Good morning Kalimera!' he grinned at her. 'Are you hungry?'

'Err, after last night's meal, not particularly!' she laughed.

'No problem,' he said, placing a plate of bacon, eggs and fried to-matoes in front of her. 'I made what I thought you would like. Eat what you want. Leave what you want.'

Petra found an appetite she didn't think she had, and it didn't take too long before her plate was clear.

As she looked up to thank him for her breakfast, she noticed that he was gazing at her intently.

'You're staring at me!' she said, smiling, feeling both flattered and awkward at the same time.

'I'm sorry,' he said, placing his elbows on the table and resting his chin on his hands. 'Do you know what?'

She raised her eyebrows and shrugged her shoulders. 'What?'

'Every evening you come into the restaurant, and I think you look beautiful. Last night, you looked just gorgeous. I loved your dress and your make-up. Gorgeous.'

She blushed. 'No, I did not,' she laughed, waving away his com-pliment.

'No, you did,' he affirmed. 'But this morning…'

'What?' she fished, nervous as to what his answer might be.

'This morning, you look stunning.'

'Don't be daft,' she scoffed, feeling her cheeks heat. 'What, shorts, T-shirt and no make-up? You must be joking!'

'I have not seen you in the morning before. I am usually just wak-ing up at this time. I think the morning suits you best. Simple, natural, perfect. This is all I can say.' He grinned broadly at her as she blushed a deep crimson, totally embarrassed. She knew she had to change the subject quickly, before he said something more.

She cleared her throat.

'So, you were going to tell me what you thought of my story.'

'Well,' he said, sitting back from his empty plate but continuing his thoughtful pose.

'I was surprised by your story. It is a fascinating one. I think either what you said is true, or you are simply a very good storyteller.'

'OK,' she said, unsure whether to be disappointed or relieved.

'So?' she uttered.

'So, I think you are both,' he said. 'I believe what you told me, and I think you told it well.'

Flustered by how intensely he looked into her eyes, she glanced down at the table and shuffled in her seat. She picked up his empty plate and stacked it on top of hers.

'I think,' he continued, placing his hand gently over hers to grab her attention. 'Look, I think I will not say this right. I am very tired. We finished last night, like always, at about four o'clock in the morning. I tried to sleep. I was thinking about you and what you told me. I tried to figure it out, what happened, and what the mist and the wind meant, and why your hair changed colour. I think it is beautiful, by the way.' His smile dazzled her, as it always did.

'So did you work it out?' she asked, almost hopefully.

'I don't know,' he shrugged. 'Maybe. I don't know.'

'OK,' she said. 'Well, I have no answers, so tell me what you think.'

He drew a deep breath. She fiddled with her hair distractedly, nervous at what he might say. She hoped he'd be kind.

'I think these are strange things,' he said. 'You said that the lady who brought the stone to your house was looking for somewhere it could rest for always. Right?'

'More or less. Sort of…' she nodded.

'Then I think that if its nest was disturbed, if it was under threat, then it might look to find somewhere safer. Does that make sense?'

She listened intently, trying to piece together his words with the story she knew.

'So maybe it chose you as a host?'

'A host?' she asked. 'What does that mean?'

'You said your distant ancestor passed her stone to her daughter, and then she to hers and so on,' he said, circling his hand repeatedly. Petra nodded.

'But maybe, in the first place, the stone was waiting to be found? Maybe it was just that your ancestor was the lucky one who picked it up. It found her, not she found it? You understand?'

'I am sort of following; I think…go on…'

'So, then it eventually found its way to your farm. And it managed to get your other ancestor to lay it to rest there. It had all the ladies in your family to look after it, for many, many years, right?'

'Uhumm…'

'So maybe then, when it was under threat of being discovered, it had to find a way to escape. So, there you were, jumping up and down right above it, with threatening ropes all over the bridge, so what was it to do?'

Petra stared at him, wide-eyed.

'So, I think,' he continued, spreading his hands to emphasise the point. 'It chose you to escape through. You are called stone, after all, like it's original rescuer. You were the next logical carrier for it. Does it make sense?'

Petra held her hand over her mouth.

'Do you mean that the stone has a life of its own? How can that be? That doesn't make any sense at all to me!'

'OK,' he said, 'so we will talk about stones.'

'Sorry?' she said, 'I'm getting lost here. Not following your logic at all now.'

Matthaios flattened his hands on the table, as though making a point.

'Well, stones,' he began, 'stones come in many shapes and sizes. Some have pretty colours, like the one you talked about. But they all have one…erm…thing they share. Is that right? Yes, that is it.'

He stopped and took a breath, while he thought of the right way to say what he wanted to tell her.

'See, they don't go away. They change, but they are still there. Does that make sense?'

'Erm…not really. Sorry!'

'I wish I had more words. See, I speak Greek. I think in Greek. Is easy in Greek!' he told her. 'What I mean, you can break a stone, but then you have more stones. They are just smaller, right?'

'OK,' she said, trying to understand where he was going with this.

'So yes,' he continued. 'Nothing is gone. If you can grind a stone, then you have dust. It does not go away. You can grind it as small, small, small…but it is still there.'

Petra gave him what she hoped looked like an encouraging smile.

'What I mean, it is still the same stone…but changed. See? It is still there but…erm…different. Dust will blow away in the wind. Then it just spreads out all over the world. If it is fine enough you can breathe it in, or take it through your skin. Like…like…'

He slapped his forehead in frustration.

'Oh, what is this thing…you know, stuff to throw on babies, like after a bath…'

'Oil?' she suggested

'No! No, not oil…powder to dry…'

'Oh,' she said, talcum powder?'

'Yes!' he said, snapping his fingers, 'yes, the talcum powder.' He took a breath.

'So, this what I think. The stone was threatened. It was disturbed. It changed, and is gone into you.'

Petra ran her hand through her colourful hair again.

'So, what you're saying is, the stone is inside me? And the colours in the stone are in my hair now?'

'Yes! This is what I think!' he said, nodding enthusiastically.

Then he shrugged his shoulders, and spread his hands. 'I might be wrong, but…'

'That's a lot to think about,' she said, puzzled. 'I think I need to work this through in my mind. I…'

'I'm sorry,' he told her, standing abruptly, and shuffling their plates. 'I'm sorry, my English is too bad…'

'No, seriously, I understood what you meant. It's just a lot to take in. Anyway, your English is much better than my Greek! All I know is, "good morning" and "thank you", and stuff like that.'

'So,' he asked her, sitting back in his chair again. 'So what is Greek for "good morning?"'

'Kalimera!' she said, with a confident smile.

'And, "thank you?"'

'Efharisto, I know that one too!'

'So,' he tested 'What does "Se agapó" mean?'

'I don't know that one,' she said, shaking her head. 'What does it mean?'

'Never mind,' he muttered, for once looking shy. 'I will tell you one day.'

'No, you must tell me now! C'mon then, what does it mean?' she said

'OK,' he said quietly, shrugging his shoulders. 'It means, "I love you…"'

'Oh, you cheeky thing!' she said, sitting back in her chair, wagging her finger at him, and laughing. 'I nearly fell for that one!'

He laughed, as he leant across the table and took her hand in one of his. His other hand cupped her face. He stroked her cheek gently with his thumb.

'Anyway, you have a lot to think about.'

'You know, I wonder if it's the same with places?' he asked, his face thoughtful. 'Like, you think you choose them, but really, maybe they choose you? Maybe if you are somewhere and you don't feel comfortable, even if you've been there a long time, this place is telling you to move on. And if you go somewhere and feel completely at home, though you've only just arrived. Maybe that place is telling you that you need to be there. You understand?'

'I think so…sort of…' she sighed.

He squeezed her hand gently, and continued, 'Christina said you were thinking you should go home soon. Please stay a bit longer. Please don't go home yet. We have more to talk about. I really, really like you, and I want to know you more.'

She smiled up into his sparkling eyes.

'I'll think about it, but I'll have to go home at some point.'

'But if the Home Stone is inside you now, you are at home wherever you choose to be, no?'

He smiled, and let go of her hand. He stroked her cheek one last time, and sighed. He stood to his feet and collected their dishes.

'I'd better clean up here before the others get cross with me,' he said, laughing.

'Come here for dinner tonight? I will take a break later. Then we can talk some more. Please?'

She nodded, and offered to help with the tidying.

'No problem,' he said, removing the plates from her hand. 'See you later.'

Later that evening, once service had died down and there was little for him to do, other than tidy things away, he came to her table and asked if she'd like to go for a walk.

'Just a short walk,' he said. 'I don't have long.'

They walked up to the crossroads and back again, deep in conversation. Once they were clear of his family's view, he took her hand in his, and held it firmly as they walked. They talked about all sorts of things, everything and anything. She was drawn to him more and more. She decided that it felt good, more than good, and she hoped he felt the same.

As they neared the restaurant, she squeezed his hand and asked, 'So, when will you have another evening off? I've decided what I would like to cook for you.'

'You don't really have to do that,' he said. 'It's not really important. We can go out for a meal somewhere if you want?'

'Absolutely not! I'm honestly not that bad a cook,' she told him, crossing her arms. 'And I want to prove it to you!'

He laughed, and said he would have a word with his dad and let her know tomorrow.

Just before they arrived back at the restaurant, he turned and took her into his arms and kissed her.

'See you tomorrow,' he said, smiling broadly at her.

She found that she could hardly breathe, let alone speak, so she just nodded.

He walked in through the main entrance to the restaurant. She continued to the corner and stepped into the lane.

As she passed the side entrance to the restaurant, she peeked in.

He was standing there watching her, smiling. She smiled back and continued walking, though her legs didn't quite feel like they belonged to her, and she had to concentrate hard, making sure not to stumble on the flagged walkway.

50

The next morning, Petra woke to a loud banging on her front door.

'Seriously!' she muttered to herself. She rolled out of bed as quickly as she could, bumping her forehead on the bedside table.

'Ommph!' She rubbed her head. 'Hang on,' she called out. 'I'm coming!'

She quickly pulled on one of the beach dresses she'd thrown over the back of the bedroom chair and unlocked the front door.

'Christina!' she said, surprised. 'Sorry, I must have overslept!'

'No problem, my darling, I could not sleep so I got up early and made you breakfast,' Christina said, waving her hand over the balcony table. 'See? You would like some?'

While Petra fetched some plates and cutlery, Christina explained, 'It is too hot now, this weather. This is too hot for me. I do not like it to be so hot. This is why I like to come to the village to spend time.'

She continued to chat and serve breakfast for Petra.

It was a dish that Petra had never seen before. It looked like baked eggs, tomatoes and some other vegetables cooked in a roasting dish, and Christina, with one hand balanced on her hip, dished up a generous portion.

She served none for herself.

'Aren't you having any?' Petra asked. 'Look, there's far more here than I could possibly eat. I will feel uncomfortable eating all this to myself. Please have some.'

'I don't like to eat much when it is too hot,' Christina shook her head. 'I will not eat. But I will sit here and drink my water.'

Petra shrugged, and resignedly picked up a fork.

'You know I live in Corfu Town, yes?' continued Christina. 'It is too hot there now. Hotter than here! There is no air. I cannot breathe. I cannot sleep. It is a problem for me, this heat.'

She sipped some water from her bottle, and twisted in her seat so that she could see Petra better.

'You like this?' she asked, indicating the food, and giving a very satisfied smile when Petra nodded. She couldn't reply because her mouth was too full.

'So, Petra, I want to take you out this morning,' she continued. 'You have not left the village yet to explore, I think. This I cannot allow. You must see more of Corfu while you are here. You like ice-cream? I will take you to Kassiopi. It is not very far. On the way back I will take you to my favourite ice-cream shop. You will like it.'

Petra felt that she couldn't refuse, despite having already experienced some of Christina's erratic driving on the journey from the airport.

'Thank you, Christina. I would like that very much!'

'Good. We will do this. I will go and change my clothes, then we will go, OK. Afterwards I must go to Corfu Town to check on my husband. He works very hard, you know. I must be there often to look after him. I made a tray of eggs like this for him also. It is in my freezer now. I will take it with me to give to him tomorrow morning. He likes these eggs too.'

Just as Petra finished her last mouthful of food, it started to rain.

She jumped from her chair and ran next door to one of the larger apartments. There were comfortable, soft furnished chairs all along the balcony, which was much larger than her own.

All around the balcony there were clear plastic sheets rolled up like window blinds, and ready to drop down to shelter the balcony in case of rain.

She grabbed hold of the long, hooked tool which wound them up and down, and frantically turned it to lower the roller blinds. When one was at ground level, she unhooked the tool and ran to the next sheet. After a few minutes, all of the plastic sheets were down and sheltering the chairs within.

'Thank you, my darling. Thank you! It would have taken a long time to dry these chairs.'

'It's OK,' said Petra. 'I just couldn't see all these lovely things being ruined by the rain!'

'I will change now,' Christina told her. 'The rain will stop in a minute and we can go, yes?'

Christina had parked her car slightly further up from the restaurant, with two wheels on the pavement in an effort to avoid scratches from passing cars and trucks.

It was a large car, and as far as Petra could tell, quite a new one. Like almost all of the cars Petra had seen in Corfu, it was covered in a layer of dust, only partially cleared by the recent downpour of rain.

As they approached the vehicle, Petra automatically went to open what she thought was the passenger door, forgetting that in Greece cars drove on the right.

'You want to drive maybe?' Christina laughed.

'Oh, sorry!' Petra replied, embarrassed, walking quickly around the car. 'I'm still not used to being in cars with the steering wheel on that side.'

Once they closed their doors, Petra reached for the seatbelt. She noticed Christina didn't.

'I cannot wear these things,' she said. 'It is not comfortable for me.'

Petra, remembering the drive from the airport, said, 'We have to use them in England. We have no choice. I'm used to it, and I really wouldn't feel comfortable without.'

Christina just shrugged. 'Up to you,' she said, turning the ignition key.

The air-conditioning whirred into action, blowing out cold air, while Christina slid the automatic gear into reverse and pressed the accelerator very firmly.

At the last minute, she turned her head to see where she was going, as the car reversed quickly out into the main road. She muttered under her breath when a van sounded its horn several times in an effort to stop her backing into it.

'Ach!' she exclaimed as she waited impatiently for the road to clear. 'You see what I mean? These drivers!'

The drive to Kassiopi was uneventful, and Christina enjoyed pointing out some of the local landmarks along the way. Petra found it very interesting, but rather wished Christina wouldn't look away from the road for quite so long, while she recounted her stories.

Kassiopi, Petra thought, was a really pretty place. Like the village she stayed in, it had once been a fishing port. Now, like many other places on the coast, it was almost entirely devoted to catering for the tourist trade.

They spent an hour or so there, sitting on a bench overlooking the harbour. While they sipped from their water bottles, they chatted about all sorts of things.

Christina had had a really interesting life, and Petra found herself liking her more and more.

Christina seemed just as interested in Petra's life, her family and her friends. She was especially interested in knowing what Petra's ambitions were, and she listened intently as Petra outlined her plans, and hopes and dreams now that she had graduated.

'To be honest,' Petra told her, 'I don't really have any firm plans at the moment. I'm sort of happy to go with the flow. I haven't really thought too far into the future. I never do. I guess I'll just have to see what happens, and if I like it, I'll do it. If I don't, I won't!'

'OK,' said Christina simply. 'Sometimes it is good to be flexible, eh? Now, you would like ice-cream?'

As they settled into some soft, comfortable chairs outside of the ice-cream shop, Christina asked what flavours Petra liked best.

'So,' Christina told her. 'Here they do some wonderful ice-cream. We come here often, my husband and me. My favourite is the waffle with the flavour ice cream you like. You want to try?'

The ice-cream the waitress brought to their table was enormous.

'Oh my goodness, Christina!' Petra exclaimed. 'It's soooo much! It looks wonderful, but I'm really not sure I would be able to eat all this!'

Christina waved away her concerns. 'Eat what you want. Leave what you want. It doesn't matter, OK.' She smiled. 'Enjoy!'

While they slowly took their time and consumed their ice-creams, Christina spoke, 'So, you are finished with university now?'

Petra nodded. 'Yep!' she said 'All done, thank goodness. I really enjoyed it, but I must admit I'm glad it's finished.'

Christina nodded. 'Matthaios also was happy to finish university I think.'

Petra looked up, and raised her eyebrows.

'Oh, I didn't realise he had been to university. What did he study?'

'He finished last year,' Christina told her. 'He studied architecture. He did well, Constantinos told me.'

'Why isn't he working as an architect, then? It would be a shame to waste it. Doesn't he want to be an architect?'

'It is difficult for him, to find a job here in Corfu,' said Christina. 'His father paid for his university. Matthaios helped in the restaurant as much as he could when he was at home, but it cost his parents a lot of money and Matthaios wants to pay them back.'

'I'm sure,' Petra said. 'I had to take on a huge debt to pay for my course. If I ever get a job, I will have to start paying it back. It'll take years!'

'Is not the same here,' Christina told her. 'Here the students, or their parents, have to pay immediately for everything. Is a lot of money. *A lot of money!*' Christina rubbed her thumb and middle finger together. 'You understand? Children work hard at university, and then they try to pay back their parents. So, Matthaios works for his father all the hours he can, and he looks for an architecture job as well.'

'I hadn't realised,' Petra replied. 'I imagined he was just a waiter...'

'That's what he does, like his father did all his life. It is the family business.' Christina shrugged. 'Next will be Antonis for the university. His father will pay for him also. This is how it is. The business pays for all. Then everyone works hard to win back the money.'

'No wonder they all work so hard!' Petra commented. 'There is always more to people than you think, isn't there?'

'Yes, there is,' smiled Christina, leaning forward in her chair. 'So tell to me, did you do jobs while you were at the university?'

'Well, anything I could, really,' Petra nodded, smiling at the memories. 'I did all sorts of things. I did some waitressing. That was alright, though I wasn't very good at it. You have seen those waiters who can balance half a dozen plates on their arms and not spill a drop. Well, that wasn't me. I could just about manage one plate! I enjoyed it, though. I did some bar work, but that really didn't suit me. Then I did housekeeping in a hotel. Making beds, getting rooms ready for customers, that was nice. I think that was my favourite job. I enjoyed that. So yeah, I've done all sorts of things.'

'Like my sons,' said Christina. 'They did not want university, but they all have worked hard. Two of them have their own shops. Their father helped them start, but they work hard to pay him back. My other son works for his father. I am happy for that, because my husband works very hard and needs my son's help. I try to help all. It is what we do. We work hard!'

It was late afternoon by the time they arrived back at the apartments. As they passed the side door to the restaurant, Matthaios beckoned to Petra.

'I have tomorrow evening off,' he said. 'Is that OK? Too soon?'

Christina brushed past her. 'I will go now! I will see you tomorrow.'

Petra waved to her. 'Thank you, Christina, today was wonderful!'

Christina waved back at her, over her shoulder.

'Tomorrow night?' asked Petra, looking at Matthaios. 'Yes, that would be great. See you then!'

51

Petra woke early. She had a lot to do, and she was determined to get it right.

She'd written a list for the shopping she would need for their evening meal. Now all she had to do was to find out where to buy the ingredients. She opened the apartment door, and looked out to where she would normally find Christina.

Her customary chair was empty. Petra's shoulders sank a little. *Oh well*, she thought to herself, *I'll just have to search for the groceries myself.*

She'd decided that she would make him her braised steak dish. She'd done it before for her housemates, and they'd seemed to enjoy it. At least they'd said they had.

Suddenly, doubts sprang into her mind. What if they'd only said they'd enjoyed it just to make her feel better? Maybe they hadn't liked it at all? Other recipes flashed through her mind, but she quickly rejected them, one by one. *No, I singed the bottom of that one*, she thought alarmingly.

In the end, she made her mind up to just plough ahead and see what happens. *Whatever, if he doesn't like it, he just won't ask me to cook again, will he!*

In the end, he'd just have to put up with it. Or maybe she'd run and tell him not to come after all? No, she really wanted him to come. Even if the food turned out to be inedible.

She scanned the apartment's small kitchen. She reckoned she was really lucky. It certainly wasn't, like some other apartments in the village, what Christina always referred to as *'cheap basic'* accommodation. She pretty much had everything she needed. A cooker, fridge, washing machine. Almost unbelievably, there was even a dishwasher. She checked the cupboards for utensils and checked things off, in her mind.

There were enough plates and cutlery, but there were also sharp knives, graters, measuring jugs, saucepans and a couple of roasting dishes.

She gazed at the roasting dishes for a few moments. Would they be big enough? She wasn't sure. She shrugged. Not much she could do about that. If Christina turned up in time, she could always ask her if there was a bigger one somewhere. If not, she'd just have to make do.

She made herself a cup of tea, and took it out onto the balcony. She took out her list and gazed over it.

Without Christina to turn to for advice, she'd just have to find everything for herself. She decided she would start with the supermarket over the road. Nikos, the owner, seemed to have a pretty wide range of goods, so surely, he would be a good place to start.

Nikos actually was a good place to start. She managed to find a few of the things she needed, and he told her where she would probably find the rest.

She hastily popped her shopping into the apartment and set off for the next leg of her shopping expedition.

Nikos had told her that there was an excellent butcher's shop at the crossroads, but that they closed at around lunchtime, and were unlikely to open up again in time for her to cook.

'Just tell them what you want. They will cut for you. No problem,' he had told her. What he hadn't explained, was that the butcher didn't speak much English at all, and she found herself doing all sort of mimes to try and describe what she wanted.

Eventually, she got him to understand, well, more or less. She emerged sometime later with some tasty looking beef steaks. The butcher had even trimmed off the fatty edges for her.

She walked back to the apartment, and put them in the fridge, and set off again for the vegetable shop. That was a longer walk, but feeling satisfied, she eventually returned with her whole list complete.

She glanced up at the clock. It wasn't quite lunchtime; she knew she had plenty of time.

She made a sandwich and retreated to the balcony to eat her lunch in the warm rays of the Greek sun.

As she ate, she ran through timings for her cookery, so that everything would be ready just as he was due to arrive. Then she thought about how she would set the table, how she would place the chairs on the narrow balcony, and which of the many lovely wine glasses in the apartment she would use.

'Oh my God!' she said out loud. 'I forgot about wine!'

A few minutes later she returned from Nikos's shop with a bottle of red and a bottle of white. She would just have to hope one of them would be to his taste.

As she sat on the balcony, forcing herself to take deep breaths, but feeling a growing sense of panic, Christina arrived with a flourish of bags and with her small laptop tucked under her arm.

Christina fell into her customary chair, groaning about the traffic, and the stupidity of pretty much every other driver on the road.

Petra's mind was elsewhere with dinner plans. She interrupted Christina's monologue, to ask if she had a bigger roasting dish.

'Yes, yes,' said Christina, clearly intrigued. 'I will find.'

She disappeared into one of the larger apartments further down. Petra could hear her clattering and banging, only to emerge a couple of minutes later, triumphantly holding a large dish above her head.

'See Petra!' she shouted. 'See, I told you we have everything!'

Christina handed her the dish over the balcony railing. 'Now. Tell me. What are you cooking?'

Petra explained about the dinner date, and what she wanted to make for him.

'Ahh, OK,' said Christina. 'You want help? You can do this? Oh my God Petra! I will come and help.'

Petra quickly shook her head, and explained that she really wanted to do this herself.

Christina gave her a look that implied her full understanding of the situation.

'This Matthaios,' she said, nodding. 'He is a nice boy. You like him very much? You want to impress, yes?'

When Petra nodded in return, Christina continued, 'OK my darling. You will be fine, but if you want help, I am here. OK.'

She started to laugh. 'It is good to cook for your man. This is how I won my husband! Listen, I like very much when people cook in their apartments. Most people go to restaurants all the time, or buy gyros from the shop round the corner. It is nice to do these things, but it is expensive, you know? But some people cook here.

'I remember one of my customers, Brenda. She came here for many years with her husband and their friend Sue. Nice people.'

Christina nodded to herself thoughtfully, reminiscing.

'Yes, nice people. Maureen knows them. So, the first year they came, one day they said they wanted to cook and asked if I would come to dinner. Me, I thought English women cannot cook. So, I told her no, but they asked again and again on other days, so in the end I had to say yes.

401

'Brenda said she would cook lasagne. I thought this will be awful. I told to my friend Lena, but she said I should go and pretend it was nice. So, the night came for the dinner. I was sat outside number one apartment talking to customers. Brenda's husband came to say to me that dinner was ready. Then he offered me his arm, so he could walk me to the apartment like I was royalty! It was so funny!'

Christina laughed at her recollection of the memory.

'So, I sat down. The table looked nice, and the lasagne looked fine, so I thought maybe this would be OK.

'They had bought garlic bread from the restaurant. I saw Antonis bring this. I told Brenda she should make her own, it is easy. She should save her money. Do you make garlic bread?'

Petra shook her head.

'It is very easy,' Christina continued, waving her hand dismissively.

'One day I will show. Like I said, me, I thought an English woman cannot make good lasagne. I was wrong! It was the best lasagne! And then her husband walked me back to my chair. I went and told Lena it was good, and she told me, *see*. I laughed and laughed that night!'

By now, Christina was laughing so much she almost fell from her chair, which made her laugh even more.

Petra checked the time again.

She had prepared everything she needed to.

She had fried the steaks, chopped and fried the onions, made and added the stock and transferred everything to Christina's large roasting dish. She had peeled the potatoes and prepared the vegetables.

The oven was on, warming to the right temperature.

She had plenty of time now, she thought, for a cool drink and a few minutes relaxation on the balcony.

Christina asked how she was getting on. 'Now, my darling. I must talk with you. There is something I want to know.'

Petra turned her head in her direction, intrigued.

Christina leant forward in her chair, but decided she was still too far away for a quiet conversation. Others might hear, and she wanted to keep this between them.

She pulled herself up the step, to join Petra.

'Go and put your food in the oven and we will talk.' She smiled.

Petra did as she was told, and went and sat beside Christina.

'These things take time to cook,' Christina said. 'Slow is good. I know these things, OK.'

Petra looked at her, both intrigued and a bit nervous about what Christina might want to tell her.

'So, come on then, Christina, what do you have to say? Is it something about Matthaios? Is he married or something? Or are you going to tell me you want to close down, and I have to go home?' she probed.

'No, my darling.' Christina laughed. 'Nothing like that. Now, I want to tell you.'

Petra nodded several times. Christina leant towards her conspiratorially.

'Listen, listen,' she began. 'OK, so, I live in Corfu Town, yes? This driving is too much now. It takes one hour to come here. It takes one hour to go home. This makes me crazy. It is too much for me. You understand?'

Petra nodded.

'My husband has his business. He is very busy. I need to help him now. I do not need to drive here, drive there. Always worrying about small things here, when there are big things there. You understand?'

'I err...I think so.'

'You are right. Usually, I would close this place in a week or two, open again in spring. Now though, many, many people ask if I would stay open all year. They want to come even in the winter. But now I cannot. It is too much for me. So, I have decided.'

'Decided on what?'

'Listen Petra. I like you. I want to make you manager here, so the apartments will stay open all year.'

'Oh! Crikey, Christina. I wasn't expecting that!'

'I know, I know my darling. I made up my mind yesterday but I have been so busy. There was no time to talk.'

'Wow, I don't know what to say…'

'Listen, I will give you a small apartment, and a small salary. Not much, maybe but plenty for coffee, food, clothes. Then a bonus at the end of the year.'

'But I haven't any experience, Christina. I wouldn't know what to do!'

'I will show you. I will come now and then, and there is always the phone. I will get you a Greek phone, it will be cheaper. And of course, Constantinos is here. He is a good man.'

Petra sucked in a deep breath.

'I'm not sure what to say. Thank you for the offer, Christina, but I need to think about it.'

Christina laughed.

'Of course, my darling. Of course. Talk with your parents. Talk with Constantinos. Talk with Matthaios. Let me know in a few days, OK?

'Right now, I will go and buy you a phone. Tomorrow we will work out bookings for the winter. All will be fine!'

Petra looked shell-shocked.

'Listen, Petra. I know people,' she said, tapping her nose with her finger. 'I know people. I know who to trust. I trust you, OK,' she said in a serious tone.

Christina chuckled.

'OK. So, tomorrow. Not tonight. Tonight, you must cook for your man! Go and check your food!'

Petra nervously checked the potatoes. The last thing she needed was to have them run out of water and burn. They were fine, and nearly done. She reduced the heat to a minimum.

She checked the water level in the saucepan with the vegetables and switched them on.

She glanced at the clock for the millionth time. Everything should be ready in perfect time.

'Oh my God!' she muttered. 'I forgot to get changed!'

She dashed into the bedroom. Luckily, she had already chosen what she would wear for the evening.

She threw it on, and checked her make-up in the mirror. She sighed. It would have to do.

Christina opened the apartment door, leant inside and called to her while she was changing.

'Listen Petra, I will go now, to see my friend Lena. From the tourist shop. You know her? I want to see if she did well this summer. I will see you later, OK?'

They exchanged goodbyes.

Petra was just finishing mashing the potatoes, when he rang the doorbell.

She closed her eyes momentarily, struggling to steady her nerves, then called to Matthaios to come in.

'Hello Petra. Kalispera!' he yelled, as he opened the door.

He was carrying a bottle of wine that he had brought from the restaurant. 'Mmm, dinner smells great! What have you made?'

With slightly shaky hands, she plated their dinner. Out on the balcony, he poured their drinks.

'I'll be there in a minute,' she called. 'How was your day?'

She finished serving, while he was talking, and carried his dinner out to him. She walked carefully to avoid spilling any.

Then she fetched her own, and sat down beside him.

'I don't know how you do it, carrying hot plates of food around, without spilling any,' she said, as she settled into her chair.

'Believe me,' he replied, laughing, 'I've spilled a few plates in my time!'

'Now,' she said nervously, as he picked up his knife and fork, 'I hope you like it. If you don't, just leave it.'

'You must be joking!' he said, pointing at his plate with his knife. 'This looks delicious! It smells delicious, and I'm starving! Let's eat. Yammas!'

He helped her clear the table once they'd finished, and loaded their empty plates into the dishwasher, while she switched on the kettle to make coffee.

'Was that alright then?' she asked, 'and you don't need to be polite.'

As the kettle started to warm up, he crossed the narrow kitchen and wrapped his arms around her. 'It was absolutely perfect,' he muttered into her hair. 'Just like you.'

'You're mad!' she giggled.

'Yes, I am,' he said, grinning broadly, 'I am mad about you, for sure. And now I'm mad about your cooking as well. I hope you will invite me again?'

She grinned back at him, then brewed the coffee.

'Oh,' he mumbled, offering her a small box. 'I wanted to give you this. It is just a small thing, but I thought it would suit your eyes. And, now I look again, it also suits your hair. I just loved the colour. I hope you like it.'

She opened the box to find a necklace of blue stones. It was just a simple thing, but she loved it.

'Oh, my goodness!' she exclaimed, as he placed it around her neck. A shiver of pleasure ran down her back, as much from the warm, gentle touch of his fingers as from the blue stones themselves, which had sparked another reminder of the constant blend of coincidence and continuity she'd felt since their first date. 'Thank you so much! I absolutely love it! The colour is just perfect.'

As they sat at the table on the balcony, sipping their coffee, she told him about Christina's offer.

'Wow,' he exclaimed, leaning forward in his chair. 'That is unexpected. She always said she would never open over the winter season.'

'So, what do you think? Will you take the job?'

She tilted her head to one side. 'I don't know,' she admitted. 'It's all a bit sudden. I really haven't had a chance to think it through yet. There's a lot to consider.'

He poured them both another glass of wine, and nodded his agreement.

'Yes, there is a lot to consider,' he said thoughtfully.

'What do you think I should do?' she asked.

'Well,' he said, staring at his glass.

'Well, what?'

'So, I think you will have to decide. As I see it, you have two options.'

'And what would those be?' she asked, taking a long sip of her drink.

'Well, if you go home. Then you would find somebody you like, settle down and have six kids.'

Her jaw dropped and her eyes widened, as she started to laugh. 'Seriously?'

'Yes, seriously,' he said, grinning widely, but trying to look serious.

'And what would the other option be?' she asked.

'Well, the other option would be that you stay here, and maybe have those six kids with me.'

By now she was laughing uncontrollably.

'Six kids. *SIX!*

She was bent over, her sides hurt with laughter, tears flowing down her face. He was laughing too, whilst trying desperately to keep a straight face.

Eventually the laughter subsided. She groaned, holding her ribs.

Matthaios took a deep breath.

'OK,' he said. 'I'd settle on five.'

The laughter erupted from her again, she could hardly catch her breath.

'Oh my God,' she was eventually able to say. 'You are so funny. Five kids? I can tell you right now, that's not happening!'

They talked, and laughed, and the conversation went on for hours, until eventually it grew chilly, and she had to excuse herself, while she grabbed her cardigan from the bedroom.

By the time she got back to the table he had already cleared their coffee cups and glasses.

'Oh! I'm so sorry. I didn't mean to spoil the evening.'

'You didn't,' he said, 'but it's getting late. It was a wonderful meal, and a wonderful evening. Efharisto bella. You have had a busy day and unfortunately, now I still have work to do.'

He held his arms open, welcoming her to embrace him. She did gladly, folding into him, curling her arms round his neck. His encircled her waist. She felt comfortable, and didn't really want the evening to end.

'Thank you so much for tonight,' he whispered. 'Dinner was wonderful. I really love being with you.'

She looked up into his dark brown, almost black eyes, smiled, and whispered, 'Me too.'

'So,' he said, tilting his head back to look at her better, 'four then?'

'Oh my God!' she gasped, burying her face into his neck. 'You really don't give up, do you!'

'Nope,' he said simply. 'Not where you are concerned.'

He pulled away, whispering, 'Goodnight my darling'

As he walked towards the edge of the balcony, she called after him, giggling, 'Two if you're lucky!'

He turned, looking back at her and nodded, smiling broadly. 'Two it is then!'

As he walked down the lane from her apartment, he turned again, and she heard him call quietly back to her.

'Kalinychta Petra! Remember this. Whatever you decide, stay here or go home. I will always be here for you.

'Always and forever.'

She leaned over the balcony, and whispered very loudly, 'Se agapó!'

He looked back at her, his smile lighting up the pathway.

Then, just when he thought he was out of sight, she saw him give a skip and punch the air above him. 'Yes!' she heard him yell in the darkness.

She beamed, and blew him a kiss, even though he couldn't see,

She sat down at the balcony table again and smiled to herself, knowing that she'd already made up her mind.

52

Petra always loved Greek Nights at the restaurant.

Even after all the years, the sound of Greek music, played loudly through the speakers, something about it excited her soul.

Her foot tapped as she clapped along in time with the beat of the music. For her, it always seemed as though there was no better way to get people in the mood for fun.

All around her, people were clapping at the same time, their dinner ignored to join in on the merriment.

The whole restaurant was enjoying the spectacle of the two handsome young men, who were dancing perfectly in time to the rhythm.

Petra was certainly one of them, watching the young men, but for a very special reason.

Tonight, for the first time, her sons had taken the lead in the dancing, instead of their father. Her eyes glistened with pride.

Matthaios had taught them to dance well, and they were performing the dance, a sirtaki dance, at first slow but building in speed and flamboyancy, it was perfect.

Andreas, the eldest, glanced over at his mother and smiled at her.

Petra felt a wave of emotion. She looked down at her daughter, Rania, and nudged her shoulder with her elbow, nodding towards the boys.

Rania looked up at her mum and beamed. She wore the same smile as hers.

While the boys were dancing, Constantinos emerged from a back room, clapping in time with the music. She heard him shout 'Opa!' as he clapped vigorously.

He bent to pick up a discarded plate from one of the nearby tables. Petra could see from his smile how proud he was of them, his grandsons and granddaughter.

She reached forward to gently restrain him from lifting the plate.

'No, Papa,' she told him, sweetly but firmly, 'the boys have everything covered. You don't need to worry anymore, OK?'

Petra thought for a moment that he might argue back, as he often did, but instead, he just smiled remorsefully back at her.

'Sorry, Petra,' he smiled warmly, 'old habits…'

'I know, Papa,' she said. 'I understand.

'When you've worked hard your whole life to build a good business it's not easy to sit back and watch others do your job. It's been the same for Christina, since she retired last year. She still comes here nearly every week, just to see what's going on. When I see her come, I go and sit with her. We talk, but all the time she's watching the cleaners. When I come back here, I can usually hear her shout at them because they're doing things the wrong way!'

They both laughed, but as she turned back to watch the dancing, she saw out of the corner of her eye, he had disappeared again into the kitchens. She just knew that he wouldn't be able to help himself, and he would soon be shouting at the kitchen staff to hurry up with the last orders for dinner.

She shook her head and smiled at the thought.

Rania had volunteered to make a video of their dance, using her mother's mobile phone, which meant that she had to keep still for once.

The thought occurred to Petra to send a copy to her mum, after the evening had finished. She knew her mum would enjoy seeing her grandsons dancing so well. She'd see them practicing with their father over the years, but hadn't yet seen them dance in the restaurant in front of an audience.

Petra rejoiced as she thought of how much pleasure her mother would receive from seeing the video. She couldn't wait until her parents could come over on holiday and visit them again this year. They'd been almost every year since Petra had moved to Corfu, almost twenty years ago, although of course, they were getting older now, she was sure they wouldn't miss this one.

It was the middle of September, and nearing the end of the season.

It wouldn't be many more weeks before Matthaios decided that the numbers frequenting the restaurant didn't warrant doing a Greek Night, but she felt sure that she could persuade him to wait long enough so that her parents could watch the boys dancing.

Her mum loved the boys, the first of her grandchildren. Andreas was eighteen now, and Spiros nearly sixteen. Both of them were almost as tall as Matthaios. They had their father's broad smile, they had his dark brown eyes, and the same dark brown, wavy hair.

Petra sometimes thought they might be a bit too handsome for their own good, but she was so proud of how all the girls always seemed to swoon and fawn over them.

More so, as they weaved their way with increasing expertise between the tables, helping to deliver steaming plates of delicious food.

Rania, on the other hand, had inherited far more of her mother's looks. She had the same round face, a similar complexion and to Petra's surprise and disappointment, the same rainbow-coloured hair.

Petra had often wondered if her children would inherit her rainbow hair, and had been pleasantly surprised when the boys hadn't.

When Rania was born with rainbow hair, it had come as something of a shock to Petra, but it made her all the more determined to give her as much love and support as she possibly could. To her, it really didn't matter what her kids looked like. The were her kids, she loved them to bits, and the rest of the world have to keep their opinions to themselves.

Once the dance had finished, and the music subsided, the boys went straight back into their roles as waiters, collecting plates and laughing with the customers.

Petra seized the moment to send the video to her mum. Nobody would miss her for a few moments, and she would soon be back, running around to help with restaurant duties.

She hugged Rania tight, and retrieving her phone, she popped into the back room to send her message. As soon as she opened her phone, though, she could see that she'd missed a text from her sister Martha.

Petra, please call me as soon as you can. Urgent! Doesn't matter what the time is xx

She glanced quickly at her watch. It was ten o'clock.

She calculated the time difference. It would be about eight o'clock back at home. Martha had said it was urgent, so Petra decided she should ring her back straight away. She flicked through the contacts section of her phone, took a deep breath, and pressed the call button.

'Martha?' she prompted. 'I got your text. What's the matter?'

'Oh God, Petra...' She heard her sister sob into the mouthpiece. 'It's Mum. I'm so sorry...she had a heart attack. She's gone, Petra!'

Petra stifled a wail as she ended the call.

The room span, and she grabbed a chair to steady herself, so she didn't fall to the floor. She sat shakily, covering her face with her hands.

Matthaios walked through carrying a heavy tray of empty plates.

As soon as saw Petra, he put the plates down, and ran to her side.

'Bella!' he said loudly, wrapping her in his arms. 'What's the matter? What's happened?'

Petra gulped between the heavy sobs, and told him the news.

'It's Mum,' she said, through her heavy tears. 'It's my mum! Martha called and said she'd had a heart attack, while she was cooking Dad's dinner. She died before the ambulance could get there!'

Matthaios sat down on the chair next to her, still holding her in his arms. 'Oh my God, my darling,' he told her. 'I'm so, so sorry…'

They stayed there for a good few minutes, while she recovered from the initial shock of her mother's death.

Matthaios subtly waved the other waiters past, so that they could deliver their loads without disturbing them.

After Petra had managed to recover and stop sobbing, he looked at her in the eye.

'OK, so you go home. Take Rania with you. We will finish everything as quick as we can, and then in the morning I will book the next available flight.'

She didn't need telling twice.

As he stood up, Matthaios asked one of the others to send Rania to her mother. She'd been giggling with some of the younger girls at one of the tables, but came straight away.

'I need you to take Mama home please. She's had some bad news, and this is not the best place for her to be right now. Look after her for me.'

Rania asked her what was wrong as they left the restaurant by the side exit, and asked her mother again as they walked up the road.

Petra made her wait, until they reached the main road, she sat her down on a bench and told her. At first, Rania was inconsolable.

'But I loved Yiayia Brenda,' she repeated countless times, as she sobbed into her mother's lap. 'Why did she have to die?'

All Petra could do was to hug her daughter tightly, stroking her bright-coloured hair.

'I know, my darling, I know,' she told her through her own tears. 'It's just not fair.'

They sat together until their tears subsided.

Rania got up and seized her hand.

'Come on, Mama,' she pulled on her mother's sleeve. 'Papa told me to look after you. Let's go home.'

There were more tears, after they closed the front door, and Petra let her daughter snuggle up with her on her bed.

'Do my brothers know?' Rania asked.

'Papa will tell them when they've finished closing up.'

Rania nodded. Her eyes were sore and red, but sleep managed to find her, as she dozed off in her mum's arms.

***

In the morning, Petra woke up to find Rania still curled up beside her.

She got up, and walked into the kitchen to put the kettle on for her morning tea.

She only half filled the kettle, knowing that she was the only one in the house who liked it. The others would be up much later, after their usual late finish at the restaurant, and she would make them coffee when they were awake.

As the kettle slowly started to warm, she wandered into Rania's bedroom.

Matthaios was in Rania's bed, fast asleep. She smiled, knowing that he would have found his wife and his daughter fast asleep in their bed. He'd done the same thing many times before, when the kids were teething, or when they were poorly with colds or the flu, and he'd never complained.

He was never a complainer. She knew, though, that it wasn't because he wasn't bothered about where he slept, but as he had often said to her in the past, his family was the most important thing in his life. Her and the kids came first, no matter how tired he might have been. Their comfort always came first.

She left him to sleep, until he was ready to stir, while she retired to the kitchen with her laptop to search for flights that might get her to an airport and back home.

There weren't many flights with seats left, and as she was pondering what to do next, running through a plan in her mind, Matthaios entered, still wearing shorts and a vest. He quickly realised what she was doing.

'Any luck?' he asked. 'It won't be easy to find seats for both of us at this time of year.'

'Both of us?' she asked in return.

'Of course, both of us,' he said, raising his eyebrows. 'You think I'd let you handle all this by yourself? Of course not, it will be the two of us. Papa has said he will mind the restaurant. He'll have the boys and Giannis to help him. He'll be fine for a few days.'

Petra's eyes opened wide. 'Matthaios, you cannot possibly expect your father to mind the shop,' she told him. 'He's getting old now. He's tired! He needs to rest now, after so many years! No, you can't allow Papa to do that.'

'He'll be fine,' Matthaios replied, shrugging his shoulders. 'He'll have plenty of help…'

'Absolutely not!' Petra told him firmly. 'He's officially retired now, and he is NOT allowed to work! You know what the government would do if they found out! He would be in so much trouble, and so would we!'

He tutted. 'The government and their stupid rules! How would they know anyway?'

'Believe me, they would find out! Remember what happened when the guy from the supermarket in Acharavi went to pick up stuff from the wholesalers in Corfu Town? He got caught on the way back. He got a big fine and they threatened to stop his pension! And this is our restaurant. Everything we do is very public. Everything we do can be seen! No, this will not happen to Papa! I will not allow it.'

'Then what am I supposed to do?' he asked plainly. 'How am I supposed to help you, to support you through all this, if I cannot be there with you? This is crazy.'

Petra reached over the kitchen table and took his hands in hers. She looked at him seriously.

'You, my darling,' she said quietly, squeezing his hands gently, 'you will be here. Looking after everything. Taking care of the kids. Keeping everything together, just like you always have. You are my rock. You keep me anchored to reality. I need to know that you, our kids, everything will be here to come back to. I need to know that my "normal" is still here. You understand?'

His shoulders dropped resignedly.

He frowned, and told her, 'I suppose you're right. But you will still need support. Who will you take with you, Andreas or Spiros?'

'No, you will need them here with you. Spiros has to go to school. It's an important year for him. He can't afford to miss it. Andreas still has a few weeks before he goes to university, and it's still too busy to close for the end of season. No, you need their help. I will be back as soon as I can, OK?'

In the corner of her eye, she noticed that Rania had crept through the doorway, still in her nighty.

'I can go with you, Mama! I will be there for you.'

Petra smiled at her daughter. 'Thank you darling,' she said 'but I'll be fine. You have school...'

'Please Mama,' Rania pleaded. 'You always promised I could go there one day. Now I can be useful!'

'Sweetheart, I know you would be, but it's important you go to school. I'll be back before you know it.'

'But it's not fair,' Rania protested, 'the boys have both been there, and you always promised I could go. Please?'

'I did take you. Don't you remember? You were maybe four, I think. Papa came with us.'

'But that was years ago!' Rania pleaded. 'All I can remember about it was sitting on Yiayia's lap by the range. I remember there was a big table, but that's all. Please, please may I go with you.'

'Matthaios, will you tell her please! She really does have to go to school.'

'Look,' said Matthaios, laying his hand firmly on the kitchen table. 'You will take Rania with you. If I can't go with you, then Rania will go with you. I will talk to the school.'

Petra could see that there was no point arguing any further. She sighed, resignedly. 'Alright, then.'

Rania was jumping up and down in excitement. Petra took hold of her shoulders to calm her down.

'But listen to me,' she said. 'This is not a holiday. Everybody will be upset. Everybody will be quiet and teary. It really won't be a place for children and noise, OK? Is that clear?'

Rania nodded at her mother vehemently. 'Yes, Mama!'

'And – and this is important, Rania – you will have to speak in English all the time. Nobody understands Greek, and it would be dis-respectful to not speak English.'

'Yes, Mama. I will be quiet, and I will speak English all the time,' Rania said, beaming gratefully into her mother's face.

'Are you sure?'

Rania smiled, and hugged her mother. 'Yes, Mama. But most of all I will hold your hand when you need me to.'

Rania ran to her bedroom to start choosing clothes to take. Petra shook her head slowly as she watched her go, wondering to herself, not for the first time, how she could ever have helped create such caring children.

***

The next couple of days unfurled in a whirlwind of activity.

Petra had talked to Martha over the phone about appropriate clothing for their mother's funeral, and they'd decided between them both that whatever they chose, should include yellows and blues. They were summer colours, and summer had always been their mum's favourite season. She really wouldn't have been happy with everyone wearing black.

Petra took Rania shopping to her favourite clothes shops in Acharavi, and eventually, they had agreed on suitable attire.

Afterwards, they'd gone to have their hair trimmed. Just enough to get rid of the dead ends, rather than anything too radical. Petra knew instinctively that, given their colouring, and given that they both had quite straight hair, anything flamboyant just wouldn't have suited them.

Since her hair had changed from light brown to rainbow, she had insisted that the hairdresser should gather the clippings together, and put them in a bag for her to take home. When she got home, she always placed them into a little leather bag she'd found in one of the tourist shops in the village. It was a tanned gold colour, which she loved.

As they left the hairdresser, Rania asked her, 'Why do you always do that, Mama?'

'What, darling?'

'You know, why do you gather up all your hair clippings to take home?'

419

Petra shrugged. 'I dunno, really,' she said. 'I just think, that it's not really my hair to throw away. Know what I mean?'

'No, not really,' came her daughter's reply.

'Well, my hair was always light brown. This rainbow hair, well, it doesn't really feel like my hair. Like it belongs to somebody else. I don't know, just sounds stupid when you put it into words, I guess.'

'So, what are you going to do with it though? Are you going to keep it forever?'

'I hadn't really thought about it. It just didn't seem right to throw it away. This rainbow hair happened when I was at home. Sort of reminds me of home. Does that make sense?'

Rania looked at her mother quizzically.

'Well,' Rania said, after a few minutes thought. 'Maybe you should take it with you? Take it home? You don't go there very often, so maybe now might be a good time?'

'Mmm,' Petra said thoughtfully, 'I'll think about it…'

Matthaios drove them to the airport. He helped them get their bags out of the car, and onto the walkway near the entrance.

'Seems like we've been here before,' he said, as he gave his wife and daughter a hug and a kiss.

'Look after each other. I'll be here when you need me. I love you both so much.'

Inside the airport, Rania's mouth opened wide.

'It looks busy today!' said Petra, as they moved further in.

'So many people!' Rania replied, looking amazed. 'Where do we go? What do we do!'

'Tell you what,' Petra said, smiling at her daughter. 'Stay close to me. Do what I tell you, don't wander off. Then we'll be fine, OK?'

'Sure,' said a wide-eyed Rania, somewhat hesitantly, moving closer to her mum as they approached the first queue.

'Mama?' Rania asked, as they stood quietly in the second queue, the one where security guards stood.

'Mmm?'

'Why are all these people staring at us, Mama?'

'Are they darling?'

'Yes!' Rania hissed, 'they keep pointing at our hair!'

'Oh that,' said Petra, in a matter-of-fact voice. 'Don't worry about that, my sweet. They're just jealous.'

'Why, because we have different hair to them?'

'Exactly. Their problem, not ours.'

'Yes, but…' Rania continued, 'why are we different?'

Petra looked down at her daughter and smiled.

'Tell you what, how about I tell you why we're different once we are in the air. It's probably about time I did.'

Rania nodded, and smiled at her mother. She caught hold of her arm, just before the man at the security gate beckoned them through.

'Thank you,' Rania mumbled.

'What for?'

'Just…thank you for being my mum.'

53

It was raining outside as they climbed down the steps to the tarmac.

'Why is it so cold?' asked Rania, pulling on the coat that she didn't think she'd needed but that her mother had insisted she carry with her.

Petra laughed. 'Welcome to England!' she chuckled as their feet touched the ground. 'Don't worry, you'll get used to it...'

'I'm not sure I want to, if it's always this cold,' Rania muttered, as they walked towards the terminal. 'I don't remember it being this cold, last time.'

'Well, it was summer then,' her mother reminded her, 'and you were only small. You only really remember the best bits of things that happen when you're young.'

As they emerged from the security section, Rania caught her arm urgently, and started waving at the crowd of people waiting to meet the arriving passengers.

'Look, Mama! There's Aunty Martha! No, not that way, over there. Look!'

Then, as Petra noticed her sister in the crowd, she too started waving frantically.

'Welcome, you two!' Martha called as they approached.

'It's so good to see you both! Did you have a good flight? I bet the weather in Corfu was better than this, eh?'

Martha never stopped talking as she helped them drag their cases towards the car park. By the time they found her car, their feet were squelching in their soaked shoes.

'Sorry about all this rain,' she told them. 'Seriously, it was lovely up until last night. She rolled her eyes. 'Typical, eh?'

They loaded the bigger cases into the boot of Martha's car, and quickly piled their hand luggage onto the back seat next to Rania. In the front seats, Petra kicked off her shoes and put her bare feet on the carpeted floor. Martha changed her shoes for a spare pair she'd brought with her.

'We can put your shoes and coats by the kitchen range to dry off when we get home. They'll be dry in no time.'

Petra glanced behind, to see her daughter sat gazing out of the window, her headphones already in place and her head nodding in time with whatever music she was listening to.

'So, how's Dad now?' Petra asked her sister, as they drove.

Martha sighed.

'I dunno. He's been very quiet since it happened. Not like Dad at all. He isn't dealing with it at all well, really. He has been out to help John with the milking a couple of times, but most of his time he just sits at the kitchen table nursing a cup of tea and staring at nothing in particular. I'm getting quite worried about him now. I've been thinking maybe I should call the doctor, but he won't hear of it, whenever I mention it.'

'It must have been a heck of shock for him, I guess. Well, let's face it, it's been a shock for all of us, hasn't it. While we're here, maybe the extra company might help. I'm glad he's made the effort to help John sometimes, though. A bit of normality won't have done him any harm at all.'

Martha's husband John was from solid farming stock.

He'd grown up on his parent's farm, and after he and Martha had married, he'd helped their father as much as he'd helped his own parents with their farm.

He was a man of few words, but he'd worked incredibly hard to keep both farms going, and since only him and Martha had shown any real interest in farming, their father had grown to rely increasingly on him, as the years progressed.

Now, as Gerald had got older, his age had begun to impact on the amount of work he could manage. John had pretty much taken over running the place. As far as Petra could tell, he was doing a pretty good job of it.

'Are the boys home now?'

Their twin brothers, Chris and Paul, had both left home years ago. They'd gone off to university, and had never really looked back.

Chris lived in London. He was an electrical engineer, and married with a couple of small kids. They'd come home several times to spend Christmas and summer holidays with his parents.

Paul, on the other hand, had moved further away, and hadn't been home at all since he moving to Melbourne, his new wife's hometown. He'd always told them it was just too expensive, and that it was way too far to travel with small children.

Petra could easily sympathise with that, having brought her own children home for occasional holidays when they were smaller. That had been trying enough, and it was only a three-hour flight. She couldn't imagine what it would be like having to spend twenty-four hours in the air with them.

'Chris has called a few times,' Martha told her. 'He'll drive down the morning of the funeral. He said he might stay overnight, and go home the following morning.'

'Will Joanne come with him?'

Martha nodded. 'I believe so,' she said, 'I think she told me they're going to leave the kids with her mum.'

'And Paul?'

'Yes, I hope so. He said he's trying to book flights, so that he can be here a few days. He'll be travelling on his own, though.'

Petra frowned. 'I'm not surprised. I'm sure it would be pretty expensive for them both to come, even if she actually wanted to.'

'I know what you mean,' replied Martha. 'She's a strange one, that Julie. I only met her a couple of times before they relocated to Australia, and she never seemed bothered about getting to know us.'

'Well, as long as Paul comes, that's the main thing. It's been a long time since we saw him. It would be nice to catch up. It wouldn't seem right if he missed the chance to say goodbye to Mum.'

'Ooh! I remember that tree!' Rania yelled excitedly, leaning forward in her seat as Martha manoeuvred to park her car under the branches of the copper beech.

Martha laughed, as they started to pull the cases out of the boot.

'Yep, it's still there. Nothing much changes around here.'

'Only the people change,' Martha said quietly. Petra leant over and wrapped her arms round her sister.

Martha returned her hug warmly. 'Right! Let's get you inside, where it is warm. Cup of tea?'

They put the cases in the hallway.

'I'll ask John to pop them upstairs later, if that's OK?'

As they walked into the warm kitchen, Rania pushed past her mother and rushed towards her grandfather, who had just risen from his chair as he heard them come in.

'Grandad!' she called. He enveloped her in his arms and smiled up at Petra.

'Oh, you're a sight for sore eyes Pet,' he said, eventually breaking free of Rania's grip to move the kettle further onto the range, so that it would boil.

'Hi Dad!' said Petra, taking Rania's place in his arms. 'How are you doing?'

He gave a small shrug and a half smile. 'Well…' he said, 'been better, I suppose.'

She squeezed him in her arms a few moments longer, then broke away to sit down at the table, while Martha brewed their tea and poured a glass of milk for Rania.

Rania looked up at Martha and said something to her in Greek.

'English, please Rania,' Petra said quickly, raising her eyebrows sharply to her. It was only natural that her kids would speak Greek as their first language, but she'd done her best to make sure they could at least converse in English.

'Sorry Mama,' Rania whispered, she asked her question again, this time in English.

'Sorry Aunty Martha. I was asking when Jenny and Mark will be home?'

Martha glanced at her watch. 'They'll be home soon,' she said. 'I didn't know if there might have been delays at the airport, so I asked a friend to drop them home from school.'

Jenny was about the same age as Rania, and Rania had always got on well with her cousin, whenever Martha and her family had been on holiday with them. Mark was a couple of years older than the girls, and usually ignored them if he could.

'Please may I go and watch TV?' Rania asked, feeling a bit out of place with the grown-ups.

Martha smiled, and asked if she remembered where the front room was. Rania told her she didn't really remember, but that she was sure that she'd find it.

As she opened the kitchen door to enter the hallway, Petra caught her eye.

'Remember what we talked about, Rania? This is their house, so they get to choose what they want to watch, OK?'

Martha looked at her quizzically. 'Well, technically, I suppose it's your house now, really,' she said. 'After all, you're the eldest daughter, and now that Mum's gone, you're the guardian of the bridge...'

Before Petra could answer, John popped his head in through the back door.

'Oh, hi Petra,' he said cheerfully. 'Good to see you! Sorry, I'd give you a hug but I'm afraid my overalls are covered in...'

'Do not even THINK about coming in here with those filthy boots on!' laughed Martha.

Petra chuckled, and told him he could have his hug later, when he'd had a chance to clean up.

John smiled sheepishly. 'I was just going to ask Dad if he wanted to come and help with the milking?'

'Is it that the time already? Aye,' Gerald told him, easing himself out of his chair. 'I'll get my kit on.'

Once the men had gone, Petra took Martha's hand.

'Look,' she said, 'the way I see it, is this. My life is in Corfu. Has been for years. I'm happy there. You're the one who's put the time and effort in here. I've seen Mum and Dad maybe for a few weeks a year when they've been with us on holiday. You're the one who's had to deal with the farm, and with them getting older, and now with all this too.'

'Yeah, but...'

'No *but's,*' Petra said firmly. 'No, this is your home, not mine. It's your house. End of story, OK?'

'But the bridge!'

'Well, a fine old mess I made of that, didn't I?' Petra declared. 'I'm the one who let all the magic go away. I really don't deserve to be its guardian. Anyway, I'm not living here. You are.'

They heard the front door open, as Martha's children arrived home from school.

Martha looked at Petra. 'We'll talk more about all of this later, alright?'

'OK.' Petra nodded. 'So can I help get dinner ready?'

'No need,' Martha replied. 'Already sorted. I made Bolognese sauce this morning. All we need now is some pasta.'

'See what I mean?' Petra laughed and looked at her sister knowingly. 'You're always so totally organised...very annoying!'

Later that evening, after the children had gone to bed and John, and their father had moved into the front room to watch TV, Martha and Petra finished washing the dishes.

'So,' announced Petra. 'I suppose we'd better talk about the elephant in the room, eh?'

'What?' asked Martha.

'The funeral,' Petra replied sadly. 'It's only a couple of days away. What are your thoughts about afterwards? Do you want to go to a pub or something, or do you think here would be better?'

'Oh, I think here, don't you? I mean, it's what we did after grandad's funeral, and Mum was always more comfortable in her own home. What do you think?'

'Yes, I totally agree.' Petra nodded in agreement. 'We'll do it here. We can do the catering between us, can't we. Let's write a list of what we'll need to get. Are you ok to go shopping in the morning?'

'Sure,' said Martha, reaching for some paper and a pen. 'But before we start, I'd been meaning to ask. Is Matthaios coming to the funeral?'

'No,' said Petra. 'He wanted to be here, but I told him he can't expect his dad to look after the restaurant without him. He's retired now, so he's not officially allowed to work. So no, Matthaios and the boys will stay home and carry on as usual.'

'That's a shame,' said Martha. 'Mum really liked him, and I'm sure you could have done with his support, eh?'

'I guess so,' said Petra. 'But here we are...'

Martha looked at her thoughtfully. She picked up her pen and started to scribble words on the page.

'So...' she said. 'Bread, ham, cheese and what else do people have at these things? Tinned salmon?'

They both looked at each other and grimaced.

'Nah...maybe we'll forget that one...so...pickled onions, pickles, tinned pineapple, cocktail sticks...'

54

The day of the funeral arrived.

Petra glanced out through the kitchen window as she filled the kettle.

It was raining, and she stood for a moment to watch tiny rivulets of water running down the glass.

When she looked up, though, she noticed some small patches of clear sky between the grey clouds. *Oh well*, she thought to herself, *the weather certainly suits the mood…*

Petra and Martha sat down at the kitchen table, sipping their early morning tea. They'd had a late night, preparing the buffet, consoling their dad and each other, and reminiscing about their mum and their lives in general, but they'd still managed to wake up early.

Martha had cooked breakfast for John and their dad, who they'd managed to persuade to go and help with the early morning milking.

The girls, Jenny and Rania, had followed them out a bit later to feed the chickens and collect the eggs, but before they left the house, Martha had made sure that Jenny was wearing her watch.

'Ten o'clock, girls please, no later, OK?' she'd ordered them, followed by a chorus of, 'Yes Mum!' and 'Yes, Aunty Martha,' as the door closed behind them.

'There,' announced Martha. 'That's them sorted for a bit. Now then, what's left to do? Have we forgotten anything?'

'I don't think so,' Petra told her, looking around the room. 'I can't think of anything.'

After a long pause, Martha placed her hands on the table.

'This is all a bit much really, isn't it?'

Petra sighed, and leant over the table to gently grip her sister's hand.

'Yes, it is really. I guess we just have to go through the motions. We just have to get things right for Mum. I think you've done that, Martha. I think you've done everything superbly. Thank you.'

There was a knock at the front door.

Martha called back to Petra. 'It's Chris! Oh, thank goodness!'

Chris had put on weight since she'd last seen him, but Petra thought he looked well.

He was wearing jeans and trainers, topped off with a damp, hooded rain jacket. He carried a small overnight bag in one hand. His suit, in a dry-cleaner's bag, dangled from his other hand.

He hugged both of his sisters, and asked Martha if she'd heard from Paul.

'No Joanne?' Martha questioned.

'Sorry, sis,' he told her, looking glum.

'She was going to come, but one of the kids has an ear infection. Bloody typical. She sent her apologies, but she really didn't feel comfortable leaving him with his grandma. Sorry!'

'Oh well,' Martha told him. 'At least you're here. No Paul though, he won't be here. Missed his flight, apparently. If there ever was one booked.'

'Really?' Chris said, his eyes widening. 'Well, he didn't make much effort then, did he? Not even for Mum. I ring him sometimes, but I can't remember the last time he ever called me. We were always so close, but he's been really strange since he married what's-her-name.'

'I know, but never mind.'

431

Martha grimaced, glancing at Petra.

'We'd hoped that Mum passing might have brought us all together again, at least for a little while.'

'Well, I'm here, anyway,' Chris told her affectionately. 'So, is there anything I can help with? Anything I can do?'

'Just you being here is enough,' Martha said, smiling. 'Cup of tea?' she offered.

'Oh, yes please.' Chris nodded gratefully, looking at Petra. 'Where are the kids? I guess John and Dad are out with the cows, but is anybody else here? Matthaios?'

Petra was about to explain why Matthaios couldn't be with them when the doorbell rang, followed by a loud knocking at the door.

Martha was busy making tea for Mark, so Petra jumped up, and ran to the door.

She nearly fainted.

'Matthaios! Oh my God, Matthaios,' she shrieked. 'How? Why! What are you doing here.' Her words came out all jumbled.

She buried her face in his chest.

He wrapped his arms around her, with a huge smile on his face.

'You seriously didn't think I'd let you do this all by yourself, did you?'

Once she released her grip on him, he held up a bag to show her.

'Look,' he said. 'I brought my best suit. I hope I'm not too late.'

'Honestly, my darling,' Petra choked, hugging him even closer, 'you can't believe how happy I am you're here! I've missed you so much. But how did you manage to come? I hope you haven't left Papa in charge, have you?'

'Who is it, Petra?' she heard her sister call from the kitchen. She pulled him through the door and into the kitchen.

'Look, everybody!' she called. 'Matthaios is here! My Matthaios!'

He sat down at the table.

Martha placed a cup of coffee in front him, as Matthaios explained what had happened.

'Well, of course, Papa told me I should have come with you. He said it was my responsibility to look after you, to support you. But I told him, *No Papa, I cannot! Petra told me I must stay*! I told him he was retired, and Petra told me you cannot do this. I will stay and see to everything. Petra will come back when she is ready. All will be fine, but he would not hear it. I told him I was to stay with him, as Petra had told me.

'He called Eleni, my cousin, and told her. So, Eleni is come to the restaurant. She will be in charge while I am gone, and Papa will be in charge also. I think it is good that I must fly home again tomorrow, otherwise they will kill each other!'

He raised his eyebrows, and laughed. 'So, Eleni is there, and so are the boys, and Papa, and Giannis. All will be fine…I hope!'

'That is an awful lot of travelling,' said Petra. 'You will be exhausted! But what about Eleni's restaurant? How will they manage without her?'

'Kostis is in charge. He has other waiters, so no problem. They will be fine,' he assured them.

'Everybody is so kind,' said Petra. 'I will have to do many favours, when we are back, to return their kindness.'

'Look,' said Matthaios. 'Everybody has troubles. Then everybody helps. It works out. No problem. But now I am here for you, where I should be.'

'And I am so, so grateful that you are. And so will Rania.'

'I hope she has behaved herself?' asked Matthaios. 'She promised she would, but she is very young…'

'She has been perfect,' Petra assured him. 'Honestly.'

'She has,' confirmed Martha, as the back door swung open and two very dirty young ladies burst into the room.

'Papa!' Rania screamed as soon as she saw him. 'Papa!' She ran into his arms, almost knocking him from his chair. 'Papa! You came!'

***

Martha glanced up at the kitchen clock.

'Shall we wash the cups?' she asked her sister, eager to have something to do other than drinking tea.

While they were busy at the sink, Petra saw Martha lean heavily on the worktop.

'You OK?' she asked her, concerned.

Martha shook her head briefly. 'Not really. I'm not looking forward to this at all.'

Petra put her arm around her sister's shoulder, and squeezed her gently.

'I know,' she told her quietly. 'But we can't do anything about it. Let's just try and keep busy, eh?'

Martha nodded, and mustered a small smile.

'Right, you lot!' she announced, turning to face the room. 'Time marches on. Things won't do themselves.

'Listen, when we went shopping, we got some yellow silk carnations for the men, and yellow corsages for the ladies. I'll go and bring them down, and we can put them on our coats when everybody's ready to go. Chris, come with me and we'll find somewhere you can get changed.'

Petra took her sister's lead, and suggested that it would be a good time for their dad to go and put his suit on.

'I'll check you over when you come down,' she told him. *Just like Mum always used to do,* she thought to herself, blinking away a tear.

Once the girls had been dispatched, to quickly shower and get ready for the funeral, Petra suggested that perhaps it was probably time that she and Matthaios should go and change as well.

Matthaios hung his suit on the back of the bedroom door, and pulled his jumper off, as Petra took her dress out of the wardrobe.

Matthaios cleared his throat. 'How is your father doing?'

'Not very well, I'm afraid,' Petra told him. 'He just sits and stares into space a lot of the time. It's really not like him at all, but I guess it's all been such a shock.'

Matthaios nodded slowly. 'Maybe he should come and stay with us for a while? It might help if he's not here at home, all the time surrounded by memories.'

Petra agreed, and promised to ask him when the opportunity presented itself.

'Tell him that when he is with us, we will dance, him and I,' said Matthaios warmly.

'Typical Greek!' smiled Petra, shaking her head. 'Any excuse to dance!'

'Well, it is in my heart, and my soul, this dancing. It might not do too much good, but it can do no harm either,' Matthaios told her. 'It always makes me feel better.'

An hour or so later, they were all sat around in their best clothes, quietly waiting for the cars to arrive, none of them knowing quite what to do or say.

They heard a car pull up outside the front door.

Martha walked through the hallway, and prised the door open to see what was happening.

To her astonishment, she found Paul stood on the doorstep, looking slightly flustered, a finger poised, ready to press the doorbell.

'I'm so sorry, I'm so late,' he stammered, as Martha grabbed his arm and pulled him in for a hug. Behind him, his taxi pulled away, just as a row of black cars pulled into the courtyard.

'It's been a heck of a few days, and I was so worried I'd miss it…'

'You'd better get changed super-fast!' she ordered, pointing at the stairs.

'OK,' Petra said, pushing him up the stairs. 'I'll get him sorted!'

'Which room?' he asked.

'Doesn't matter. Anywhere!'

Paul was red-faced as he pulled on his suit trousers. His sister was already holding his shirt open, getting it ready for him.

'Oh, just get on with it,' Petra told him firmly. 'I've seen you in a lot less!'

'God, what a mess!' he said, panting with effort. 'I'm so sorry for all this. Our neighbour, Michael, said he'd drive me to the airport. He's another Brit. Archaeologist, I think, works at the university…'

Petra hissed at him. 'Just hurry up!'

'I thought he'd understand how important it was for me to get to the airport in time,' Paul continued, not heeding his sister's caution.

'I told him he was going the wrong way, but he just kept tapping his nose and saying he knew a short-cut. Some bloody short-cut! He kept going the wrong way! Idiot! By the time we got to the airport, they'd closed the gates. I had to book the next flight I could get.'

Petra passed him his tie, and held his jacket open ready. 'Right…shoes! Come on! Hurry up, Mum's waiting!'

'Sorry,' he said. 'Cost me a bloody fortune, this trip!' he mumbled, as they ran down the stairs. 'Sorry everybody.'

'It's fine,' Petra told him. 'You're here. Take a deep breath…'

He looked out of the open doorway, at the parked cars, he sighed. 'I'm so sorry, Mum…'

Towards the end of the service, the celebrant invited the congregation to join with him in a few moments of quiet reflection.

Petra looked across the middle aisle, to where her sister was sitting next to their dad. To the other side of her, were John and their children.

She wondered how Martha was holding up, and whether she, like herself, would be glad when this was all over.

Next to where the celebrant stood, facing the central aisle, their mum's coffin was festooned with the yellow flowers of the family's wreath. *Mum would have loved those flowers;* she thought to herself.

She herself was sat between Rania and Matthaios. Alongside Matthaios were Chris and Paul.

She looked over towards them, but her view was partially blocked by her husband. *It doesn't matter*, she thought, *at least I know they're here.*

She felt Rania's hand shaking, as it had all the way through the service.

Rania had taken her hand as they had entered the small chapel, and hadn't let go of it since.

She glanced upwards, towards a small window in the side wall, and found herself gazing intently through it at the rain falling outside, interspersed with patches of bright sunshine.

As she watched, a rainbow appeared between the falling rain and the rays of the sun, and she couldn't help but smile.

Thank you, Mum, I'm glad you're alright. I'm glad you've found your way.

55

Petra looked out of the kitchen window.

It had been raining on and off for most of the time she'd been at Home Farm, but today it was sunny and fairly warm.

Copper leaves had started to gather on the cobbled flags of the courtyard.

'It always makes me feel a bit sad, this time of year,' Petra said wistfully. 'You can feel summer starting to ebb away. Mornings are beginning to feel chillier. Autumn is well on the way, isn't it. Oh well…'

Martha nodded.

'You were always more of a summer person, weren't you? Then again, it's all part of the circle, isn't it? The years just go around and around…'

Petra agreed. 'It's quiet now, isn't it? Now that everybody's gone?'

Matthaios had flown home the day after the funeral, worried about the chaos he might find when he got back.

Chris had taken him to the airport, as he was travelling home to London, and Paul had left for the train station just that morning, on his way to catch up with friends before flying home to Melbourne the following day.

'Will you be alright here by yourself? Once we fly home tomorrow?' Petra asked her sister. 'It's been a hectic few days, hasn't it?'

'It sure has,' Martha told her. 'But yes, of course I'll be alright. It'll be just the same as normal. Just us and the kids and Dad. I'm used to it.'

'But there won't be Mum for you to talk to.'

'I know…but we're all going to have to just get used to it, aren't we? Oh look, enough of this. You'll be having me crying in a minute, and I don't want to cry any more tears. I want to enjoy the last few hours, in the company of my favourite sister.'

'I'm your only sister!' Petra reminded her, laughing.

'I know…but you know what I mean. Look, let's take the girls for a walk, shall we? Blow away the cobwebs a bit.'

'Good idea,' said Petra. 'Anyway, there's something I want to do while we're still here, up at the bridge. Something Rania suggested. Well, not exactly suggested, but something she said has given me an idea. May I borrow a trowel?'

Martha's eyes piqued in curiosity. 'Why on earth would you need a trowel?'

Petra explained as they walked. The girls had gone on ahead. Their legs were younger and more energetic than their mothers'. It gave them a chance to talk without having to answer a constant stream of questions.

'You see,' she started hesitantly. 'Well, it might seem a daft thing to do, but ever since my hair turned the colours of the rainbow, I've been saving up all the clippings every time I had my hair trimmed.'

'Why on earth would you want to do that?' Martha's eyes sparked.

'I know, weird huh. The thing is, do you remember what happened that day? When my hair changed?'

'Well, yes, of course I do. It was really odd, what happened.'

'Well, I hated it. I hated my hair. I wouldn't go out for weeks. It took me a long time to get used to it…'

'I know, Mum was really worried about you. So was I,' sighed Martha.

'I know.' Petra nodded, knowingly. 'But I couldn't shake it off, this feeling that I hadn't chosen it. It was just sort of imposed on me, but I couldn't do anything about it.'

Martha pressed her lips together. 'I can imagine how you must have felt.'

'After a while, though, I just sort of came to terms with it. I reckoned that there was nothing I could do, so I'd just have to live with it. Then I went back to Corfu. And then Matthaios took me out to dinner, and it was something he said on the walk home that got me thinking.'

'You are *not* going to ask me to imagine what happened next, are you?' laughed Martha.

'No, nothing like that!' Petra smiled, catching her sister's meaning. 'No, we'd been playing this silly name game for ages, where he had to guess what my name was.'

'I remember you told me this once actually...'

'Anyway, in the end, that evening, I told him my name. Then he told me what the name meant in Greek; Petra means 'stone'. Then I told him the story of how my hair changed, and the next day he told me that maybe the Home Stone had felt threatened by what happened that time with Michael. We spoke about how it may have sort of invaded me. Would that be the right way to put it?'

Martha shrugged. 'But what has all that got to do with saving your hair clippings?'

Petra continued. 'So that got me thinking, maybe he was right? I mean, at first, I thought he was just humouring me, you know, because he fancied me, but I started thinking maybe the stone really had chosen me to carry it to safety? I figured that maybe my rainbow hair was the stone, that it didn't really belong to me, and I should save the clippings. Stupid, right?'

'I don't know,' said Martha, shrugging her shoulders, 'it seems a strange sort of logic, but if it made sense to you. What are you planning to do with it now? You must have saved quite a lot of hair clippings by now?'

Petra reached into her pocket, and brought out her leather bag to show her. It was about the size of her palm, and quite hard, the hair was pressed firmly inside.

'I'm thinking it might be a while before I come back home again, so I'm going to bury it by the bridge. I'm sort of returning it to where it should be. Does that make any sense at all?'

'It makes as much sense as everything else, I suppose. So that's why you wanted a trowel?' her sister said in a low voice.

Petra nodded. 'Can't do any harm, can it?'

Once they were inside the stone circle, Petra made a beeline for the bridge. The ground surrounding the base of the bridge was hard-packed and stony, and it took quite a bit of effort to make any sort of hole at all, let alone a deep enough one.

As they dug, the soil started to move a bit easier, and eventually she declared it ready.

With Martha and the girls watching, she planted her little leather bag at the bottom of the hole, and started scooping the soil and stones she'd disturbed back into it.

Finally, she stamped the top layer of earth down with her boot.

'There,' she muttered to herself. 'It's done.'

'What happens next, Mama?' Rania asked.

'Hmm…to be honest, darling, I have no idea. But it's done. Come on, let's sit on the grass for a while and Aunty Martha and I can tell you stories about times we used to spend here when we were kids.'

They sat away from the bridge, on a patch of grass that seemed a little bit drier than the rest.

After a while they were all laughing, and giggling at the various stories that the special place brought to their recollection. The sisters realised there were so many things they'd forgotten about over the years, and it felt good to reminisce.

'Don't you miss all this? You know, the farm, the bridge? Solstices, equinoxes and all that?' Martha asked her at one point, as they sat gazing over the bridge.

'Oh, I meant to say before. The weatherman last night said it was the Autumn Equinox today. About half past one, he said, though I've no idea how they get it all so exact!'

Holding her hand out in an exasperated fashion, Petra looked at her sister and raised her eyebrows.

'Now there!' she said, shrugging her shoulders. 'Years ago, I'd have just known when the equinox was automatically. Now I need reminding. Nowadays, the equinoxes and solstices just pass me by. I really don't feel connected to it all anymore.'

Martha gazed at her in sympathy. 'But even then, don't you miss it?'

'In a way, I suppose I do,' she said. 'But like I said before, my life is in Greece now, with Matthaios and my kids. I think I'd miss them more than I miss being here. Know what I mean? I miss you guys, of course, but this?' she asked, waving her arm around her. 'No, sorry. Apart from the memories, I don't really feel it anymore.'

'But what about if something happened to you while you're not here? I mean, do you believe what Mum always told us about people crossing the bridge when they die? I'd hate to think you'd be too far away to do that, to join me and the rest of the family. If it's true, of course. I really don't know what to believe about all this stuff.'

Petra looked at her seriously.

'Well obviously it's crossed my mind, but I really don't have time to think about it much.'

Martha nodded, frowning.

'But even so…'

'Look,' Petra told her. 'I know what I saw when Grandad died. At least I think I do. And then there was all that stuff that happened with Michael…so I suppose there is something here. Something. I just don't know what to believe, really. Anyway, remember the rhyme Grandad used to tell us about guides?'

'No, what?' Martha's eye's crinkled in confusion.

'You remember. It was about looking out for a stranger by the midnight gate?'

'Not really…'

'Well, I do. I remember the second verse especially.'

'How did it go?' asked Martha

'It went something like this…

Beware the stranger at the midnight gate
He hovers near. He won't be late.
So when you pass you need not roam,
For he has come to guide you home.

He knows the way, though near or far,
For he knows where the ley lines are.
While those you left still mourn their loss
He'll find the bridge, and help you cross.'

Martha smiled.

'So I'm not going to worry about being a long way away when my turn comes. If it's true about the bridge then I'll get help to come here. So, what's the point of worrying.'

Eventually, the conversation waned, and Petra took her phone from her pocket and started writing a text to Matthaios.

443

She knew he'd got home safely, but she wanted to know how everybody was, and to remind him that he was to collect them from the airport tomorrow. She told him that she really couldn't wait to get home, to get back to normal again.

While she was typing, Rania grabbed her arm suddenly.

'Mama.'

Petra grunted, but didn't look up. 'Hang on darling, nearly finished.'

'Mama! Quick, I need your phone!'

'What? Why?'

'I need to make a video. Quick Mama!' Rania tugged her sleeve hard.

Petra didn't look up. 'What Rania? What's so urgent?'

'Mama! *Look*!'

Petra looked up quickly, in the direction Rania was pointing at.

A mist had begun to surround the bridge.

'Oh!' she gasped.

'What is it, Mama? Aunty Martha?'

'Crikey…' was all that Martha could utter, watching as small flecks of colour started to move through the growing mist.

'Look, Mama! It's getting closer!' Rania yelled excitedly.

Petra could see that Rania was right, the mist had started to drift away from the bridge, fast approaching them.

'I don't like this, Mum,' whispered Jenny, squeezing Martha's hand and cowering. 'What's happening?'

'I think…it's starting again!' Petra marvelled. 'It won't harm you. Just watch…'

By now, the mist had reached their feet. The colours moving through it were growing brighter and swirling more quickly.

'It's beautiful Mama! Is this what you saw before?' Rania asked, entranced.

Petra just nodded, watching in amazement, as the mist enveloped them completely.

A rainbow of vibrant colours surrounded them, moving rapidly in a circle, weaving between their awe-struck faces.

The moment seemed to last forever, but the mist eventually disappeared.

'Wow!' exclaimed Rania. 'Just wow!'

'Well,' said Martha, a little breathless. 'I've never seen anything like that before! That was amazing.'

As Martha glanced over towards her sister, her jaw dropped.

'Oh my God, Petra! Your hair! It's brown again. And Rania's too!'

Rania looked up at her mother's hair. 'I've never seen it brown before. Papa will be surprised.'

Petra couldn't think of anything to say, she was lost for words. She had become so used to her rainbow hair; it was going to take a bit of getting used to. Brown hair again.

After a few moments, she stood and pulled Rania to her feet.

'I think I need a cup of tea,' she muttered. 'Or maybe something a bit stronger...'

Martha sighed, and came to walk beside her sister. 'Me too!'

As they walked down the hill towards the house, Rania suddenly stopped.

'Damn!' she said loudly.

Her mother looked at her sharply.

'Language, young lady!'

'But I never made a video!' Rania told her. 'You never gave me your phone, so I never recorded it! I wanted to show Papa and my brothers what it looked like...'

Petra put her arm round her shoulders. 'Never mind, darling. We can take photos of our hair to show them. That'll be enough of a surprise, I'm sure.'

445

'I told you I should have my own phone, Mama! Why can't I have my own phone? I'm old enough now. Everybody else at school has their own phone, so why not me?'

'We've talked about this before, Rania. Maybe for your next birthday, alright?'

'But it's just not fair Mama!'

'Stop now, please Rania. It's been a strange day, let's just get back to the house and send Papa some photos, eh?'

'And what am I going to tell my friends at school? They've all been begging their parents for rainbow hair like mine! Now I won't be different anymore!'

'Rania darling, please. Enough already.'

Petra smiled to herself, knowing that, just like her daughter, she would miss her rainbow hair more that she'd secretly like to admit.

Petra paused briefly, and turned to take one more look back at the bridge, knowing it might be quite a while before she found herself here again.

As she looked, she could see a band of rain approaching.

'Uh-oh,' she said. 'Looks like we're going to get wet in a minute!'

Just at that moment, the clouds parted briefly to allow a bright ray of sunshine to break through, and a rainbow began to form. Petra could see that one end of it was planted pretty much where the bridge was.

She couldn't see the other end at all. It disappeared over the horizon.

'Wow!' she exclaimed. 'That must be the biggest rainbow I've ever seen! Just look at it! It's enormous!'

Rania and the others looked up at where her mum was pointing.

'That's just amazing, Mama.' She gasped in delight. 'Where does it end?'

'I don't know,' Petra told her. 'I can't see the other end!'

Rania thought for a moment. 'I wonder if it goes all the way to Greece, Mum? All the way to our house?'

Petra smiled, and put an arm around her daughter's shoulders.

'Well maybe it does, my darling,' she whispered. 'Maybe it does. Imagine that.'

Acknowledgements

This book has been about ten years in the making. It's been a long journey, and of course I have relied on help from a number of people along the way.

Firstly, I must thank my several beta readers for their valuable insights, suggestions and encouragement, at various stages of the story's development. I'm going to resist the temptation to name individuals – I wouldn't want to cause them any embarrassment, and in case I might inadvertently omit somebody…but they know who they are, and they know that I'm grateful to them.

I'm so grateful to Luca Cordina for allowing me to add a layer of much-needed realism to one of the important scenes, by using the name of his delightful Caffee Cordina in the story….and yes, he really does serve probably the best lemon cheesecake ever!

I'm also grateful to our various wonderful friends in Corfu, who unwittingly influenced some of the fictional characters in later stages of the story. I hope I've captured at least a reflection of their warmth, friendliness and generosity.

I absolutely need to acknowledge my wonderful editor, Charlie Mackenzie, whose incisive comments, questions, hints and suggestions have, I feel very strongly, helped to make the story far richer, and deeper than it would have been without her intervention.

Last, but certainly by no means least, I want to thank my wonderful wife, Brenda, who over the last ten years must have patiently read and critiqued every word of this book, at least a hundred times over.

I would not have been able to write it at all without her patient support and endless encouragement.

Stephen Mossop was born in Lancashire, raised in Cornwall, and now lives in East Devon with Brenda, his wife of nearly fifty years. He enjoyed a varied and successful career, initially designing and fitting kitchens – but after deciding, at the age of forty, that a change of direction was needed, he went on to gain a degree from Lancaster University. This enabled him to establish a new career in librarianship, and over time he rose through the ranks to become Head of Library Services at the University of Exeter, from which role he eventually retired in 2014.

Since then, he has been able to dedicate himself full time to honing his writing skills, publishing a series of 'management' text books and articles alongside a broad range of fictional works.

His passion for writing started early – as a teenager he edited and published *Riff-Raff Poetry Magazine*, and over the years several of his poems and short stories have been published in major anthologies.

Storytelling comes naturally to him – ask his kids, who are never quite sure if he's making things up…